T0059155

# BURIED

*Deception*

# OTHER TITLES BY AMANDA MCKINNEY

## Steele Shadows Series

## Road Series

## Broken Ridge Series

## Berry Springs Series

*The Woods*

*The Lake*

*The Storm*

*The Fog*

*The Creek*

*The Shadow*

*The Cave*

## Black Rose Mystery Series

*Devil's Gold*

*Hatchet Hollow*

*Tomb's Tale*

*Evil Eye*

*Sinister Secrets*

## Stand-Alones

*Lethal Legacy*

# BURIED
## *Deception*

# AMANDA
# MCKINNEY

Montlake

This is a work of fiction. Names, characters, organizations, places, events, and incidents are either products of the author's imagination or are used fictitiously. Otherwise, any resemblance to actual persons, living or dead, is purely coincidental.

Text copyright © 2022 by Amanda McKinney
All rights reserved.

No part of this book may be reproduced, or stored in a retrieval system, or transmitted in any form or by any means, electronic, mechanical, photocopying, recording, or otherwise, without express written permission of the publisher.

Published by Montlake, Seattle

www.apub.com

Amazon, the Amazon logo, and Montlake are trademarks of Amazon.com, Inc., or its affiliates.

ISBN-13: 9781662500558 (paperback)
ISBN-13: 9781662500572 (digital)

Cover design by Caroline Teagle Johnson
Cover images: © Anna Gorin / Getty; © Douglas Sacha / Getty; © Nick Brundle Photography / Getty; © plainpicture/Design Pics/Carl Johnson / plainpicture

Printed in the United States of America

*For Mama: here we go.*

# Chapter One

## Mia

There's this quote, "Don't let your struggle become your identity," from author unknown.

I suspect the author is unknown because they know that the statement is total bullshit.

This pithy little quote was likely coined by someone who grew up with a silver spoon in their mouth and, in a desperate attempt to fit in with today's self-loathing youth, felt the need to pretend that they understood the trials and tribulations of those less fortunate. Those ill-fated individuals who have had the unique misfortune of experiencing multiple traumatic events in their lifetime.

To be clear—by traumatic events, I'm not referring to a momentary break in your Wi-Fi connection or having to settle for a chai latte because the local juice bar no longer sells your organic, gluten-free, non-GMO, nonirradiated, kosher green juice.

Traumatic events, or TEs, are slightly more dramatic, such as threatened death, serious injury, loss of a loved one, or sexual violence.

If Author Unknown had spent more than five minutes researching, they would have learned that there are indeed physiological changes our bodies undergo after such events.

You've likely experienced it yourself at some point in your life—dilated pupils, flushed skin, pounding heartbeat, shallow breathing, and trembling. For me personally, this happens every time I stand in front of a crowd. Whether I'm speaking to five people or a hundred, my body responds as if day one of the apocalypse were upon us.

This automatic response serves as a survival function by preparing the body to either fight or run—hence the term *fight or flight*. After the event, the body returns to its normal state.

*Most* of the time.

The issue is when the effects of this trauma don't go away on their own. Slowly metastasizing like an incurable disease, the trauma takes over our bodies—literally. It becomes us, more often than not leading to chronic mental illness, such as PTSD.

This is my specialty.

These are my people.

Author Unknown had no right to advise these people not to allow their struggle to become their identity, because for them, it's clinically proven to literally become that.

This quote is quite possibly the single reason I became a psychologist. Because I know, all too well, the power that such events can have on the human psyche.

I first became interested in psychology in my teens, devouring self-help books like most self-absorbed teens devour diet pills or social media. I did this because I was, well, fucked up and wanted to understand why. Why my brain seemed to operate on its own, uncontrollably, as if a separate entity from my body.

It was this obsession that laid my path.

You see, I could lie and say I became a psychologist to help others, but the true reason lay far deeper—or shallower, you might say.

Why am I a therapist?

Because I'm broken. Plain and simple. It's true—those who can't do, teach.

In a way, you could say that somewhere along the line I accepted my fate, the exact opposite path I suggest my patients travel. This was done subconsciously, of course, brick by brick, one by one, stacked around me over the course of many years, solidifying that so-called armor that most of us wear. Us being the weak ones unable to address and move on from the inevitable vicissitude that is life.

It's a dangerous way to live; I know that now. And as much as I wish I could say that it was my strength and all my infinite wisdom that finally released me from the binds of the past, I'd be lying. My salvation, my savior, came in the form of a man they called Chief.

This is my story, my fall from grace, my unwilling surrender.

My capture.

# Chapter Two

## Easton

I rolled to a stop at the edge of a dank and pestilential swamp, bloated with recent rain. A jacked-up Chevy marked the end of a cluster of trucks and emergency-response vehicles that crowded the small clearing, their haphazard parking a hint of the chaos to come. A Lone Star flag hung limply from the bed of the truck. The faded red, white, and blue sagged dispiritedly in the still, humid air. Cool but sticky. Suffocating.

In a never-ending battle, the chilled air and warm swamp water collided in a thick blanket of fog, slowly weaving through the gnarled cypress trees, their long, crooked branches silhouetted like ghostly fingers in the waning light. Spanish moss dripped from the limbs, swaying in a breeze I didn't feel.

It was typical weather for the changing seasons. The day had been warm and humid, interrupted by a late-afternoon thunderstorm followed by a swift drop in temperature.

Something was in the air that evening, an ominous electricity punctuated by a setting sun that glowed like a pink ball of fire through the haze, casting a peachy echo through the dense forest.

It was unnatural. Unnerving.

I didn't like it. I've never been a man who believes in ghosts or any invisible force beyond the realm of humanity. I do, however, believe in signs. I believe that Mother Nature guides us—but only if you are perceptive enough to receive her messages.

And that night, she was screaming at me.

Forgoing my jacket, I grabbed my pack and stepped out of the truck, not bothering to lock it.

Urgent, excited voices echoed in the distance. Lots of chatter, questions, confusion. Fear. Likely a crowd of well-intentioned idiots trampling the scene.

Sheriff McNamara emerged from between two trucks, his broad shoulders tense, his expression hard, his focus that of a man being pelted with questions from every angle.

As usual, the lanky fifty-two-year-old was dressed in his formal sheriff uniform, pressed, pinned, highly decorated. I, on the other hand, was wearing khaki tactical pants that hadn't been washed in days, scuffed boots, and a faded T-shirt with pit stains. McNamara's trademark high-and-tight was thinner than the last time I'd seen him, yet the top was combed to perfection, no strand out of place. A body I'd been told could once move boulders was now stringy and lean but no less effective.

We fell into step together, his urgency palpable. As usual, the Skull County sheriff bypassed pleasantries and small talk, this perhaps being my favorite thing about the man.

"Thanks for coming on such short notice, Chief," he said, aggressively swatting at a swarm of gnats swirling in front of his face. "I'm sorry I couldn't get into the details over the phone. Goddamn reception is shit out here by the swamps."

"No problem. What've we got?"

"Seventeen-year-old girl, local high school student, reported missing three hours ago. Name's Courtney Hayes. Plays the flute in the band, runs track, and is a rising star on the swim team. Washes dishes at the local diner on the weekend. Her car is parked at the trailhead, where I've set up command."

"Have you established PLS?"

"Yes. Courtney was last seen leaving the high school after band practice yesterday afternoon. Friend we talked to said Courtney had mentioned going for a jog at the Black Cat Trail. I deployed an officer immediately."

We veered into the woods, stepping onto a footpath covered in dead leaves, freshly worn by dozens of boots. Thankfully, McNamara had diverted the volunteers from using the main path that led to the trailhead, instead having them use a shortcut through the woods. Too bad he hadn't diverted the vehicle traffic the same way.

"You said her car is here?"

"Yes. A beige Nissan Altima, one pothole away from falling apart. Two tires are low, left-side mirror hanging by wires."

"Messy on the inside?"

"No, ironically." McNamara glanced at me. "Sparkling clean. Why do you ask?"

"A clean interior tells me Courtney took pride in her vehicle, her most prized possession, perhaps. A banged-up outside suggests money is an issue with her family, so she does the best she can by keeping what few things she does own clean."

"Okay, where you goin' with this, Chief?"

*Chief.* An annoying and imperious moniker I'd been given after founding the LYNX Group, a combat-tracking training facility and volunteer search-and-rescue team.

"This helps me put together a picture of who she is," I said. "And therefore where she might go. Typically, someone who meticulously cares for their car—whether old or new—isn't someone who's reckless, selfish, or juvenile."

"You mean not someone who would run away from home at a moment's notice?"

"Right. Or wander too far off the trail, for that matter."

"Good point."

"Are there any other vehicles in the lot?" I asked.

"No."

"Tire tracks?"

"Too many to get a solid read on the type of tread. You know as well as I do this is a busy trail. The new loop they just put in—the one that skirts your property—has caused a renewed interest in the area."

"And in my land."

"If I've told you once, I've told you a million times—you need to use some of that government-grant money to build a fence on your property line. Or just call us, instead of scaring the shit out of trespassers."

I didn't bother telling the sheriff how much it would cost to fence in eighty-seven heavily wooded acres. Or explain my only enjoyment in life came from watching the LYNX Group operators chase trespassers off the land wearing Bigfoot costumes—if Bigfoot carried a Smith & Wesson.

"Is her car locked?" I asked, returning to the point.

The sheriff nodded. "And nothing seems out of place as far as we can see. No apparent struggle of any kind, inside or outside the car."

"Cell phone inside?"

"No. Not that we can see. We're keeping our distance from the car for now."

I looked over at him, the implication heavy. Sheriff McNamara had instructed his team to stay away from the car to avoid contaminating potential evidence in the event this missing-girl case took an ugly turn.

"Do you suspect foul play, McNamara?"

"There's nothing to indicate that as of this moment," the sheriff answered, a canned, emotionless, and automatic response. One that he'd delivered a thousand times over the course of his highly decorated career.

7

Fourth-generation law enforcement, Sheriff Andrew McNamara was a legend around the small town of Skull Hollow. His unwavering commitment to the job and intolerance of stupidity and nonconformists made him both highly respected and highly feared by all who crossed into his county. He and I had met years earlier while stalking a group of tweakers who had taken up residence in the bayou. Turned out McNamara's father and mine had served together in the navy years earlier.

Although little was known about the sheriff's private life, it was rumored that he'd missed the birth of his twin girls to personally oversee a group of unruly teens, who'd decided to throw a pot-smoking bonfire party in his woods during a fire ban, collecting every piece of litter from their party spot, as well as the three-mile trail that led to it. I think McNamara was on his third wife at the time.

We got on well.

My gaze shifted to the direction of the trailhead, barely visible through the crowded pines and thick underbrush. The Black Cat Trail was definitely not a place for a young woman to jog alone. Especially lately, and especially considering the number of alternative trail options in the area.

"Do you know why she came here, specifically?" I asked.

"No."

"Was she meeting someone?"

"Don't know."

"What time did she leave band practice?"

"Around four thirty yesterday afternoon. Mom called nine-one-one three hours ago, worried that her daughter didn't come home last night."

"It's six thirty at night. You mean to tell me the girl has been missing for nearly twenty-four hours, and the mother just called it in?"

The sheriff rubbed the back of his neck, an unusual sign of stress from the man. "The mom—Bunnie Hayes—has a record. Petty theft, possession, and a DWI."

"Bunnie, you say?"

"Yep."

"Real name?"

"Yep. Fifty-one years old, Skull Hollow native."

"Who took the call?"

"Cheryl from dispatch. Story goes that the mom called nine-one-one after calling one of Courtney's friends, who told her Courtney had mentioned going to the Black Cat Trail. This, for obvious reasons, triggered the mother's concern. Cheryl routed the call to us, considering it's out of city limits. This is all included in the incident report I emailed you thirty minutes ago—you get it?"

"Yes. Just confirming details. Where's the dad?"

"Chet Hayes is currently locked up in the state penitentiary."

"You verify that?"

"Yes. Spoke with the warden myself, immediately after I got the call."

"What's he in for?"

"Drugs."

"Mom got a boyfriend?"

"Not sure."

"Courtney got a boyfriend?"

"Not sure yet."

"What did her coworkers at the diner say?"

"That Courtney doesn't say much, a shy gal. They don't know if she had a boyfriend, a crush—hell, some didn't even know her last name. Our best bet is with the mom, but unfortunately she gave us little to go on. I get the vibe she's not very present in her daughter's life, to say the least."

"Sounds like Courtney is a bit of a loner. Is the mom here?"

"Just showed up. Her car is the beat-up black Accord parked crooked in the ditch with the ass hanging out. Started celebrating five o'clock a bit early, best guess. That or on pills."

I clenched my jaw. I already didn't like this case. "Does she seem worried about her daughter?"

"She's definitely amped up about something. I've got my female sergeant, Rosa, interviewing her now, after I didn't get too far with her."

"Bunnie doesn't trust men."

"I'd say that's an accurate statement. Anyway, she started babbling something about therapy. According to Bunnie, Courtney recently called a local mental health facility requesting an appointment. The Dragonfly Clinic . . . you heard of it?"

"I have. What did she call them for?"

"Mom's not sure. She saw the number scribbled on a notepad on the kitchen counter. Thinks maybe Courtney was depressed."

"Who did Courtney see at the clinic?"

"The name Dr. Frost was scribbled next to the number. Dr. Mia Frost, from Austin, I assume. Moved here several years ago, started the clinic—owns it, I think. Specializes in treating PTSD and building psychological profiles of criminals. She's been in the news for doing some weird new-age alternative shit—hypnosis, I think." He sniffed. "Bought old Merle's cabin a few miles west."

"West of the swamp?"

"Yeah, close to your land, come to think of it. Anyway, she's kind of a hermit, I think."

"Did you call her?"

"Left a message, spoke with the office manager there—Stella Bloom is her name. Apparently, our missing gal had scheduled an appointment with Dr. Frost for next week."

"What for?"

"Office manager wouldn't say. Spouted some bullshit about client confidentiality. Quite a brusque young woman."

"Word of the day?"

"Yep."

We walked a moment in silence.

"Don't you have a group of National Guardsmen in town to take your tactical-tracking course?" the sheriff asked.

"I do." And I instantly didn't like where this was going.

"When did they arrive?"

"A few days ago."

"How many?"

"A group of six."

"What do you know about them?"

"Everything. And I also know that you are not a man to beat around the bush."

"The timing is interesting, that's all."

"Do you have any reason to think that one of my trainees is involved here?"

"Not necessarily, but the entire town will, once word gets out."

"I'll handle it."

"I know."

"So . . ." I inhaled, compiling a mental timeline and diverting his attention away from my company. "Courtney Hayes was last seen leaving the high school at four thirty yesterday afternoon. Didn't go home, didn't call anyone that we know of. Mom is aware that her daughter didn't come home but waits until three hours ago to call the cops. No current evidence that Courtney is either, one, a victim of foul play; two, injured and unable to call for help; or three, simply lost in the woods."

"Correct."

"Is there any trace of Courtney after leaving band practice, aside from her car sitting by the trailhead right now? Any social media posts?"

"Her last post was Wednesday, a close-up picture of a bunch of wildflowers. No caption."

"Where from?"

"Can't tell."

I chewed on this a minute. "Is there anything to make you believe Courtney could be suicidal?"

"Everything's an option at this point."

I nodded, scanning the woods. "How many volunteers do you have for the search?"

"About a dozen so far. They're being briefed right now. My team is staging the area, and I've got two others securing the trailhead and making sure no one touches her damn car. Other than that, everyone's waiting on the infamous chief of LYNX Search and Rescue to dole out orders."

*Infamous.* Another moniker, this one perhaps deserved.

"All right," I said. "I don't want a single person to place a foot on the trail until we establish direction of travel, understood?"

"I know that already. It's not the first time we've worked together, Easton."

"Have you called in your dogs?"

The sheriff nodded. "The handler should be here soon."

"Who?"

"Sandy Griffith."

"Good. She's good. Did Mom bring a scent piece?"

"Yes, Courtney's pillowcase. I considered drones—"

"No. Useless. The cover is too thick." I gestured to the canopy of trees overhead.

He nodded. "Exactly my thoughts."

We looked over our shoulders to the distant roar of motorcycles entering the woods.

"Your team?" McNamara asked.

I nodded, and we stopped.

"I'm deploying my six-man hasty team to hit the ground running immediately. They'll combine with your searchers." I paused for approval, and the sheriff dipped his chin. "My newest member, Dane Stratton, will stay at the command post to field updates and change the plan accordingly."

McNamara shrugged. "It's your show. What will you do?"

"Search. I'll meet you at command in ten minutes." I turned and began walking in the opposite direction.

"Where are you going?"

"To meet my team—a quarter mile out."

The sheriff frowned, glancing in the direction of the clearing where everyone else had parked. "Why there?"

"Didn't want them destroying tracks or evidence if it ends up we need to search for some."

The sheriff bristled, catching the dig.

"We'll get started in ten minutes," I said over my shoulder, maneuvering into the weeds, avoiding the path. "No one touches that trail, McNamara. Not a single boot."

"Got it. Hey, Chief?"

I glanced over my shoulder.

"You good?" he asked.

Ignoring his question, I bit my tongue and veered into the woods, slipping into the shadows.

Into the darkness of the past.

# Chapter Three

## Easton

I glanced up at the trees overhead, the gaps in the darkening canopy spotlighted by the pink sunset. My pace quickened. Nighttime isn't when you want to find yourself in this part of the woods.

Known as the Piney Woods, the dense coniferous forest stretches over fifty thousand acres across eastern Texas, southern Arkansas, and western Louisiana. Considered one of the most diverse and endangered ecological communities in the United States, the region includes nine different ecosystems, from longleaf pine forests to cypress-lined bayous. From rolling hills with steep ravines to flat wetlands.

Sixty inches of rainfall per year supports dense vegetation that includes loblolly pines, sweet bay magnolias, flowering dogwoods, and my personal favorite, bald cypress trees that spear up from the murky swamps, their limbs draped with Spanish moss. Tourists claim it gives the woods a haunting, ghostly appearance.

Feels like home to me.

Nature lovers flock to the area, not only for the stunning scenery but also to glimpse one of the many rare species of birds and amphibians. Or the bears, or the 150-pound panthers known to stalk the woods.

The most popular and fearsome fauna of the area, however, are the elusive alligators that hunt the freshwater swamps and marshes.

Black Hills Bayou, one of the most popular tourist destinations in the state, is home to eleven hiking trails that weave through miles of dense forest and wetlands. It wasn't my first time being called to the area to assist local law enforcement in a missing-person case.

There's something about the area that draws people, pulling them beyond the designated trails to the murky, bottomless swamps. Most hike, camp, and fish without issue. Some, however, succumb to the brutal, untamed wilderness of the forest, a dark side that I know very, very well. A side that came out in full force on that late October evening, the day that would change the course of my life.

The breeze picked up, sending a rainstorm of brittle brown leaves tumbling down from the treetops. Ahead, a silhouette emerged from the fog, a pack secured on his back, a pistol in his belt.

"Put the gun up," I said as the six-foot-three, 250-pound former Special Ops Marine strode toward me.

"Put yours up," he said.

"Mine is in my boot."

"Mine is on my belt."

"Hide it."

"No."

"Beckett—"

Ignoring me, Beckett Stolle shrugged out of his pack, pulled out a bottle of water, and began chugging, exposing yet another gun secured to the opposite side of his belt.

"*Jesus*, Beck. There are already at least a dozen volunteers on site. I don't need you walking up like goddamn Yosemite Sam."

"Then you hired the wrong person, Chief." He winked with a cocky smile the exact moment a streak of sunlight broke through the trees and sparkled off his perfectly white teeth. As if he didn't look pretty enough.

Beckett Stolle and I had served together in the Marines, sharing several tours overseas, one with me as his supervisor. In the military, Beckett had been known as a loose cannon, hot tempered and impatient, with a penchant for breaking the rules. This, combined with his monstrous frame, made people clear any room he entered like Moses parting the Red Sea—aside from women, of course, who fell to their knees. He was a cocky, smooth-talking son of a bitch but also the most dedicated, hardworking, tenacious man I'd ever met in my life. Beckett never gave up on a mission. Not ever. Death would take him first; this vow was literally tattooed on his arm.

Beckett was a talented tracker with an uncanny—and somewhat unnerving—knack for predicting the enemy's next move. This instinct had saved many lives over the course of his military career and had carried over seamlessly when I'd hired him to head up the search-and-rescue division of my company.

Within weeks, the job had turned into a full-fledged partnership, with me owning 51 percent of the company and Beckett 49. In a few short months, we'd secured a contract with the United States government to teach select soldiers and federal agents the specialty of combat tracking and to occasionally assist in black-op extraction missions. In an instant, it seemed, Beckett and I were working fifteen-hour days and sleeping at our desks, the partnership with the government blowing the company—and our bank accounts—out of the water, so to speak.

The company grew almost as quickly as our reputations.

Over the years, we'd developed a good-guy-bad-guy partnership when it came to operations. I was the CEO, the face of the LYNX Group who accepted nothing but perfection, while Beckett, officially named COO, was the brass knuckles who implemented the perfection I demanded.

"Where's everyone else?" I asked.

"On their way."

A few shouts echoed from the other side of the woods.

"Sounds like more than a dozen volunteers," he said. "Who's running the show?"

"McNamara."

Beckett's dark eyebrow arched. "Anyone else with him?"

"Not sure." I yanked a windbreaker with the LYNX logo from my pack and thrust it at him. "Here. Tie this around your waist."

"Why? To hide my gun? Are you serious?"

Beckett yanked the coat from my hands and raised it into the air, examining the object as a toddler might their first stalk of broccoli. Then he threw it on the ground in the same manner.

"Wear it, or I'll put you on command post. I'm not doing this shit with you right now, Becks. Let's go."

After the full minute it took him to swallow his pride, Beckett plucked the coat from the ground. Muttering words I hadn't heard since MARSOC, he haphazardly tied the coat around his waist like a preteen wrestling into his first jockstrap. He looked like a nineties pop star, plus two hundred pounds.

I updated Beckett as we quickly made our way to the clearing by the trailhead where the sheriff had set up post.

"Jesus *Christ*," Beckett muttered through clenched teeth as the rendezvous site came into view.

We slowed our pace, taking a moment to assess what would soon be our search group.

At least two dozen people crowded the small space, draped in their best "search and rescue" gear. Cowboy hats, canvas Carhartt jackets (a few with the price tag still hanging off the sleeve), starched Wranglers, and pleather hiking boots straight out of the box.

The men hovered over maps that had been spread over tailgates while the women filled thermoses with coffee that one of the volunteers had brought. A few stared blankly into the woods as if having no clue what they were doing there.

Klieg lights were being erected in the corners, attracting swarms of bloodsucking bugs. They would soon be our only light.

"Who the hell brought a kid?" Beckett muttered.

An unruly toddler stumbled around the tall underbrush, ripping at the grass, then chewing a few strands.

"Who knows."

"Well, have someone put a tracker on her. I don't care to hunt for two missing people tonight."

"It's a boy."

"What?"

"The kid—it's a boy."

Beckett frowned. "It has long, curly hair."

"It also has a penis."

"What?"

"He's naked from the waist down."

The toddler waddled out of the brush, diaper in one hand, a clump of mud in the other.

Beckett grimaced. "God, I hope that's dirt."

I sighed.

It was a disorganized clusterfuck, unfortunately not unlike most incidents we were called to the field to assist in.

Beckett and I paused at the sound of heavy footsteps coming up behind us.

Two men emerged from the tree line, followed by six more marching single file, like soldiers, each wearing matching khaki tactical pants and green shirts with the LYNX logo—the face of a black panther.

Dane Stratton, former woodland firefighter and newest LYNX member, led the group, scanning the thick underbrush as he walked. Always looking, always analyzing.

Alek Romanov, grandson of a former Russian mob boss and current CFO of the LYNX Group, followed closely behind. One hand held a hand lamp while the other gripped a Ka-Bar knife. He swatted wildly at the air ahead of him with the knife, missing the back of Dane's neck by half an inch.

"Goddamn mosquitoes," Alek muttered, scowling at the blood streaked on the tip of his knife from where he'd sliced a mosquito in half.

"You're late," I said as we fell into step together, our small, well-trained LYNX volunteer team following in a line behind us.

"One of the boys twisted their ankle on the obstacle course," Alek informed me. "Had to deal with that shit."

"The boys" was what we called the trainees enrolled in our combat-tracking course.

"Which one?"

"Samson."

"Pussy," Beckett said, adding his opinion, though no one had asked.

Pussy or not, I didn't care to have any bad press, even if nothing would come of it.

Our lawyer had drafted an ironclad nondisclosure agreement that I insisted be signed by every single person who set foot on our property. The paperwork also ensured that the LYNX Group couldn't be held responsible (or sued) for serious injury—or death—that was incurred while on our land or under our supervision.

Regardless, the unconventional and extreme tactics we used in our training courses had bred hot gossip, generating more press for us over the years than I was comfortable with. What we did behind the gates wasn't meant to be exposed. It was meant to turn out the best soldiers and trackers possible. I took the job very seriously, because saving a life should never be by chance.

"Did you fix him up?" I asked Alek.

"Did what I could do. Called in Doc Winters. She was taking x-rays when I left."

"Does she think it's broken?"

"Don't think so; just making sure."

Beckett swatted at a gnarly bug the size of a tangerine—same color too. "You owe me twenty bucks."

Alek lunged forward, slicing the massive bug with his knife. A game, I realized. Not self-defense.

"Don't owe you shit," he said, wiping the blade down his thigh.

"You will when Samson quits."

"He won't quit," I said. "I won't allow it."

We stepped into the clearing.

"Oh, you've gotta be kidding me," Alek mumbled, mirroring Beckett's opinion on the motley crew of volunteers the sheriff had dredged up for the search.

Heads turned as we approached. Conversation halted and whispers ensued—the normal reaction to the approach of three former special ops soldiers and the grandson of an infamous Russian crime lord.

"Is that the mom?" Beckett asked quietly.

The woman standing alone by the trees was shivering under layers of blankets, although it was sixty degrees outside. Her face was ghostly pale. Oily brown hair draping in tangled strings over bony little shoulders. The woman appeared ten years older than her fifty-one years, her face bearing deep lines and acne scars that suggested a hard life.

I wondered if that kind of life had trickled down to her missing daughter.

"You got the profile?" I asked Alek.

He grunted a yes, scowling at the team of novices with thinly veiled revulsion. As usual, the local volunteers assumed that more boots on the ground to find a missing person was a good thing. Wrong. Not when the searchers knew very little about how to properly execute a search and rescue.

In most cases, well-meaning volunteers actually hamper an investigation instead of providing value. Precious evidence and tracks are trampled, destroying clues that might otherwise lead to the missing person's location, as well as clues that would help lead to whoever is involved in the disappearance, if something nefarious has happened to the person.

It wasn't our responsibility to train the volunteers the authorities selected to help in a missing-person search, but it was always our goal to prevent these volunteers from destroying spoor or evidence.

As an SAR volunteer unit, my team was called in by local law enforcement as needed, usually after intel had already been gathered. It was up to law enforcement officials to manage the case of the missing person. It was only up to us to manage the search-and-rescue operation and locate that missing person—not handle the investigation.

However, it never took long until my team began to grow impatient and annoyed by this constant battle of egos. After all, my men had built their careers on saving lives, each highly skilled in various areas. And because of this, LYNX went above and beyond the call of duty, whether the local officials appreciated it or not.

It was a delicate dance, a pissing match that I had to meticulously manage. The thin lines of authority blurred the moment our teams came together, and mine often stepped over that line to get the job done.

It was expected at this point.

Sheriff McNamara turned from his position at the end of a tailgate, his tall, gangly silhouette towering over the crowd, his sharp gaze fixed on me.

But I was focused on his chief deputy, Chris Mason. The motherfucker I'd put in the hospital twelve months earlier.

My goal had been the morgue.

# Chapter Four

## Easton

Sheriff McNamara ignored the phone buzzing on his hip as he approached. "Beckett, Alek, Dane." He nodded to the team behind me. "Good to see you all. Glad you could make it. I trust that Chief Crew has briefed you, but I have a few updates . . ."

McNamara's voice faded as my focus narrowed on Deputy Mason.

His blond hair glinted under the artificial light, spiked and gelled to perfection. He'd put on weight, I noticed, the county-issued short-sleeved shirt stretching at the seams over a puffed-up chest and swollen biceps. The thirty-three-year-old minor-league dropout had bulked up since our last meeting.

Something inside me took this as a challenge. One I welcomed.

"Chief, if you wouldn't mind . . ." McNamara broke through the savage thoughts racing through my head, gesturing to the volunteer who'd just walked up with a clipboard and pen.

I scribbled my name on the sign-in log and handed it to Beckett as we fell into step beside the sheriff.

"As I was saying," McNamara said, now that he had my attention again, "Courtney was last seen at band practice, wearing the clothes she wore to school. So assuming she changed clothes for her jog, unfortunately we don't have a physical description of what she was wearing when she disappeared—"

"Incorrect." Beckett scribbled illegibly on the clipboard and thrust it back to the volunteer, who stumbled backward at the enthusiasm of the delivery. "Courtney Hayes was wearing a neon-pink tank top and black leggings, Lululemon is my assumption, based on the reflective dots down the sides and the current popularity of the brand. She was wearing navy Nike running shoes with a white swoosh and a green scrunchie on her left arm. Her hair was pulled back in a braid."

"How the hell do you know this?" McNamara snapped, clearly defensive that he was unaware of such important details.

Beckett gnawed off the tip of a Slim Jim. "I asked around."

I scowled at Beckett to cool the attitude. Damn the man and his aversion to authority—and his obsession with sodium, for that matter.

Regaining control of the conversation, I said, "Immediately after I received your call, I advised Beckett to check with the gas stations between Courtney's apartment and the trailhead."

"Why?"

"We're trackers, Sheriff. We don't wait for evidence to tell us where to go; we begin tracking the moment we know the path. We knew Courtney was headed to the Black Cat Trail. We knew there was a chance that she possibly needed gas or a bottle of water on her way. So we checked. Sure enough, she stopped for a Gatorade."

"Cool Blue, to be exact, and a pack of gum—Juicy Fruit," Beckett added as Alek slayed bugs in the air like a damn samurai next to him, unnerving every single person watching.

*Jesus.*

Continuing, I said, "She was recorded at the gas station at four forty-one, placing her at the station after band practice."

The sheriff watched me, his jaw twitching, obviously not liking that his team had overlooked this. I, however, wasn't surprised.

Checking the gas station had been overlooked simply because no evidence pointed in that direction. The police were not trained to *think* like the quarry (the missing person) they were tracking. And that was a huge difference between us and the cops. Police operate on black-and-white facts, on computers and technology, while searchers operate on primitive instinct. A method known as man tracking, or combat tracking, to be exact.

Today's soldiers and law enforcement are the product of modern, technologically oriented armies who rely on things like drones, hacking, and artificial intelligence. Everything relies on technology. This in an effort to enhance our power, but ironically, it only strips us of the most powerful tool we have—our instinct.

Primitive man developed the skill of tracking simply because they had to. Visual tracking became vital for survival, whether it was for hunting for food, protecting the tribe, or attempting to locate another competing tribe. Our most primal instinct is slowly being erased from our biology and replaced with reliance on technology.

This doesn't sit well with me, which is why I set out to change it by starting my own company.

McNamara led us to his truck, the volunteers stepping back as we approached.

Beckett swiped clean the tailgate, making room for Dane to assemble the maps he'd printed and marked before leaving the office.

Alek handed me a laptop as my team of six began readying itself for the hunt.

McNamara leaned in, Deputy Mason keeping a safe distance from the end of my fist.

"All right, listen up." I pulled a pen from my pocket and pointed at the location circled in red on the map. It was of the gas station. "This is the PLS, point last seen." I trailed the tip of the pen along each line drawn outward from the circle. "These three paths indicate the three options Courtney could have taken to the trail." I then drew a line that connected the high school to Courtney's apartment. "Based on the location of the gas station relative to her apartment, we can assume Courtney ran home to change clothes after band practice."

The sheriff cut in. "Local PD dispatched two patrol units to the apartment building an hour ago. Last update I received says they interviewed the neighbors, but none recall seeing her. They had the super unlock her apartment." He glanced at his watch. "As of twenty minutes ago, there was nothing to indicate an altercation of any sort took place or that she left against her free will."

"No one saw her?" Beckett asked to confirm.

"No."

"Doesn't mean she wasn't there," I said. "How long does it take to change clothes?"

McNamara cocked his head. "Well, with my last wife—"

"Let's assume Courtney doesn't use the pantry as a shoe closet."

"Right."

"Six minutes, average," Beckett cut in. "Three if the clothes are already on the bed . . . or the floor, for that matter."

We turned to Beckett. He grinned, then winked.

Dane rolled his eyes.

I shook my head. "My point is that it doesn't take long to change, meaning it's not surprising a neighbor didn't see her."

A breeze blew past, and I studied the darkening sky. "We need to get a move on."

I clicked into LYNX's tracking software on my laptop. A detailed satellite map filled the screen. I pointed to the red circle in the middle.

"I've named this area at the trailhead the LKP, or last known position, considering her car is parked here." I zoomed in on the map. "We're working off the assumption that her direction of travel is the trail itself. Based on that, I've created eight search segments branching out from the LKP, labeled A1, A2, A3, and so on. My six-man hasty team will begin searching each segment immediately, while Dane remains here at the command post and works on a more detailed search while setting up operational periods for each team. He'll work with your K9 as soon as Sandy gets here to establish that route as well. My team will cover this area—"

"Why is that area highlighted?" Mason asked, finally speaking, his voice like shards of glass slicing down my spine.

"It's the path my team will take."

"Why them?"

"It's considered hazardous terrain," I said carefully, controlling my tone. "I've established it as a high-probability area. The shading calculates the angles of the slopes, which means higher chances for injuries, such as falls and twisted ankles."

"My searchers can handle it," Mason said, his tone defensive.

I felt Beckett bristle next to me.

"I'm not talking about your volunteers," I said, controlling . . . controlling, controlling. "I'm referring to Courtney. Our missing person might be missing simply because she fell, injured herself, and is unable to return to her car. My men will handle searching this route. End of discussion."

Dismissing him, I refocused on the map, catching McNamara shoot Mason a look laced with warning.

"According to the sign-in log, you have sixteen volunteers and four uniforms, excluding yourselves. I want one of your men or women with the teams in these particular search segments." I tapped each location with the tip of my pen.

"Why those?" Sergeant Rosa asked as she walked up.

"To cover our asses," Beckett said.

"These segments are the most likely paths someone on this trail would take. If Courtney is being held against her will or something far worse has happened, it becomes a crime scene. In which case it's better to have an officer on hand to record the scene."

Rosa nodded, her face paling.

Yes, it was a bad time to be a woman on the Black Cat Trail.

I turned to McNamara. "With your permission, I'd like to get started immediately."

He gestured to the crowd. "They're all yours."

McNamara stepped back, giving me the floor as the LYNX hasty team melted into the woods. Mason disappeared between the trucks.

"All right." I focused on the motley crew of volunteers standing before me, wide eyed and bushy tailed. "Tonight we're searching for Courtney Hayes, a seventeen-year-old local who was last reported seen at the high school and at Skull Crossing Gas Station, at four thirty yesterday afternoon."

I recited the details of her clothing as Dane passed out a collage of images he'd printed from her social media accounts.

"Tonight we're going to operate in eight teams of two, each team identified by a number. Before you set out, you are to locate your team's—or number's—quadrants for the search. I trust that all of you know how to use your GPS. Once you plug in the coordinates, you will begin the search. You're searching for something that's out of context in nature, such as disturbed or bent grass, overturned rocks, footprints, broken leaves. If you see any of this, report back immediately, and this becomes the new LKP—or last known position of Courtney Hayes."

I paused as a man the size of a backhoe hocked up whatever the hell was stuck in his throat. A woman missing a front tooth gagged like a cat.

I cleared my throat, fighting my own gag reflex. "As you know, Black Hills Bayou is home to dozens of bayhead swamps, typically found at the base of hills where rainwater drains and settles. The saturated, muddy soils are prime for prints—the holy grail of a search and rescue. Watch for shoe prints. As mentioned, Courtney was wearing running shoes, which usually have a very distinctive tread. Our challenge here, folks, is that Courtney likely wasn't the only person on this trail in the last twenty-four hours. Her prints will be mixed with others. However, based on the height and weight we pulled from Courtney's driver's license, I estimate her shoe size to be smaller than the average woman's, around size five. This might look like a child's print to you. Keep an eye out for that."

Dane stepped forward. "According to her social media accounts, Courtney Hayes enjoys spending time at the lake and river. She also recently joined the swim team. Meaning Courtney isn't afraid of water, so don't assume that there's no need to visually search the swamps and creeks that line the trails."

I nodded. "My team and I have identified two choke points within the search location—two bridges that anyone on the trail would have to cross—which I will deploy my men immediately to search."

The naked toddler ran in front of the crowd, flinging what we all hoped was mud into the air.

"Can someone please get that kid?" Beckett said.

A woman emerged from behind a folding table that held doughnuts—because setting up glazed carbs, guaranteed to elicit sugar crashes among the volunteers on whom Courtney's life depended, was what was most important at that moment.

"Micah! Come here!" she called out, her voice shrill.

Loudly, I continued, "In your bags, you'll find high-visibility yellow vests and baseball caps. On each vest is a clip-on strobe light. Wear these, turn them on, and don't take them off. Remember, we *want* to be seen, not only by Courtney, assuming she's responsive, but by hunters who might think we're deer. This will also help us to see each other should our paths cross. Also included is bug spray, water, food, an extra radio, and a first aid kit. In the front pocket is a handheld thermal imager. It detects body heat—the presence of another person. This will help as the sun goes down. If you don't know how to use them, meet with Dane before you head out."

Beckett began passing out the prepacked backpacks we freely supplied at every search we assisted in, a decision we'd made after the seventh incident when a volunteer had gotten either hurt or lost while searching for a missing person. I didn't have the time or patience for that kind of incompetence.

"Be cognizant of your surroundings at all times, and remember, in these parts of the woods, you aren't at the top of the food chain. You're merely an intruder in the vast wilderness of the Black Hills. In the water, you'll find brain-eating amoebas that enter the body through a cut and eat human brains. Flesh-eating bacteria called vibrio also thrive in these swamps, as do water moccasins, spiders, and scorpions. These you can easily avoid by staying out of the water. The two predators you can't avoid are alligators and mountain lions. So, I repeat, be aware of your surroundings at all times. When—"

"One more thing," Beckett mumbled around his fifth slab of jerky. "We're closing in on night, the conenose bug's favorite feeding time. They bite humans around the mouth and eyes and are commonly infected with disease-causing parasites. So keep an eye out—or closed— for those bastards. Trust me on this."

"That reminds me," I said. "It's deer season as well, so the deer will be active. Don't let them spook you." I glanced at my watch. "We'll search for four hours, until ten o'clock, at which point we'll call it off for the night and begin again at first light tomorrow morning. Sheriff McNamara, Deputy Mason, and LYNX team member Dane Stratton will remain at the rendezvous site, fielding information and incoming calls. My team and I will be out with you. Check your packs; add anything else you need—medications, whatever. We head out in five. Any questions?"

The crowd didn't move or speak, half of them focused on the knife Beckett was using to clean the beef from his teeth.

"All right then—"

"I have one." A short, burly volunteer with a bottom lip full of dip flicked up his wrist. "What about the Black Cat Stalker?"

"Yeah . . . I was thinking the same thing," someone from the crowd added.

"What if he's out there?" another asked.

"Are we using thermal imaging because you're expecting to find her dead body?" This was yelled from somewhere in the back.

"Is there a link between Courtney's disappearance and the Black Cat?"

Sheriff McNamara quickly stepped forward. "No." He waved his palms in the air to quiet the crowd. "There's currently no reason to believe the Black Cat Stalker is connected to Courtney Hayes's disappearance."

"Oh, come on," a woman barked from the back in a deep, gritty voice that accompanies a two-pack-a-day habit. "In the last few months there've been three reports of women being spooked by a man in black on this very trail."

"I understand, Mrs. Bodean," McNamara yelled over the chatter and suspicion. "But at this time, we have no reason to link the two."

The crowd erupted into an uproar.

"But this is the fourth incident out here in less than two months!"

"Yeah, there's gotta be a connection!"

I watched the sheriff closely, the flex of his jaw, the way his throat worked in a deep swallow. There was no way McNamara hadn't considered that Courtney's disappearance and the faceless man the town had dubbed the Black Cat Stalker might be connected. Unfortunately, gut instincts weren't solid enough for public statements.

Mine, however, was screaming at me that the disappearance had everything to do with the Black Cat.

Over the last two months, three women had reported being out on a hike or a jog when a man, dressed in all black and wearing a black bandanna around his neck, had suddenly appeared behind them. "Out of nowhere," they'd all said.

This man had followed them closely before eventually disappearing into thin air, earning him the moniker *the Black Cat Stalker*. All three women had been scared out of their minds and reported the incidents.

Were there more unreported incidents? Very likely. But so far, the Black Cat Stalker had done nothing more than scare the women.

So far.

# Chapter Five

## Easton

We set off just as the sun slipped beneath the horizon, the eerie peach glow settling between the trees.

Nighttime searches weren't ideal, for many reasons, but particularly for those conducting the search. I wasn't worried about Beckett, Alek, or my hasty team . . . I was worried about the volunteers. One twisted ankle, one snakebite, could throw off the entire search, prolonging the rescue of whoever needed it the most.

The volunteers were edgy that night, with a disjointed undercurrent of anxiety and fear. A primo headspace for making mistakes. I didn't like it. I needed everyone to be on their toes, their sole focus searching the terrain for clues that would lead to Courtney Hayes's whereabouts, not looking over their shoulders for the Black Cat Stalker.

Beckett and Alek split off, disappearing into the woods to search the two bridges in the area. I continued alone, exactly the way I preferred to hunt.

I adjusted my headlamp, its yellow beam of light distorted by the fog. Careful to stay to the side of the trail, I followed the narrow gravel path like an animal after its prey.

The woods closed in around me.

The *tap-tap-tap* of a woodpecker echoed through the pines. A luminescent tangerine shimmered on the swamp just ahead, the last of the sun's rays like spilled paint spreading across the black surface. The only breaks in the thick, murky water were the trees rising from it like bony, cracked fingers.

It was the less traveled "creepy" path in the bayou, one that had been avoided since whispers of the Black Cat had begun spreading like wildfire.

I'd assigned myself to this route, not only because my gut told me that a woman who enjoyed the water would likely be pulled to this trail but also because I was intimately familiar with it. A fact that everyone knew and no one spoke of.

Almost immediately, I picked up shoe prints in the moist soil. Small prints, athletic tread, spaced widely apart. A woman jogging.

I glanced at the GPS. To the east was a narrow, winding road twisting through the pines.

My heart skipped a beat, memories pummeling through my head like a train crash, one cargo car after another.

Chills ran over my arms.

The thunder, the lightning, the rain. The mangled car twisted around a tree. Chunks of her hair caught along the tree limbs.

The blood.

Closing my eyes, I exhaled slowly, envisioning my breath pushing away the memory as if it were nothing more than smoke.

Because that was all it was. Life, death. Gone in the wind.

Refocusing on the prints, I scanned the path from left to right as I journeyed deeper into the forest, where the prints began to widen. I imagined Courtney hitting her stride, sweat beginning to bead on her forehead, her muscles loosening, the runner's high setting in.

A trio of deer burst from the tree line, leaping over the trail, tails up.

*Danger.*

I stopped.

The swamp hugged the trail, a thin green layer of duckweed coating the stagnant water. Intrusive moss dripped from the cypress and tupelo trees that thrived in the slough, their skeletal limbs interconnecting like an army, reminding me whose territory I was in.

My senses sharpened.

I wasn't alone. Something or someone was close by. I could feel it in my bones.

I pulled the SIG from my boot, clasping the grip, adjusting to the weight in my hand, and slowly did a three-sixty scan of my surroundings.

The forest was a loud bustle of activity, flashes of movement flickering in the growing shadows. Creatures making their last rounds before nightfall and letting me know I wasn't welcome.

Once I was certain I was in no immediate danger, I moved forward with two focuses now. One, not losing Courtney's prints, and two, watching for whatever—or whoever—was hunting *me*.

The footprints on the trail suddenly became closer together, as if the runner had slowed down instantly. Had she seen something ahead? Scared, perhaps?

A surge of adrenaline pulsed through my blood, the same feeling I got right before something big was about to happen.

My pace quickened as I followed the prints around a sharp bend in the trail. The woods were darkening by the minute.

I zeroed in on a break in the weeds a yard ahead of me, next to the rotted trunk of a fallen tree. Visually, I followed the path of the disturbed grass, which led into the trees. Then I followed it back to the trail, where I noticed the soil was overturned in several spots.

Something had happened there, no doubt about it. A struggle of some kind.

Lifting my gun, I scanned the woods as I approached the rotted tree, where a green scrunchie lay saturated in mud a foot off the trail.

I clicked on the radio secured to the neck of my high-vis vest. "Crew to Stolle. Beckett, you there?"

A second ticked by, followed by a crackle. "Stolle to Crew. Here."

"I've got her," I said. "Green scrunchie on the side trail that leads down to the swamps. About a half klick west of the main trail."

"Do you have visual?"

"Negative."

"Okay, I'll inform lookout of the new LKP and have Alek head that way. He's closer. Estimate seven minutes."

"Copy. Anything on the bridge?"

"Negative. I'll head that way too. See you soon, bro."

I clicked off, knelt down, and studied the erratic prints in the overturned mud. There were two sets of shoe prints, undoubtedly a scuffle of sorts. One pair of prints belonged to the small jogging tracks I'd been following, the other to much larger hiking boots. I studied the tread. A backpacking boot, I discerned, based on the deep heel indentations into the mud and the high cut of tread.

I shifted position to focus on the bent grass. Unfortunately, the prints were not as clear there, but it was obvious that the hiker, who had come from the woods, had gone back in the same direction.

But where did the small prints go?

It was as if the jogger had disappeared into thin air. Or had her attacker carried her body into the woods?

On my feet again, I waded through the tall weeds, using my headlamp to follow the tracks.

I knelt down again.

No blood, no hair. Using the tip of my finger, I traced the outline of the print, which was no deeper than the ones on the trail. This suggested that the hiker hadn't had extra weight on them when they'd gone back into the woods. Courtney hadn't been carried, and she also hadn't been dragged.

So where the hell was she?

I returned to the point of the scuffle behind the fallen tree. She hadn't gone any farther down the trail.

*What the hell?*

I pulled the flashlight from my belt, clicked it on, and used the wide beam to scan the weeds for a body. There was none.

I slid the light back into its holster to free up my hand, returning to my headlamp as the only light. Turning, I focused on the murky swamp.

A minute passed as I stared at the water.

Slowly, I walked to the edge of the swamp and peered down at the black water, my reflection distorted under a yellow pool of light shimmering on the surface.

I paused, listening.

Felt the air against my face, the humidity against the back of my neck.

Listened to the cicadas click and buzz against the growing night.

I felt her. Close.

I could *feel* her.

As if being pulled by instinct, I stepped into the swamp, my foot sinking into the mud, a circle of waves pulsing away from the movement. Thick, black water engulfed my ankle. I scanned the surface for any predators lurking below, though I knew it was pointless. I was in their territory, invading their space. They had the upper hand.

I took another step, now calf deep in sludge. I glanced into the trees as a blue heron took flight, its large gray wings flapping against the silence.

*Whomp, whomp, whomp.*

Another step, then another.

I stopped, the hair on the back of my neck standing on end. My finger slid over the trigger of my pistol.

Slowly, I turned, my senses in overdrive trying to discern what or who had gotten the drop on me. As I turned, the light from my headlamp slowly swept along the edge of the swamp. A pair of eyes glinted in the light, like an animal caught. Trapped.

But it was no animal.

Curled into the fetal position under an overhang of bushes and gnarled roots, Courtney Hayes hid in the shallow waters of the swamp, hugging one knee to her chest, the other stretched in front of her, completely underwater.

Barely visible if not for the white of her round, horrified eyes, Courtney was covered from head to toe in sludge, her once-vibrant pink tank top now serving as makeshift camouflage. She was sopping wet, with long brown strings of hair snaking down her face. Vomit had settled around her, coating the water in chunky brown liquid.

Her entire body shuddered as she saw me, fear rolling off her in waves. Her lip was bloodied, as was her knee, and that was just what I could see. She looked like a creature from some sci-fi film.

Carefully watching her, I holstered my gun and lifted my palms. "Miss Hayes, my name is Easton Crew, a member of the local search-and-rescue team. I'm here to take you home, ma'am."

The shaking of her body turned to violent palsied shudders, her eyes staring at me, yet through me.

That was when I realized Courtney was in shock and likely had been for a while. Her vital organs weren't receiving adequate blood flow. She needed immediate medical care to avoid serious tissue and organ failure.

I spoke slowly and clearly as I carefully began to approach. "Miss Hayes, are you hurt?"

Her eyes widened as I drew closer.

"Miss Hayes—"

I stopped. Every muscle in my body froze as the water moved next to her.

"Courtney . . . *Courtney*." I repeated her name until I was sure I had her focus. "I need you to stay still—completely still—and I need you to focus on me right now. Can you do that?"

She blinked. A good sign.

"Courtney, don't move." I slowly slid my hand into the pocket at my knee. "I want you to look at me, and me only. Focus on me."

I watched the black water moccasin slide to a stop next to a root less than six inches from Courtney's elbow, the moment another slithered down from the mud above, next to her head. Courtney had found herself close to, if not in, a snake nest, a fact she apparently didn't realize.

Her trembling was causing the water to vibrate, drawing attention from nearby predators. She was a wounded animal caught in the swamp. A sitting duck.

"Courtney, I want you to listen to the sound of my voice and do as I say. We're going to take a deep breath together. Right now. Inhale." I slowly pulled the bag from my pocket. "Exhale . . . inhale . . ."

The shudders began to ease from her body as I slowly inched forward.

"That's right. Good girl. Right here. Focus here . . ."

The snakes moved closer.

"Don't move, okay, Courtney?"

This time, she nodded. Something was registering. I just hoped it wasn't the snakes.

"Good job. Stay still." I slowly brought my arm back and then hurled a handful of tiny balls into the air.

Courtney jerked as the tiny balls splattered the surface.

Snakes, at least six of them, scattered like mice, whipping across the water in the opposite direction. I lunged across the water, black muck splashing into the air, onto my face.

Chaos erupted from somewhere behind me, a heavy splash followed by something popping against the water.

Courtney screamed, a bone-chilling shriek that cut the air like glass.

I had no fucking clue what was going on behind me. My sole focus was on saving Courtney from the den of snakes.

The woods turned into a circus, birds and deer scattering, screaming, into the night.

I grabbed Courtney under the arms and pulled her out of the water, leaping out of the swamp and falling to my knees behind the tall grass. Cradling Courtney in one arm, I pulled my gun with the other hand and spun around.

My headlamp flashed across the swamp, where, next to a thicket of cypress trees, a scaly tail whipped against the shallow water, charging Beckett, who was using his body to distract an alligator that had been seconds from making me his nighttime snack.

Alek burst from the side of the trail, gun up.

I shifted, blocking Courtney's view as two deafening blasts echoed through the woods, followed by quick, urgent chatter between Beckett and Alek. I didn't have to worry about the alligator anymore.

Courtney fell limp in my arms.

Alek ran up and dropped to his knees beside me. "She hurt?"

I repositioned our bodies so that she was in my lap, keeping her head elevated against my chest, getting my first good look at her. Courtney was ghostly pale, her skin covered in angry red bites and an oozing red rash. I hoped to God it wasn't the sign of an infection spreading. The good news was that none of the wounds appeared to be snakebites.

"Get her some water."

Alek slipped out of his pack as my gaze landed on her shoeless foot, then on her ankle, the size of a cantaloupe. Even underneath the sludge and dirt, I could see that it was already ten shades of purple.

"Broken," Alek said as he unscrewed the lid of his thermos. "In several places, if I had to guess."

Beckett jogged up, holstering his gun. "You already call it in?"

I shook my head. "Not yet."

He pulled his radio and stepped aside.

I refocused on Alek. "I need you to search the area, specifically by the fallen tree, over there. Look for the track that leads into the woods. Her attacker fled through the woods to the west."

"You're sure she was attacked?" He glanced at her ankle. "Didn't just fall and hurt herself?"

"I'm sure. She was paralyzed with fear when she saw me. Something happened to her, more than just a fall. Check the prints that intersect with hers. They're hiking boots. Not just traditional hiking boots but backpacking boots. Whoever did this isn't a novice hiker. It's someone who does a lot of outdoor stuff."

Beckett returned. "McNamara and Mason are on their way."

I jerked my chin to the massive alligator now floating belly up in the swamp. "Thanks."

Beckett dipped his chin. "Always wanted to try gator jerky."

"You're sick," Alek mumbled, slowly pouring water against Courtney's blue lips.

We didn't have ten minutes to wait.

I cradled her small body in my arms and stood. "I'll meet them midway. You guys search the tracks in the woods. Report back to the rendezvous site in an hour."

Courtney shifted her weight in my arms, snuggling against my chest. It was then that I noticed the waistband of her pants, twisted and ripped as if hastily pulled up.

Beckett noticed the same thing, saying nothing.

My stomach roiled.

The Black Cat Stalker had done more than just scare this girl.

# Chapter Six

## Mia

It was a bleak, dreary afternoon. Gray clouds swayed around the withering treetops like a ghostly virus spreading through town. The storms from the day before had blown in chilly temperatures and a fog so thick it was as if you could reach out and touch it. The air was cold and heavy, weighted with the kind of mist that fools you into thinking you don't need a raincoat but then slowly soaks you within minutes. The gloom of the weather mirrored the unease rippling through town after one of their own had been found near death in a swamp the day before.

My knuckles were white around the steering wheel, at the textbook ten and two o'clock position, despite being parked for almost an hour. I could no longer feel my fingertips, though I'd yet to slide on the gloves lying on the seat next to me.

The meeting was scheduled for four thirty, but for some reason, I'd arrived at the Skull Hollow Sheriff's Department at three.

The clock on the dashboard read 4:17 p.m. as I turned back to the redbrick building ahead of me, my mind spinning.

*You're wrong, Mia.*

At 4:22 p.m., I wiped my palms on my jeans, the friction of skin against rough fabric sending tingles up my arms.

*It has to be a coincidence.*

At 4:27, a sheen of sweat broke out over my skin. I grabbed my purse and slid it onto my lap.

*It's not happening again.*

I began counting the seconds in my head.

*Twenty-six, twenty-five . . .*

I grabbed the door handle.

*Twenty-four, twenty-three . . .*

The moment the clock clicked to 4:29, I tossed my keys into my bag, banished my nerves, and forced myself out of the Jeep. My senses ignited with the sharp scent of fallen leaves, the musty smell of damp earth. My heart started to race.

*You're wrong, Mia. It's not happening again.*

"Shut up," I muttered through clenched teeth, cursing my brain, which had a mind of its own.

Inhaling, I jerked back my shoulders and strode across the pitted parking lot. Why? Because I had a job to do.

⁓

Despite the cool temperature outside, the white room was stifling, the air heavy with the nauseating scents of burnt coffee and wet paint, courtesy of the renovation underway in the sheriff's department. I hoped fixing the furnace was next on the list.

*White.*

Regardless of the attempt to revamp the department, someone—likely a man—had decided to keep the interview room walls white. A stark, blinding white.

Perhaps the willfully ignorant schlemiel had heard that white was a symbol of purity, peace, and innocence. A fresh start.

Incorrect.

I knew from experience that sitting in a small white room did nothing to calm one's mental state. Quite the opposite, actually.

If the decision maker had spent two seconds researching the color, he would have learned that white is most commonly associated with cold or emptiness or a harsh, sterile environment. It is quite possibly the worst color for fostering the nurturing, safe environment necessary for interviews—or confessions, for that matter.

I stood behind the newly installed two-way mirror, taking a moment to observe the patient in the white room, as I did before any interview.

Courtney Hayes sat in a plastic chair behind a white folding table, picking nervously at her fingernails. Every few seconds, she'd stop to chew on them between her swollen, split lips.

Her left leg, encased in a black cast from the knee down, was stretched awkwardly to the side, propped on an upside-down trash can. A pair of crutches lay on the stained tile floor. On the table were an unopened bottle of water, a box of tissues, a phone, and an audio recorder.

A bike cop I recognized from around town lingered in the corner, no more than nineteen, I guessed, his curious, anxious gaze fixed on Courtney's back. He was undoubtedly wondering what to expect from his first time assigned to a woman on suicide watch.

The girl was a tad over five feet tall, small in stature and extremely skinny. According to the incident report, Courtney was seventeen years old, although based on her size, she looked no more than fourteen. The vintage Metallica T-shirt and bubblegum-pink sweatpants she was wearing were two sizes too big for her frame, giving her a skeletal appearance.

Her arms and neck were covered in nasty red insect bites, some of which had been bandaged. Her pixie-like face was gaunt, pale, her eyes sunken in, one swollen from the gash bandaged above her eyebrow. Her hair had been washed overnight at the hospital and was now hanging in thin chestnut waves down her back. A thick line of black peeked from the roots, suggesting a lack of resources to keep up with her adopted hair color. A fresh patch of acne colored her jawline, the outer effect of extreme stress, although I knew the damage below the surface would be much more devastating.

Courtney was much too skinny. I cataloged this immediately, considering she said she'd been out for a jog.

I began pacing, studying the teen while mindlessly smoothing my clammy palms against my clothes.

I'd chosen a casual outfit for the interview, a fitted black dress shirt tucked into a pair of skinny jeans. Rather than wearing heels, I'd opted for flats. I wanted to ensure my height matched Courtney's as much as possible, which wasn't difficult considering I was only two inches taller than her five feet one. I'd pulled my hair into a messy topknot and chosen to wear my glasses, wide-rimmed tortoiseshell. As with every one of my interviews, my outfit had been meticulously chosen, piece by piece, after studying the file of the patient—or victim.

According to the case notes Deputy Mason had sent me the evening before, Courtney had been transported directly to the emergency room after being rescued from the swamps at Black Hills Bayou. At the ER, she'd received a thorough medical examination, including a rape kit, and had been treated for shock, multiple lacerations, hundreds of insect bites, and a broken ankle.

Page one of the report detailed the multiple lacerations and contusions over her body. Courtney's ankle had suffered what's called a trimalleolar fracture, an all-encompassing diagnostic term for fracturing all three bones at the base of your ankle. She'd been taken into surgery immediately, where the doctor had performed a bone graft and inserted two pins into her ankle. It would be months until she could walk without assistance and longer before she could run again—if ever.

The rape kit, a process of gathering and preserving physical evidence after a suspected sexual assault, showed that Courtney's inner and outer thighs were speckled with small, round contusions similar to fingerprint depressions, suggesting forced compliance. However, the genital exam noted no injury or penetration to the urethra, perineum, labia, hymen, or clitoris. Regardless, samples had been taken and sent off for analysis.

But page two told a very different story.

Further examination showed significant abrasion and tearing both around and inside the anus. Specifically, a friction injury called shearing was noted, where significant and repeated back-and-forth force of an object separates the top layer of skin from the bottom of the epidermis. Foreign particles had been discovered inside the tiny lacerations, most notably dirt, insects, and pieces of cork cambium—the bark of a tree branch.

Not a speck of DNA, fingerprint, hair, or semen had been found outside or inside Courtney's body.

While the full report had yet to be released, the preliminary report said enough.

The medical report had taken me thirty minutes to read. Not because of its length but because of the number of times I'd had to walk away and recenter myself so that I wouldn't vomit on the paperwork.

And I had yet to finish it.

Courtney had been given a cocktail of pain medication, antibiotics, steroids, and benzodiazepine and had fallen asleep shortly after, sleeping through most of the first night. At her doctor's urging, the police had not been allowed to interview Courtney until she was in stable condition.

According to the confidential report, Courtney's mother had remained by her daughter's side at the hospital—until they'd arrived, together, at the sheriff's department the following afternoon. Bunnie Hayes remained in her car, chugging coffee and smoking like a freight train, while her daughter was wheeled into the sheriff's department, where Deputy Mason interviewed Courtney about her attack.

Correction—*attempted* to interview.

Courtney didn't say much, only that she'd been attacked by a masked man with a knife while jogging and that she didn't recognize her attacker. She had yet to use the word *rape*, despite the evidence in her medical examination report.

She had yet to accept it.

The small town of Skull Hollow was in an uproar. Gossip ran rampant, citizens blaming the horrific attack on the mysterious Black Cat Stalker and demanding his head on a stick. Although the coincidence was too great to ignore, sexual assault did not fit the Black Cat's MO.

This was when I'd been called in. The cops had discovered that Courtney had recently scheduled an appointment with the Dragonfly Clinic *before* her attack, citing anxiety as the reason. The appointment had been scheduled for the following week. Not only was this interesting, but it also presented an opportunity.

The hopes were twofold. First, that Courtney would feel more comfortable opening up to a woman—one she had already reached out to and was familiar with—and in tandem, that I would build a psychological profile of her attacker to help narrow down the suspect pool and catch the son of a bitch.

Something that I had very little faith in.

∽

I inhaled deeply, my fingertips digging into the ledge below the two-way mirror, steeling myself for what I was about to do.

My heart began to race, that insufferable, suffocating heat sliding up my throat, the voice in my head beginning to—

*No.*

I squeezed my eyes shut.

*No.*

But the voices penetrated, as they always did.

*You're an imposter, a fraud. Nothing but a liar, a fake.*

*They'll figure you out.*

*They'll find out.*

*They'll* find out.

"No," I hissed under my breath, anger mixing with the anxiety. *"No."*

I inhaled again, forcing away the voice, willing my pulse to ease, the rage to simmer.

"You have a job to do," I whispered to myself, now staring at the girl on the other side of the mirror. "A job."

I squared my shoulders, smoothed my shirt, and pushed open the thick steel door to Interview Room One.

Courtney startled as the door opened. Her red-rimmed eyes met mine with fear, then quickly relaxed in surprise. She recognized me.

The kid cop straightened from the wall he'd been leaning against, startled as well. I nodded for him to leave, thanking him as he closed the door behind him.

Crossing the room, I assessed her as she assessed me.

"Hi." Smiling, I asked, "Mind if I sit?"

Courtney shook her head, shifting in her seat.

I pulled back the empty chair from the table, the loud squeaks of steel against tile like nails on a chalkboard. Courtney and I cringed simultaneously.

I needed to pull it the fuck together. I was the interviewer, *not* the interviewee.

I lowered myself into the chair, wobbling a bit on the uneven legs. I paused, wobbled again.

"Excuse me." I stood, plucking a handful of tissues from the box, then squatted next to the chair. "There are few things I have absolutely no patience for, and uneven chairs are one of them," I said as I stuffed the wad of tissues under the back leg of the ten-dollar metal chair. Nodding to her chair, I asked, "Yours?"

Courtney's face softened in the closest thing to a smile I was going to get, and that worked for me. She nodded.

I stood, plucked more tissues, squatted by her chair, and leveled the legs. Courtney didn't flinch—and this was exactly what I was hoping for. It was men who scared her, not women.

My stomach rolled as I settled back into my chair. Courtney began fidgeting with the hem of her faded Metallica tee.

"Can I get you some water? Tea or coffee? Do you drink coffee yet?"

Courtney shook her head.

"You will soon enough, trust me." I opened my bag to pull out the Diet Coke I'd gotten from the break room vending machine and passed it to her. She unscrewed the lid and took a deep sip, then another.

"Good?"

"Good."

"Courtney, my name is Mia Frost, and I'm a therapist. I believe you called my clinic last week requesting an appointment."

She nodded.

"I'm sorry I wasn't able to get you in sooner and especially that we have to first meet under these circumstances."

"That's okay." The teenager lowered her gaze, fidgeting now with the label on the Coke.

I inhaled . . . and began.

"I know that many different people have met with you, asking all sorts of questions . . . uncomfortable questions. And I'm sorry you've had to go through that. Please know that if at any point during our chat today you need a break or simply want to stop talking, you absolutely have the right to do so. Also know that in my line of work, there's nothing you could tell me that I likely haven't heard before. There's no surprise, no judgment, on this side of the table; I can promise you that."

After receiving a slight nod but no eye contact from Courtney, I continued.

"My purpose here today is to understand more about what happened to you on the Black Cat Trail. Using that information, I'm going to build a psychological profile of the man who attacked you so that the cops can have a better idea of who they are looking for."

Courtney looked up with a slight flicker of interest. I adjusted my pitch accordingly at this point, to explain further and keep the interest I'd unexpectedly piqued.

"You see, I look at things a bit differently than the officers that you've spoken to. Their main focus is to gather evidence, as well as facts and figures. Undoubtedly, those are the most important pieces to solving a case and finding the bastard who committed the crime."

Her lip twitched.

"But what I do is different. I listen to your story and try to get into the mind of the offender—the man who attacked you. I try to understand him, why and how he did what he did, why he picked you specifically. Then I build a profile of this person to help the police narrow down the suspect pool, so to speak. I also try to predict what the bad guy might do in the future, and when, so that no one else gets hurt. So by combining the police's fancy facts and figures with my profile, we can narrow down the search drastically and in a much quicker fashion. Does that make sense?"

Courtney nodded. I now had her full attention.

"Great. Now, with your permission, I'd like to record . . ."

When I reached across the table to the recorder, Courtney immediately leaned back as much as the chair would allow, retreating and withdrawing from the conversation. The interest I'd had a second earlier was gone.

I pulled back my hand, studying her for a minute.

Her once-pale cheeks were now flushed from the heat of the room, tiny beads of sweat forming at her hairline. I saw myself in her in that moment. I remembered the bright, unforgiving lights, the faces, the voices, the questions, the bitterness of the terrible coffee I'd been given.

The eyes staring at me.

The pity.

God, the *pity.*

I tilted my head to the side. "It's hot in here, yes?"

"Yeah." Courtney nodded, a bead of condensation dripping through her fingers from the Coke bottle she was gripping like a lifeline.

"Hang on just a sec."

I pushed out of my chair. She watched me as I strode across the room and opened the door. Peering out, I looked up and down the hallway, ignoring a few confused glances from cops sitting in the bullpen.

I turned back to Courtney, grinned, and jerked my head to the hallway. "Come on."

She gaped at me.

"Come on," I whispered, my grin widening.

Courtney pushed out of the plastic chair with more energy than I would have guessed from her composure just seconds earlier, proving just how badly she wanted out of that damn room. After assisting her in sliding the crutches under her arms, I helped her hobble across the white room.

Courtney paused dramatically behind me in the doorway, like an excited teen about to execute their first "sneak-out." I made a flamboyant show of checking up and down the hall again.

I pictured a small grin curving her sharp pixie face, if only in my imagination.

"Okay," I whispered over my shoulder. "Come on, let's do this."

Courtney followed as I hurried down the narrow hallway and pivoted into the break room. I grabbed a bottle of water from the counter, paused, then glanced at her with a smirk, nodding to the open box of doughnuts on the break room table.

She nodded feverishly, her eyes twinkling.

I quickly grabbed a stack of paper towels, and together, we piled doughnuts onto our napkins like children stealing from the cookie jar.

Balancing everything in a stack in my hands, I grabbed another bottle of water and whispered, "Come on."

The grin that split her face was absolutely glorious. I'll never forget it.

Courtney followed me through the back door, into the cool, dreary afternoon, which somehow was also glorious after sitting in that damn room. Together, we gulped the cool, fresh breeze, a gift from Mother Nature welcoming us to the freedom of the outdoors. The mist had subsided, thankfully, and in the distance, a line of sapphire blue suggested sunshine was on the way. We crossed the parking lot to a picnic table hidden underneath mature oak and pine trees.

I could practically hear Courtney relaxing behind me. Hell, I was too. I'd just settled Courtney onto the bench when the door flung open.

"Hey! What's going on?" Deputy Chris Mason stalked across the parking lot like a storm cloud about to burst open.

Courtney shot me a panicked look. Apparently, she was as fond of the deputy as I was. I winked at her, then turned to the man and smiled broadly.

Chris Mason, age thirty-three, had transferred to Skull Hollow from Cooper County in northwest Oklahoma after his department had downsized due to budget cuts. A borderline narcissist, Mason had a head nearly as swollen as his biceps, which he liked to show off by wearing too-tight shirts that stretched like the Incredible Hulk's. Although nothing was incredible about this man.

I'd met Chris at the local pizzeria one evening while waiting on my double-cheese hand-tossed. He was alone at the bar. In under one minute, the man had made his way to me like a moth to a flame, standing uncomfortably close while he ordered another Pabst.

In under five minutes, I learned that Chris was a former baseball player whose minor-league career had been ended by a torn Achilles on game four of the Triple-A National Championship Game—*ten years* earlier. I learned that Deputy Mason could squat a clean 325, had just purchased a brand-new Silverado, and had a cat named the Rock . . . after—you guessed it—the Rock.

Mason was the kind of guy who manscaped in the shower and felt the need to prove his masculinity by offering bone-crushing handshakes, using big words, and making gay jokes. The only thing Chris Mason asked about me in that entire five minutes was if I was free Friday night.

I'd said no, wrapped my slice of pizza in a napkin, and turned and walked away. And that was that.

I'd been surprised when he'd called, requesting my services to assist on Courtney's case, and couldn't help but wonder if there was more to it. Because Chris Mason wasn't the type of guy to take no for an answer.

$\sim$

"We're just getting some fresh air," I said to the deputy, meeting him next to a spray-painted camouflage 1985 Datsun King Cab pickup with a vanity plate that read *EASYRDR*.

"Can I talk to you for a quick second, Dr. Frost? Over there."

"I'll be right back," I said over my shoulder to Courtney before following Deputy Mason to a nearby dumpster barely out of hearing distance from the teenager now devouring a jelly-filled doughnut.

Propping his hands on his hips, he glared down at me. "What the hell are you doing?"

"I'm interviewing the witness, exactly as you called me in to do."

"Are you? Because it looks like you've taken our only witness of the Black Cat Stalker for an impromptu picnic."

"Do you have children, Deputy Mason?" I asked, even though I already knew the answer. Mason's messy divorce from his beautician wife, along with all their dirty laundry, which included rumors of infidelity, had been the hot gossip in Skull Hollow for almost all of last year.

"No, I don't have kids," Deputy Mason said defiantly, as if I were going to question or argue this.

*As if.*

"Well, if you did, you would know that aside from raging mood swings and debilitating confidence issues, teenagers despise authority. Putting this poor girl in an interview room after she was brutally attacked and expecting her to obediently sit through hours of questions is the worst thing you could do to get her to open up."

"Mia—"

"It's Dr. Frost."

Mason's perfectly sculpted brow cocked. "Fine. *Dr. Frost*, I understand that you and your staff at the Dragonfly Clinic do things differently. I understand your whole MO"—he paused for sarcastic effect—"is that you're an unconventional therapist, as is your clinic. But now isn't the time to try new things. The Black Cat Stalker is growing more notorious by the day, and this new incident just shot our town into the stratosphere."

He jabbed his fingers through his hair, the thin fabric of his T-shirt groaning against the assault.

"Maddie over at SET News has already called me seven times this morning—*seven*. This thing is blowing up, Frost. We have a certain way of doing things here, and this involves *recording* witness testimony. You can't just pull her outside for a chat. You were asked to come in to interview Courtney Hayes and build us a psychological profile—on the record. I need all of this recorded. Every single damn word of it."

Hostility brewed in my stomach, but I swallowed it. I'd learned long ago that nothing threw off a man like a woman with a cool head. I knew how to play the game. In my line of work, I had to.

"Deputy Mason, what makes you think that I'm not doing the job that you've requested of me?"

Johnny Bravo dramatically gestured to the picnic table where Courtney was licking the jelly from her fingers.

"Your interview room is stifling," I said. "Courtney is scared, vulnerable, and physically uncomfortable—not to mention intimidated simply by being here at the sheriff's department. Under these circumstances, I feel strongly that I can't get a true and accurate report from the victim without interviewing her in a more accommodating environment."

"Out here?"

"I'd rather take her to my office—"

"No. It has to be here."

"Then yes, here, outside in the fresh air, with a little food and water in her stomach. I'd like to talk to her woman to woman. This is how I'm going to build a successful psychological profile for you, Deputy Mason."

"What about recording the interview?"

I showed him the iPhone in my hand.

"You're planning to record on that?"

"Instead of the 1980s Talkboy tape recorder you have on the table in there? Yeah."

His gaze lingered on Courtney for a few seconds. Finally, I was granted approval with a dip of his baby-smooth square chin.

"Thank you," I said. "Now leave us alone. I'll have your interview for you shortly."

"And the profile?"

"Shortly."

"Define *shortly*."

"Shortly."

I turned my back on him and crossed the pavement.

Truth was, I'd already built a profile in my head. One that had haunted my nightmares for years.

# Chapter Seven

## Mia

"Let's start at the beginning."

Courtney nodded from across the picnic table, her cheeks a rosy pink, her demeanor less stressed. Her guard had been left in the Skull Hollow Sheriff's Department, in that damn suffocating white room.

It was time.

"I'm going to ask you a series of questions. You have a choice with each one. Answer them or don't—it's totally up to you. Do only what you're comfortable with, but know that the reason for this interview is to not only help find your attacker but also hopefully prevent this from happening to anyone—"

Courtney sucked in a sharp breath. "I don't want this to happen to anyone else."

A little piece of my heart shattered at that.

"Is it okay if I record this?"

"Yes," she said, her voice stronger now.

I slid my phone to the center of the picnic table and tapped the record button. I went through the mandatory introductory script, reciting who I was and why I was there, then asked Courtney to confirm her name, age, and address.

Finally, we got down to business.

"Let's start by you taking me through the day of the attack. From the moment you woke until you were found in the swamp. It doesn't have to be perfect; just take me through whatever you can remember. Tell me even the silliest things, small details, as they pop into your head. I'll ask questions as we go."

Courtney swallowed deeply, her back straightening. She took a deep breath and began. "I woke up around seven, like usual, got ready, and went to school."

"What did you wear?"

She blinked, then tilted her head to the side. "Uh, jeans and a T-shirt. And sandals—no, sneakers. My white sneakers."

"Did you drive to school or . . ."

Courtney nodded. "Oh. Yes, I just got a new car." She smiled sheepishly. "It's old but what I could afford."

"My first car was a fuchsia 1985 Dodge Shadow with purple-tinted windows and over a hundred thousand miles on it."

A hint of a smile crossed Courtney's lips.

I continued, "The fabric that lined the roof had pulled away from the frame and hung down like drapes over my head," I said.

She snorted out a laugh.

"Tell me about it." I winked. "Okay, continue."

Courtney repositioned herself in her seat, getting more comfortable by the minute. "So I went to school. It was just a normal school day; nothing weird or different happened. Then I went to band practice. And then I was supposed to meet Jamie for a jog at the Black Cat Trail."

"Who chose the location?"

"I did."

"Any reason?"

"Yeah. I'd jogged the other trails in the area already. This was the only one I hadn't."

"Sounds like a lot of jogging."

Courtney looked down. "I've been trying to lose weight." Guilt pulled at her face, and I imagined she was regretting devouring the doughnuts.

I stilled, my thoughts suddenly swerving to the moment I'd noticed how skinny she was and how, considering that, I'd cataloged it as interesting that she'd been out on a jog. The signs were there, and I was surprised I hadn't noticed the indications immediately. Courtney was not only too skinny; she was malnourished and very likely knee deep in an eating disorder. I quickly drew from my past experience, building a profile of an anorexic young adult.

Shy, introverted, resistant to change, low self-esteem. Sensation seeking and reward dependent, usually stemming from a lack of love and appreciation within the household—from, say, a disconnected mother.

This was an entirely different subject that needed to be psychologically evaluated, one that I didn't think Deputy Mason would appreciate me focusing on in this particular interview. There were more pressing matters to attend to. Although someday soon, I vowed to myself, I would circle back to this one.

Courtney lifted one shoulder. "Anyway, Jamie got in trouble for something, I think not cleaning her room or something like that. Her parents are real strict. She was grounded after school and couldn't come."

I made a note to have Mason confirm that.

"Were you supposed to meet at the trail or drive together?"

"Meet there. Like I said, Jamie's parents are pretty hard core about curfew, so she always takes her own car everywhere."

Courtney stopped suddenly, observing the woods, her thoughts somewhere else. Somewhere I really wanted her to take me. But she didn't.

"When you learned Jamie had to cancel, you decided to go on a jog by yourself?"

Courtney nodded.

"Why?" I asked.

She shrugged.

I let the silence linger. There was a lot here to unpack.

"I didn't really want to go home," Courtney muttered.

"Why?"

"My mom and dad . . . they're getting a divorce."

"Ah. I'm sorry. I'll bet that makes for a very tense household."

"It's just Mom at the house. My dad is in jail."

"I'm sorry to hear that."

Courtney shrugged, and another moment of silence passed.

"I remember when my parents got a divorce," I said. "When my dad moved out, it was just me and my mom. And she didn't handle things very well."

"How old were you?"

"Nine. I remember feeling like everything was my fault."

"Was it?"

"No, and Courtney, it's not your fault either. It's a tough time, I know, but their separation isn't your fault."

She nodded, then looked down.

"Let's go back to that day." I glanced at the red light on the phone. "So you decided to go for a jog . . ."

"Yeah. Yes. So I drove to the trail. I got there around five or so. The sun was setting, but it was really cloudy, and I remember thinking the woods were dark."

This was Courtney's instinct awakening. The one that she'd ignored.

"Do you remember anyone else in the parking lot?"

"Yes, a black truck and a blue minivan."

"Can you remember the details of the vehicles? Make or model? Old or new?"

"The truck was old . . . that's all I can remember."

"Bumper stickers?"

She shook her head.

"And the van?"

"It was like every other blue van, you know, the kind that moms drive. Oh, it had a bike rack on the back."

"Was there anyone in the vehicles?"

"I don't remember."

"Okay, go on."

"So I locked my car and slid the keys under the front wheel before I started stretching."

I bit my tongue and refrained from telling her what a terrible place this was to leave your keys. "Was anyone around you at that time? Maybe in the woods or just past the trail?"

"No."

"Okay."

"Then I started my jog."

"Did you pass anyone?"

"Yes, I passed a woman pushing a stroller."

"Was she alone?"

"Yes, just her and a little kid . . . probably the person who owned the van, I guess. Anyway, I was almost to the top of the mountain, and that's when I passed a man walking . . . coming toward me from the opposite direction." Her voice grew quieter, her shoulders drawing in.

"Are you sure it was a man?"

"Yes, I think so."

"What makes you sure?"

She thought for a minute. "I don't know; that was just my immediate reaction, I guess. The shape of the body, the way he was dressed and walked. I just knew it was a man."

"So he was walking, not jogging, correct?"

"Yeah."

"Did that strike you as odd?"

"No, I don't think so. A lot of people just walk the trails."

"Do you remember what he was wearing?"

"Yes, all black. Everything was black. He had a baseball cap on, and he had a black bandanna around his neck. Oh, and black sunglasses too. Uh, aviators, I think."

Goose bumps prickled my skin like a million little tiny ants crawling up my arms. My pulse began to pick up pace.

"Could you tell his skin color?"

"Yes. He was white."

"Beard? Mustache?"

"No."

"No to both?"

"Right. He didn't have any hair on his face."

"Where was this? Exactly."

"Just before the top of that hill before the swamps. He was coming down as I was going up." She quietly folded her hands in her lap and swallowed hard.

I wanted to stop in that moment, just walk away and let her be. But I knew the one thing Courtney needed more than privacy was for us to catch the son of a bitch.

A long moment passed.

A yellow leaf floated down from the tree above, settling onto the picnic table. She picked it up and began plucking the brittle leaf apart, piece by piece.

Her voice was tiny now, small, like a scared child, as she continued. "I veered off the main trail then, to the one that runs by the swamps. I felt . . . I think I heard something in the woods."

My stomach began to twist in knots. "Did you look over your shoulder?" I asked, focusing on the strength of my voice.

Courtney shook her head. "I just kept running, but I was really aware all of a sudden, if that makes sense."

"Yes, that makes perfect sense. That was your sixth sense, Courtney, your woman's instinct. Always listen to that little voice."

She nodded. "I started running a little faster. I wanted to get away from the area."

My pulse turned into a steady thrumming.

"Then I was by the swamps, and that's when I noticed . . . something moving in the woods."

She closed her eyes, and I wanted to close mine too.

"And then . . ."

"Then what, Courtney?"

"I . . . I . . ." Her lip quivered, her hands clasping on her lap. "I slowed, stopped—I shouldn't have. I don't know why. I think I was thinking I should turn around and get back to the main trail."

"Where did you stop? Do you remember?"

"There was this really old tree trunk next to the trail. Like a fallen tree?"

I nodded.

"There. That's where I stopped . . . he attacked me from the side—the same guy I passed on the trail." Her voice shook as her words began running together like a hysterical confession. "He jumped out of the woods and attacked me. He said he had a knife. Told me if I screamed or moved he'd slice my throat."

"Did you see a knife?"

"No, I don't think so."

"Then what?"

"I got away, tripped as I tried to run away, and fell into the swamp. And then I just stayed there, hiding."

I blinked. Courtney had just skipped over the biggest part of her ordeal. Okay, I decided, I needed to just go with this.

"How did you get away?"

"I kicked him."

"Good job."

She frowned, wiping a tear from her cheek.

"Not many try to get away. You're a strong girl, Courtney."

She sniffed.

"Did you see his face?"

"No, he was wearing a black bandanna around his nose and mouth, like a mask. And . . . I shut my eyes for most of it."

"The same bandanna he was wearing around his neck when you passed him earlier?"

"I think so, yes."

"What about the sunglasses, the aviators? You mentioned when he passed you he was wearing sunglasses."

"Yeah, he had those on, and the baseball cap too."

"Okay, so you were attacked, got away, and then you . . . fell?"

"Yeah. After I got away, I tripped and fell into the swamp. I didn't know if he was gone or not or if he was going to try to get me again, so I hid . . . there was this cave, kind of, just under the shore. I shoved myself into it and made myself as small as I could."

"How long did you stay there?"

"A long time. I realized my ankle was broken. After a few hours, after it had been quiet for a while, I dragged myself onto the trail. But when I realized there was no way I could drag myself miles back to the car, I just . . . hid again. In the best place I thought—the swamp."

"Did anyone pass by while you were in hiding?"

"No. It got dark quick."

"So you think your attacker left right away?"

"Yeah, I think so. I screamed . . . toward the end. Right before I got away. I think that scared him. But I was worried he was going to come back."

"How long did you stay in the swamp?"

"All night. I couldn't walk. Didn't have my cell phone . . . I got sick. Really dizzy. I don't remember much after that. Until he came for me."

"Who?"

"A search-and-rescue guy," she said, a hint of adoration in her tone.

"Do you remember his name?"

Courtney sniffed, then sighed, frustrated that she didn't remember the name of her apparent new hero. "No." She shook her head. "I'd thrown up everywhere . . . I think even other stuff too." She glanced at me from under her lashes.

"You have absolutely nothing to be embarrassed about, Courtney."

She took a deep breath. "Anyway, I don't know his name."

"I think it was Easton Crew," I said, recalling the information on the incident report.

She lit up. "Yeah, that's it. He, Easton—I mean Mr. Crew—found me. I don't know how. And he saved me. I heard there were snakes everywhere . . . I remember hearing him tell someone else that it was a miracle I didn't get bitten."

"And then what happened?"

"I remember other guys coming up. They made some sort of plan. And then Mr. Crew carried me back to the trailhead. I would have been dead if it wasn't for him."

As would be many Skull Hollow locals and tourists if not for LYNX Search and Rescue—if you believe the gossip, anyway. I'd heard about the "guys" within my first week of moving to Skull Hollow.

A group of former jarheads and federal agents, the men of the LYNX Group had become sensationalized over the years, mainly due to the fact they were rarely seen in public. Rumors of what secret— or nefarious—programs they conducted behind the tall gates of their compound were widely gossiped about, as were their pantie-soaking good looks.

Although, at that time, I hadn't had the pleasure of meeting a LYNX superhero, I knew the type. In college, I'd studied notes of the cases of former special ops soldiers and had even participated in a few therapy sessions.

They were all the same—thrill seekers who craved high-intensity and high-risk situations. Ambulance chasers. Macho alpha males who thrived on saving the damsel in distress and the praise and glorification that came afterward. Life to this kind of man was defined by heroic adventure and how many women they had along the way.

"So Mr. Crew carried you to the trailhead. Then what happened?"

"I remember being surprised my mom was there."

"Surprised?"

Courtney nodded. "I knew she had to work."

"Her daughter was missing. That must have been horrifying for her."

The teenager began scraping at what remained of the black polish on her nails. Talking about her mom made her close up. I made a mental note.

"And then what?"

"I was put in the ambulance."

"That must have been a relief."

"Yes, it was."

"How were you feeling then?"

"I hurt."

My stomach flopped. "I understand your back was pretty cut up, from the ground, right?"

"Yeah."

"What else hurt?"

"My ankle, and my eye." She lifted her hand to the bandage above her black eye.

I leaned forward, my heart pounding wildly. "What else?"

Courtney looked down.

"Anything else?"

As tears shimmered along the rims of the girl's bloodshot eyes, I wanted to hold her. Pick her up, hug her. Put her in my pocket where she would never experience the evil in the world again.

I also wanted to run. Retreat. Hide.

I didn't want to hear it. I didn't want to hear this part of her story. But I had to. It was my *job*.

*You're an imposter, a fraud. Nothing but a liar, a fake. You don't deserve to be here, to pretend to treat others. You don't—*

*Stop.*

*Stop.*

Stop.

I took a silent deep breath. "Can you tell me more about the attack, Courtney?"

A cool breeze swept past us, a silent urging. I sat stoic, frozen on pins and needles.

"He . . . jumped out of the weeds . . ." Courtney kept her gaze down, picking now at the hem of her shirt. "He grabbed my arm and yanked me back."

A minute of silence passed, my pulse beating like a drum in my ear.

"And then he pulled me down and dragged me behind the tree trunk. He told me that if I screamed or moved, he would slice my throat."

"Did you see the knife?" I asked again, needing to be certain of this.

"No . . . I don't think so."

Courtney hadn't seen a knife. I knew she hadn't.

"And that's when it happened . . ."

When her voice trailed off, I didn't fill the awkward, gut-wrenching silence because I knew that she needed to say it. Sheriff McNamara and Deputy Mason needed to hear her say it. What had happened to her needed to be in black and white, for them, for the courts, for the record.

"What happened, Courtney?" I whispered, leaning forward.

A tear trickled down her cheek. Her voice was so small. "He . . . he held my wrists over my head with one hand and yanked down my pants with the other. I couldn't watch." Her cheeks flared. With embarrassment. With shame.

*Goddamn the shame.*

Like a dam breaking, Courtney curled in on herself, sobbing. I scrambled out of my seat and dropped to my knees at her feet, my fists clenched so tightly against my thighs that I felt the sting of my nails slicing into my flesh.

She turned to me, tears rolling down her cheeks. "And then he pulled my panties down. He covered my mouth, forced my knees up, and raped me with a stick."

# Chapter Eight

## Mia

Back inside the sheriff's department, I stumbled into the women's bathroom, gasping for breath. The door slapped shut behind me as I lunged for the sink, my wide eyes wildly sweeping over the stalls to make sure I was alone.

Pieces of memories flashed behind my eyes. An incoherent jumble of flashbacks colliding like a train wreck in my head.

My hand trembled as I turned on the water and ducked my face underneath the stream, uncaring about my hair, makeup, or shirt. The cold water on my scorching skin felt like an explosion of glass across my cheek. I sputtered in the stream. Sweat rolled down my spine and the back of my legs as I angled my face so the water ran over my pulsating forehead.

Believe it or not, this was always the worst. Not the dizziness, the confusion, the constriction of my lungs. No, the worst part was the rush of heat that came with the panic attack. The kind of suffocating heat that felt like a wave of lava sweeping over your skin, dragging you under, slowly consuming every inch of your body while you were unable to stop it. The kind that incited a fiery rage of confusion and madness. An internal battle of trying to remember and trying to forget.

Why couldn't I remember?

Footsteps sounded in the hall.

*Shit.*

I spun around while pulling a handful of paper towels from the dispenser and lunged into the closest bathroom stall. Shutting the thin metal door as quietly as I could, I fumbled with the lock with one hand as I desperately clawed at the top buttons of my shirt with the other.

I wanted to rip it off, claw off my skin, then shove my fist through the wall.

*Stop. Stop. Stop.*

When the bathroom door opened, I froze. Inhaled and held it. The footsteps moved into the stall next to me. Slowly, I backed up, pressing my back against the wall, and held my breath until the woman finished her business and exited, the door slapping shut behind her.

Exhaling, I collapsed, my knees giving out from under me as I slid down the white concrete wall onto the bathroom floor. I pulled my knees to my chest. A tube of lip gloss and a bottle of Tylenol rolled to the drain in the middle of the floor.

My teeth clenched.

*Another panic attack.*

I took a few deep breaths, my lungs expanding like normal.

The end was coming, thank God, but soon to follow would be the anger. The rage. The disappointment in my inability to control my own body.

I rested my forehead against my knees until my breath returned and the light-headedness subsided.

Another fucking panic attack.

Another broken memory of the past.

# Chapter Nine

## Mia

I dried my blouse under the bathroom hand dryer, wiped the smudged mascara from my cheeks, and twisted my hair into a tight bun. After taking a long drink from the faucet, I popped a stick of gum in my mouth and pushed out the bathroom door. It wasn't the first time I'd had to clean up quickly after a panic attack.

The moment the bathroom door shut behind me, Deputy Mason appeared from around the corner. He'd been waiting on me.

God, I despised the man.

"So? What did you get?"

"Is she still here?" Ignoring his question, I breezed past him, beelining to the window that overlooked the parking lot.

Courtney and her mother were gone.

*Dammit.*

I'd planned to discreetly offer Courtney free therapy if she would be interested in seeing me again professionally. Properly, at the office.

I'd have to find a way to see her again. And I would. Because I was determined to ensure Courtney didn't turn out like me.

I scanned the street, then finally turned and offered Mason my attention. Half of it, anyway. "I got everything you wanted from Courtney."

"Did you get a description of the guy?"

"As much as she could recall, yes. It's all recorded."

"And your psychological profile of him?"

"As discussed, I'll have my profile to you first thing tomorrow morning."

"What do you have so far?"

Deputy Mason was unsatisfied, and I was officially out of patience. I stepped around him. "I'll have my report tomorrow morning."

I made my way to the deputy's office, where I'd been instructed to leave my purse while interviewing Courtney. But he chased after me.

"Come on, Doc. You have to have an idea of the type of guy he is or at least something floating around in your head already. Something to help us."

Mason was correct. Despite my personal rule to sleep on a profile so that not a single detail was missed, at that moment, I could have given the deputy everything he was asking for. Hell, I even had a physical image of the offender sketched in my head—nothing that would hold up in court, of course, but nonetheless, I could have delivered even more than Deputy Mason expected.

But the impatient bastard was going to have to wait until I'd had at least one glass of wine and an hour to put my thoughts on paper. The ones I would allow him to read, anyway.

As we stepped into his postage-stamp-size office, Mason quickly bulldozed his way around me, cutting me off because it was unacceptable that *I* lead the way into *his* territory. He squeezed behind a cluttered, scratched-to-hell mahogany desk, leaving me at the door in a cloud of Cool Water cologne.

Deputy Mason was a walking stereotype of the worst kind of alpha male—arrogant, narrow minded, and uncompromising. And for the cherry on top, he drove a tiny sports car with three hundred horsepower to make up for the deficiency in his pants.

Borderline narcissist? No, full-fledged narcissistic personality disorder. In my humble professional opinion, anyway.

"Phone," he demanded, extending his palm.

I pulled my cell from my pocket and, after a brief pause, clicked it on. This hesitation surprised me. I was protective of Courtney and our interview, which meant I was allowing my emotions into a case.

That wasn't good.

I clicked on the file of the recording and handed him the phone. "There it is. Everything you asked for."

Mason snatched the phone from my hand, pulled a USB cord from the floor, and inserted the tip into the end of the phone. A few clicks of his mouse later, he began transferring the audio file onto his computer.

"Three minutes to download. Give me the CliffsNotes."

"Mason, I told you I would have the profile for you first thing tomorrow morning. It's vital that I spend time organizing my thoughts so that my profile is as accurate as possible and I don't send you down the wrong trail."

"We don't have time for you to organize your thoughts."

Because there were so many, he meant? Or because I was slow at doing so? I assumed the latter.

"If this is the Black Cat Stalker," he said, leaning into his computer, willing the file to transfer faster, "he's stepped up his game. In the worst way possible. The motherfucker will be charged with first-degree aggravated sexual assault *and* battery—do you understand . . . shit, Frost, I can't even remember the last time we charged someone with aggravated *sodomy* in recent history. That shit doesn't happen around here. We have no time to lose in this case."

He was right. Aggravated assault is unfortunately far too common, but aggravated sexual battery—defined as when the offender uses a foreign object to penetrate the sexual organ or anus—is far less common.

And in Courtney's case, her anus was the only organ penetrated, which made this case even more bizarre, gruesome, and sensational.

Why only that organ? And why a stick? Did the object have significant meaning to the offender? Why no penile penetration?

Did this open the door to consider if the offender could possibly be female?

The possibilities were endless, each as disturbing as the next.

Mason was also right that time was of the essence—I felt it in my gut.

I took a deep breath, and despite every instinct in my body telling me not to, I gave him my preliminary thoughts. My first mistake of many.

"I believe that you're looking for a disorganized offender."

Mason glanced up from beneath thick black lashes, studying me for a second. This surprised him, and I wasn't sure why.

"Go on."

"Off the record, right?"

He rolled his eyes in a dramatic, effeminate fashion. "Yes."

"In contrast to an organized offender, who plans his or her crimes and typically leaves very few clues, Courtney's recollection of what happened suggests her attack was spontaneous—not planned. Therefore suggesting the offender is a disorganized personality."

"Why? What makes you say that?"

"One, Courtney passed her attacker before he—let's assume it's a male for now—"

"She was sexually assaulted, Dr. Frost. Of course it was a male."

"You don't think females are capable of sexual assault?"

He paused, opened his mouth, thought better of it, then closed it and nodded at me to continue.

"The fact that he passed her before circling back to ambush her suggests a 'wrong place, wrong time' scenario. The offender saw Courtney and *then* made the decision to attack. This points to a disorganized offender, one that attacks off the cuff. Her attack wasn't personal, had nothing to do with her personally. My assumption here is that there was something about Courtney that triggered him, perhaps a thought that was already festering in his head."

I began pacing, restless energy accompanying my now-racing brain.

"Hell, maybe that's why he was out for a hike in the first place. He was mad about something, likely a woman, or maybe about something that bruised his ego, and needed to blow off steam. Perhaps he was already considering assaulting a woman—especially if he had done it before—and *bam*, Courtney presented herself. Wrong place, wrong time."

"And you're saying this makes him a disorganized—"

Whirling around, I glared at Mason. "I'm not done. Courtney's attacker also didn't wear a mask. According to her statement, the man was Caucasian, had no facial hair, and was wearing a black bandanna around his neck and sunglasses when he passed, most of his face on full display. A man who was planning to rape a woman would have made more of an effort to conceal his identity."

"But she said the man who attacked her wore a mask."

"The black bandanna that was around his neck. He simply pulled it up."

"But that points to an organized killer. Because he was wearing it in the first place."

"Incorrect. Bandannas, or neck gaiters, whatever you want to call them, are often worn by runners or hikers to wipe sweat from their face during hot temperatures or, in the winter, to warm and protect their face in cold temps. Bottom line, if the offender was organized, he wouldn't have shown his face when he first passed her."

"What about the fact that he was wearing all black?"

"Have you ever been to a yoga class before? Many people, women in particular, wear black exercise clothing because it's slimming."

᛫ "But we're assuming the Black Cat is a man."

"Maybe he has insecurity issues, is self-conscious about his weight. Feels more comfortable in black."

Mason shook his head, not buying it. After all, a badass man like himself didn't worry about such trivial things.

"Also," I said, "if the Black Cat had planned the attack, he likely would have been carrying a weapon of sorts: a gag, tape, a syringe full of drugs, zip ties, anything that could easily slip into his pocket."

"But in her initial statement, she claims that he threatened her with a knife."

"And yet she didn't see the knife, Deputy."

He glanced out the window as if considering this information, then refocused on me. "You used the word *recollection* a few seconds ago, referring to Courtney retelling her story."

"Ah. Yes."

"Why that word? What do you mean?"

"Recollection, as in what Courtney actually *remembers* from her attack."

"You think she's not telling us everything?"

"It's plausible. Dissociative amnesia is very common with traumatic events such as this." I looked down, my stomach suddenly swirling.

*No*, I thought. *Not now. Pull it together, Mia.*

I inhaled and forced eye contact. "She could have mixed up details or left out some altogether."

"Well, that fucking sucks."

"For you or for the patient?"

Mason's dark eyes narrowed at the dig. "So you think this is what she has? Amnesia?"

"No. I'm simply saying it's an option and something to consider. Give the girl time to digest, to cope."

*If she would ever cope . . .*

"We don't have time," he snapped.

"I'm not talking weeks, just a day, maybe two. She needs to rest, begin to absorb what happened. She's given me a lot to work with, including details of the assault."

"And these details tell you what?"

"Well, for one, the way in which she was assaulted suggests an extreme disrespect, hatred, and disgust for women or perhaps the act of sex and/or intimacy itself. This kind of savage behavior doesn't just appear in someone. It's embedded in their psyche, likely at a very young age. Want to know what I really think? Our offender has a past—no question about it. Maybe even a criminal record, but definitely a difficult childhood. I'd bet my life on it."

"What else?" Finally, the deputy was interested.

Now solidly in my comfort zone, I nodded and continued. "As I said, disorganized offenders show little or no sign of planning, which is what I see here. The victim triggers something in them, like a switch being flicked on. They're typically under the influence of drugs or alcohol and are prone to overkill with the attacks. In other words, the rush they get from their spontaneous act completely overtakes them in the form of uncontrollable rage, like the horrific cases you've read about where the victim is stabbed thirty times. Courtney triggered something in this guy."

When the computer dinged, indicating the file was done downloading, Mason detached my phone from the cord and handed it back. "Okay, but that doesn't necessarily give me an idea of who to look for."

"Okay, well, broadly speaking then, DOs tend to move a lot and, because of this, have multiple addresses, multiple phones listed. So you could possibly be searching for someone who just recently moved here or is only here temporarily. Start there."

I watched as Mason's wheels began to turn.

"DOs are commonly mentally ill and/or socially inadequate. They typically have a low IQ, and they're usually introverts, living alone by either choice or divorce. Look for people who have recently divorced, maybe. DOs are insecure creatures, overanalyzing and questioning situations, and often feel that they are sexually incompetent. They don't think things through and flee the scene immediately."

Mason's brows popped up. "Which means they're messy."

"Not necessarily. Are you familiar with the Whitechapel murders in 1888?"

"You're talking about Jack the Ripper."

"Exactly, one of the most notorious and sensationalized serial killers in the world. Jack the Ripper was responsible for at least five brutal slayings of prostitutes in London. His story is studied ad nauseam within psychology."

"Why?"

"Because police conducted their search under the assumption that Jack the Ripper was a highly organized killer. They assumed this because his victims were all prostitutes—to them, this pointed to planned attacks. Thing is, the Ripper mutilated each woman differently. Some were brutally sliced over and over, some stabbed multiple times, and in some, he removed the organs. In each one, the cuts were different. And they were messy, indicating that the Ripper had no clue what he was doing. Studies have now suggested that Jack the Ripper was quite the opposite of someone who meticulously planned their attacks, and what we would now call a disorganized killer. Today's assumption is that something triggered the Ripper, and he went out and killed. And despite his attacks being disorganized, unplanned, and messy—as you would say—he was never caught. It remains one of the greatest unsolved mysteries of our time."

A moment stretched between us.

"So you see, just because our offender's attacks are random, it makes him no less slippery. Don't ever underestimate the mind of an evil, sick human being, Deputy Mason."

"Noted." The room fell silent as he studied me intently, his gaze trailing over the lines of my face.

I took a step back, registering the throbbing between my temples. "I'd like access to the files of the three other women who reported run-ins with the Black Cat Stalker on the trail, and also, I'd like to see their pictures. My guess is that they're all very similar in appearance."

He frowned. After a second, his eyes widened. "You're right. All the vics are young women, late teens to late twenties, and are remarkably similar. Brown hair, skinny."

"And all are joggers, or into fitness, at least, considering they were all on hiking trails."

"Yes."

I nodded.

He contemplated me another moment, for the first time seeing me as a partner, not as an adversary. "Access granted. I'll email you their reports this afternoon, and images."

"Thank you. And I'll get you my report as soon as possible, and I'd appreciate if you would keep me up to date as the investigation progresses."

"Just get me my official psychological profile, and we'll go from there."

"Thank you, Deputy. I'll—"

"Have a good evening, Dr. Frost." Mason dismissed me abruptly, settling into his oversize office chair.

I didn't argue. I grabbed my purse and hurried to the parking lot, my mind racing, my stomach in knots.

*Have a good evening.*

I wasn't sure what the night had in store for me, but I had a feeling that none of it was going to be good.

# Chapter Ten

## Mia

After interviewing Courtney, I left the sheriff's department. Despite the bathroom-panic-attack hangover, I drove straight to the Black Cat Trail to immerse myself in the scene of the crime while mentally solidifying the profile I would deliver to Deputy Mason.

I couldn't get it wrong.

There are many stages and methods in building a psychological or criminal profile.

The first and most urgent step is to study the crime scene. One can do this by interviewing the first responders, studying the incident reports, or studying the scene itself. This vital stage provides immediate and tangible information about the crime, which can include the time and day the crime occurred; the location; the weapons used; the type of crime (sex, homicide, etc.); and the age, race, and sex of the victim.

If or when the victim's identity is revealed, they become the next focus, or stage, in building the offender's profile. By understanding the victim, one gains great insight into the offender.

Who are they? Who is their family? Are they gainfully employed? Where? Why that path? What are their hobbies, beliefs? What insight do their friends have on why or how the incident happened?

Then comes the tricky part, stage three, as the profiler begins to dive into the very risky world of assumptions. What are the possible motives for this crime? Who fits into this possible scenario? And most importantly, why?

While these first few stages provide a plethora of useful information, I've found that there's no better way to get into the dark, twisted mind of a criminal than to walk in their shoes. Go where they go. See what they saw. Imagine the crime; become it. Feel the victim; feel the offender. Though one is always louder, both open pathways of thought and insight that can't be derived from pen and paper.

I'm leaving out a stage. The one that was perhaps most pertinent to Courtney Hayes's case—though unbeknownst to the investigators. This stage is comparing the crime to similar past crimes.

Had there been any crimes like this one? When? Where?

Was there a connection?

Was it possible . . . all these years later?

*No. It's impossible. Isn't it?*

I pondered that very question the entire day following the interview and into the evening.

Over a glass of wine, I continued my investigation by scouring not only Courtney Hayes's social media but that of her friends, their friends, and every family member in between. For hours I worked, researching, printing, organizing, forgoing dinner and my nightly jog while flashbacks blurred past and present.

By the time I reached the bottom of the bottle, my dining room wall had become a full-blown crazy wall. Images of Courtney Hayes, her mother, her father, and the three other women who had reported run-ins with the Black Cat Stalker were tacked onto multiple corkboards using thumbtacks. Red lines slashed the boards like bloody lacerations, connecting one link to the next.

In the center was a picture of myself. On the dining table lay a red velvet bag.

I worked long after the sun went down. After reaching the bottom of the bottle, I opened another, clumsily poured another glass, and went outside to sit on the back deck.

It was a cold autumn night. A full moon had risen in the black sky, spotlighting the trees and casting long shadows across withered, dying grass.

I wasn't sure how long I sat there that night. I never am. I just wait until I'm so tired or drunk that I can hardly hold my head up, then drag myself to bed. Sometimes, the sun rises before then, and I drag myself to work.

Scanning the woods at the edge of the short backyard, I lingered on the bare pink dogwood tree smack dab in the center.

I took a sip of wine, forcing myself to look away. Instead, I focused on the maple behind it. Usually vibrant with the season, the red maple was different this year, dry and almost colorless. Bleak and sad, as if it had simply given up. Its long, gnarled branches pushed their way into the surrounding pines, their needles brown and brittle.

Death. Everything was dying.

A pitiful rusty-red leaf dropped from its branches, fluttering slowly through the air as if it had all the time in the world. No worries. No troubles. It didn't care that within seconds it would hit the cold, wet ground, then slowly shrivel up and disintegrate into nothing.

It was the forty-second leaf I'd watched fall that night.

With my head fuzzy with wine and my body wired with memories, I pulled the small red velvet bag from my robe pocket. Inside were six stones, two twigs, and one brown feather. Inconspicuous items to most, life-changing relics to me.

I set it on my lap and glared at that goddamn dogwood.

Another symbol of the past.

# Chapter Eleven

## Easton

It was night two of tactical tracking, the last course in level three of the LYNX Group's combat-tracking training. My students were growing tired, and I was growing irritated.

This portion of the business was my baby. My passion.

While the search-and-rescue arm of the business centered on finding a missing person, combat tracking was solely focused on hunting the enemy—often while they were also hunting you. The course was built in a way to recalibrate soldiers to focus on their primal instincts, which were slowly being replaced by technology. Stealth, patience, and perseverance were crucial to not only surviving but also protecting those around you. Tracking a man wasn't just about you—it was about your brothers next to you. It was about working together as one impenetrable unit with a singular focus.

Tracking men who wanted you dead wasn't for the faint of heart. It took courage, brass balls, and more than that, obedience. I took teaching this lost art extremely seriously, which was why each course that I handled had a twist.

This week's group of trainees ("boys") consisted of a team of hand-selected National Guard soldiers who had been placed on active-duty special work orders to complete my course before leaving for active duty overseas. For some, their first tour.

They were young and naive and certainly capable of sneaking out of their barracks and assaulting Courtney Hayes—according to the sheriff's implication, anyway. While I'd supplied the sheriff with everything I had on each of the soldiers, I planned to conduct my own internal investigation.

One thing I'd learned in the military was that you could never be too careful.

It was ten o'clock on a dark, bitterly cold autumn evening, the coldest of the season thus far. The sudden drop in temperature was unexpected by the group but welcomed by me. Weapons were easier to hide under layers.

We'd set out from base camp at dusk and had spent the first part of the evening hiking through the forest, studying the effects of natural light on tracks. How the shifting sun affects what you see. Though I wanted to press forward, the men were hungry and needed to rest before their final exam.

*They'll toughen up*, I reminded myself. They'd have to if they wanted to continue in the military.

The campfire popped and hissed in front of us, bright-orange flames licking up into the black sky speckled with stars. Leaves from low-hanging branches swayed in the updraft, casting shadows along the dirt floor, playing tricks with light. The air smelled of burnt leaves and wet earth.

It was a full moon that night, the hunter's moon, they call it.

I sat on the edge of a boulder, sharpening my knife, while the men huddled together on the opposite side of the fire. Their skin and clothing were covered in dirt and grime, a few with angry red scratches down their necks from a day of hiking.

The hushed voices suggested the intense conversation wasn't intended to leave their circle, and the occasional glances my way suggested the topic of this conversation was me.

I wondered what the gossip was this time. There was plenty in my past to be discussed. Some true, some not, some buried under ten feet of sand.

I'd been told my reputation preceded me, but I didn't give a shit.

As long as this resulted in my men giving 100 percent of their best selves, I couldn't care less what was said about me. I'd learned long ago that judging a man's competence based solely on his reputation is like betting on the man with the nunchucks. It only matters if he knows how to use them. It's all an illusion. Reputations, titles, fame, medals, awards—they're fickle, devious little bastards.

Something these men had yet to learn.

One man's gaze lingered on me longer than the rest. The self-appointed leader of the group, a young man named Henrick Taylor, a six-foot former linebacker who shot snot rockets in the bathroom stall, still laughed at his own farts, and chewed tobacco like bubble gum. He was always the first to step in line, the first to speak up, the first to get on my damn nerves. Next to him sat Jay Ruiz, a twenty-year-old Texas native, and a kid named Dave Schultz.

Then there were the outcasts.

Wearing a worn do-rag and a tank top, despite the temperature, Lucas Miller sat on a nearby tree stump, his sleeves of tattoos on full display. Lucas didn't say much, but when he did, everyone listened. Next to him, Shane Davis was asleep on the ground, wearing a T-shirt that read OMELET THAT SLIDE. Enough said.

Rounding out the group of six was Benji Green. He was two inches taller than my six feet three yet half my weight, with red hair and freckles and a fresh tattoo of a panther coloring his bony forearm. Benji was the wallflower, the loner. The target. Henrick had immediately identified Benji as the weak link and therefore refused to acknowledge his presence. Benji was the black sheep of the group, and past experience told me he was the one to pay attention to.

It hadn't taken long for the men to form a bond against me, as most students do against their teachers. I welcomed this for a few reasons: One, nothing solidifies a brotherhood faster than a common enemy. Two, this detachment allowed me to step back and observe the boys, mentally cataloging and recording the interaction among the men.

A hierarchy, with Henrick at the head and me as the enemy, had been internally established, whether they realized it or not. This was also common with my groups.

The interesting thing here was that, more often than not, this self-appointed leader wasn't the smartest or the most qualified of the group. He was simply the most confident, gaining compliance from his peers for no other reason than this. It wasn't until this self-appointed leader was placed in a real-world, quick-thinking situation that his true self would be revealed. In the end, he was the quickest to fall. The weak link among men. A man who had yet to understand the thin line between confidence and cockiness—a thin line called the ego.

Most people were rarely able to operate from a truly unbiased and clear head. Rarely able to separate themselves from the situation.

This was where I came in. I trained my boys to see the bigger picture, see beyond what you expected to see.

Some got it, and some didn't. Some would never get it.

Pride was the enemy.

It was Henrick Taylor's biggest enemy. There was a spark that I recognized from my younger days. Unfortunately, I also recognized the unbridled arrogance and the immortal sense of self as if I were staring in a mirror.

It was the kind of cockiness that made you reckless. A loose cannon. The kind of self-righteous bullshit that cost lives. I had little patience for this. And Henrick Taylor was about to learn that the hard way.

"Up." I sheathed my knife and pushed off the rock.

The men jumped to their feet, but I wasn't pleased. I examined the man who had lingered a bit too long before following orders.

"In class today we studied conclusive signs, footprints or trace evidence, that can be directly linked to the quarry—your enemy. Stuff your grandma could pick up. Now, in the darkness of night, we're going to review inconclusive signs that are equally important when tracking your quarry. Inconclusive signs are less obvious than conclusive. They are signs that most novices overlook, such as broken twigs or bent grass. The goal here is to use all of your senses to find and read each sign, or spoor, create a profile of your quarry, put yourselves in their shoes—then go where they go and find them."

I glanced at Henrick before continuing. "If you've read the combat-tracking manual, you know that there are four main buckets you must master for a successful hunt. One and two, know the terrain and the local fieldcraft. This is done by obtaining maps, aerial photos; speaking with local law enforcement, farmers, tour guides, you name it. Ask them how they would use the terrain to survive. Food? Shelter? Weapons? It's important to approach these people with humility. *We* are learning from *them*."

I paused a moment to let that sink in.

"Three, know the local weather, and four, know the enemy. Before a hunt, try to learn your subject's motives, his habits, his tactics. Again, this is done by forming friendships and trust with the locals and law enforcement. There's one thing that's guaranteed to impede even the savviest tracker's mission—that is a pissing match between us and them. In search and rescue, the time spent comparing dick sizes and intelligence can literally cost someone their life. In combat tracking, it can cost many, many lives, including our own. Do you understand?"

The team nodded in unison.

"Tonight, we're focusing on the physical aspect of tracking. This requires stamina, concentration, and an eye for detail. Specifically, we'll be studying tracks, perhaps the most important—and easily destroyed—pieces of a manhunt."

I knelt down, fisted a clump of dirt in my hand. While slowly letting it fall from between my fingers, I said, "When we find a print, how do we know it belongs to our quarry and not someone else or an animal? This is important. I know several missions that have failed because someone spent days tracking prints that belonged to something other than their quarry."

I reached into my pack and pulled out a deer hoof, then pressed it into the dirt. "Ungulate walkers are hoofed animals, like deer, horses, and cattle." Next, a coyote's paw. "Digitigrade walkers walk on their toes and heel pad. Examples of this are dogs, coyotes, lynx cats. Lastly, there are plantigrade walkers, or heel strikers, because that's the first thing that hits the earth. Humans, bears, and raccoons are examples of these kinds of walkers. Tonight, you're tracking a man, so you will be searching for plantigrade tracks."

Standing, I pulled a map from my back pocket. "A word of caution. We're not using the trails. You'll track your quarry through the densest part of the forest, over and through multiple rivers and swamps. There are no medics on standby tonight, and any trouble that you find yourself in must be resolved by a teammate. Is that clear?"

When they all nodded, I shrugged into my pack.

"Beckett Stolle and Alek Romanov have set up the course for you to complete tonight. You'll be split into two teams. The first to capture the quarry wins. It's as simple as that. Use anything and everything to your advantage, including night-vision goggles and thermal imagers. Stolle and Rom are scattered along the course to observe as you proceed, and I'll be watching from a distance. The team leaders will pick their teams, two teams of three. Team One's leader is Henrick Taylor. Team Two's leader is Benji Green."

A groan rippled through the crowd.

We flipped a coin, and Henrick got first pick. Within minutes, the teams were set, with Henrick Taylor, Jay Ruiz, and Lucas Miller on

Team One, and Benji Green, Dave Schultz, and Shane Davis on Team Two.

"How long is the course?" Schultz asked while zipping up his vest.

"However long it takes."

After checking equipment, the teams split into two different routes, both with identical clues to track, both leading to the same target—a case of Budweiser, a lifetime supply of Slim Jims (donated by Beckett), and certification of course completion. This victory pack was located exactly 10.7 miles out, though the men didn't know this.

The course was, by far, the most strenuous test of the five-day training. The students would be tracking until the early-morning hours, unbeknownst to them. Their patience, energy, and mental aptitude would all be tried.

I hung back, allowing the teams to get a head start before beginning my track. I had yet to be caught by a group of trainees. We had an ongoing wager on this at the office that involved a pair of nipple clamps, a diamond-studded ball gag, and a pink jockstrap.

Never was a fan of pink.

The voices faded, the flashlight beams growing dimmer against the trees as the teams trekked into the woods, looking for their clues.

After bringing up their locations on my handheld digital tracker, I started my own journey through the brush. For every mission, there was one team I focused on more than the other, and there was no question which team that was on that night.

Henrick's blustery voice echoed through the trees, something about the latest football game on television.

For hours we hiked, me following Team One while keeping tabs on Team Two. The woods grew silent, the jokes and small talk petering out as fatigue began to take hold.

At that time, both teams were even in terms of pace. Then an argument broke out in Team One.

Drawing my knife, I slipped through the trees and crept up on the side of the group. I listened to the team argue about recently discovered tracks and which path to take. Henrick demanded his path, and the rest of the team suggested another. To no one's surprise, Henrick took off on his own, disappearing into the woods, following the path he'd deemed the best.

I hunkered down and jogged through the underbrush, slipping past the rest of the team from shadow to shadow. They'd decided not to follow Henrick but to pause and reassess while he pressed forward, walking over twenty minutes on his own.

*Idiot.*

I followed his wide, pissed-off stride closely through the terrain. I noted every twitch in his jaw, every time he fought to turn around and check to see if his team had chosen to follow. Even though Henrick knew he was breaking protocol by leaving his team, he kept going, right into a small clearing surrounded by tall pines.

His scream shattered the silence.

Birds scattered from the trees, and an armadillo bolted out of sight.

I remained hidden in the shadows as Henrick, now hanging upside down from a tree, desperately clawed at the rope secured around his right ankle in a feeble attempt to release himself from the trap he'd gotten caught up in. The one Beckett had expertly laid only hours earlier, a trap he insisted on in every single course to prevent the trainees from making the same mistake he'd made during his first year in the Marines. A mistake that had almost cost him his right foot and his life.

"What the *fuck*, man?" Henrick barked as I stepped into the clearing, into the beam of his frantically waving flashlight.

"You misread your target." I slowly circled the man dangling six feet in the air, secured only by his right ankle. "Congratulations, Henrick. You've been successfully tracking a family of deer for the past hour, a fact you would've known if you'd listened to your team or paused for one minute to question yourself a single time on the path. If you'd done this, you would've seen the markings on the trees made by bucks rubbing their antlers against the bark and then would have known you were on the wrong path."

"That's *bullshit*," he spat out, long brown strings of tobacco flinging from his lips. His eyes blazed as hot as his temper. Henrick didn't accept failure.

"You should consider yourself lucky," I said, circling his head. "Stolle considered using a bear trap."

"Crazy son of a bitch. Okay, *fine*—lesson learned. Cut me the fuck down."

"No, sir. The rules were clearly stated. If any one of your team members, including yourself, finds themselves in trouble, it's up to the team to resolve the issue." I pointed at him with my knife. "If I were you, I would focus on steadying your breathing. Right now, the blood is pooling in your chest and skull, causing pressure to build in the brain and behind your eyes. Your heart is having to work three times harder to pump your blood."

His brown eyes rounded like a fearful child's.

Biting back a grin, I said, "Prolonged inversion can lead to strokes, seizures, blindness, or in some cases, asphyxiation. You don't have high blood pressure, do you?"

"L-let me down, Chief. *Now.*"

"Now would be good, but no can do."

Henrick struggled against the rope, sending himself into a dizzying spin as he dangled from the end. "I could die from this!"

I reached up, grabbed a fistful of his hair, steadied him, and pulled his swollen red face to mine. "Then let's hope you gained enough respect from your teammates to make sure that doesn't happen."

Henrick blinked, these words like a slap to his face.

"The thing is, Henrick, the only thing deadlier and more poisonous than the enemy you're tracking is your own ego. It will kill you, destroy every goal and dream you have. Learn to control it, to use it to your advantage. You have a lot to offer, but you have more to learn. You have failed this course, Henrick Taylor. I'll send notice of your failure to Sergeant Jones at your National Guard unit within the hour."

"No." Pathetic, he squeaked out the word.

I released my grip on his hair. "Your bags will be outside your bunker. A car will take you to a local motel, where you'll wait for the rest of your team to complete the course. Then you will fly back to Louisiana as scheduled."

"No!" Henrick fought against the rope again, rage contorting his face.

"Good luck to you, son." I turned my back and began crossing the clearing.

"Don't leave, Chief! You—you better not leave me here." More garbled groans came as he spat and hissed, his tone rising in unbridled panic and anger. The kid was losing it.

The first step in rebuilding.

Then—

"Get me down or I'll *kill* you, Chief."

I stopped and turned, my eyes locking on his. "Not if you can't track me in the first place."

# Chapter Twelve

## Easton

Pausing, I glanced at my watch, then took one last look over my shoulder at Henrick fighting a losing battle with the nylon rope.

At the sound of heavy footsteps entering the clearing, I turned. His team had heard his screams and had decided to help him, despite Henrick's arrogant and impetuous decision to set out on his own.

It took his team nearly an hour to remove Henrick from the trap, thereby ensuring their loss. The underdog, Benji Green, took home the trophy that night.

In the end, Henrick was lucky that his team decided to help him. This was also a good thing for me, because my thoughts were already elsewhere, my body craving another hit. I slipped into the woods, my focus purely on feeding my latest addiction.

And an addiction she was, this no-name woman I watched from behind the veil of pines that lined her backyard. I didn't know a thing about her, just that her dark eyes and hair the color of honeycomb had captivated my every waking thought since I'd first seen her months ago.

Dreams, fantasies, nightmares, she'd induced them all, enslaving my imagination. There was something about the woman, an aura, that drew me like a moth to a flame. Except it wasn't bright or joyful. Her aura was dark, heavy, and quite honestly, disconcerting.

I'd become obsessed with this woman, her sudden presence in my life filling some fucked-up hole that I didn't know how to fill otherwise.

She intrigued me. Some days, I wondered if that was all it was. She was simply a mysterious distraction with no strings attached. Other days, I wondered if it was more.

The first time I'd seen her, I'd been observing a group of trainees, much as I'd been on this night. I'd emerged from a stinking bog when a warm summer breeze had swept past me. This was the first time I'd smelled her. A soft scent out of context from the nature around me. A scent that didn't belong there.

Jasmine.

I pivoted off course and followed the scent, silently slipping through the woods that I knew by heart. The sweet fragrance led me off my land and into the area known as Black Hills Bayou.

I stopped and inhaled, trying to find the scent again. Instead, I heard the sound of a woman crying somewhere in the darkness.

After securing my night-vision goggles, I followed the muffled sobs to a small cabin nestled in a thicket of pines. I realized then that the woman crying had no light around her. No flashlight, no illuminated cell phone, nothing. She was in total darkness, curled into the fetal position in a small patch of grass at the base of a dogwood tree. She appeared to be cupping something in her hand. Circled around her body on the ground were what appeared to be strategically placed sticks and rocks.

My hand froze around the radio. My immediate instinct was that the woman wasn't hurt or in danger—just very, very sad.

I instinctively took a step back. Injuries and danger I was trained for, but a crying woman I was not.

I scanned the surroundings, noting the small cabin and the silver Jeep parked next to it. A small neighboring house was twenty yards away, barely visible through the trees. No light was on, no one watching me watching her.

I refocused on the woman.

The situation was odd enough that I hung back, assessing before forming a plan. Something told me this woman didn't want to be found. She simply wanted to be left alone, although my military-trained instinct was to go to her.

Instead, I watched her. Perplexed. Entranced, perhaps. Not understanding what the hell this woman was doing crying in the dark in the middle of the woods at one in the morning.

I couldn't make out her features through the darkness, only that she was short, small in stature, and lean. Early thirties, although that was just a guess. Long golden-brown hair with unruly, tangled waves shimmered under the streaks of moonlight. She hid behind this hair, I noticed, the silky strands concealing her face from me, from the world.

It shocked me that she had no light whatsoever. It was as if the woman was intentionally allowing the darkness to engulf her, along with a pain so severe it was almost palpable.

What had brought her to this moment?

Through my night-vision goggles, I watched her as one might an elusive endangered animal, observing the shuddering rise and fall of her chest until she finally stopped crying.

Thankful for this, I relaxed a bit, as dealing with a crying woman had never been my strong suit. It wasn't lost on me how ironic it was that the recipient of a Purple Heart could be rendered completely helpless and incapable by a crying woman.

I'm not sure how long I watched her that night, but I couldn't tear myself away. I responded to this woman on a visceral level, something deep inside me physically feeling the pain around her.

I was instantly addicted, connected to this person in pain, though I didn't understand why or how—only that I couldn't let go.

So I'd gone back the next night, and the night after that. Every night after work, I'd hiked through the woods to check on my mystery woman.

Over the weeks, I'd learned that she lived alone, aside from a yellow pet bird that occasionally perched on her shoulder while she enjoyed her evening wine on the deck. She always came outside right at dusk, when the sun was setting.

I knew her schedule—when she went to work, what day she got her groceries, and that she'd recently taken up some sort of online fitness class, which she would do in the evening before her first glass of wine. I knew when to expect her on the back deck, the blanket she'd throw over her lap, and finally, the time that her drowsiness would finally win the battle and she would drag herself inside to bed.

One time, she'd forgotten to lock the door.

I'd locked it for her. And every night since that night, I ensured that her doors were locked so she could rest safely, easily, during the few hours of sleep she allowed herself.

The few hours of peace.

⁓

I glanced at my watch again. That night I was pushing it. It was late.

I broke out in a jog, following a footpath I'd worn through the trees, fearing that I might miss my woman and spend the rest of the evening wondering if she was home, asleep and safe.

Finally, that sweet scent of jasmine carried on the cold night air.

She was up—I hadn't missed her.

I slowed as I drew closer to the backyard I knew better than my own. Every blade of grass, every tree, every cracked board on the weathered wooden deck. The single chair with the navy pillow, the table and the citronella candle on it.

Silently, I made my way behind the thick trunk of the massive maple tree, the grass withered around the roots from hours of me standing in that exact spot. Watching her, watching nothing.

A dim light from the living room windows silhouetted her small frame, wrapped in a flannel blanket, curled on the chair on the deck. The wineglass she was holding glinted in the light as she took a sip. The candle flickered on the table next to her, casting yellow licks of light against pale alabaster skin. Her hair was unusually messy that night, thick waves like drapes around her face.

I leaned against the tree and watched the same scene I'd seen a hundred times over. The woman, alone, sitting on her porch, staring at the dogwood tree in the center of her backyard.

She was crying.

Why, I wondered. Why was she upset? *What happened?* I wanted to scream out, wanting to know more.

I watched as she pushed herself out of the chair and picked up something from the table. A bit unsteady on her feet, she made her way off the deck and into the backyard.

She was dressed unusually for that time of night, trading her evening uniform of a baggy T-shirt and sweatpants for a thick sweater over dirt-covered jeans and hiking boots. Mud caked the bottoms of her boots, clumps falling off as she stumbled across the yard.

She'd been out that afternoon. Hiking, somewhere in the woods. With who, I wondered? And she was obviously drunk. Again, with who?

A pang of jealousy pricked my chest. I quickly pushed away the odd feeling, chastising myself for the ridiculous emotion. I didn't even know her.

I shifted farther behind the tree trunk as she approached the dogwood tree in the center of her yard. I wanted to call out to her, for her to turn to me. See what I felt when our eyes met.

My pulse rate picked up as she dropped to her knees, emptying the contents of the red velvet bag—the same stones, twigs, and brown feather that she'd had the first night I'd seen her.

And just like that night, the woman arranged the items just so, lowered herself clumsily to the ground, and softly wept.

*You're not alone. My woman, you're not alone.*

An owl hooted overhead, and something twisted deep in my stomach. A sudden unease, a portent of something to come.

# Chapter Thirteen

## Easton

The next morning, I woke on the couch when my cell phone rang. Groggy, I picked it up.

"We've got another one."

I sat up, dragging my fingers through my hair. It was 6:04 a.m. The last I remembered seeing the clock, it had been just after two. An icy chill had settled in the office overnight, a prelude to a biting winter to come.

The sheriff continued, "A man, reported missing an hour ago. Last seen on the Black Cat Trail."

I blinked, setting my boots on the floor, unlaced but still on my feet. "Related?"

"Not sure. But another missing person within days of Courtney Hayes's attack doesn't make me feel warm and fuzzy inside."

"Do you have any suspects?"

"Not yet. And no, nothing to point to any of your trainees—currently, anyway. And not that I should tell you that."

The relief hit me hard—a reminder of just how much my business meant to me and how losing it to bad press wasn't an option.

"Deputy Mason brought in that head doctor from the Dragonfly Clinic, Mia Frost, to interview Courtney and get a sense of the type of suspect we're looking for," McNamara continued, and I got the sense he needed to talk. Needed to iron out his thoughts to someone other than his hardened, shortsighted team. "Mason thinks we're looking for a disorganized offender."

"Meaning someone who is impulsive?"

"Right. And specifically, someone who moves a lot, from town to town or state to state. Maybe moved to Skull Hollow recently, or someone who has only lived here a short time."

"That's a start."

The sheriff snorted, and I was ready for him to get to the point of the call.

"How can LYNX help?"

"Gus Bynes and his son reported seeing a silver Jeep Wrangler, newer model, parked in a cove off the trail yesterday while out hunting. A secluded area not common to locals or tourists. Seemed out of place and suspicious—their words exactly. Called us when they heard the gossip that someone else was missing. Curious if it belongs to you or one of your operatives? Your office manager or anyone on your team?"

"No."

"*Dammit,*" he snapped, abnormally expressive. "Have you seen a silver Wrangler lately around your land? Or any idea who it belongs to?"

I paused, dark eyes and long chestnut hair tickling my memory. My brain suddenly jerked awake, my thoughts zooming from zero to ninety in an instant.

"No," I lied.

"All right. Well, if you see a silver Jeep Wrangler in the area, let me know. Or hell, anything that feels off. I'll shoot you the notes from dispatch. Keep a lookout. Could be related, could not, but let me know if you see anything."

"Yes, sir."

# Chapter Fourteen

## Easton

The house was like something out of a Thomas Kinkade painting.

Small and quaint, the cabin appeared as if it had sprouted from the woods around it, its stone walls almost invisible under the vivid green vines that snaked up the sides, reaching all the way to the shingled roof. Cut out of the greenery was an arched doorway and two beveled windows with sheer curtains obscuring the view inside. Knotted tree branches wrapped the tiny structure as if hiding it.

*Hiding it* . . . coincidence? If so, add it to the list that had played on repeat in my head since the moment I'd hung up the phone with Sheriff McNamara.

Coincidence that a man had gone missing in the same area Courtney Hayes had been sexually assaulted.

Coincidence that the nameless woman I'd been secretly observing for months drove a silver Jeep exactly like one that had been spotted close to the man's last known location.

Coincidence that I'd caught this extremely upset woman crying under a dogwood the night before.

Something that resembled nerves kicked in my stomach. I didn't like this. I couldn't remember the last time that anything had made me nervous, especially not a woman.

I realized then that I didn't want to meet this mystery woman. Didn't want to come face-to-face with the reality of my late-night addiction. I didn't want to make her *real*. This confirmed my assumption that the woman had no place in my life other than as a distraction, one that I wanted to keep badly—*as is*.

Everything about that morning felt wrong. Off.

My odd emotions, the nerves, the coincidences. The fact that I'd lied without hesitation to the sheriff, protecting a woman I didn't even know. More importantly, why had I done it, and so instinctively?

It also felt wrong that I was about to introduce myself to this woman under the guise of a stranger, when in fact, I'd spent many hours watching her through the trees like a sick fuck.

For a fleeting second, I considered turning around and aborting the ill-conceived plan I'd devised while in the shower. But no, I was in too deep now. Within seconds after hanging up with the sheriff, I'd been behind my laptop, searching public records for the name of the woman who lived in the cabin next to my property line.

According to my research, Dr. Mia Frost was born and raised in Dallas, Texas, to a mother who'd worked days at the public school and nights at the hospital and a deadbeat, noncommittal father who'd changed jobs every six months before leaving his family for good on Mia's ninth birthday. After high school, Mia and her mother moved to Austin. She attended the University of Texas there, earning her doctorate in psychology and graduating with honors.

During college, Mia befriended a woman named Jo Bellerose, a psychiatrist who also graduated from UT. After graduation, the two left the city for the remote Piney Woods of eastern Texas, where they opened the Dragonfly Clinic, a mental health facility in the small town of Skull Hollow. The clinic's unconventional—and in some cases, very controversial—approach to therapy had gained national attention, most positive but some negative. Now, she was in the spotlight, once again, for being brought in on the Courtney Hayes case to offer her expertise.

Dr. Frost had no criminal record, no warrants, no speeding tickets. Not married, no kids.

Nothing special.

*Nothing special*, I reminded myself.

I turned onto the driveway. It was a cloudy, crisp autumn morning. A muted shade of gray exposed a small yard covered in brown leaves. A narrow pebbled walkway led to a freshly painted bright-red door. No lights appeared to be on inside.

Unlike the rutted road that led to the house, the rock driveway was smooth and obviously well maintained, as was the shrubbery around the house. The roof appeared to be new as well.

*Must have a man in her life*, I thought as I rolled to a stop behind the silver Jeep Wrangler. After double-checking its tags, I cut the engine.

I checked my watch—7:17 a.m. It was early, but this was my only free time that day. I had classes scheduled that morning and multiple courses in the afternoon, capped off by a team meeting at the shooting range afterward. Typical workday.

A chorus of what sounded like a million glasses shattering greeted me as I pushed out of my truck. I counted four glass wind chimes hanging from the eaves of the house. Funny, I hadn't noticed the sound when visiting her from behind the shadows of the maple. Then again, my vision had been tunneled on her—*only her*.

I wondered who could live with such racket. My idea of relaxation was a hurricane-level box fan six inches from my face.

This was when I noticed the bird feeders, dozens of them hanging from trees and scattered across the small yard on fancy little stands. At the side of the cabin stood the Four Seasons of birdhouses, a six-story—*six*—monstrosity on four legs.

The place appeared completely different in the light of day, and this unnerved me. Why hadn't I noticed the details before? What kind of trance did this woman place me under?

Aside from the mariachi band dangling from the eaves, the property appeared to be quiet, and I wondered if she was home.

I knocked on the door. A few birds squawked angrily from a nearby tree, which was the first sign that I was unwelcome.

I knocked again. No answer.

I glanced at the silver Jeep, then attempted a peek through the window. Nothing.

I considered my appearance and how this might play into a woman not answering her door. If the army-green T-shirt, stained tactical pants, and scuffed boots weren't unappealing enough, the sawdust covering my hair from spending the evening in the shop, working on a new outdoor obstacle course, completed the unprofessional look.

Professional. Another illusion.

I frowned, calculating the last time I'd showered. Took note of the time.

I raised my hand to knock one last time when a voice registered from somewhere in the house. A loud female voice, excruciatingly monotone, as if reading a script or reciting commands.

Frowning, I took a step back and peered in the window again, unable to see beyond the sheer curtains. There was a pause in the one-sided conversation, then a robotic laugh of sorts that sounded more like a goat bleating, before it continued again. There was no way this voice belonged to the delicate woman who cried herself to sleep under trees.

*What the hell?*

I knocked again. Waited.

I stepped off the stoop and slowly made my way around the cabin, careful to avoid the perfectly trimmed shrubbery. The voice grew louder, as did the squawking bird that was following me from the trees above.

I rounded the back of the house, then halted when I saw the silhouette of a woman pacing back and forth inside the open window. I quickly ducked against the side of the house as I listened.

"The conscious mind focuses on the present moment and exactly what we are paying attention to at that moment, such as sights, sounds, thoughts, activities, tasks. Science has proven that a human mind can only be consciously aware of a few things at a time. However, hypnotherapy works with both the conscious and subconscious mind—at the same time, merging them together, if you will."

I focused on the assertive, crotchety sound of the voice, nothing like the one I'd fantasized about in the shower. Quite the opposite, in fact, as this was the voice of a domineering alpha female, the kind with something to prove. The kind with insecurities that ran a mile deep.

"The subconscious mind carries all of our memories, beliefs, and habitual patterns. Things like tying your shoe or riding a bike. Traumatic memories, ones that cause conditions like PTSD in particular, can become trapped in the subconscious and can result in adverse reactions when we are presented with a stimulus that reminds us of the traumatic memory."

Peering through the blurred view of the sheer curtain, I shifted my stance. I knew instantly it was her, standing in front of a selfie tripod, staring into a camera that was attached to a laptop sitting on a desk.

Her long honey-brown hair was pulled into a tight bun. A few unruly pieces had escaped, framing a porcelain-white face. Earphones dangled from each ear. She wore a starched, blinding-white blouse with a floppy, feminine tie around the neck. Below that, she was wearing a pair of baggy, tie-dyed mesh basketball shorts two sizes too big. On her feet were a pair of ridiculously fluffy slippers in the shape of two kittens.

I couldn't make out the screen of her laptop, but it was evident that she was giving a virtual lecture of sorts—from only the waist up, obviously.

"Hypnotherapy works with both the conscious and subconscious minds to aid in emotional and behavioral changes to better one's life. When the patient is under total relaxation and then taken through the traumatic event step by step by the therapist, this helps to weaken the barrier between the conscious and subconscious. Meaning the patient is no longer fighting their own thoughts. They are being guided through them and therefore more easily seeing what truly happened."

God, that voice. Jarring. I swore I knew it from somewhere.

"It isn't a state of unconsciousness, rather a state of heightened awareness. It is very, very powerful . . ."

*Powerful*—then it hit me. Dr. Mia Frost's voice reminded me of an instructor from the Marine Special Ops School, where I'd spent the most grueling nine months of my life. Sergeant Seaman, a forty-two-year-old former wrestler, and the first woman in the school's history to win the knockout challenge two years in a row.

I shuddered at the thought, the fantastical image of perfection I'd built of this woman in my head quickly dissipating with each passing second.

"Hypnotherapy has been proven to be particularly helpful with those who suffer from PTSD. I—"

As she paused and went silent, staring intently into the camera, I found myself waiting with bated breath.

"Yes, that's correct," she said finally. "A session can last as long as ninety minutes, if the patient is responding. I recommend two or three weekly sessions at first, then slowly taper down over the course of a month. And for an outline of what we recommend for each of those sessions, I'll hand the metaphorical mic over to Dr. Vaughn with the Silver Anchor Clinic for Mental Health . . . You're welcome."

Dr. Frost stood still with a fake smile plastered on her face until the screen went black. Immediately, the earbuds were ripped from her ears, and with an exaggerated exhale, she doubled over, gripping the edge of the chair for support.

A grin caught me. Apparently, Mia had a fear of public speaking. This amused me, although I wasn't sure why.

She straightened and turned toward the window. I ducked, pressing my back against the cold stone wall. I scrutinized the dogwood, its bare branches bleak against the green backdrop of the pines. I pictured all the times I'd seen her sitting underneath it and became more curious than ever what this woman's story was.

# Chapter Fifteen

## Easton

Staying low, I jogged back to the front door and knocked again.

No response.

I leaned forward and listened. When I heard nothing, I knocked again, this time louder, my irritation growing rapidly.

I spied movement from the neighboring house. Someone was crossing the front lawn, the silhouette obscured by the dense trees that separated the two homes. An old black K10 4x4 with tinted windows was parked to the side of the small redbrick house.

According to my research, the home belonged to Louise Littles, otherwise known around town as Old Lady Lou. A seventy-seven-year-old Skull County native, although she said she wasn't a day over sixty. Sometimes fifty, depending on the size of the wineglass she'd chosen for the day. A widow of fifteen years, Lou worked mornings at the DMV, knitted blankets in the evenings, and was rumored to know every piece of gossip that came through Skull Hollow. She was also rumored to be a witch, but I couldn't vouch for that.

I'd raised my hand to knock one last time when the door jerked open—only as much as the security chain would allow.

"How may I help you?" the robot recited from the other side of the door.

I wondered if Mia had a sister. A twin, visiting from boot camp, perhaps. Or maybe temporarily in town while Mia cared for her after her reassignment surgery from human to cyborg.

I squinted through the crack, hoping to glimpse a view of the face obscured by shadows. The home was dimly lit by the natural light of what appeared to be a floor-to-ceiling window somewhere past her. Tiny little shadows moved along a gleaming hardwood floor.

"Dr. Mia Frost?"

"How may I help you, Mr. . . . .?"

"Easton Crew. Does Dr. Mia Frost, a psychologist with the Dragonfly Clinic, live here?"

"Maybe."

I blinked. "Is this your silver Jeep parked out here, under the tree?"

"It's a little early for maieutics, don't you think?"

"You mean answering a question with a question? No, do you think it's too early for that?"

There was a pause on the other side of the door. I grinned, ridiculously proud of myself for winning a battle with what appeared to be a very intelligent, very high-strung individual, who, if I had to guess, didn't lose often.

Finally, she said, "I'm kind of busy."

"This won't take long."

"I didn't assume otherwise." *(Ouch.)* "You seriously think I'm going to open the door to a total stranger?"

"Depends on your definition of a stranger. As I said, my name is Easton Crew, owner of the LYNX Group."

"You mean LYNX Search and Rescue?"

"Yes, that's a part of the business."

A second of silence passed, and I got the sense that she knew who I was. I wasn't sure if that would work to my advantage or not.

A few strands of her hair peeked from behind the door as she shifted to look at me through the peephole—for an abnormally long amount of time.

I cocked a brow, staring back, then glanced over my shoulder at the rusted, beat-up Ford behind me. Had she been expecting a blacked-out Maserati with a vanity plate? Because that one was in my garage.

"What does *the group* do?" Mia asked, testing me.

"Top-secret spy stuff." My patience was waning.

"Show me your ID."

"ID?"

This maieutic response was met with a slamming door.

Too early, indeed.

I reached into my wallet, pulled out my driver's license, and pressed it against the windowpane.

The curtains fluttered. After a pause, the chain was lifted and the door slowly opened.

The first things I noticed were two charcoal-gray laser beams pinning me in place, leaving no question whose territory I was in. Everything else blurred around them, like a pair of graphite crystals against a swirling, hypnotic backdrop.

I was rendered speechless by the almost-black irises, which seemed out of place against an alabaster almond-shaped face and pale-pink lips that would put the Rolling Stones to shame. She was still wearing the same mismatched outfit, except now, instead of thinking it odd, I wanted to see what the kaleidoscope of colors would look like hanging from my bedpost.

My attention was pulled over her shoulder, to a ray of sunlight sparkling off one of the largest birdcages I'd ever seen in my life. The massive floor-to-ceiling structure vied for space among a dozen indoor plants, giving the room an aviary-like appearance. The walls were lined with nature photography, each a picture of a random bird in flight.

She cleared her throat.

*Dammit. Focus, Easton.*

"Miss Frost—"

"Doctor."

My brow cocked with delight. Quite the pair of brass balls, considering the woman had almost doubled over in a panic attack after giving a lecture with exactly zero people in the room.

My gaze was drawn again, but this time to a neon-yellow bird casually padding across the living room floor behind her, completely uninterested in me or anything else around it, not a care in the world. Like a self-absorbed college roommate oblivious to anything that doesn't involve jungle juice or Netflix marathons.

Suddenly, a spine-tingling quack came out of the little monster. "Miiiiia . . . *Mia! Mia! Mia!*"

Without waiting for a response, the bird waddled out of sight.

I forced my mouth closed.

"That's Goldie." A grin tugged at those pink lips. "She's a parakeet."

"She . . . talks."

"Yes, when she's having feelings."

"That's the creepiest thing I've ever heard in my life."

"No, creepy is a man standing outside your window listening to you give a hypnotherapy lecture." Her gaze swept over me, lingering on the gold ring I wore on my pinkie finger.

I shoved my hand into my pocket. "Well, you didn't answer your door."

"Exactly."

We regarded each other a moment, both registering the weird, instant chemistry bouncing between us. Hers more annoyance than lust, perhaps, but chemistry nonetheless. It intrigued me.

"I didn't realize you were the hypnotherapist of your clinic," I said.

"And I didn't realize you were a Peeping Tom."

"I'm not, trust me. I simply overheard after I knocked."

"Impressed?"

I tilted my head to the side. "Remains to be seen."

She snorted, but not humorlessly, in a "you're so pitiful like everyone else" kind of way.

"Ah. I see I'm not the only skeptic you've crossed," I said.

"Let's put it like this. A week after introducing the new therapy, I spent two days scrubbing the words *voodoo witch—witch* spelled *w-h-i-c-h*—off my office window."

"Small town, small minds."

"And a small education budget, apparently. I can assure you what I do isn't sorcery. Voodoo wasn't what brought five hundred of the world's top mental health professionals to a virtual summit this morning to discuss research- and science-backed evidence of the efficacy of hypnotherapy as a *cure* for PTSD."

"That's a lot of STEM before eight a.m."

"The conference is being streamed over several countries, several time zones. Half the attendants are in the UK."

*I'm a pretty big deal* was the only thing she left off that sentence. Or maybe she did say it, but I couldn't hear her over the noise from the aviary that was her living room.

"Are you here for hypnotherapy?" Her hip cocked with attitude, those baggy basketball shorts flipping in the air. "Because off first impression alone, you're not my ideal patient."

"And why's that, Doctor?"

"Because you're too supercilious."

In a sarcastic show of deep thought, I rubbed my chin. "Quick to label the stranger—interesting. Sounds like your subconscious talking there, Dr. Frost. Is there something about me that reminds you of a trapped memory? A trigger, perhaps?"

"Yes, you're definitely making me think of a certain type of trigger."

I grinned at her ability to go toe-to-toe with me. "No, I'm not here to talk about hypnotherapy. I'm here to talk about a man who was reported missing early this morning."

The muscles in Mia's neck tightened. Something sparked in her eyes, so slight that if I hadn't been watching, I would have missed it.

"No. I hadn't heard," she said a bit too quickly—a bit too interested. "Are you working with the cops?"

"Kind of. We—LYNX—specialize in human tracking—"

"Trafficking?" she squeaked.

*Christ.* "No. We specialize in human *tracking*—not *trafficking*. Combat tracking, to be exact. We work closely with local law enforcement when something like this happens."

She scanned the lines of my face, as if assessing my very existence and how it fit into her life at that moment.

"Have you seen anyone in the woods lately? Wandering off the trail, perhaps? Maybe someone you've never seen before?" I asked.

"Was he last seen around here?"

"Close by. The woods around the Black Cat Trail."

Something in her eyes flashed. "The same area Courtney Hayes was attacked?"

"Yes."

I wasn't sure if she knew that my team had found the missing teen, but there was definitely something about this new disappearance that made her suddenly uneasy.

"When did this man go missing?"

"Reportedly two nights ago . . . the night a silver Jeep Wrangler was spotted parked in a cove close to the swamps."

She blinked, then glanced at her Jeep a few yards away. I watched her wheels turn with this plot twist.

"That was you, correct?" I asked.

"No."

"No? The mud on the tires suggests a different story." I jerked my chin to the pair of hiking boots just inside the door. "And the same mud caked on the bottom of those boots—size seven, if I had to guess—suggests whoever owns those boots recently went on a hike."

If looks could kill, I'd be dead. Right there on Dr. Mia Frost's doorstep.

Peering over my shoulder, at my truck, the woods, her Jeep, then back to me, she was seconds from closing the door in my face.

"What's the missing person's name?" she asked. "The man's name?"

"Cullen Nichols."

Her gray eyes rounded, and every instinct in my body surged to life.

"Cullen Nichols?" she repeated. "Are you sure?"

"Yes, ma'am."

"Who reported him missing?"

"His housekeeper. Arrives at his house every morning at six o'clock to wake him up and begin breakfast. According to her statement, he's always there, and if he's not, he lets her know in advance. On the second morning that she didn't see him and hadn't heard from him, she called the police."

Mia blinked, processing.

I reached into my pocket and handed her my card. "My number's on there. Call me—"

"No, Mr. Crew, I haven't seen anyone or any unusual vehicles around here or during my visit to the Black Hills Bayou. Now, if you'll excuse me—"

I opened my mouth to question what she'd been doing in the woods in the first place, but the door slammed in my face. Deep in thought, I swept a hand over my mouth.

Not only did Mia Frost know the missing man, but something about him made her emotional.

I turned and crossed the pebbled walkway to my truck, questions pummeling my head.

What was the connection between Dr. Mia Frost and Cullen Nichols? Secret lovers, perhaps?

And how did her role in interviewing Courtney Hayes—*another* missing person—play into all this? Or was it simply another coincidence?

But most importantly, what the hell was this woman hiding?

# Chapter Sixteen

## Mia

The sun never came out that morning.

A heavy blanket of thick clouds colored the sky a dreary gray, like an ominous presence moving in. Tiny beads of water blurred the windshield as I sped down the narrow two-lane road, my body vibrating with the adrenaline of five espresso shots.

Cullen Nichols was missing.

My fingers gripped the steering wheel as I accelerated too fast out of a hairpin turn.

*Cullen Nichols.* There had to be a mistake. There was no way he was missing.

It was impossible.

It couldn't be related.

It was *not* related.

*It's not related.*

I cracked the window and turned up the radio, willing the white noise to mute the voices in my head.

The moment Easton Crew had disappeared down the dirt road, I'd thrown on a black wool pantsuit and matching heels before sprinting out the door.

The mist had transformed into full-blown sprinkles of rain by the time I turned onto the main drag of town, lined with newly restored historic brick buildings, manicured trees, and potted shrubs. It was the hub of Skull Hollow, home of the county courthouse, a tall stone building that resembled the Alamo. There was also a post office, a barbershop, an auto-repair garage, a twenty-four-seven barbecue joint that declared itself the best in the state, and finally, a western dive bar called Jolene's that hosted a once-monthly Scorpion Shot night that drew drunks and thrill seekers from all over the region.

Despite the cold autumn morning, the street was busy, the sidewalks lined with cowboy hats going about their business and a few dreadlocks waiting in line at the diner, tourists in town to experience the splendor of the Piney Woods in autumn.

I flicked on my turn signal and turned onto a narrow paved driveway that cut through a patch of pines, their long-needled branches creating a tunnel overhead. Mist danced through the trees, blurring the large gray structure at the end of the drive.

The gravel lot was empty, to my surprise and relief. The clinic didn't open until nine, but it was unusual that no one was in yet.

I slid into my designated spot behind the back door of the Dragonfly Clinic, otherwise known as my baby.

Location had been key when I'd moved with my business partner, Jo Bellerose, a psychiatrist who collected cigars like most women collected shoes, to southeast Texas with the intent to open a mental health facility. Texas, and its surrounding states for that matter, had the highest prevalence of mental illness—and the lowest rates of access to care, especially southeast Texas. And after a recession and a pandemic, the need for mental health was greater than ever.

And there we were, breaching an untapped market in hopes of pulling people out of the darkness while making a decent living at it.

The moment I'd seen the dilapidated gray barn in Skull Hollow, I knew it was perfect.

Yes—*barn*.

The two-story structure had once been part of the largest personal property in the area, before the owners died and their children decided to split the property. They offered it for commercial sale piece by piece, thereby expanding the business district of the small town. It was a big deal for Skull Hollow and highly controversial.

The southern-plantation-style mansion at the center of the property sold first. A widow from Arkansas bought it and turned it into a lavish bed-and-breakfast. The rest of the land sold quickly, with plans for a large portion to be developed into a park and an outdoor recreational facility to cater to the tourists and nature lovers who traveled to the area.

The old barn with its shabby exterior remained unsold, however, lingering like the redheaded stepchild that no one wanted.

Until I saw it.

I purchased the dilapidated structure on the spot, emptying my savings and putting up my condo in Austin for collateral. Jo and I relocated to Skull Hollow and began renovations the next week.

We hired Jo's mother to head up the renovations. The newly divorced wife of a southern real estate mogul had plenty of time on her hands and, more importantly, plenty of money to fund the project at an interest rate that no bank could match.

In four months, Melinda Bellerose had turned the weathered barn into a stunning two-story sanctuary with exposed beams, gleaming hardwood floors, and floor-to-ceiling windows that flooded the space with warm, natural light. The modern open floor plan downstairs had been split into a waiting area lined with potted plants and lush carpets, a kitchen / break room, and two offices.

One office was occupied by Stella Bloom, our office manager; the other by our newest hire, Luna Raimi, a cognitive behavior specialist and yoga instructor. Jo and I shared the upstairs in two spacious offices where we met with clients.

Three years after opening its doors, the Dragonfly Clinic had become the premier mental health facility in the region. Jo and I had plans to expand the business into nearby cities within two years.

It was an exciting and terrifying time, during which a mixture of guilt and self-loathing slowly ate my insides like a virus. Despite the company's success, I awoke every morning waiting for what I thought was the inevitable to happen. For my unworthiness to be exposed. I couldn't understand why I was being afforded such success. Me, undoubtedly the least deserving person to advise others on how to live their lives.

It was a constant internal battle, anxiety warring with greed in my head. A dangerous, volatile combination, fragile enough to shatter at a moment's notice. I knew that one day I would wake up to that other shoe dropping.

And why did I feel like that moment was coming far too soon?

I grabbed my briefcase, locked up the Jeep, and crossed the gravel parking lot, the light rain frizzing the wisps of hair that had escaped my topknot. My heels crunched on the gravel, a few brittle leaves spinning in my path.

After unlocking the back door, I pushed it open, noting the fresh scent of Pine-Sol lingering in the air. Stella had likely stayed late the evening before, scrubbing the office from top to bottom in her own unconventional form of therapy.

I hurried through the stone kitchen, down the glass-walled hallway, and up the stairs to my office in the west corner suite. Usually at this time of morning, my office was awash in the bright, happy shades of dawn. That morning, though, it was colorless and cold. I clicked on a floor lamp, set my briefcase on my desk, and made my way across the room to the freestanding birdcage that stretched to the exposed ceiling beams. I'd spent an entire month's paycheck on it.

Despite the darkness flooding the room and my head, I smiled. "Good morning, my babies."

The string of tiny mirrors in the cage caught the light from the lamp, sparkling on the Dragonfly Clinic's mascots, six colorful parakeets that had single-handedly calmed more patients quicker than a snort of Xanax.

The birds squawked gleefully, jumping from perch to perch, excited at my arrival, and my smile grew.

"I'll play with you guys in a bit. I've got some work to do."

After quickly refilling food and water dishes, I clicked on my computer and settled behind the desk, mindlessly straightening a stack of folders as the system booted.

I inhaled, then clicked into my patient files. "Okay," I whispered, nerves fluttering in my stomach. "Cullen N—"

The front door flew open, and voices flooded the building.

"Uh-oh, smells like Stella had a bad date."

"Dear God, did she use an entire bottle this time? God, I can't stand that smell—isn't there a lemon scent we could buy her or something?"

"I kind of like the smell."

"You can smell? I figured your nose was desensitized years ago."

"I don't inhale the cigars, Luna."

"Sure you don't. Is she here?"

"No, but Mia is somewhere. Mia!"

The voices drew closer as I feverishly clicked through my folders. "Mia!"

Two pairs of shoes clomped up the staircase.

*Dammit.*

I glanced up as Jo and Luna stepped under the arched doorway, the differences between the two women never more evident than on that day.

Fresh off her motorcycle, Jo wore a black leather jacket and matching combat boots laced over her skinny jeans. Her long dark hair was tied into a topknot, with a folded silk scarf around her forehead to keep the flyaways from tickling her cheeks.

Not surprising, in all her black leather glory, it hadn't taken long for Jo to gain a reputation in Skull Hollow as someone not to be messed with. Funny thing is, the gossips didn't know that her leather jacket was couture and cost $4,000, her boots were fresh off the Alexander McQueen runway, and the silver jewelry that circled her wrists and each finger? Platinum. And if you looked closely enough, you could see the black diamonds sparkling in the eyes of her skull earrings.

In contrast to Jo's chic biker-chick appearance, Luna wore a baggy sweater over yoga pants and a pair of Uggs about ten years past their prime. In her hand was a recycled paper cup filled to the brim with a green-colored substance. Her blonde hair was braided to the side, emphasizing high cheekbones and a beautiful long, thin neck. Luna was the passive earth child to Jo's femme fatale.

"Whoa, why so serious? You okay?" Luna asked, politely lingering in the doorway until invited inside.

Jo, however, barreled into the room like a silverback gorilla. "Does this have to do with Courtney Hayes?" she asked, also picking up the vibes I was apparently putting out. "Did you meet with her again?"

"No, and I'm not sure. I mean, no, I didn't meet with her again." *Was* there a connection? My stomach rolled for the hundredth time. "You guys remember Cullen Nichols, right? My client?"

"Yeah." Luna finally stepped into the room, greeting the parakeets with a quick smile and a jerk of her chin.

Jo frowned. "The short redhead with glasses and more sway in his hips than Tyra Banks?"

I rolled my eyes. "He's effeminate."

Jo raised her hands. "Hey. Whatever."

"And he was married."

"I believe that's called a beard." Jo winked, then sobered. "He's an accountant, right? Works out of his home. Amateur photographer on the weekends. Shy guy, doesn't talk much. Started coming here last year . . . for treatment of PTSD, right?"

"Right."

Jo was always on point. It was my favorite thing about her.

"Well, what's going on?" she asked.

"He's gone missing."

"What?" Luna stepped to the edge of my desk, next to Jo.

"Yeah." I began chewing my lower lip, a nasty habit I had when I was worried. "Last seen or heard from was two days ago. No clues, nothing. Just—gone."

"Vacation, maybe? Moved?"

"No. No way. He has, like, four appointments scheduled out with me. And according to his housekeeper, he didn't pack his luggage, so no vacation. He was very diligent about letting her know when he wouldn't be there. She's the one who called it in."

Jo tilted her head. "When was the last time you talked to him?"

"Last week, during our last appointment."

"Did he mention leaving town?"

"No."

"What about his family?"

"No kids, and the ex-wife lives in Canada now. They divorced a decade ago and have no place in each other's lives anymore. His mom and dad are deceased. I'm assuming the cops already called the ex, but she must not have offered much additional information."

"Anything abnormal about the last appointment you had with him? Did he say anything? Seem off?"

I paused, considering the question I'd mulled over since the moment I'd slammed the door in Easton Crew's face. "No, I don't think so. I was just about to review my notes and recordings from our last few meetings. See if I could pick up anything I might have missed. That's why I'm here so early."

Unlike most therapists, I recorded each of my sessions and reviewed the audiotape immediately afterward. This gave me two perspectives—the one the client intended me to see and the one hidden behind the mask of perfection. Ninety percent of what we say isn't in the words themselves; it's in our tone and body language.

"How do you know this?" Jo asked, probably surprised she hadn't heard the gossip at the bar the night before.

"A guy—man—showed up at my door this morning, asking about him."

"A guy man?" Jo's brow cocked.

"The guy that runs LYNX Search and Rescue."

"Easton *Crew*?" Luna squeaked.

My brows popped as Jo smirked at the childlike grin spreading across Luna's pixie face.

"Sorry." Luna raised her palms as if to surrender to the emotions. "But that guy is *hot*."

"I hadn't noticed," I said, avoiding the topic.

As usual, Jo saw right through me.

Butterflies had surged in my stomach the moment his name rolled off Luna's lips, my body betraying my brain's effort to tuck his image away in a metaphorical box deep in my mind, then toss away the key.

I'd be lying if I said I hadn't noticed how attractive the man was in a rugged, alpha, "throw you over his shoulder" kind of way.

If you like that sort of thing. And I do.

The polar opposite of the dapper, pretty-boy models who graced the covers of fashion and health magazines, Easton Crew had a weathered, ruggedly handsome face, with unkempt hair and a five-o'clock shadow that somehow made him even sexier.

Then there were his eyes, a murky hazel green with a piercing intensity that made goose bumps race over my skin, evoking a primal response that left me questioning if he was friend or foe. Even in silence, the man emanated a kind of hyperaware alertness, giving away the years he'd spent running special ops in the deepest depths of hell.

And underneath the clothes he obviously hadn't washed in weeks was the outline of a body carved from granite, with thick, broad shoulders and a muscular chest that made me want to claw my finger-nails into it while riding his . . .

*Dammit.*

Yes, my heart had actually fluttered the moment I'd seen Easton Crew. The emotion had been fleeting, however, and followed immediately by utter humiliation.

The man had seen me at my absolute worst. My house in total disarray, cluttered and messy, inhabited by a loud group of birds that I knew was ten too many, but the truth was, I couldn't help myself. And at the crux of it all, me half-dressed in an outfit worthy of a psych ward.

It was the first time a man had visited my house since I'd moved to Skull Hollow.

What did that say about me?

What did Easton think of me?

Why did I care so damn much?

*Stop it*, I told the voices in my head. *Just stop it.*

I needed to relinquish whatever carnal feelings I'd immediately had for this man. I didn't do relationships—not that he was willing or had even suggested the slightest bit of interest. I wasn't good at them, proven by repeated failure and eventual surrender.

Life was easier being single, without having to get too close, disclose the real you, the one you kept hidden from the world. Because then, why would he want me? Why would anyone want me? I was damaged goods.

A man like Easton Crew would never like me. He was too good for someone like me.

"And he's single, too, right?" Luna said, yanking me from my thoughts.

"Yeah, he is. I know he is." Jo pulled her smartphone from her pocket and clicked it on. The resident queen of social media, Jo needed nothing more than your height and hair color to uncover where you lived, your financial situation, your personality type, and your vaccination status. Social media, and the internet for that matter, truly was a terrifying plethora of information.

Her fingertips flew over the screen. "Or maybe recently divorced, something like that. Regardless, I know he's single. Let me just—"

"If I give you his number, will that help move this conversation along?" I said. "Because I'd rather be figuring out what happened to my missing client than what Easton Crew's current relationship status is."

"Sure, give it to me," Luna said. "His number—I'd love to have it."

A pang of possessiveness stabbed through me, which angered me. I rattled off the number with more attitude than intended.

"Aha!" Luna jabbed her finger at me. "You *memorized* it. That means you like him, Mia." She laughed. "I don't want his damn number. It was a test, and you just failed miserably, sweetheart. You *like* him."

I'd just opened my mouth to say whatever was necessary to shut this conversation down when Jo raised her phone into the air as if discovering the location of the Holy Grail.

"Got him! Yep, he's single." She refocused on her phone. "No, not divorced, but he was engaged . . ."

"Engaged?" I asked, despite myself.

This surprised me. Easton didn't seem like the type of man to get down on one knee for a woman.

And why didn't that turn me off?

"Yep." Jo glanced up conspiratorially under long black lashes. "But she died not long ago."

"*What?*" Luna and I asked in unison.

"How?" I asked.

"Not sure. The news article doesn't go into detail, but I get the vibe it was unexpected."

"Like cancer or something?"

Jo shrugged.

"So . . . not murder or anything like that?" Luna asked, reading my thoughts exactly.

"Article doesn't say."

I made a mental note to research this immediately—right after Cullen Nichols.

"Car accident," a voice yelled from downstairs, startling us all.

"Stella?"

"Car accident," Stella called out again with about as much emotion as one might when sharing the weather forecast.

I looked at Luna, who looked at Jo, who looked at me.

"Come up here," Jo yelled over her shoulder.

A few seconds passed as Stella finished whatever she had been so stealthily doing downstairs before padding quietly up the stairs. Her curly red hair was piled on the top of her head, away from her face, highlighting a new pair of tortoiseshell glasses. She wore a yellow sweater over a pink skirt and bright-red heels to complete the look. As usual, the woman was dressed in a kaleidoscope of colors. Anything else would have been cause for concern.

She was obviously tired, her puffy red-rimmed eyes contrasting with abnormally sallow skin. I wasn't the only one stressed about something.

"Yep," she said, stepping into my office. "Easton Crew's fiancée died in a car accident. It was bad."

"You look bad." Jo frowned, giving Stella the once-over.

"God, you're a bitch." Stella breezed past her to the birdcage, greeting the Dragonfly mascots.

Jo smirked.

"The office looks good," Luna said to Stella, probing while also giving her the once-over.

"Thanks." Stella stuck her finger into the cage, petting the green parakeet she'd named John. After John Deere—her father had been a lawn mower salesman. "Couldn't sleep."

"I have pills for that," Dr. Jo said.

"Great. Where? In your purse, your desk, the console in your car, or in that little safe you keep hidden under your desk?"

Luna sucked in a breath, and the room fell silent. Eyes widened, and gazes darted around the group. It was an unspoken question among us. What the hell did Jo guard so fiercely in that safe? No one dared ask, but I knew time would tell. Her secrets would come to light someday, just like I feared mine were going to.

"Anyway," I said quickly and too loudly. "Bad . . . you said the car accident was bad. How do you mean? What happened?"

Stella turned from the birdcage and gave Jo the scorching glare we were all avoiding. "Rumor is they'd just gotten engaged not even a month or two before. She'd moved here from California, I think, or Florida—one of the sunny states—and wasn't used to the curvy roads. Slid off the road during an ice storm, crashed into a tree, hit her head, and died. She had to be cut out of the vehicle."

"No shit?"

"No shit."

"How long ago was this?" I asked.

Stella shrugged. "A yearish ago, I think."

"Did they have kids?" I asked—not that it mattered or had absolutely anything to do with the conversation.

"I don't know. Don't think so, considering they'd only been engaged a minute."

"Wow. That's sad." Luna wrapped her arms around herself.

I pictured the small gold band I'd noticed on Easton's pinkie finger and wondered if it was his fiancée's.

"People die. It's a circle of life," Jo said. "Now, back to the matter at hand. Cullen Nichols."

"What about Cullen Nichols?" Stella asked.

"He's missing."

Stella's brows arched as she joined Luna and Jo in front of my desk.

Growing impatient, I continued. "Anyway, have you guys seen him in town? At the bar? Grocery store?"

Luna and Jo shook their heads, while Stella seemed to take a second to digest this new information.

"Was he only seeing you for PTSD?" Jo asked, and I nodded. "From what? What happened to him?"

I shifted in my seat, considering the file that was suddenly blurred on my screen. "An . . . assault. When he was young."

A moment of silence stretched out, hovering uncomfortably in my office.

I blew out a breath, released my weight against the back of the chair, and folded my hands behind my head. "It just doesn't feel right."

"What exactly?" Jo asked.

"The fact that Cullen showed no desire to leave town during our last meeting—or signs of distress, for that matter. Nothing to make me think he was about to leave, for any reason, or that anything bad might happen. I've had—God, I don't know how many appointments I've had with him. A lot. I know him well enough to pick up on anything. I think I do, anyway."

"Where was he last seen?"

"The woods around the Black Cat Trail."

The air in the room instantly shifted.

"Are you saying Cullen has gone missing in the same area Courtney Hayes was raped?" Luna asked.

I slowly nodded.

"So this points to the Black Cat Stalker, doesn't it?" she said. "This would be—what—the fifth case associated with him in less than a few months?"

"If Cullen's disappearance is related, then yes."

"Let's not jump to conclusions here." Jo narrowed her focus on me. "Are you going to meet with Courtney again?"

I shrugged. "I submitted my psych profile of the Black Cat Stalker to Deputy Mason the next day and haven't seen her since."

"I'd like to read the profile."

"That's the thing . . ." I blew out a breath, scrubbing my hands over my face. "Cullen's disappearance changes everything. If his disappearance is connected to the Black Cat Stalker, my profile is totally fucked. Inaccurate. So far, the Black Cat has targeted young athletic females who are brunettes, which is what I based the bulk of my profile on."

Jo sighed. "And an overweight, balding, forty-something-year-old accountant doesn't fit this."

"No. It's a completely different MO. But what are the freaking odds he went missing in the same area? It's got to be connected, right?"

Only in rare cases would a rapist switch from targeting females to targeting males. Regardless, my gut told me something was very wrong. Very off. And I'd just hand delivered a profile that was quite possibly incorrect and could throw off the entire investigation.

Courtney Hayes deserved better . . . she deserved justice. And for some reason, I felt like Cullen Nichols held the key. I needed to find him, not only for my own sanity but to confirm if there was a link between him and the Black Cat. Because it sure as hell didn't seem to fit.

"Anyway, I'm going to listen to our last few sessions again. See if I missed anything." I nodded to the paper cup in Luna's hand. "Go finish that nasty wheatgrass organic double shot of collagen you have in your hand, and we'll regroup in a bit."

"You got it, boss."

"Need anything right now?" Stella asked.

"No, thanks."

When the trio stepped out of the office, Jo paused, then turned back and leaned against the doorframe. "Hey . . . question."

She studied me in a way that suggested she knew I was leaving something out. Little did she know exactly how many things I was leaving out.

"Why did this Easton guy go all the way to your house at the ass crack of dawn to ask you about Cullen Nichols? And why him, a search-and-rescue guy? Why not the cops?"

I forced myself to hold eye contact. "He said they asked him to help in the search, so . . ."

"Yeah, but why him—to *your* house?"

"Because I live close to the trail, I guess. He asked if I'd seen anything suspicious over the last few days."

"But why *him*?"

It was a good question, one that I'd wondered as well. Easton had told me that a group of hunters had reported seeing a silver Jeep parked in the cove. Okay . . . but how had Easton Crew known *I* owned a silver Jeep? And why hadn't he just forwarded this information to the cops so they could handle it? Why had he handled it himself?

Too much to dissect. I needed to focus on Cullen.

Wanting this conversation shut down, I shrugged and shook my head. There was no way in hell I was going to tell Jo, or anyone, the real story. She'd ask why I'd been in the woods in the first place. And if I told her that I'd spent the last few days searching for clues about the Black Cat Stalker, she'd ask more questions.

Why was I inserting myself into the Courtney Hayes investigation, and secretly at that?

Why did I care so much? she'd ask.

Why? Was it personal?

I couldn't—wouldn't—go down that path with her, or anyone. Not when I'd spent the last decade deliberately tucking it away.

Jo stared at me a minute. "Okay, then. Talk soon."

She knew that I knew she didn't believe me. But being the good friend that Jo was, she didn't pry. Jo had secrets of her own, after all, and boundaries were easily kept when there were plenty of skeletons in your own closet.

I waited until Jo's footsteps had disappeared down the stairs before refocusing on the computer monitor. My mouse's pointer hovered over Cullen's file, but then, as if having a mind of its own, the arrow slid to a different file.

My hand trembling, I clicked into the past.

I examined the black-and-white photo of a sixteen-year-old girl with a beaming smile that I no longer recognized. Shiny light-brown curls fell over her shoulders, and she had a massive trophy in her hand.

The next document, a medical report.

*Victim in horrific attack . . .*

Goose bumps spread over my skin like an army of fire ants, and a feeling of doom settled in my stomach.

I knew myself well enough to know that I wasn't going to let this go. I had to get answers. I had to know if there was a connection between my past and the present.

And it started with finding Cullen Nichols.

# Chapter Seventeen

DOCTOR: Do you feel like talking today?

PATIENT: [*No response.*]

DOCTOR: This is the fourth time you've come to see me . . . maybe the fourth time's a charm?

PATIENT: [*No response.*]

DOCTOR: I'd like to understand why you're not opening up to me. The fact that you continue to show up for our meetings and then schedule follow-up appointments suggests to me that you have something to say. Perhaps a lot to say. I'm here to listen. I'm here for you.

PATIENT: [*No response.*]

DOCTOR: Okay. Let's go back to the documentation you completed online before your first appointment. Among other questions, you were asked if you had been exposed to one or more events that included threatened

death, serious injury, or sexual violence.
You marked *yes* to this question. You were
asked if you experienced recurrent memories
or dreams of this event, therefore causing
you stress. You marked *yes*. You were also
asked if you avoided any scenarios that
you associated with this trauma. Again,
*yes*. And lastly, you were asked if the side
effects of this trauma affect your day-
to-day life, for example, through anxiety,
difficulty sleeping, or destructive behavior. You marked *yes*. Your responses here
suggest you're suffering from severe PTSD.
Do you think that's the case?

PATIENT: [*No response.*]

DOCTOR: Okay, then. Today I thought we could
play a little game. How does that sound?

PATIENT: Fine.

DOCTOR: Great. This game involves pulling memories from the past. Please understand that
there are no right or wrong answers here,
and there are no trick questions. This is
just me asking you simple questions, and
then you simply responding with the first
thing that pops into your head. Sound good?

PATIENT: Sure.

DOCTOR: All right, here we go. I'd like you to
tell me the happiest or most joyful memory
you have.

PATIENT: You mean . . . recently?

DOCTOR: Whenever. What was your first memory that
came to mind when I asked that question?

PATIENT: Well . . . I guess when I was . . . around seven years old. I went on a camping trip.

DOCTOR: That sounds like a good memory. Who was on the trip?

PATIENT: My mother, father, and our dog, Bandit.

DOCTOR: Just curious, why do you call your mom and dad your mother and father?

PATIENT: Why do you ask?

DOCTOR: Feels formal, that's all.

PATIENT: [*No response.*]

DOCTOR: Okay. And you have no siblings, correct? If I recall from your paperwork correctly.

PATIENT: Correct.

DOCTOR: How about friends?

PATIENT: No.

DOCTOR: None on the camping trip, or none in general?

PATIENT: Both.

DOCTOR: That must be lonely. Any reason?

PATIENT: [*No response.*]

DOCTOR: How often do you think about this camping trip?

PATIENT: I dream about it a lot.

DOCTOR: Tell me about the dreams.

PATIENT: They change from time to time.

DOCTOR: It doesn't have to be exact. Is there a recurring theme in the dreams?

PATIENT: My father showing me how to start the fire . . . it was autumn when we went . . . when I see a fire in a fireplace, I think of him and usually have dreams that night.

DOCTOR: And what feeling does this bring you? When you think of your father?

PATIENT: [*No response.*]

DOCTOR: How about when you think of your father teaching you how to build a fire? Can you remember how you were feeling then?

PATIENT: Happy . . . worthy.

DOCTOR: I'm sorry—you said "worthy"?

PATIENT: Yes.

DOCTOR: Why worthy?

PATIENT: I don't know . . . I guess because I had his attention.

DOCTOR: And this was something he usually didn't offer you?

PATIENT: [*No response.*]

DOCTOR: These dreams, are they vivid?

PATIENT: Yes.

DOCTOR: What about during the day, when you're awake. Can you recall that camping trip in detail? Building the fire in detail?

PATIENT: Most of the time, yes.

DOCTOR: Okay. Now I'm going to flip things on you a bit. Is that okay?

PATIENT: Do I have a choice?

DOCTOR: You always have a choice.

PATIENT: [*No response.*]

DOCTOR: Now I want you to tell me the most traumatic or frightening memory you have.

PATIENT: This is a trick question. You said no trick questions.

DOCTOR: Okay, fine, we don't have to talk about that yet. Instead, I'll ask you some questions about your symptoms associated with the traumatic event you indicated on your paperwork. Is that okay?

PATIENT: [*No response.*]

DOCTOR: First, I'd like you to tell me how this traumatic or frightening moment, or moments, made you feel?

PATIENT: [*No response.*]

DOCTOR: Did it make you feel sad?

PATIENT: [*No response.*]

DOCTOR: Scared? Fearful?

PATIENT: Yes.

DOCTOR: Did it hurt?

PATIENT: Yes.

DOCTOR: In your heart?

PATIENT: Yes.

DOCTOR: In or on your body?

PATIENT: Yes.

DOCTOR: Where?

PATIENT: [*Silence.*]

DOCTOR: When did this event happen?

PATIENT: A long time ago.

DOCTOR: When you were a child? A teen—

PATIENT: A long time ago.

DOCTOR: When you think about this traumatic event and feel scared or fearful, what do you do to combat those feelings?

PATIENT: [*No response.*]

DOCTOR: Perhaps that's how you respond, by not responding at all? Outwardly, anyway? Some say you might keep it all in?

PATIENT: [*No response.*]

DOCTOR: How often do you think about this traumatic event?

PATIENT: Every day.

DOCTOR: Any particular time of day?

PATIENT: At night. At dusk. During the sunset.

DOCTOR: That's very specific. Why?

PATIENT: Because that's when it happened.

DOCTOR: Dusk, where?

PATIENT: The woods.

DOCTOR: Did this traumatic event also happen during the camping trip you mentioned
earlier?

PATIENT: [*Silence.*]

DOCTOR: These dreams you mentioned earlier . . .
are they nightmares?

PATIENT: [*No response.*]

DOCTOR: How often?

PATIENT: Almost every night.

DOCTOR: So it affects your sleep. What about
the daytime? Do you think about it during
the day?

PATIENT: Yes.

DOCTOR: Do you have flashbacks?

PATIENT: [*No response.*]

DOCTOR: Tell me . . . do you ever feel like it's
happening all over again? Or that it could
happen again?

PATIENT: [*No response.*]

DOCTOR: [*No response.*]

DOCTOR: Are you okay?

DOCTOR: Are you feeling okay?

∽

DOCTOR: Okay . . . I'm going to touch you, okay? . . . I need you to sit down on the floor, come here, yes, good. Now, rest your back against the couch and put your head between your knees. You're having a panic attack. Focus on your breathing. You're safe. You're okay. I'm right here. Inhale . . . exhale . . . inhale . . .

∽

DOCTOR: Do you have prescribed medication for panic attacks?
PATIENT: [*No response.*]
DOCTOR: Inhale . . . exhale . . . good, great job. You're doing great. Now, I'm going to get a bottle of water from the fridge in the corner. I'm not leaving. Just walking across the room.

∽

DOCTOR: Your color is coming back. Do you feel better?
PATIENT: Yes.
DOCTOR: Is this your first panic attack?
PATIENT: No.
DOCTOR: How many have you had?
PATIENT: I don't know.
DOCTOR: A lot?

PATIENT: Yes.

DOCTOR: Is this what drove you to come to see me in the first place?

PATIENT: Yes.

☙

DOCTOR: You know, the sooner you tell me what happened to you, about whatever this traumatic event is that brought you to my door in the first place, the sooner I can help you. I'm here to listen. I'm here to help you. You just have to let me in . . . you just have to let someone in.

# Chapter Eighteen

## Mia

The property was like something out of a James Bond movie. A sprawling compound speckled with sleek modern buildings, insane obstacle courses that looked more like torture chambers, and dozens of jacked-up trucks, ATVs, and motorcycles. A helicopter pad, a few horses in the distance, and a cow thrown in for good measure.

The main attraction, though, was the office, otherwise known as the LYNX Group headquarters.

If a building could be a man, this was it. Masculine, utilitarian, monochrome, an expansive structure made of glass, steel, and concrete with sharp angles that looked like they could prick you if you got too close. It was imposing and intimidating, an exact representation of the CEO himself, Easton Crew.

The hard lines on the building shimmered in the late-afternoon sunlight, the brightly colored leaves of the surrounding trees reflecting in the windows.

There were no plants or flowers, no shrubbery, no welcome sign, no thoughtful decorations, no femininity whatsoever. Just steel and concrete out in the middle of nowhere.

There was also no guest parking, so I edged onto the side of the asphalt driveway and cut the engine. I grabbed my keys and phone, then paused. Despite myself, I flipped down the visor to check my makeup.

That morning, I'd opted for a knee-length beige pencil skirt and a white silk blouse. I'd chosen my most expensive pair of peep-toe heels, because a drunk homeless man had once told me they looked "hot" on me.

And why did I care about being hot that day?

The moment I'd decided I was going to reach out to Easton Crew for help, I'd begun planning my outfit immediately. Eleven wardrobe changes later, I'd settled on the formfitting skirt suit that tiptoed the fine line of inappropriate business attire.

Why? I wanted to redeem myself from the train wreck he'd seen at my house.

Fine. I also wanted him to think I was pretty.

*Damn it all to hell.*

My hand froze as I was raking through my hair, my pout turning into a scowl as I internally chastised myself for being so damn nervous about meeting him again.

I'd spent the entire morning researching his company, his past, the men of his company, and their pasts . . . borderline stalker behavior that I'm not particularly proud of.

I slapped up the visor. "Get over yourself. Who gives a damn what Easton Crew thinks of you. *Jeez,* Mia."

I was pathetic.

With a mental kick in the ass, I pushed out of my Jeep.

It had been two days since the CEO of the LYNX Group had shown up on my doorstep asking if I knew anything about the missing man named Cullen Nichols.

Two days of nothing, no sign whatsoever of my missing client, which meant he'd now been missing for four days.

Two days of the small town of Skull Hollow in an uproar, panicked mothers demanding answers on the whereabouts of the brutal rapist known as the Black Cat Stalker.

Courtney Hayes had yet to leave her home, unwilling or perhaps unable to go out in public. Or to return my calls, for that matter.

I had a list of questions I wanted to ask her, most likely disturbing and inappropriate. It was probably a good thing she hadn't answered.

In the meantime, I'd barely slept or eaten, my thoughts consumed by the Black Cat Stalker, Courtney, how my client Cullen tied into this mess, and more importantly, where the hell he was.

I'd become desperate, searching his file for any coded comments he might have made, clues that I might have missed as to where he could be. I kept circling back to a comment Cullen had made months earlier about photographing a remote cliff known as Yellow Rock.

It was a stretch but one that I'd decided needed to be explored nonetheless.

A gust of cool wind spun through my hair as I stepped in front of my Jeep, noticing how quiet the property was despite all the fanfare.

I glanced at the four-car garage attached to the side of the building. All four bays were open, revealing two black custom utility trucks that looked more like mobile command centers than vehicles. The LYNX logo was printed on each tailgate. In the next bay were two of the biggest, most equipped ATVs I'd ever seen, with more logos. And in the final bay, a blacked-out Humvee with more bells and whistles than a private jet—which I assumed was parked somewhere next to the helipad out back.

Apparently, contract work with the government paid well. Very well.

A concrete sidewalk led from the driveway to the front of the building, which was lined with glass walls. I passed what appeared to be a conference room and glanced inside. Gleaming dark hardwood floors ran underneath a long, modern table and chairs with steel accents. A phone sat in the middle of the table. A rock wall enclosed the back. The room was pristine, uninviting. Ice cold.

I followed the walkway to a shiny metal door that read THE LYNX GROUP, LLC.

The door was locked. Next to the handle was a small intercom. I lifted my finger, then stilled with the sudden feeling that I was being watched.

I glanced over my shoulder. Nothing.

I pressed the intercom. A minute passed, then another. I pressed it again.

Movement from the woods caught my attention. I turned just as a woman rounded the front of the garage, a tool bag in one hand and an ax in the other, a backpack slung over her shoulder.

The woman was like a lotus emerging from the swamp, her face, neck, and arms covered in mud. But her short platinum-blonde hair was spotless, a luminescent glow against the grime. She was wearing a skin-tight tank top that emphasized cleavage I'd kill for, camouflage army fatigues, and combat boots. She was tall and slender with toned muscles and a hard look that suggested she'd started her day with CrossFit instead of a quiet cup of coffee like most humans. Midtwenties, I guessed, but the glint in her eyes suggested a wisdom beyond her years. A past, maybe?

There was something about her that instantly struck me. Like I'd known her in another life, or perhaps she had a place in this one not yet revealed.

When our eyes met, hers narrowed.

I smiled. "Hi there. I—"

Without a word, the woman disappeared into a side door I hadn't noticed on the garage.

*Well, then.*

I cleared my throat, refocusing on the steel door ahead of me, and pushed the button again and again. Nothing. Frustrated, I heaved out a breath.

I imagined Easton scrutinizing me from the other side of a security camera hidden somewhere nearby . . . probably pointing right up my nose.

He—someone—had to know I was there.

Embarrassment from being dismissed stirred with anger.

This time I bypassed the intercom and pounded on the door, my resolve stronger than ever to look the man in the face once again. Because this time, I was wearing my peep-toe heels, dammit.

And this time, I truly needed his help.

# Chapter Nineteen

## Easton

Mia Frost was a woman who wouldn't tolerate being ignored. This was evident by the hole she was wearing on my front stoop, pacing back and forth like a rabid animal. I watched her—*studied* is perhaps a better word for it—trying to discern which of her many personalities was the real one.

She was a surprise on all counts, and I wasn't someone who was easily caught off guard.

The woman I had watched from my hiding place behind the pines was sad, despondent, and most often, drunk. The woman I fantasized daily about in the shower was sweet, agreeable, and mild mannered, with an affinity for DIY and single-topic conversations. But in reality, the woman I'd met was an uptight ornithophile with an electronic larynx and a serious anxiety problem. And messy.

Dammit, nothing was worse than a messy woman.

Today's Mia was determined, impatient, headstrong . . . interesting. She was a woman who expected to be responded to immediately, something I was sure she'd grown accustomed to quickly with a face and a body that rivaled Natalie Portman's in *Star Wars*.

I watched the sway of her hips, squeezed by a tight, conservative skirt that reminded me of my first crush, the school librarian, Mrs. Kleinschmidt, a timeless beauty despite the unfortunate surname . . . or perhaps sexier because of it.

I was contemplating this comparison when Beckett stepped into the doorway, a folder of papers in one hand, a cup of coffee in the other, and a Glock 22 secured on the waistband of his tailored Brioni suit.

"Hey, Chief. We got a visitor."

I glanced back at the big screen mounted on the wall, displaying a black-and-white grid of the property's CCTV cameras, including the one where our guest was now gnawing at her fingernail.

"I see that."

"Never seen her before."

"Name's Mia Frost. She's with the Dragonfly Mental Health Clinic across town." I decided to leave out the part that I'd spent over an hour researching her when I should have been doing any one of a million other things.

"Oh—that place that sells hypnosis shit and CBD?"

"CBT, Becks, not CBD. They specialize in hypnotherapy and cognitive behavior therapy, not pot."

"Guess I should cancel my appointment then. Want me to let her in? She looks . . . oddly pissed."

Cocking my head, I focused on the screen. "No. Give her a few seconds."

Beckett stepped deeper into my office, following my gaze to the screen. We watched her pace, huff, sigh, pivot, and repeat, studying each movement as we would one of our trainees who'd been caught midbreakdown by one of our security cameras during a particularly brutal survival-training exercise.

Just then, the front door swung open. I sat up as Alek, all six feet four, 260 pounds of muscle, welcomed Dr. Mia Frost with the same hospitality as a pit bull at a junkyard.

"Dammit." I turned to Beckett. "I told you never to let him answer the door."

Beckett grinned.

"What the hell has he been doing?" I looked back at the screen, where Alek was dressed in camo army fatigues, covered from head to toe in dried mud and debris.

"He's been down at the new rappelling course, working day and night on it for a few days. I think he slept in a cave last night. Loren's been helping him this morning."

"I can smell him from here. Tell him to take a break, shower, eat, and ensure that he never answers the door again."

"Whatever you say, Chief."

I leaned forward, anxious to see how this interaction was going to go.

To my surprise, Dr. Mia Frost didn't flinch as the grandson of a former Russian crime lord stepped nose to nose with her. She stood her ground and stared him down—or up, I should say—as if a worthy adversary, and in that moment I decided she was. Her little fists curled at her sides, her weight shifting to her toes, ready to fight. An interesting automatic response to a man. I thought back on her inhospitality when I'd visited.

Mia didn't like men. Or was it that she didn't trust them?

Mia said something to Alek, her expression sharp, her jaw tight. He responded in kind, and then they glared at each other like two boxers in a ring.

My attention was pulled to camera three, where Dane Stratton was speeding up the drive, as usual. Also as usual, he skidded to a stop next to the front door.

Alek and Mia turned as the former firefighter unfolded himself from the Tahoe and crossed the driveway. I took note of the new suit he was wearing, as well as the new wing tips and aviators, a stark contrast to the ill-fitting suits he'd interviewed in months earlier.

He and Alek dipped their chins in acknowledgment, and something inside me was spurred to life as I watched Dane give Mia the once-over, a head-to-toe scan of everything she offered.

I shifted in my seat.

Dane disappeared inside.

I watched Alek refocus on Mia and take a step back, saying something to the effect of *Come back when you have an official appointment.* When he started to close the door, I leaned forward and clicked the intercom button.

"Dr. Frost, to what do I owe the pleasure?"

Her focus snapped to the black intercom next to the doorknob. "You and I have very different definitions of pleasure, Mr. Crew."

"It's Chief around here."

Beckett chuckled, and I couldn't fight my smirk.

She turned her deadpan face to the security camera looming over the door.

"Do you have an appointment?" I asked, realizing I was enjoying this little game. I must have been bored.

"No."

Alek glared up at the camera with annoyance.

"May I take five minutes of your time, Mr. Crew?" Mia asked in a condescending tone that made my dick jerk.

Grinning, I said, "I have three."

She dipped her chin to Alek in approval of this, as if he worked for her. Alek shot a glance at the camera before taking a step back and ushering her over the threshold.

Beckett shook his head, then refocused on business. "I spoke with Henrick Taylor this morning, as you requested. Says he didn't leave his hotel except for food and a run after you cut him from the course."

"You verify this?"

"Best I could. The Blue Pine doesn't have security cameras. I spoke with the manager, who confirmed seeing him in the parking lot, quote, 'a few times.'"

"That's it?"

"All she had in her. The woman is one staircase away from complete heart failure. What goes on in her motel is the least of her worries."

"Did she see him two nights ago, specifically?"

"I asked, but she couldn't recall."

"What about Jay Ruiz? You speak to him? That kid never leaves his side. Henrick gets off on it."

"No, Chief, I didn't. Figured me asking if he knew his buddy's whereabouts a few nights ago when a young woman was brutally raped would raise questions. You're wanting me to go under the radar here, right?"

"Right."

"Any specific reason you think Henrick could be involved in what happened to Courtney Hayes?"

I peered through the window at the woods, where the last time I'd seen the kid, he'd been threatening to kill me. "Bottom line, the LYNX Group was hosting a group of men from out of town when Courtney Hayes was raped and Cullen Nichols went missing. I'm just staying a step ahead of it. I'm surprised the cops haven't been here yet to interview each of them, to be honest."

Beckett snorted. "You're surprised?"

Truthfully, no, I wasn't. The small-town sheriff's department was stretched thin as it was. Add deer-hunting season into the mix, and local law enforcement was already working double shifts. Likely, McNamara had passed the information I'd supplied him on each trainee onto a part-timer, who'd run a quick background check and called it a day.

Not that I was complaining.

"Did Henrick pick up on the fact you weren't just calling to check on him?"

Beckett tilted his head to the side with the closest thing to an eye roll his masculinity would allow.

"Right." I nodded.

"Before we hung up, he said he wants another shot at the course."

"No."

"You still mad he threatened to kill you?"

"If I got mad every time someone threatened me harm, I'd be more maniacal than Captain Marvel in the waiting room." I jerked my chin to the security screens.

Beckett laughed. "He's pretty damn determined not to go back home being the only one who failed your course."

The ego.

"He should have thought of that before ignoring the rules."

Beckett nodded. "I'll take care of it. I'm assuming you've got Loren checking into everyone on the team?"

I nodded. "So far, no record for anyone. Not even a speeding ticket."

"I don't know whether to be proud or disappointed about that."

"Becks, you're the only person I know that actually went to jail for speeding tickets."

"Hey, that got me a plaque on the wall."

"I think it's a dartboard. You slept with the mayor's daughter, remember."

"Ah." He angled his head thoughtfully to the ceiling, then grinned. "Come to think of it, leaving her house was when I got one of the first speeding tickets."

"God, you're an ass."

"This from the man making a woman wait on his front stoop so that he doesn't have to engage in an actual face-to-face conversation." Beckett glanced down at the folders in his hand. "Anyway, we've got that group of four state troopers coming in this afternoon, earlier than intended."

"How early?"

"Four hours. I adjusted their package to include land navigation. By the way, one is friends with Deputy Mason."

My lip curled in disgust.

Beckett laughed, knowing far too well my disdain for the deputy. "I know. They were even roommates for a while."

"Roommates?"

"Yep. Apparently Mason lived in Lubbock for a few months before moving down here."

"Texas? I thought he transferred from Oklahoma?"

Beckett shrugged and frowned, wondering where I was going with this.

Where was I going? My head started spinning with McNamara's words . . .

*". . . we're looking for a disorganized offender."*

*"Meaning someone who is impulsive?"*

*"Right. And specifically, someone who moves a lot, from town to town or state to state. Maybe moved to Skull Hollow recently, or someone who has only lived here a short time."*

"Chief?"

I shook my head, refocusing on the current moment. "Are you taking them out?"

Beckett nodded. "Taking Dane with me. He's ready, Chief. Alek and I have spent months with him now. He's ready to lead his own course."

Glancing out the window, I leaned back in my chair and steepled my hands under my chin. The former wildland firefighter was physically at his peak, likely the strongest and healthiest on the team. Mentally, though, there was something about the kid that gave me pause. Dane was too quiet, too . . . something.

"No," I said.

"No? But—"

"One more month. The kid's still hanging on to something he needs to let go of before he can be fully engaged."

"Maybe Dr. CBD can help with that."

I snorted, cataloging the possessive pang that shot through me. "Anything else?"

"Nope. I'll keep you updated." Beckett jerked his chin to the monitor. "She looks like fun."

He disappeared down the hallway.

I picked up the phone and dialed Loren, our young, eccentric office manager slash sleuth extraordinaire.

"Hey, Chief."

I winced. Her voice was particularly perky that morning.

"Loren, I need a favor."

"You got it."

"Thanks. I need you to get me every address Deputy Chris Mason has lived at over the last ten years. I also need you to pin his whereabouts for the last week. Every single day, every hour, every night. I want to know what he did, where he went, who he talked to, and what he was wearing. Literally."

"That's going to take some time . . . I'll have to hack into—"

"I need it ASAP. It's important."

"I'll . . . see what I can do."

"Thanks."

After locking my computer, I grabbed my cell phone and made my way to the small waiting area next to the conference room, where we took all our walk-ins. We didn't get many.

Mia wasn't in the room.

Frowning, I looked over my shoulder toward the restroom. Surely, she could hold whatever it was that she needed to do for three minutes.

A breeze that I shouldn't have felt inside the office swept past me, carrying with it the scent of jasmine.

I turned. A svelte, elegant silhouette stood on the balcony that over-looked the rolling hills of the tactical courses. Mia's back was to me, her hands resting on the rail as her hair lifted in the breeze, a sapphire-blue afternoon sky framing the delicate curves of her body.

My scrutiny dropped to her legs, long and lean, and then to the four-inch heels, sexy as fucking hell. I was reminded of the way she'd made me feel the first time I'd seen her, the way she'd pulled me in like a magnet, and how that feeling had grown into an intense attraction in the weeks following.

There was something about the woman.

I quietly stepped onto the balcony and watched her for a moment.

"It's beautiful out here," she said, keeping her back to me while acknowledging my presence. Mia Frost didn't miss much.

I stepped next to her and rested my forearms on the rail. A moment passed as we viewed the autumn trees, the sunlight shimmering through translucent reds and yellows.

Mia turned, a strand of hair blowing across her alabaster face. Our eyes met, and a snap of electricity crackled between us.

"Mr. Crew," she said, and my balls literally tingled at the sound of my name rolling off her lips. "It's good to see you again."

Despite the rehearsed, strong tone, the doctor's throat worked with a deep swallow, her nerves betraying her.

When I straightened and turned fully toward her, she glanced at the gold ring around my pinkie finger.

"Are you always this formal, Dr. Frost?"

"Only when I want something from someone."

"It must be important for you to drive all the way out here without an appointment."

"I thought unannounced drop-ins were kind of your thing."

I grinned.

"And by the way, your guard dog was much more obnoxious than mine."

"I apologize for Mr. Romanov and his lack of hospitality."

This time, she grinned, and that undercurrent of flirtation, sexual tension, began to hum between us.

"Speaking of unruly characters," she said, "who was Imperator Furiosa back there?"

I frowned.

"The woman in army fatigues with the short platinum-blonde hair."

"Ah. That would be Loren, our office manager."

"She must have gotten her hospitality training from Mr. Romanov."

"I'll advise her to serve cookies next time. So," I said, leaning against the rail. "What is it that my company and I can do for you, Dr. Frost?"

"You came to my house—unannounced—two days ago, asking about my client Cullen Nichols."

"Your client?"

"Yes."

My brows arched. *The plot thickens.*

She quickly continued: "You said that Sheriff McNamara had requested your assistance in the search."

"That's right."

"Well?"

"Well what?"

"What have you found? Not him—not Cullen, correct?"

"Was Sheriff McNamara not able to provide this information to you?"

"I spoke with him this morning, and while he wasn't exactly forthcoming with information, he implied that they have no leads. When was your last search for Mr. Nichols? And where? Where exactly was your last search?"

There was a sense of urgency in her voice that suggested desperation, confirming my suspicion that she was emotionally invested in Cullen Nichols. Only because he was her client? Or was it something more?

"Don't you think you should leave this to the authorities? Especially considering the potential connection to the Black Cat Stalker?"

Mia opened her mouth to say something but quickly closed it, deciding against disclosing whatever secret she kept on the tip of her tongue.

"Is there a relationship between you and Cullen that goes beyond therapy?"

"No. When did you last search for him, and where?"

"The evening before I came to your house."

Her jaw dropped. "Are you serious? Days ago?"

"When it comes to working a missing-person case, our search-and-rescue division takes orders directly from local law enforcement. We searched on the day that they asked us to search but didn't find anything. They didn't ask again."

"So that's that?"

My head tilted to the side as I regarded her closely. "No, I don't think so, considering you're standing here right now."

Mia lifted her chin like a defiant child expecting an argument. "Well, I have a specific location I'd like you to search."

"Where?"

"Are you familiar with Yellow Rock?"

"Yes. A bluff three miles from the Black Cat Trail, three miles from where we were instructed to search for him."

"Correct. Sheriff McNamara would like you to get a team of your men there to search—track, whatever—as soon as possible."

"McNamara requested this? Am I missing a call or an email or something?"

"Apparently so."

I pulled my phone from my pocket and scanned the missed calls and emails. There was nothing from the sheriff. I hadn't missed anything. I never missed anything.

I slid my phone back into my pocket and considered her. "Listen, Dr. Frost, I don't have time for games. Why don't you just give it to me—"

"Fine. I went to the sheriff's department this morning and spoke with Deputy Mason, requesting that they search Yellow Rock."

My shoulders stiffened at the name, a flash of possessiveness surging through me at the thought of *her* being in proximity of *him*.

"Mason told me that they had their hands full with the Courtney Hayes case and reminded me that there's technically no reason to think Cullen didn't just pack up and move away."

"But you don't believe that."

"No, I don't. The deputy suggested I reach out to some local search volunteers for help, and considering you know this area better than anyone else"—she spread out her arms—"here I am."

"Did Mason tell you to reach out to me specifically?"

"No."

"To LYNX specifically?"

"No."

A moment stretched between us with me studying her and her studying me.

"And—to be clear—Cullen Nichols is only a client of yours, correct?"

"Correct."

*Liar.* The subtle shift in her hips, the brief avoidance of eye contact, gave her away. Cullen Nichols was definitely not just a client.

"Why Yellow Rock?" I asked.

"I believe it has . . . symbolic meaning to him. He goes there from time to time to photograph it. To reflect and think about the past, I think."

"What past?"

"A painful one, one that I'm not at liberty to share with you. But I think the location needs to be searched immediately."

My gaze trailed down her body, her legs, to those heels that I wanted to see discarded next to my bed. Her cheeks were flushed.

"You can't hike in those."

"In what?"

"Those shoes."

"Who hike?"

"You hike."

She blinked rapidly. "Me?"

"Not up for it?"

"B-but I thought, assumed, you would dispatch one of your teammates to—"

"Not up for it?" I repeated.

"S-sure. I mean, yes, I am."

"Good, because my team is busy this afternoon, and I don't have the time it would take to search alone."

This was bullshit, of course. Yes, I was busy, but in truth, I wanted to know more about the relationship between Mia and Cullen and if this somehow connected to the Black Cat Stalker.

I turned and began across the balcony. Over my shoulder, I asked, "Size seven?"

"Size seven what?"

"Your shoe size."

"Oh. Yes. Now? We're going now?" Heels clicked quickly on the balcony as she chased after me.

"You said it was urgent. Stay here. I'll be right back."

The tapping of her heels stopped.

I felt her gaze hot on my back as I disappeared down the hallway, jasmine on my mind and a foreboding in my gut.

# Chapter Twenty

## Mia

I insisted on taking my Jeep for two reasons.

One, to reclaim my sense of control, which this man seemed to be able to dissolve with a simple lick of his lips. And two, I'd recently had it washed and detailed by the local Boy Scouts, and a ridiculous part of me wanted Easton to see this immaculateness after seeing my house (and me) in such disarray.

But nope, Chief Macho-Man Easton Crew demanded that we take a LYNX company truck—a blacked-out dually with an ATV secured to a trailer on the back—claiming the control he consistently demanded.

Easton had given me a pair of men's hiking boots that laced all the way up my calf. They fit, and I wondered who on his team had such small feet. I politely declined the tactical pants and LYNX logo sweatshirt—kind of cute—which were both three sizes too large for my frame. No way in hell was I replacing the outfit that had taken me three hours to assemble with one that would make me look like a bag lady.

I grabbed a granola bar from the console of my Jeep and stuffed it into my purse while Easton readied the truck. I hadn't planned on hiking through the swamps that afternoon and instantly regretted skipping lunch.

By the time we loaded up, the wind had picked up, bringing with it clouds and a chill in the air that made me second-guess declining the sweatshirt. The sun hung low in the sky, soon to dip below the trees, slowly stealing the light.

Easton turned onto a narrow dirt road hidden under a thick blanket of dead leaves. Weeds lined the sides, slowly closing in on us the deeper into the woods we drove. The gossips were right—Chief Crew knew these woods like the back of his hand.

We stayed silent most of the short drive, an awkward energy between us that neither wanted to address or, rather, knew how to navigate. Easton's focus was fixed on the road ahead, and I got the feeling his mind was racing. With what? I wondered.

When we parked under a thicket of pines in a small clearing just off the road, I pushed out of the truck, my boots landing with a heavy thud on the moist dirt. I snorted, considering my appearance and the irony that the mismatch wasn't unlike the first time he'd seen me. Slick business on top, hot mess on bottom.

I couldn't win with this guy.

After smoothing my skirt, I made my way to the tailgate, where Easton was organizing a backpack that was surely half my weight.

His gaze flickered to me.

"What?" I asked.

"I kind of liked the stained basketball shorts better."

Glaring, I said, "It was a video conference. They could only see the top of me, you know."

"Shame."

I blinked, trying to read the subtext from a man who seemed to speak in code.

Easton pulled the pack from the bed of the truck, unzipped the side pocket, and retrieved a large green can. After a quick shake of it, he squatted and aggressively sprayed my bare legs with cold, sticky goo.

Letting out a shrill scream, I jumped back. "What the hell is that?"

"Bug spray. You'll need it. Trust me," he said, and I felt a weird tickle in my stomach. "Come back and turn around."

"I think I'm good—"

"Come here."

I closed the few feet between us and turned, my ass inches from his face. My cheeks heated. This time, the burst of spray against my legs felt tingly. Erotic. Avoiding his scrutiny, I stepped away.

After spraying himself down, Easton picked up his pack and zipped the side pockets closed. "Ready?"

"No pack for me?"

"I've got it."

"Thanks. Okay, so what do I do? Do you want me to just—"

"I want you to stay beside me. Watch for anything that looks out of place in nature, like bent weeds, broken twigs, footprints. Stay close to me at all times, and don't venture off on your own. Got it?"

"Got it, Chief." I saluted.

His brow quirked, and I noticed he didn't correct me. "It's about a mile hike to the bluff from here. I didn't see his SUV parked anywhere along the way."

I hadn't even thought to look. "How do you know what Cullen drives?"

"Rule number one: always know everything you can about the person you're hunting."

*Hunting.*

"How did you know what I drove?"

Easton shrugged into his pack, turning away, and my internal alarm went off.

"Easton. How did you know what I drove? You said the reason that you came to my house was because someone reported seeing a silver Jeep where Cullen went missing. How did you know that Jeep belonged to me?"

He stuffed a bottle of water into a side pocket. "I know everything about everyone who lives around my land. Let's go."

Fair enough, but there was something in the way he turned away that made me want to circle back.

*Later.*

I tightened the laces on my boots and steeled myself for the treacherous hike to come.

Easton and I set out, me in my eggshell-colored fancy skirt suit and combat boots, and him in all his rugged, manly search-and-rescue gear.

The forest was ripe with the musty scent of damp earth and fallen leaves. The air seemed colder in the woods, heavy with a wet humidity that chilled me to the bone.

We walked slowly, me obediently at his side.

Within minutes, Easton appeared to slip into some alternative personality with laser focus and heightened senses, like a dog on the hunt. Acutely aware of everything around him—around us. His steely gaze swept from side to side, cataloging every rock, tree, fallen branch.

Occasionally, we paused to examine something, a leaf or a twig, then continued. I simply followed his cues, not knowing what I was watching for—or doing, for that matter. The woods darkened as we journeyed deeper into the thicket on an invisible trail that Easton seemed to know by heart.

My mind began to drift as my gaze turned upward to the trees. A flock of blackbirds scattered as we passed, breaking the stillness of nature, the silence between us.

I caught Easton taking me in intently, as if I were the quarry we were tracking.

"No camera today?" he asked.

"Why do you ask that?"

"The pictures in your living room. The birds. You took those, yes?"

I nodded, a strange feeling of insecurity creeping up.

"They're good."

I looked away. "Thanks."

"So where is it? Your camera."

"It's in my car." I slid him the side-eye. "You know, the one I suggested we take."

"Mine is better suited for the occasion, trust me."

"You say that a lot."

"Say what?"

"'Trust me.'"

"What's with the birds?" he asked, ignoring my observation. Avoiding it, perhaps.

I shrugged. "I like them."

"I like tacos, but I don't live in an adobe."

"Oh, okay, so you're funny in the woods?"

"I'm funny often."

"On purpose?"

One corner of his lips lifted, and I grinned.

"The birds, Doctor," he urged, and it was then that I realized he was studying me as much as I was studying him.

I stayed silent for a few steps, wondering how I should tackle the question. The woods seemed to still around us, waiting with bated breath for my response.

Would I be honest? Or would I fool him as I had so many others?

Making a decision, I began the spiel I'd spent years perfecting.

"I studied bird therapy in college. Birds are scientifically proven to be soothing creatures, a type of natural therapy, and it works. At my suggestion, several of my clients have erected birdhouses or feeders outside their windows. It's something—aside from drugs and alcohol— they can do or focus on in times of stress. Within minutes of watching the birds, the patients are calmer. I've watched it happen in my office. I have yet to meet a single client who has taken my suggestion and regretted it."

"Okay . . . so *you* having an aviary in *your* living room means one of two things. Either you go above and beyond for your clients, personally testing every therapeutic method on yourself first. Or that you—*yourself*—are in dire need of being soothed."

"I take my job very seriously. I don't test anything on my clients unless I've tried it myself," I said in this delicate dance of distraction. "You've heard of equine therapy?"

"Horse therapy?"

"Yes, it's common with autistic children and adults with PTSD. It's completely revolutionized how therapists do their jobs. Taking it off the couch, if you will."

"Nothing wrong with a little couch time."

"Your motto?"

"Not lately."

My brows arched, and he winked.

"Anyway, watching birds gives us a moment of pause, reminding us to breathe, to refocus. Like equine therapy, it's proven to lower blood pressure and heart rate. But it goes deeper than that—*shhh*." I gently grabbed his arm, lifted my finger to my lips, and pulled him to a halt. "Stop. Listen."

We paused, listening to the nature around us.

"Do you hear that? The birds singing in the trees—they're happy and calm. You can feel it, hear it. This sound alone has a calming effect like nothing else."

"It tells you you're safe," he said, peering at me.

"Yes." Something in my heart fluttered, and I stepped back.

"I use that in my training," he said, "the absence of nature as a sign. Birds, if you will. I teach my students that their lack of presence or noise indicates something very important in tracking—that something is close by that they deem unsafe. Whether it be a predator, a thunderstorm coming, a tornado, a person, whatever, when birds are quiet it means something."

"That's right. And when they sing, we know we're safe." I smiled. "See? There you go. Birds for the win. Plus, they're really pretty."

We started again through the woods.

"Not many people would call the brown-headed nuthatch pretty," Easton said.

"You know your native birds."

"I know the woods, nuthouses included."

"It's nut*hatch*. And beauty goes far deeper than outward appearance, Mr. Crew."

"Spoken like a psychologist."

"No, spoken like someone who is trained to dissect every minute detail of someone's outward appearance as a path of reaching the inside."

"And what does my outside appearance say about me, Dr. Frost? Because I can see that's where this is going."

"Have you done any therapy before?"

"No." He looked away, and I cataloged this behavior as a hint of something deeper. "I don't need to pay a total stranger two hundred dollars an hour to dissect my deepest, darkest secrets."

"Two hundred an hour? Excuse me while I adjust my rate sheet." I searched for a smile, but there was none.

"Back to the assessment of my outward appearance, Dr. Frost," Easton said, suddenly very interested in what I thought of him. Or sensitive to it, maybe?

"Well, from the little I know of you, I'd say you're all an act."

His brows popped. Amused? Pissed?

No, exposed.

"That's right," I said, smirking at his reaction. "It's all a show. This carefully constructed charade that you've got it all together, that there's nothing you can't handle, that you're, dare I say, infallible."

"Infallible."

"Right. You ensure that everything seems perfect from the outside, while inside it's a disorganized mess. You ensure that you portray an overly confident, meticulous, always-in-control man. But I call bullshit."

"Bullshit, huh?"

"Yep. My assessment of you, Mr. Crew, is that you're two seconds from phoning it in."

"I'm now officially two seconds from phoning this conversation in."

"Hey. You asked."

I'd hit a nerve. My assessment might not have been spot on, but there was truth to it. I could see it in his eyes, the way his shoulders tensed when I'd suggested he was about to give up. Easton's past as a decorated soldier suggested the man was no quitter, but I knew far too well how time—and things—changed a person.

I thought of his fiancée's car accident, her death, the ring he wore on his pinkie finger, and wondered how badly her passing had affected him. Easton Crew was searching for something but didn't know where to look.

At that point, I decided it was best to bite my tongue.

We walked deeper into the thicket, losing light with each passing minute. Things unsaid lingered between us, I could tell, with him as much as with me. I studied him, building my psychological profile of the man behind the armor.

My mind raced as we passed the swamps, skeletal cypress trees sprouting from the still, stagnant water suffocated by a thick layer of green duckweed. Then we made our way to higher elevation, evident by the deep burn of my thighs.

The terrain became more difficult to travel through, the brush so thick I had to physically push through it. My legs were cut to shreds, an itchy-hot pain. The ground became rocky, threatening to twist an ankle if I wasn't laser focused on each step.

Ahead, craggy boulders crowded long thin pine trunks. We were getting close to Yellow Rock, the bluff that marked a deep ravine that was speckled with sharp, pointy rocks covered in moss when it wasn't flooded.

Finally.

"Go on," he said.

"What?"

"Go on."

"You mean, continue with the assessment I started thirty minutes ago?"

"Yeah."

"Didn't seem like you were too interested then."

"I'm not. But I can tell you're about to internally combust with this unsaid psychoanalysis."

"Hey, if you can't take it—"

"I'll manage. So I'm about to phone it in, have a midlife crisis . . ."

"I didn't say *midlife crisis*."

He shot me a look.

I feigned innocence. "No, I would never suggest you're going through a period of psychological distress brought on by some significant midlife events."

"Of course you wouldn't. Because it would be extremely irresponsible of you to make this kind of assessment of someone you've only recently met."

"Right."

"But?"

"But there are certain insights you learn almost immediately when meeting someone."

"Such as the person is about to, quote, 'phone it in.'" He reached into his pack and pulled out a navy-blue LYNX windbreaker. "Here. Put this on. You're shivering."

"Thanks." I slipped into the coat, which swallowed my frame, leaving only a thin line of my beige skirt visible just below my knee. I didn't care because, truth was, I was cold.

I zipped it up, inhaling the collar. It smelled like him. Butterflies set flight in my belly, and I caught him checking me out.

"These boots are really comfortable, actually."

"Good." He dipped his chin, tearing his gaze away.

"Anyway, you don't realize how much you can read from a person at first meeting. For example, while every one of your coworkers at the LYNX Group wears a suit to the office, you, the CEO, choose to wear faded T-shirts with pit stains—"

"My T-shirts do *not* have pit stains."

"Left pit, the Hanes you wore to my house Monday morning. Pit stains."

"Pit *stain*, as in one."

"Semantics."

"Better than two."

"Is it? Anyway, while everyone you work with takes pride in their appearance, you wear left-pit-stained shirts, dirty tactical pants, and ATAC boots."

"Incorrect. Alek answered the door looking like the Unabomber. Do you not remember this?"

"Yeah, I do, but it was because he'd been in the woods with your gal Mad Max. In every picture I could pull of this Alek guy, in relation to the LYNX Group, he's wearing a suit, just like the other men."

Easton seemed to think on this a minute. "My ATAC boots are new."

"Exactly. Brand new means that you take pride in those boots and that you're quick to replace them as each pair wears out. That furthers my presumption that nasty workmen's clothes is all you wear—meaning that you don't care."

"Why were you researching my company?"

"I'm not in the habit of making unannounced drop-ins on people, or companies, that I don't know." I swooped down and plucked a small blue feather from a rotting fallen tree branch. "Ah, look." I held the feather up to the light, examining the vivid blue colors. "A bluebird feather. Beautiful little songbird. Don't see them much. Anyway . . ."

"There are a lot of men who don't wear suits, you know."

"Why don't *you* wear a suit? That's what I want to know."

"Because they're only slightly less uncomfortable than this conversation."

I jabbed a finger in the air. "But you *used* to wear them."

He frowned.

"Yep. And this is where the assessment began. In every image I could pull up of you before a few years ago, if not in army fatigues, you were dressed to the nines, shaking hands with heads of state, foreign leaders, supermodels, the whole nine yards. One article even suggested you were going to run for president one day. Now, though, the most expensive thing in your closet is a Hanes tagless six-pack purchased from the local Walmart."

His focus remained ahead, but I saw the twitch in his jaw, the tension in his brow.

"I'm right, yes?"

Easton shrugged. "Life has a way of throwing you curveballs."

"Yeah, I know all about that. Trust me."

He glanced at me, and it was my turn to look away.

I cleared my throat, pivoting back to the subject—him. "I'm just saying, when I compare what I see in you to what I've seen in hundreds of patients I've treated, you've got *midlife crisis* written all over you. A secret internal crumbling, if you will."

"A secret crumbling. Sounds ominous. You get all this from your study materials from UT?"

My stomach dropped. Easton had researched *me* just as I'd researched him.

His words from earlier filtered back into my head: *Rule number one: always know everything you can about the person you're hunting.*

He'd researched my past.

I felt myself stiffen, and suddenly, I wanted this little adventure to be over.

"You grew up in Dallas," he said, reading me. "Then moved to Austin, where you attended college, graduated at the top of your class. Shortly after, you opened a mental health facility in the middle of nowhere and quickly grew it into a successful regional clinic. You're a single woman, rumored to be a hermit, have no kids, never been married, and have built your life around finding alternative therapies for PTSD."

My pulse was kick-started. Before I could catch myself, I asked, "Is this all you uncovered about my past?"

"Stop." Easton's hand darted out, grabbing my elbow.

I froze and followed his gaze to the outline of a footprint in the mud.

# Chapter Twenty-One
## Mia

Easton crouched down, studying the dirt. "See, here?"

With his finger, he outlined the almost invisible print but didn't touch it.

"This is the corner of the heel, a boot, and you can see the tip of the toe here. And a bit of the tread here, but not quite enough to gauge the type of boot . . ." His voice trailed off before he continued, as if talking to himself now, working out the details in his head. "But I'd say the shoe size is about a nine."

"A woman?"

"Maybe."

"Cullen is kind of a short guy. Do you think it could be his? I think that's close to the shoe size he would wear."

"Yes, it's his shoe size."

"How do you know?"

"Assumption, based on the height from his most recent driver's license photo that I had McNamara send me before we left." Easton stood. "Stay there. Don't move."

After marking the print with a small yellow flag, he then carefully stepped away and began scanning the forest floor from left to right. He paused, taking note of something else.

"What is it? What do you see?"

Carefully, he stepped through the brush and knelt down, becoming almost invisible in the tall grass. "Someone was here too."

"Someone else?"

"Not sure. Do you know if Cullen dips?"

"Dips what?"

"Tobacco."

"No."

"No, you don't know, or no, he doesn't?"

"No, he doesn't. I'm sure of it. We discuss things like that, physical addictions, extensively in my sessions. He drinks; that's it. Can I come over?"

"No, stay there. Hang on."

Easton stood, pulled a small plastic bag out of his backpack, then knelt again. After a minute, he stood and made his way back to me.

"Did you just bag up the tobacco?"

"Come on."

"Why?"

"Why what?" Easton breezed past me.

"Why did you take the dip?"

"This way." He reached back, his palm open, and my hand slid into his. It felt more intimate than it should have, considering we were tracking a missing person. Carefully, he guided me around the track. "Stay right behind me, close."

"What's the significance of the dip? It's so annoying when you don't answer my questions."

"It's significant because it indicates someone was with or close to Cullen Nichols before he was reported missing. Assuming the footprint is his."

"What are you going to do with it?"

"Not sure yet. For now, focus on these tracks."

He held on to my hand, leading me through the brush, following a trail that I couldn't see. The trees closed in around us, blocking the waning light. I didn't care, though. I was preoccupied by the feel of my hand in his and why he wasn't dropping it . . . and how much I didn't want him to.

"So is this how you track?" I asked quietly at his back, not wanting to break his intense concentration.

"Technically, yes. The easy way. Finding a print is like hitting gold for a tracker." He paused, then knelt in front of another print that I didn't see. "Yes—the tracks belong to a man."

I swatted at a bug zipping around my face, then bent forward, putting my hands on my knees as I studied the overturned earth. "How do you know for sure?"

"Women and men have very different tracks. Women's gaits are closer together and their feet more pigeon toed. Men, on the other hand, have wider strides and walk in a more straightforward manner. Their toes point straight ahead."

"And these tracks indicate the latter?"

"Exactly. This person was on the move, walking with intent, not simply meandering through the forest. He had a purpose and, based on the path, was likely familiar with the terrain." He pointed to another divot in the mud. "See? The prints are deep and long, which means they're moving quickly."

"Couldn't that just mean he's tall?"

"No."

"Why?"

"Because the size and length of the print isn't typical for someone who's very tall."

We walked a few more steps, and the track became more visible to me.

"Only one person . . ." Easton's pace quickened as he followed the tracks. "And no drag marks."

He was like an animal on the hunt, his body seemingly spurred to life with an energy and adrenaline I could feel radiating off him. I felt like I was watching something magical happen—a person transforming into their most primal self, an animal, doing exactly what they loved the most, something that was as basic to them as inhaling breath.

"If these prints belong to Cullen, he's not lost," I said. "He knows this part of the woods. So if not his, do you think they could belong to the Black Cat Stalker?"

"This location would be out of the Black Cat's normal hunting grounds. All of his victims were on the trail. What did Mason say when you suggested he search it?"

"Not much. Just what I told you—that I should team up with some local searchers to check it out."

"Mia." He glanced over his shoulder, disappointed in me about something.

"What?"

"Do you think it's odd that Deputy Mason suggested that you, a woman with no emergency training whatsoever, go hunt for a missing man in the same woods where a savage rapist is rumored to be hiding?"

"Now *that's* quite the assumption, Mr. Crew."

He kept walking.

"Do you think Mason was, what? Setting me up for something?"

Under normal circumstances, being set up by law enforcement was an idea I would never entertain. But considering how Mason had treated me while I'd been interviewing Courtney Hayes, this kind of devious behavior wasn't a stretch to imagine. But why? To what end? And why was this Easton's concern?

When he didn't respond, I pressed. "Do you not trust him?"

"Absolutely not."

"Why?"

"I want you to stay away from him."

"Why?"

Easton planted his feet and spun around. "Because I told you to."

I blinked, then took a step back.

He turned and resumed his tracking. Although I wanted to know the story between the two men, it was obvious that Easton would rather swallow glass than talk about the guy.

We walked in silence until he asked, "Do you think it's connected? Courtney Hayes's attack and Cullen's disappearance?"

"I don't know. It doesn't fit the Black Cat Stalker's MO. He likes young, athletic, female brunettes. Cullen Nichols doesn't check a single one of those boxes. Even so, I can't ignore the timing of it all—it seems to be a hell of a coincidence. Two people missing within days of each other, one raped by the Black Cat, the other still missing."

"And you don't believe in coincidences?"

"No, I don't."

"Me either."

We walked a few more minutes in silence.

"It's been a while since these tracks were left." Easton gestured upward to the birds swooping from tree to tree, the squirrels skittering. The rustle of a darting deer sounded somewhere in the distance. Their presence indicated the lack of a threat. "I think these tracks were made two, maybe three days ago. Likely at night, based on the raccoon tracks dried in the print."

"So this person was potentially hiking at night, in the dark."

"Yes."

"And there are only two reasons someone would hike through these woods, alone, in the middle of the night," I said. "They were either running away from something—"

Easton caught my eye. "Or hiding something."

We surveyed the bluff just beyond the trees.

"That's Yellow Rock, there," I said.

"Let's go take a look then."

# Chapter Twenty-Two

## Mia

A trio of birds scattered as we stepped onto the Yellow Rock bluff.

Slowly, Easton cataloged every detail around us like a bloodhound on the hunt. Nerves tickled my stomach as I followed him, moving from one clue to the next, then eventually to the edge of the bluff.

My heart started to pound, as if my body knew what was coming next before my head did.

Easton grabbed my hand again, and together, we peered over the edge.

I don't remember the scream, only the carousel of memories flashing in my mind.

# Chapter Twenty-Three

## Mia

Without thinking, I lunged forward, my immediate instinct to help my client overwhelming.

Cullen lay sprawled out over the rocks, his arms and legs contorted, red rivulets snaking from his body like tentacles.

My attempt to descend the bluff was thwarted by two arms wrapping around me like a vise. I was lifted from my feet and pulled backward, a strong, commanding voice speaking quickly in my ear, but I couldn't make out the words.

I was absolutely freaking out. Crazy, uncontrollable. In the throes of a mounting panic attack. I fought wildly as Easton dragged me away from the edge of the cliff.

"*Mia*. Mia, *stop*. Focus. *Stop*."

*Stop.*

*Stop.*

*Stop.*

As the words began to register, my panic slowly waned.

I was spun around. Two hands gripped my face.

"*Focus, focus, focus,*" he said, and the repetitive phrase began to penetrate the hysteria.

I blinked, my eyes locked on his.

"He's—he's down there, Easton. He might be alive." My voice came out in a breathy whisper, barely able to form the words.

"Yes. And I need you to calm down so that I can help him."

I nodded, mentally latching onto Easton's calm, controlled demeanor.

"We don't get reception out here, and I didn't pack my sat phone in the bag. I need you to go back the way we came."

Blinking madly, I tried to understand what he was saying to me. "Go back where?"

"To the truck. We had reception there. If for some reason you don't, I need you to call from the sat phone in the glove box. I need you to call for help."

"But I don't know the—"

"Yes, you do. I marked the path with small red flags on the trees."

"You did?"

"Yes. Look for them at your eye level, not mine. You'll see them. Follow the trail."

My mind raced. I hadn't even noticed Easton marking our path. Why had he done that? Had he known that I was going to be returning to the vehicle alone?

Why did something feel wrong in my gut?

He thrust a key fob in my hand. "When you get back to the truck, call nine-one-one. Don't hesitate. We've got about ninety minutes of light left. You're going to need to hustle." He began tightening the straps on his pack.

"What are you going to do?"

"I'm climbing down."

I peered at the edge of the steep drop-off.

His hands cupped my cheeks, pulling my attention back to him. "Focus, Mia. We need to see if he's alive, and this is the quickest way to do that. Now, go get us some help."

I nodded.

Easton pulled the gun from his belt and cocked it, the harsh, jarring sound echoing through the woods as if punctuating the stress of the moment. He handed it to me. "Do you know how to use it?"

I tried to remember the last time I'd shot a gun. Years earlier, during a self-defense team-building class. "I . . . I think so."

"There's no safety. All you have to do is point and shoot. There are nine rounds—nine shots. If anyone comes up to you that you don't recognize, tell them you're going to shoot if they advance. Listen to that gut instinct inside you. If you believe you're in danger, shoot, Mia. Do you understand?"

I stared at him like a deer caught in the headlights.

"Mia." A spark of concern like panic lit his eyes. "If you believe you're in danger, shoot. Don't hesitate."

"What if—"

"No. You're strong, Mia. You can do this."

Easton's hands cupped my face again. The look on his face was no longer panic but desperation. Like a boy not wanting to let go.

Butterflies swirled with the nerves in my stomach.

"*Fuck*—Mia," he snapped as if losing a battle in his head. Then he crushed his lips to mine.

One hand dropped to my chin, holding me in place as he devoured me in a way that obliterated the air in my lungs, the strength in my knees. His other hand slid to the back of my head, threading through my hair, gripping, tilting my face where he saw fit.

Locked in his grasp, I was his. Submissive and willing, lost in the most beautiful way.

In that moment, I was nothing. I was everything.

His kiss was like him, commanding, dominant, charged with such intensity it rendered me absolutely powerless. I was being *taken*, willing, unwilling, there was no question. In that moment, all my worries, my pain, my sadness, my anxiety, lifted from me like a suit of armor being shattered into a million little pieces. I didn't worry about control, because he had it. I didn't worry about my safety, because he had it. I didn't worry about anything—because he *had it.*

It was the first time in my life that I felt small, fragile, like I didn't have to take on the entire world—because Easton *had it.*

When he pulled away, I stumbled, my knees giving out. We stared at each other, his chest heaving, his eyes ablaze with heat.

Stunned, I was speechless, as if my mind had somehow recalibrated in that minute following the kiss. Every fiber of my being changed in an instant, now that I'd experienced something so momentous that nothing would ever be the same again.

"Go," he said, breathless.

I inhaled, then nodded.

"Go."

He turned, knelt down, and lowered himself over the edge.

My heartbeat skittered, my worry no longer for Cullen Nichols but for the man risking his life on the side of the bluff. The man who I knew, without question, had just taken a piece of my heart.

My pulse roared in my ears.

"Go," he said, pausing before moving lower. "The red ribbons are eye level. Once you get back to the truck, call the police, get into the vehicle, and lock the doors. Stay there until I get back. Do you understand?"

"Yes. Yes, I understand."

"Good. Go. Quickly."

# Chapter Twenty-Four

## Mia

As it turned out, I obeyed only one of Easton's commands.

I followed the red ribbons—exactly as Easton had said—although I didn't make it to the truck. The moment my cell phone connected with reception, I called 911 to convey our location and that we'd found the missing man, Cullen Nichols.

Once I'd confirmed that someone was on their way, I ended the call and retraced my steps back to the bluff. I wasn't dressed to descend the bluff as Easton had, nor did I have the skill set, so I pivoted, jogging parallel to the bluff until the steep slope flattened enough that I could safely climb down.

There was no dusk that evening, no sunlight to guide the way, only a dull gray light dimming with each passing minute. The clouds had thickened, the winds increased. My hair whipped around my face as I hastily and recklessly descended the slope, using the vines and prickly bushes growing from the crevices of the rock to assist my descent.

The moment my boots hit the rocky ground, I sprinted across the narrow bottom of the ravine, focused on Easton's silhouette leaning over Cullen's body, hardly visible in the waning light.

My heart pounded as I drew closer.

Easton looked over his shoulder at me, his face twisting with emotion. Relief, I guessed, mixed with anger that I hadn't obeyed his order to stay in the truck.

"I'm sorry, I—" My babbling cut short as I hurried closer, not at all prepared for what I'd run up to.

Cullen's face was grotesquely bloated, swollen, and covered in bites, bruises, and angry, crusty wounds. One eye was completely swollen shut, his lip split down the middle. The T-shirt and jeans he was wearing were torn, covered in debris and dried blood. His exposed skin was colored with oozing red rashes from the insects that had been swarming over him, in what I could only imagine was hours of lying helpless by himself.

But he was alive—barely conscious and in no position to talk, but alive.

"He's been beaten badly," Easton said, almost as if to himself.

"*Beaten?*" I shrieked.

Easton knelt on the rocks, cradling Cullen's head in his lap, helping him breathe. With his other hand, he dabbed at the man's wounds with some sort of antiseptic he'd retrieved from his pack.

"He didn't fall?" I fell to my knees next to them, a strong sour scent of urine rising in the air. Cullen had soiled himself, several times by the smell and look of it.

"No, I don't think so. His injuries aren't congruent with a fall, even from the bluff. Someone kicked this man's ass."

"Are you sure?"

"From someone who's been in more fistfights than I can count, yeah, I'm sure."

This made more sense to me than Cullen falling from the bluff, considering he'd been there many times before, but it also alluded to something much more nefarious.

Was it the Black Cat? Could the same man who'd attacked Courtney Hayes also have attacked Cullen?

"What's the ambulance ETA?" Easton asked.

"They're on their way," I said, my thoughts racing. "I wonder how long he's been here?"

"Well, he's been missing for almost four days now, right?" Easton lifted the backpack that lay beside him, one strap popped. "Assuming this is his pack, seems like he packed for a few nights of camping. But nothing he packed is eaten, and the tent hasn't been removed. My guess is that he was attacked the first night he set out."

"Are you saying he's been lying here for more than *three* days?"

"Appears that way."

"Someone left him out here to *die*, Easton."

Anger ignited in my veins. I inspected the bluff above, the dark woods looming behind it.

Cullen Nichols had been attacked in the woods and left to die. Just like Courtney Hayes.

Just like me.

# Chapter Twenty-Five

## Mia

The cops and medics approached with the subtlety of a marching band through the woods, destroying the stillness of nature, bringing chaos, confusion, and a dizzying strobe of flashlights.

I stood to the side, watching the medics tend to Cullen's wounds as he slowly regained consciousness, only to be pelted with questions while everyone tried to understand what had happened. He didn't say much, other than a fervent refusal to go to the hospital for a thorough examination.

This didn't surprise me. The emergency room held very bad memories for Cullen. Hell on earth wasn't going to make him go there.

Obviously familiar with the first responders—friendly, even— Easton offered his assistance, working seamlessly alongside the men and women crowding the scene. Every few seconds, he glanced back at me, then returned his focus to whoever he was speaking to.

I eavesdropped where I could, gathering small pieces of the story here and there. It went something like this: Cullen had planned an overnight hiking trip to photograph the change of the seasons. Sometime in the middle of his hike, he'd been attacked from behind. Cullen had engaged his attacker, who'd been wearing, quote, "black clothes, a black hat, and a black bandanna."

The Black Cat Stalker.

Except this time, according to Cullen, the Black Cat had worn the bandanna around his neck during the attack. His face had been exposed.

Cullen didn't recall much else, no details or visual descriptive clues that could help build a physical picture of the perp. A side effect from the blows to the head, per the medic, but I had another hypothesis. One that these small-town blunt instruments wouldn't understand.

I watched Cullen closely, questioning if he was even aware that I was there. He was unsteady, groggy as he came to, but there was something about his confusion that seemed off, more than just getting his ass kicked. I wondered if he'd been drunk or high on drugs or pills. I made a mental note to call the pharmacist, Dr. Ashby, to check if Cullen had filled any prescriptions other than the antidepressant Jo had prescribed him when he'd begun coming to the Dragonfly Clinic. The doctor owed me a favor after I'd talked his wife off a ledge during a particularly aggressive booze-filled mental breakdown the Christmas before.

Night had fallen, engulfing the woods in a pitch blackness so thick it was as if you could reach out and touch it. The site was poorly illuminated with flashlights and cell phones, casting long black shadows across an already creepy scene.

The autumn wind blew relentlessly, hollowing through the narrow valley, whipping leaves and debris into the air. Destroying evidence, Easton had pointed out.

My legs had gone numb, my fingers stiff, from the cold.

After Cullen was stabilized, a new obstacle presented itself—getting this two-hundred-plus-pound man back up the ravine and through the woods. This was when Easton stepped in, easily taking control of the entire situation before anyone realized it.

He was a master at this, I realized. A sneak attack you never saw coming. Cool, calm, collected, luring you into safety while slowly reversing the roles to where he became the authority before you even realized what had happened.

He demanded constant control and was gifted it, every time.

There was no question Easton Crew had been built for moments like this. I watched the few women who were there scrutinize the former soldier / current hero with keen interest and little hearts in their eyes.

And yet, he'd kissed me.

*Me.*

What did it mean? Anything at all?

The night had turned into one confusing out-of-body experience.

Cullen was secured to something called a Stokes basket, a portable stretcher-like basket used to carry victims through rough terrain.

One by one, Easton guided the team up a steep path on the far side of the bluff. I watched him closely, his seemingly innate ability to make everyone fall in line when he spoke. The way his attention split between the team and scanning the terrain, looking for tracks or evidence, clues that would help find the Black Cat Stalker. A sick psychopath who appeared to be scaling up his attacks at an alarming rate.

It didn't make sense.

Cullen Nichols didn't fit the Black Cat's target victim—the one I'd mapped out so eloquently to Deputy Mason—and now the location didn't fit either. The Black Cat Stalker had only stalked and assaulted women on the Black Cat Trail, hence the name.

Why deviate from the script? Why Cullen? A male? Why Yellow Rock, miles away from the Black Cat Trail? Why *now*?

I began to question everything, and I wasn't the only one.

It was obvious Easton doubted Cullen's story, evidenced by his cold, dispassionate attitude toward the victim. I'd noticed it immediately, the skepticism as he watched Cullen speak and move. The rough, hostile touch as he'd strapped him to the basket.

There was something about Cullen that Easton didn't like. Because he was a male in therapy, maybe? Did that make him less of a man in Easton's estimation? The thought bothered me. Did Easton think less of Cullen because he'd voluntarily sought therapy?

I didn't like it. The judgment. The . . . something I couldn't put my finger on.

But Cullen wasn't the only man Easton didn't care for that night. His dislike—disdain, more like—for Deputy Mason was more apparent than ever from the moment the man had shown up at the scene an hour late.

Easton's demeanor had changed in an instant, a sudden urgency to move this dog-and-pony show along. The men avoided each other like the plague. Others noticed it, too, I saw. Men glanced at each other as Mason approached.

I was losing count of all the things I was making mental notes to follow up on.

In summary, it was a fucked-up night. Nothing about it felt right.

With Easton leading the way, we navigated through the woods, flashlights bouncing along the uneven terrain, the darting flashes of light against darkness making me sick to my stomach. We walked in single file, quiet, unnerved, as we slowly made our way back to the clearing, now filled with trucks and emergency-response vehicles.

Cullen again refused to be taken to the hospital and, in an aggressive show of defiance, wrestled his way out of the stretcher and wobbled to his feet, gripping a truck for support. There was nothing they could do. The man refused help, along with a ride to his car, which he'd said was parked on the east side of the trail. An uncommon place for locals to park, I noted. Another thing that felt odd, in addition to his dazed state that seemed to be more than just physical pain and fatigue.

There was confusion, awkward pauses, the team not knowing how to handle the unusually disgruntled man.

"I'll take him home," I said, stepping forward seconds before the situation reached the boiling point. "He's a patient of mine at the clinic. He's comfortable with me."

Easton suddenly came out of nowhere, his gaze on Cullen, who was now staring at me.

Deputy Mason closed the few feet between us, and the crowd hushed. "I think it's best if I—"

"I'll take him," I said again. "He can—"

"I'm not going to the damn hospital," Cullen snapped in a weak, gritty voice.

"I know," I said. "I'm just going to—"

Easton interrupted, stepping in front of me. "I'll take care of it."

Mason took a step back. "Fine. Just make sure he comes to the sheriff's department for an interview first thing tomorrow morning. This man came face-to-face with the person who raped Courtney Hayes. I need to talk to him the second he's willing."

Easton and Mason glowered at each other, sending the hair prickling on the back of my neck. Finally, the deputy turned and motioned to everyone to get a move on.

I quickly stepped to Cullen and gently wrapped my hand around his biceps. "Come on, let's get you out of here."

Cullen blinked, his red-rimmed, glassy eyes taking a second to adjust on me.

Engines roared to life around us, puffs of exhaust pluming into the night sky.

Easton opened the back door of his truck. Together, we helped Cullen inside.

When Easton slammed the door, I startled, a rush of annoyance and anger zipping through my veins.

"I don't know what your plan is, but we're not taking him back to his car, and we're not taking him home," I snapped at Easton's back as he rounded the back of the truck.

"Get in."

"Did you hear me?"

"Get in."

"Easton, I'm not going to leave him alone," I hissed, stomping after him.

He turned, his icy glare slicing mine in half. "Are you seriously this close to all your clients?"

The ambulance maneuvered around us, the driver nodding as he passed.

I leaned in so that no one could hear. "Listen, someone attacked Cullen and left him for dead."

Anger brewed in my belly like the beginning of a hurricane, slowly twisting, turning, dredging up the past. "But he didn't die. Am I the only one who worries that the Black Cat might come back to finish the job? Especially considering Cullen could possibly identify him?" My words trembled as I spat them out, heat rising up my neck. "Dammit, Easton, he was left for *dead*."

"So what's your plan?"

"I don't have one. I just know that I'm not taking Cullen to his house, where he'll be alone. Cullen already struggles with PTSD—this could send him over the edge. He's scared, emotionally unstable, and possibly still in danger. I don't care what the sheriff's office thinks—or doesn't, for that matter." I shook my head, creating a plan as I spoke. "I'll take him to my house, let him rest, take care of him, and . . . we'll just tackle this thing in the morning."

Easton turned and yanked open the passenger door. "Get in."

Growling, literally, I took his hand and climbed into the truck.

The door slammed. Easton stalked around the hood, clearly fuming.

Since when had we crossed the line into bickering like a married couple?

The kiss.

*Damn the kiss.*

I glanced back at Cullen, whose head lolled against the headrest, his eyes closed. His breathing was heavy from the exertion of the rescue.

Easton started the engine, shoved the truck into drive, and hit the gas, jostling Cullen in the back seat. After checking Cullen's car to ensure that it was still locked and hadn't been vandalized by whoever had attacked him, we made our way out of the woods. The cab remained silent as we drove down the lonely, dark roads.

Cullen had fallen asleep quickly in the back seat, and I realized how tired I was. My body suddenly feeling like a wet blanket, I mentally laid out my plan for the next day.

I'd let Cullen sleep in my bed, and when he was ready in the morning, we'd go to the sheriff's department to meet Deputy Mason for an interview and get that out of the way. Then I'd take him to his car.

Easton, however, apparently had very different plans. I opened my eyes just as we were turning onto the long paved driveway that led to the LYNX Group headquarters. I glanced at the clock—11:28 p.m.

"What are you doing?" I whispered.

"Mia," he said, *not* whispering, "you're crazy if you think I'm going to leave you alone to care for a man who was supposedly just beaten almost to death in the middle of the woods. We don't even have any details of what happened. You aren't—"

"You don't believe him?"

"I'm just saying there's a *lot* to unravel here. And if Cullen's attack is linked to the Black Cat Stalker, then I don't want you alone with him—or with anyone who has anything to do with the stalker."

"Easton, I'm fine. I know how to handle myself. I've lived alone for years now."

He shook his head, his jaw clenching. "You know, for someone who creates psychological profiles for a living, you sure are missing a huge detail in this case."

"Like what?" I snapped like a defensive child.

"Don't you see it?"

"See what?"

"Christ, Mia. *You* look exactly like the other girls—*you* fit the Black Cat's victim profiles to a T. Brown hair, dark eyes, same height, same weight. You're an avid jogger and nature lover, just like the others."

"And so are a thousand other women in Texas."

He shook his head, clearly frustrated.

"Listen," I snapped. "Of course I've noticed the similarities, but what the hell am I supposed to do with that information? Run away and—"

"You're supposed to be more careful!" he snapped back.

I released a guttural groan, matching his frustration, then took a deep breath.

"Cullen doesn't fit the profile, though. Cullen isn't a female with brown hair, dark eyes," I pointed out. "The Black Cat is deviating off course."

"Exactly. Something's off. Cullen Nichols is staying here, under my care. And you are too. End of discussion."

"Listen. This macho-male thing might work for most women, but I'm not most women. I'm *not* sleeping in your damn office." I gestured toward the glass-and-steel building glittering in the headlights. "And neither is Cullen. This is absolutely ridiculous. I know Cullen personally, on a very deep level, and in any scenario, it wouldn't be odd that I would allow him to sleep on my couch, or vice versa, if this happened to me. He's a client, yes, but I also consider him a friend. He has no one, Easton. And bottom line, friends help friends."

"You're forgetting something in this scenario."

"What?"

"Me."

Easton drove the truck around the building to the garage. The moment our headlights shone through the window, a man I recognized from the website, Beckett Stolle, strode out of a side door. He was alert, his shoulders back, dressed in tactical pants, boots, and a T-shirt as if it were two in the afternoon. He swept a concerned glance over the truck, lingering on the woman in the passenger seat—me.

Another light clicked on in the building, and then another large silhouette passed swiftly by a window. Apparently, Easton had given his team a heads-up.

"Do your employees live here?"

"Sometimes. We have sleeping quarters here." Easton rolled to a stop next to the door. "They have their own homes, but we work a lot."

The back door opened, unceremoniously awakening Cullen.

I twisted in my seat. "We're just making a quick stop. It's okay."

Cullen frowned, blinking rapidly.

"It's okay. Don't worry."

Beckett helped Cullen out of the back seat as Easton and I climbed out.

"I've got everything set up in medics," Beckett said, wrapping Cullen's arm around his neck.

Easton slipped under Cullen's other arm, but not before discreetly passing a small plastic bag to Beckett. I recognized it as the tobacco we'd found in the woods.

"What's medics?" I asked, having to jog to keep up with their long strides, despite the fact they were carrying the extra weight of a man.

"A clinic, kind of." Easton opened the door, ushering me inside.

I followed the men down a dark hallway barely lit with LED running lights along the baseboards.

Why the hell did a tracking company need a medical clinic installed in their headquarters?

Alek Romanov, wearing a midnight-blue suit, stepped out of the shadows. The gun on his hip glinted in the light. After a quick whispered exchange between him and Easton, Alek slipped away as silently as he'd approached.

I was led into a blinding-white room. In the center was a stainless steel operating table under a large silver light. The walls were lined with cabinets and the countertops laden with jars filled with various scalpels, Q-tips, and scissors. The room resembled a surgical suite more than a patient room in a medical clinic.

Easton guided Cullen onto the table as Beckett snapped on a pair of gloves.

"What . . . is all this?" I asked, helping Easton settle Cullen.

"Beckett was a combat medic in the Marines."

Easton grabbed my hand and lightly pulled me back as Beckett stepped up, masked and gloved, to slip a needle into Cullen's arm so smoothly I almost missed it. Apparently, Cullen did. His eyes fluttered before closing.

"What did he just give him?"

"Something to relax. Don't worry. There isn't a single medical procedure that this man can't handle."

"But the EMTs said Cullen was okay—banged up, but okay."

"We'll see."

I watched the former Marine slip into laser focus as he checked Cullen over, gently wiping and cleaning wounds that had already been tended to.

"This is a pretty deep gash that they butterfly closed," Beckett said.

"Think it needs more?" Easton asked.

"The laceration is uneven, jagged at the end. Yeah, it needs stitches."

Without another word, Beckett removed the bandage, cleaned the wound, then began stitching it.

The room was so silent you could hear a pin drop.

I watched Beckett as he worked, studying the tattoos that ran up his arms, one holding my attention more than the rest. It was a harrowing depiction of what I assumed was the Grim Reaper, its skeletal face contorted in a creepy grin. In his bony fingers he clutched a scythe, and in contradiction to the terrifying image of the hooded skeleton, vines of bright-red flowers intertwined on the staff, winding up the Grim Reaper's body like a gorgeous virus.

It was beautiful, yet haunting, and I wondered how many ghosts this man had in his life. How many men had he watched die while being a combat medic? How many had he held in his arms as they'd died?

According to Beckett's examination, a concussion was possible, but there was no way to know for certain. Cullen was taken to a spare bedroom in the living quarters. The lights were dimmed, barely illuminating the sparsely decorated space. The furniture was sleek and minimalist, just a bed, a nightstand, a dresser with a TV, and a chaise in the corner. The colors were monochromatic. Very simple, very masculine.

After ensuring Cullen was comfortable in bed, I stepped out into the hallway, where Beckett and Easton appeared to be arguing about something. They stopped talking immediately. I didn't like this.

Beckett scowled at me, then at Easton, then dipped his chin and disappeared into the darkness, leaving Easton and me alone in the hall.

"I'll sleep on the chaise lounge in the corner and watch him," I said.

"Beckett will keep an eye on him. He knows what to watch out for. You'll sleep in my room."

"Your room?"

Easton nodded.

"You live here?"

Another nod.

I frowned, unable to imagine someone as successful as Easton living full-time in his office. "You don't have a house?"

"Sold it six months ago. You'll sleep in my room. You'll—"

His room. His *bed*.

My thoughts immediately clouded, drifting someplace else they didn't need to be. Someplace very intimate. *No.* I needed to focus—and I sure as hell wouldn't be able to do that between his sheets.

I held up my hand. "No, you sleep. Please. Listen . . . I don't want to make this a big deal. I can promise you I'm not going to sleep; this night has been crazy. I have work I can do on my phone and things I can read. I'm just going to hang out until we leave in the morning."

"I want to understand your relationship with this man, Mia."

"I told you, he's my client."

"This is more than a patient/doctor relationship."

"If you're asking if we're in a romantic relationship, the answer is a hard no. If you're asking if we've ever slept together? Also a hard no. There's no romantic relationship between Cullen Nichols and me whatsoever, not that it's any of your business. And by the way, what's your deal with him? Why don't you like him?"

"There's no deal."

I snorted. "Like there's no deal with Deputy Mason? Shit, Easton, the crowds parted when he walked up to you, like we were in the Wild West getting ready for a showdown. And what's with the dip you found in the woods? Why not just give it to the cops?" I blew out a breath. "I can tell you think I'm not being totally transparent with you, but I'm certain you aren't with me either."

"Your business is now my business, Mia."

"And why's that?"

"Because I'm involved now."

"And that allows you to automatically run the show?"

"Yes."

I snorted. "No wonder you're still single."

"Who says I'm single?"

I stilled, staring at him a moment.

He was right; I didn't know. I had no reason to think Easton wasn't involved with another woman. He'd kissed me, yes, but that could have been a spontaneous misstep. A man with his good looks and success probably had many women.

A sickening wave of disappointment and insecurity washed over me.

I squared my shoulders and lifted my chin. "I'm going to work on the chaise lounge in here. Thank you for offering your bedroom, but it's yours."

"If you aren't sleeping in my bed tonight, no one is."

"What will you do?"

"Work."

A beat of silence ticked between us.

"Do you think Cullen is still in danger?" I asked.

Easton stepped forward, closing the inches between us, reminding me just how in control he was. Butterflies erupted in my stomach as he stared down at me.

"Or," I whispered, my gaze drawn to his lips, "is it that you think I'm in danger?"

He trailed his thumb down my cheek, sweeping it over my bottom lip, leaving a blaze of heat on my skin.

"I'm not willing to take that chance." He dropped his hand and stepped back. "Good night, Mia."

I blinked, clumsily reaching behind me for the doorknob. "Good night, Easton."

I slipped back inside the room, closed the door but didn't latch it. After a few seconds, I peeked out the crack and saw Easton standing like a sentinel in front of the door, his arms crossed over his chest. His profile was hard, icy cold, as he viewed the woods outside.

He wasn't going anywhere.

For a moment, I wondered if Easton had somehow uncovered my past. If he knew about my true connection to Cullen.

*No.*

That nightmare had been buried long ago.

Or had it?

# Chapter Twenty-Six

## Easton

It didn't take Mia long to fall asleep.

Quietly, I entered the room.

Her cell phone had fallen from her clutch, her open palm balanced on her thigh. Her head rested against the back of the chaise, tangled brown hair fanning from her face. Her lips were slightly parted, exactly as they'd been before I'd so recklessly kissed her in the woods. Full, plump, and pink. Mesmerizing. Long feathered lashes outlined a pair of big, round eyes, somehow just as captivating as when they were open.

I wondered if this was the only time her face reflected peace.

She was so small under the jacket I'd given her, and I liked the way my logo looked across her chest. Her boots were still laced, her legs tucked to the side.

That night, I watched Mia for longer than I cared to admit, my brain fluttering somewhere between the present and a very dark past.

I wouldn't let her out of my sight, I decided.

I would be smart. Vigilant. This time, I wouldn't be too late, like I had been with the last woman I'd cared about.

After covering her with a blanket, I turned my focus to the mystery that was Cullen Nichols.

The man who Mia Frost was willing to risk her own safety for.

There were too many pieces being added to the puzzle, and the problem was that none of them seemed to fit.

I clicked on my phone, checking my missed calls and text messages for the umpteenth time.

I typed a new text to Loren:

I need that information on Deputy Mason STAT. Also, need to know if he uses tobacco.

I clicked off the phone, tapped it to my chin as I gazed outside. Where the hell was she?

# Chapter Twenty-Seven

## Mia

To my surprise, I'd fallen asleep quickly, the events of the day before proving too much for my already stressed system. I awoke to Beckett speaking quietly to Cullen, who had awoken before me. Easton loomed at the edge of my chair like a guard between me and the men, his back to me, freshly showered, dressed, looking as alert and gorgeous as ever.

When I stirred, he turned and handed me a cup of coffee from the small table next to the lounge. It was piping hot, making me wonder how many times he'd refilled it while I'd slept.

Despite a solid night's rest, Cullen still couldn't remember details of the attack. He seemed as disoriented as he'd been the night before. Not himself. Something wasn't right.

It had to be drugs, I thought. I wanted to ask him but was ushered out of the room so that Beckett could check Cullen's wounds.

Easton led me to his personal suite, a bedroom and expansive marble bathroom worthy of a feature in *Architectural Digest*. White was everywhere, blinding, clean, sharp lines and angles. The fixtures, gleaming silver. The bed, a massive king under crisp white sheets. The suite was as cold and masculine as the exterior of the office.

How many women had seen this room? I wondered.

How many women had slept in the bed?

How many women had Easton kissed under the trees?

I was acutely aware of Easton's presence in his bedroom as I showered. He wouldn't leave my side.

Overnight, there had been a shift in him with me. A weird possessiveness that I'd be lying to say that I didn't like. I wanted to be his, I realized. His to kiss, hold, protect. Something about the man—our kiss, perhaps—had awoken a primal need of partnership inside me. I wanted to be with someone who valued my life as much as their own. Someone who *wanted* to take care of me, *wanted* to take away the world that seemed to sit solidly on my shoulders. Someone who willingly sacrificed their time and energy for *me*.

Easton filled those needs and wants and so much more. That morning, he guarded me like a princess, an heiress to a throne, as if I were invaluable to his very existence.

It was something I'd never felt before.

I loved it.

A LYNX sweatshirt and a pair of jeans had been laid on the bathroom counter for me. The jeans had to have belonged to his Mad Max office manager, I assumed. I hoped, anyway.

No underwear.

It was a tense morning, to say the least. Fear and uncertainty were in the air, mixing with whatever was blooming between Easton and me.

After I slipped into clean clothes that smelled like fresh cotton, we loaded Cullen into Easton's truck, and I followed them in my Jeep into town for interviews.

Ten minutes later, I paced in the waiting room of the sheriff's department, my stomach churning with nerves. The furnace still wasn't working properly, blowing a continuous stream of hot, dry air that whistled from a rusty vent.

Despite the heat, I shuddered with chills.

It was just after nine on a cloudy gray morning that mirrored the mood of the town, now rampant with gossip and fear.

*"The Black Cat struck again. Who will be next?"*

*"No one is safe, men or women."*

*"The Black Cat is the devil himself, terrorizing our town. He must be caught."*

No matter how my client played into what was happening, one thing was clear—the Black Cat Stalker was stepping up his game. His presence was more frequent, his assaults more brutal. A man without a face, the mystery of him now consuming the small town of Skull Hollow.

I glanced at the black-and-white clock on the wall. It had been forty-seven minutes since Sheriff McNamara had taken Cullen back for an interview. Easton had gone back as well, to update them on Cullen's condition overnight.

I was left in the waiting room.

There wasn't much to update.

The sound of the doorknob turning startled me.

I turned as Sheriff McNamara walked into the room where I waited, his eyes bloodshot and puffy. Lack of sleep combined with fielding calls from concerned citizens all night long, I assumed. Easton followed seconds later.

The sheriff sighed heavily and parted his hands. "He still doesn't remember anything else."

The room was quiet a moment. The only man who could help take down the Black Cat Stalker couldn't remember a thing.

"We've given him food, water, space," the sheriff said. "He's been interviewed by two different deputies. Still, nothing."

"Have you dispatched a team to recheck the scene?" Easton asked.

McNamara nodded. "They're there now." He scrubbed his hands over his face. "There's nothing else I can do with Cullen right now. If he can't remember . . . he can't remember."

"It's called dissociative amnesia," I blurted, earning both men's sudden fixed attention. "It's not uncommon after a traumatic event. It's the body's way of dealing with something extremely painful that his brain isn't quite ready to accept or acknowledge. He's blocking it out, although he doesn't realize it. It's a coping mechanism."

"How long does it last?" Easton asked.

"Depends."

"On what?" McNamara asked.

"Several factors. One, how early an intervention takes place."

"What kind of intervention?"

"Therapy. To try to bring back the memories so that he can begin to deal with them—and so we can understand more about who attacked him." I inspected the steel door, my mind racing. "I'd like to work with him. Now."

"We've had two people try to interview him—"

"Not to interview. I'd like to take him through a guided meditation to pinpoint the memories."

"You're talking about hypnosis," Easton said.

"What?" McNamara recoiled as if I'd just suggested sticking pins in a doll.

"Yes. The technical term is *hypnotherapy*. It uses visualization to help with memory recall. With your approval, and if he's willing, I'd like to try with him."

"Hang on." McNamara shook his head. "There's no way something like this would hold up in court."

The sheriff was right. Any memory pulled from hypnotherapy would be destroyed by the defense shooting more holes through it than swiss cheese.

"Understood. But I also understand you have zero leads, and this could perhaps reveal something that would help point you in the right direction."

The sheriff was getting desperate. So was I, so I gave him my pitch.

"I'm a doctor, Sheriff, not a sorceress. This is a widely accepted form of therapy that's used for situations just like this. And it's proven to be extremely accurate. I'll need about an hour—"

"Wait, how does it work exactly?"

"First and foremost, you must have a willing and ideal participant."

"And what makes you think Cullen is willing to do this?"

"Because we've spoken about it. He asked, specifically, about hypnotherapy when he first came to my clinic. I suggested waiting a while before attempting this type of therapy to build rapport between us. This is very important."

"And how is he an ideal participant?" Easton asked.

"The ideal patient for hypnotherapy is someone with high ability to focus and concentrate and, typically, someone with above-average intelligence. Cullen hits each of those marks. More than that, though, I worry that his attack will exacerbate his PTSD, and the sooner I can intervene—with drastic measures like hypnosis—the better, for him *and* for you, Sheriff, in terms of the information he might be able to provide to assist in the investigation."

"Walk me through the exact process," McNamara said.

"I will take him through several phases. First the induction, where I'll guide him into a relaxed state where he will 'let go,' if you will. Then we enter the suggestion phase, where I walk him through what I know of his attack, taking him back to that place to unlock the memories. Typically, I'd do this over a series of sessions, but we can start today. I'd like to take him to my office, to a calmer, more suitable environment."

The sheriff shook his head, his expression dark. "Absolutely not."

"Listen, you've got the entire town breathing down your neck. Women are terrified to leave their homes, and now men are too. They want answers. This can help provide that—can help lead you to the Black Cat."

"She's right," Easton said, and I glanced at him. "My guess is you've got less than a day before this thing hits the national news and the Feds invade this town. You should try everything you can to nail this bastard before he hurts anyone else."

McNamara looked outside, thoughts warring in his head. Finally, he said, "Okay. I'll agree to it under two circumstances. That it's done here, recorded, and that I get to sit in and watch the entire thing."

"No. Absolutely not. Cullen has to be relaxed, and he won't be with the sheriff watching his every move from the corner of the room."

"We can watch from behind the two-way mirror," Easton said quickly.

*We.*

McNamara sighed. "Fine. Okay, we'll give it a shot."

"I'll need a couch or a cot for Cullen to lie on. The lights need to be dimmed, and we need something for the guy to drink other than water. This *cannot* be approached like a typical interview."

McNamara looked at Easton, then back at me. "I'll have a cot brought in." He turned his back and jerked open the door. "Don't make me regret this, Miss Frost."

*Miss* Frost.

# Chapter Twenty-Eight

## Mia

I was escorted into the interview room, the same room where I'd met with Courtney Hayes days earlier. The irony wasn't lost on me. A cot had been awkwardly shoved into the corner, pulled from a jail cell. No pillow or blanket, nothing.

My jaw clenched. It was as if they were trying to sabotage me, the crazy shrink and her weird ways.

*You aren't crazy*, I reminded myself. *You aren't crazy. You are in control.*

Cullen sat across the table, pale and lethargic, but a wild energy coming from him suggested uncomfortable excitement. He was alert now. Scared.

My heart broke for him.

He watched me closely as I crossed the room, and I found myself feeling uncomfortable and nervous.

"Hi, Cullen."

"Hey," he said quietly, his voice weak.

"I understand Sheriff McNamara spoke with you already about what I would like to do. Are you sure you're okay with it?"

"I think so, yes."

"Thank you—for being open to it. I really think this can help. Would you mind lying down? It will help the process." I gestured to the cot. The setup was less than ideal, but it would have to work.

Cullen slowly rose to his feet. I stepped forward, ready to assist, but not so close as to intrude or diminish his masculinity.

Once Cullen settled in, I clicked off the lights, allowing the single window in the room to illuminate the space in a dim gray light.

I settled behind the table and switched on the recorder.

In a quiet, monotone voice, I explained how the session would proceed, taking Cullen step by step through the process. This was strategic more than anything, to begin to quiet his racing mind and adjust to the setting.

Finally, I asked him to close his eyes, and I began.

"Cullen, I'd like you to become aware of a staircase in front of you. A beautiful staircase with a polished banister. You're standing at the top of the staircase. A thick, rich carpet runs underneath your bare feet, cushioning your body, the soft threads interweaving through your toes. Look down the stairs. There are ten steps. I'd like you to walk down those steps with me. I'll count them for you, one at a time, and you'll find that with each step, the more comfortable and more relaxed you'll become. When you're ready to walk down the stairs, I want you to gently place your hand on the banister and begin to slowly descend the stairs as I count them off from ten to one."

I counted slowly, each numbered step accompanied with a reminder to relax.

"We're almost at the bottom now . . . just one more step to go . . . and here we are. Good job, Cullen. You're now standing at the bottom of the steps and feeling very comfortable, very relaxed, at peace with the world. In front of you is a large door. The door is closed, but you can open it. You have the key to the beautiful place awaiting you beyond the door. Insert that key, place your hand on the knob, turn it, and push the door open . . . now, close the door behind you, and you'll find yourself in a very special place. This place, Cullen, is where I would like to talk to you."

I allowed a moment to pass, the silence settling around us before continuing again.

"As you drift deeper into hypnosis, I'd like you to listen to the sound of my voice, focus on it, feel it. After a while, you'll find yourself being able to visualize, in your mind, the things that I'm saying to you. You will go deeper into this visualization, and there's nothing at all for you to do but relax and just let go."

My pulse started to increase, beads of sweat forming along my spine.

"I'd like you to visualize yourself walking through the woods, the trees around you, the birds in the trees. Feel the breeze against your skin, hear it moving through the trees. Remember how you were feeling, walking through the woods. What were you thinking about? Were you happy? Hungry? Thirsty? Restless? Think about what you were wearing, how your shoes felt on your feet. The sound of your clothes as you moved through the brush. Did you have your phone on you? Were you wearing a coat? Visualize yourself, visualize everything around you."

Modulating my voice, I kept it even and calm, resisting the urge to speed up.

"Remember, I'm right here. I'm right here; hang on to my voice, Cullen . . . remember how you felt walking up to the bluff. The smell around you. I know you know this place, in your heart. And it's okay, you don't have to go that far back now. Just stay with me, right here, right here on the bluff. Now, remember the descent into the ravine, the path that you took. Think about the way the ground felt underneath your feet."

My throat became dry, and I took a moment to swallow.

"I'd like you to think about the temperature of the air as you walked through the ravine. What did you see? What were you thinking of? Sit here for just a minute, Cullen, and take in the moment. If you begin to feel scared, simply cling to my voice. I'm right here. I'm not going anywhere, and you're safe, you're in a safe place. Now, I want you to remember the way you felt the moment you knew someone or something was behind you. Do you remember? That feeling? That instinct?"

His fingers began to tap against the cot.

"I want you to remember the way you felt when something touched you. When someone touched you. Remember the feeling. What did you see, at that exact moment? What went through your mind?"

Pulling in a deep breath, I kept my voice steady.

"Your cheek was struck. Your face. Your body. Remember it all, those feelings. I want you to picture yourself, the environment around you. What happened, how you felt while you were being attacked. I want you to replay it in your head. Over and over."

The tapping increased, *tap-tap-tap* of his finger against the steel frame of the cot. His eyes rolled frantically back and forth under the closed lids.

"I'm right here, Cullen, I'm right here. Stay here with me, in this place, stay here. Now, I'd like you to picture your attacker, their face, their body, their characteristics, the way they physically connected with you. I'd like you to draw a picture of this person in your head. I'm right here. You're drawing on a chalkboard now, Cullen. Draw your attacker. I'm right here, I'm right here. Draw the person, everything you can remember . . ."

After giving him a moment, I continued.

"I know you have a picture in your head now. Can you describe this person to me?"

There was a long pause.

"Cullen, who attacked you in the woods?"

Suddenly, Cullen's eyes fluttered open. His head slowly turned, as if on a spindle. A pair of glassy black eyes stared into my soul, and a chill shot up my spine like lightning.

"Cullen," I whispered, my pulse a sudden rush through my veins. "Who attacked you in the woods?"

"You," he said.

# Chapter Twenty-Nine

## Mia

What happened next was a blur, a haze of confusion and chaos.

The door swung open, revealing loud voices, and a blinding fluorescent glare filled the room as someone clicked on the lights. People filled the room.

Dumbstruck, I was in shock. Frozen in place, like a deer caught in the headlights, while all my attention funneled to Cullen.

I heard Easton's voice, loud and commanding, though I couldn't make out the words. His hand wrapped around my biceps, gently pulling me from the seat. I stumbled to my feet, my eyes still locked on Cullen, the man who had just accused me of brutally attacking him in the woods.

The man who had just accused me of being the Black Cat Stalker.

I turned to Sheriff McNamara, meeting the questioning, accusing look he gave me.

"I'm getting her out of here," Easton snapped.

"Wait," I said, suddenly jolted out of my shock.

I stared at Cullen, now standing, staring back at me with that goddamn dazed look on his face. The room fell quiet, all eyes on me.

"Cullen . . ." My voice cracked. "Cullen, I don't understand. Why?"

"No." Easton yanked my arm, pulling me from the room and down the hall.

The usually noisy bullpen was silent as we passed, curious faces peering over the cubicles. More eyes on me.

*Me.*

A hand swept to my lower back, gently pressing, guiding me out the front door. I welcomed the touch, needed it to ground me. Needed someone.

The chilly autumn air was like another jolt to my system. I stopped and spun toward Easton.

"W-wait. What the hell just happened in there? What *the hell* was that?" Panic bubbled through my system.

"I'm kinda hoping you can tell me."

"Shit. Oh *shit.*" I gripped the top of my head. "Oh my God, do you think they *believe* him?"

"You sold the efficacy of hypnotherapy pretty hard in there."

"Do you seriously think I'm the Black Cat Stalker?"

"Come on. Not here." Easton took my elbow and guided me down the steps into the parking lot.

The doors burst open behind us.

Sheriff McNamara jogged down the steps, accompanied by Deputy Mason, who had apparently shown up during the interview. "Dr. Frost. Can you hang on just a second?"

Ignoring them, Easton quickly led me to my Jeep as their boots pounded the cracked concrete behind us.

"Do you have a lawyer?" Easton whispered in my ear.

"A lawyer?" I hissed back. "Are you serious?"

"Yes. I can call mine if you don't."

I shook my head. "No. That's not necessary. I—we, I mean the business—has one. I can call her."

"Call her now. Don't say a word to the sheriff or the deputy unless she's sitting next to you. They're going to want to—"

"Dr. Frost, we'd like to ask you a few questions, if you don't mind."

"Her lawyer is on her way," Easton said as I jerked my arm out of his hold and turned to the men storming me.

"Lawyer?" McNamara frowned. "Kinda jumping the gun there, aren't you? I just have some questions."

"Where's Cullen?" I asked.

"We've got him in another room now."

Deputy Mason considered me. "Do you have any idea what that was about?"

"No questions until her lawyer gets here." Easton's tone was as cold as ice.

Annoyed, McNamara shook his head.

This was serious. But the worst part was that I couldn't wrap my head around it. I didn't understand what was happening.

Why had Cullen said I was the one who'd attacked him?

What the fuck was happening?

"Give us a second." As we reached my Jeep, Easton stood between me and the other men. "Listen to me—you owe them nothing. Talk to them or don't, but you owe them nothing."

"But I have to talk to them, Easton. I have to defend myself. I can't believe Cullen said—did this. I don't know why. It's ridiculous."

I choked out a humorless laugh at the irony that I was the one who'd put these wheels in motion by suggesting hypnotherapy. *Convincing* them to let me help.

Easton studied me. "Does Cullen have a diagnosis that would make him see or think things that aren't true? Like schizophrenia or something?"

I shook my head. "No. He only has PTSD, unresolved trauma from his childhood. I diagnosed him myself."

"Do you have an alibi for the last few nights? Aside from last night?"

I dragged my fingers through my hair, thinking. "No, I . . ." I shook my head, the panic beginning to spread like fire. "No. I don't really do much. I work late most days, go home, sometimes go for a jog. That's about it."

"Go through your phone and see if you spoke with anyone during the last few nights, someone who can vouch for you. That way if you need it, you'll have that in your pocket."

I blinked, suddenly realizing Easton wasn't questioning me. He didn't doubt me.

"Why do you believe me?" I asked before I could stop myself.

"Mia, did you beat Cullen Nichols to a bloody pulp in the middle of the woods?"

"No."

"Did you sexually assault Courtney Hayes with a stick?"

My stomach rolled. "No."

Easton dipped his chin. "Good enough for me. Now, get in your Jeep, call your lawyer, and have her meet you here as soon as possible. It's better to address this and get it done immediately before it leaks to the gossips."

"What will you do?"

"I'll be right here." He opened the door to the Jeep. "You're okay. Everything's going to be okay. Get in. Make the call. I'll make sure no one bugs you."

I grabbed his hand and squeezed. "Thank you. I mean it. Thank you, Easton. I don't even—"

He turned as the door to the building opened and two more deputies walked out, their beady eyes narrowed directly on me.

My world began to spin.

Minutes earlier, I'd been a doctor interviewing a victim. Now, I was the suspect.

Now, the past was going to be unearthed. And it wasn't going to be good for me.

# Chapter Thirty

## Easton

"Where the hell have you been?"

Loren sat across from my desk with a stack of paper in her lap and a frown on her face.

Her short blonde hair was spiked, a cap of dark roots starting to invade the bleached strands. I thought of Mia's comparison to Imperator Furiosa. True, if not for the unusually feminine yellow sundress Loren had chosen for work that day.

I'd never seen my office manager in a dress before that day.

It was our weekly time to touch base, a recurring one-on-one meeting Loren had scheduled to discuss the week's events, onboarding outlines for new trainees, payroll, expenses, my travel schedule, what snacks I wanted in the break room, when to expect my dry cleaning, and what I should eat for dinner.

Somewhere along the line, Loren's role had morphed into that of personal assistant, though I'd never asked for it and certainly never expected the role to suit her so seamlessly.

Loren had joined the National Guard at age eighteen, straight out of high school, the first female MLRS crew member in the 133rd Field Artillery Brigade. She'd enrolled in one of LYNX's tracking courses, graduated at the top of her group—and never left. I'd offered Loren a job, and she'd accepted on the spot. The company was growing, and we needed someone to manage the day-to-day. Loren fit the bill.

"I've been here, mostly," she said.

"Why have you been avoiding my calls and texts?"

"I haven't."

I blew out a breath of frustration, closed my eyes. "Just tell me what you got on Mason."

"Well, I haven't got all the information you asked for yet."

"Give me what you have."

"The deputy worked most of last week, typical ten-hour shifts, and worked overtime last weekend."

"Who did you verify this with?"

"Dispatch."

"I need a detailed outline, Loren. You know that. I need to know what he did every hour, specifically on the day Courtney Hayes went missing. Talk to people; use that charm of yours to get information. Get your ex-boyfriend computer genius to pull CCTV feed from his locations. Verify the car or truck he was driving . . . everything, Loren. And all his past addresses. I want to know every town and state he lived in."

Her eyes narrowed. "What's wrong with you?" she asked, sliding her mechanical pencil above her ear, a gesture meant to inform me that she wasn't going to continue with the meeting until I'd answered her question. "You're off."

"Off?"

"Yeah. You've got something on your mind. Spill it."

"I've got you needing to get me that information on Mason on my mind, Loren."

"More than that."

I rested my elbows on my desk, steepling my fingertips, my thoughts funneling back to the real reason for my distraction. Cullen had accused Mia of attacking him . . . had she? Could she have?

"What do you know about dissociative amnesia?" I asked.

"I forgot," she deadpanned.

"Seriously. You took psych in school, right?"

"Slept through most of it, but yeah." Loren's blue eyes crinkled in deep thought as she attempted to recall lectures that she hadn't slept through. "Dissociative amnesia happens after some sort of severe trauma . . . something so bad that the person literally can't deal with it. The brain simply blocks out the memory. Sometimes the person doesn't remember the incident at all, or even that they were involved."

"So . . . any traumatic event, right? No matter which side of the aisle you were on in this event?"

"What do you mean?"

"I'm wondering if the offender of said traumatic event could have dissociative amnesia . . . and completely forget what they did?"

"Yeah, I think so. It doesn't discriminate, so yeah."

"So the offender could literally forget, not remember what they did. Even if they, say, attacked a person. Or killed them, maybe?"

"Yep. It's like their memory wipes it clean."

"How quickly does it happen?"

Loren pulled her phone from her lap and clicked it on. Using the sleuthing superpower gifted only to women, she found the answer within seconds. "Immediately, according to this article. And it can last for years . . . says here that DA"—she looked up—"short for—"

"Yeah. Got it. Go on."

She grinned. "DA can happen to criminals when the act of violence they committed reminds them of something in their past . . . the victim is usually known by the offender . . . blah, blah, blah." She scrolled further. "The likelihood of amnesia increases with the severity of the crime. So yeah, it could happen, I guess."

Staring through the window, I was lost in thought, not really seeing the chilly, overcast, dull autumn day outside.

"This is about that girl, isn't it?" Loren asked, in a tone about the same as the weather outside.

*You mean Mia Frost? The woman I secretly watched for months, not realizing our worlds were about to collide with the force of a hurricane? The one I randomly kissed in the woods because I couldn't help myself? The woman I can't get off my goddamn mind, no matter how hard I try? The woman I spent the entire last evening—again—watching from a hallway in this very building, rather than from in the shadows behind the pines?*

The woman I'd yet to call or reach out to since watching her peel out of the sheriff's department after being interviewed for aggravated assault. Thing was, Cullen's accusation was nothing short of a metaphorical grenade being dropped in the room. I needed a second to wrap my head around it—to reconnect with the man I'd been before I'd met Mia, the one who thought more clearly, could never be fooled. My logical side had to consider . . .

Was it possible?

"What woman?" I asked in a feeble attempt to appear aloof.

Loren rolled her heavily lined eyes. "The chick who stayed the night here last night, whose door you guarded like a bulldog. The same chick you've spent the entire day with today—making you late for our meeting. And you're never late."

She was right.

I pulled in a quick breath and forced myself to focus on my office manager and the matters at hand. "Sorry. Go on."

"Thank you," she muttered, her brow cocked with attitude. "Now. Sergeant Jones has called twice, wanting to speak with you about your assessment of Henrick Taylor."

"What's there to speak about?"

"Apparently, Jones isn't pleased that you failed him from your program, as this affects where he wanted to place Henrick in his unit."

I lifted a shoulder.

"He's pissed, Easton. Says the goal should be to teach until they get it. Not just fail them."

"I couldn't care less. You can quote me on that. Henrick is just one of many to come through our course. He gets no favors from me or anyone."

"Aha!" Loren grimaced as if she'd just caught me with my hand in the cookie jar. *"Exactly."*

"Exactly what?"

"You couldn't care less about derailing Henrick's career because you feel like you owe him nothing. So why the hell are you bending over backward for some woman you just met?"

"Because Mia Frost was directly connected to a missing person. In case you've somehow missed it, that's kind of what we do here in Skull Hollow. We find missing people. She is—was—a lead."

"Oh, just a means to an end, huh?"

Something in my gut twisted, a deep unease from knowing that whatever was happening between Mia and me had become so much more than that.

"Well," she continued, "I guess since you guys found this missing person—Cullen Nichols, is it?"

I nodded.

"Right. Since he's been found, I guess you'll be less preoccupied, huh?"

"What's your problem with M—Dr. Frost?"

"I've just never seen you go out of your way so much. For anyone. Especially lately."

"Seventy-four hours, Loren." I leaned forward, days of tension and emotion that I wasn't used to coming to a boiling point. "Two years ago, Beckett and I voluntarily spent seventy-four hours straight hiking through the swamps in the middle of winter searching for a missing autistic child. We didn't eat or sleep until we found him. I believe his mother and father would beg to differ that LYNX doesn't go out of their way for people. It's what we do." I stood up, feeling the heat rise up the back of my neck. "I need that information on Mason immediately. Do you have anything else for me right now?"

"Uh." Loren looked down at her notebook, her cheeks reddening.

"Good." I clicked off my computer and grabbed my coat. "I've got something to do. Forward my calls to my cell."

Loren shot out of her chair, her plastic yellow pencil tumbling to the floor. "Where are you going?"

"Out." I strode past her.

"Wait . . . you've got two calls this afternoon." She squatted, scrambling for the pencil rolling under my desk. "One with the chief of naval operations, and another—"

"I'll be there."

"And if you're not?" She lurched into the hallway after me.

"Beckett can handle them."

Loren huffed. "You're going to check on *her*, aren't you?"

I stopped and turned slowly, meeting my office manager's glower. "There's a line, Loren. It's a very thin line, but you're dangerously close to the edge. Do you understand me?"

Her jaw clenched. "Sir."

I dipped my chin, turned, and strode down the hall, a faint warning bell going off in my head.

# Chapter Thirty-One

## Mia

I shot up in bed.

Saturated, stinking strands of hair flew into my face as my pillow tumbled to the floor. The room was pitch dark. The night-light I always kept next to my bed had finally burned out.

Frantically, I slapped the hair away from my face. My body was trembling, palsied shudders with each heave of my chest. Sweat dripped down my face. My body was soaked.

*Night terrors.*

A flash of lightning illuminated the window. A rumble of thunder followed seconds later.

Another autumn storm moving in.

My tongue felt like cotton, my mouth thick with the disgusting sour taste from the bottle of red I'd emptied before falling into bed. I was still drunk, I realized, though now the buzz had settled into an excruciating headache. Like two machetes piercing my brain.

I flattened my palms on the mattress on either side of my hips in an attempt to steady myself.

Two nights had passed since I'd been interviewed at the sheriff's department for my involvement in Cullen's attack, my lawyer at my side, Easton pacing outside the room like a caged animal.

Two nights of no sleep.

My lawyer had strongly advised that I not contact Cullen and said that he had been advised the same. If anyone reached out to me, I was advised not to say a word and call her immediately. So far, it had been crickets from both the deputy and the sheriff. Not that I was complaining. She'd also advised me to lie low, as the gossip of Cullen's "confession" had already breached the diner's front doors, otherwise known as the hub of all things Skull Hollow and the birth of all gossip.

The accusations, insults, and condemnation were crippling.

*"Mia Frost is the Black Cat."*

*"The town psychologist finally snapped."*

*"I always knew there was something weird about that girl. She's not right."*

*"Mia Frost deserves to rot in jail."*

*"Get her out of our town."*

*"Kill her."*

It was only a matter of time before someone uncovered the past my mother and I had put so much effort into burying.

I felt like a prisoner in my own home, just sitting there waiting for something else to happen.

I'd told the girls I was sick and would be taking a few days off, in hopes that the gossip hadn't reached them yet. This had been met with baskets of food, bottles of wine, and dozens of flowers on my doorstep.

Soon, they would hear. Soon, they would be back, and I'd have to talk.

The birds stirred, sensing my panic from the living room. They never got used to my night terrors. I didn't either.

I glanced at the clock—11:11 p.m.

Goldie squawked from her cage in the corner. I could just make out the yellow of her feathers in the darkness.

When I ripped off the comforter, a chill raced over my sweat-soaked nightshirt. The nights were getting colder.

Hands trembling, I reached for the glass of water I always kept on the nightstand but swiped it instead. The glass teetered and fell to the floor, shattering into a million pieces, splashing water over everything.

Cursing, I swung my legs over the bed. Gripping the nightstand for support, I stood, avoiding the broken glass.

The moment I fully straightened, my stomach flip-flopped, rolling as if I'd just taken a nosedive off a thirty-foot diving board. I lunged into the bathroom, falling to my knees next to the toilet seconds before vomit spewed from my mouth.

Wiping the slimy chunks from my chin, I fell against the cold tile floor, my sweaty arms sliding against the tile like the tendrils of an octopus out of water. I lay in dead man's pose in the pitch dark, wanting nothing more than the floor to open up and swallow me whole.

I focused on a spot on the ceiling as the question returned, barreling through my head like a tidal wave.

Was I mad?

Had I finally lost it?

Had the past that I'd buried finally metastasized, taken over, manifesting in violence?

Could I have attacked my client, who shared a past eerily similar to my own, and not remembered? Was I projecting? On him?

Could I, Mia Frost, have beaten another human almost to death—*and not remember?*

*Could I have done it?*

There were no marks on my knuckles, no injuries on my hands. Could I have beaten him with an object? A stick, perhaps, and tossed it into the woods? I'd checked the baseball bat I kept next to the front door. It appeared to have been unmoved. I'd checked my clothes for blood—none—my shoes, my fingernails. I'd even inspected my hair for specks of leaves or any sign that I had been out in the woods. I felt like I was going mad.

I'd spent the last two days scouring my old textbooks and medical journals, studying dissociative amnesia. I'd read article after article, personal accounts from patients who had experienced the memory gap. One out of five victims experienced DA more than one time in their life.

Was there some sort of predisposed condition in our brains or psyches that made us more likely to experience set responses to trauma, such as dissociative amnesia?

"You."

The single word uttered from Cullen's mouth ran on repeat in my mind.

"You."

*"You."*

YOU.

Flashbacks barreled into my head, one after the other. Only parts of memories, but each more devastating than the last.

Lying on the wet forest ground, bleeding, cold, lost.

Broken.

I was so fucking sick of feeling broken.

I was so sick of hiding my own personal battle with dissociative amnesia from my mother, my friends, the girls, my clients, Easton.

*You're weak. You're an imposter . . .*

A loud boom of thunder startled me, sending a burst of adrenaline through my veins, igniting the anger simmering below. Rain began to slowly tick against the window, quickly turning into a deafening deluge. A clock ticking down to something.

I pulled myself off the bathroom floor and stumbled to the living room. Lightning flashed outside, illuminating that goddamn dogwood in the middle of my backyard.

God, I hated it. I hated everything it represented. And I hated *me* for hating it so much.

That tree stood for everything I hated about myself.

An unnatural rage ignited inside me.

I stumbled to the tool closet, yanked open the door, and, like a junkie searching for their stash, began frantically rifling through the boxes that lined the shelves, sending tools and buckets crashing to the floor.

The birds went nuts in their aviary, only amplifying the crazed, insane state I found myself in that night. Chaos ensued, doing nothing to calm the rage, the delirium taking over my body.

Goldie screamed my name over and over and over again.

*"Mia, Mia, Miiiiiia . . ."*

I ignored her.

Finally, I found the ax buried in the back of the closet. The one I'd gotten weeks after moving into my new home, on a high of independence. With this ax, I'd planned to chop my own firewood and burn it on lazy Sunday afternoons by a fire, sipping chai lattes and reading *Cosmopolitan* until a beautiful sleep gripped me.

How wrong I'd been.

The ax felt good, solid, in my hands as I stormed outside into the raging thunderstorm, in nothing but a long T-shirt. No shoes, socks, panties. Nothing.

Dead leaves spun in the wind, whipping around my body and sending my hair spinning around my face, sticking to my cheek, my forehead. Mud seeped between my bare toes with each step, but I relished it. The mud, the dirtiness. The rawness.

I slipped on a patch of mud in front of the tree, and this only fueled my rage even more. Rain dripped off my nose as I bounced the ax in the palms of my hands a few times, testing its weight and tightening my grip against the wet wooden handle.

Positioning my feet, I steadied my stance and, with a deep inhale, swung back the ax and released the blade against the tree with a guttural howl and every bit of strength I had in me. A loud crack echoed through the rain, tiny shards of bark exploding into the air. Breath left my lungs, reverberations from the blow jarring my shoulders, my head, my entire body.

It felt damn good.

Inhaling, I reared back and did it again, and again, and again.

Tears ran down my cheeks.

I swung again and again, the tiny slice in the bark growing deeper with each blow. I imagined his face under the blade; then I imagined Cullen's face.

My palms burned as the skin ripped, but instead of stopping, I hit harder.

Heaving sobs shook my shoulders.

With each strike, I screamed vile, horrible things, releasing years and years of pent-up anger.

Releasing myself.

# Chapter Thirty-Two

## Easton

I watched Mia obliterate the beautiful dogwood tree with such violence and vigor it was as if I were watching an animal fighting for its life. Knowing it was going to die but continuing to fight.

She looked like a ghost against the dark backdrop of the forest, emerging from her natural habitat, an eerie paleness against the blackness.

Long brown hair snaked down the front of her face and down her shoulders. Rivulets of rain dripped off her nose to her chin. Her hands clung to the ax with a viselike grip, the rain red with blood as it seeped through her fingertips.

Her beautiful face was almost unrecognizable, contorted with rage and spots of mud and tree bark. I wasn't watching Mia Frost. I was watching someone in the middle of a mental breakdown.

It was like seeing myself, twelve months earlier. On my hands and knees in the rain, staring at my fiancée's dead body.

I knew exactly what Mia was feeling. The weight of a single life-changing moment, a virus, finally overcoming its host. A final and voluntary disengagement from life. An anger only a handful of us experience in our lives. The kind that changes you to the very core, makes you do things that you never thought you would. The kind that rewires your brain and turns you into someone or something else.

It was the first time Mia had stepped out of her house in two days. I knew this because I'd spent almost every second of the last forty-eight hours perched outside it. Watching from a distance, my comfort zone.

Mia's name had been tarnished, the citizens of Skull Hollow labeling her crazy or evil. Some claimed Mia was possessed. Her clinic would suffer, as would her employees, and I worried it might be only a matter of time before the doors of the Dragonfly Clinic would close for good.

Mia's life had changed in one split second.

I was worried that someone was going to vandalize her house or worse. I was ready to confront anyone who dared to knock on her door. I wouldn't care that I was caught watching.

Mia was right in her early assessment of me that I was simply "phoning in" life. I didn't give a shit about much anymore. *Except her.*

I wanted to call or text her so badly, but I didn't know what to say or how to handle it. Everything had changed the moment I'd kissed her. Not only with us but with me.

Mia Frost had a place in my life. I was sure of it; I just didn't know how or when.

*Bullshit.*

The truth? It terrified me. That was the brutal truth. My feelings for her absolutely terrified me.

I'd fuck it up. Hurt her.

I'd be too late.

*No. Never again.*

I watched Mia swing the ax with such force that it split the tree, despite her small size. I envisioned Cullen and his gruesome injuries.

Yes, Mia Frost had a side that she kept hidden from the world.

A violent side.

A very dangerous side.

# Chapter Thirty-Three

## Mia

The ax slipped from my fingers, and my knees buckled with exhaustion. I fell to the wet ground in a sobbing mess, mud seeping around my legs, between them.

What *the hell* was wrong with me?

Fisting the earth in my hands, I let the cold, wet mud slide through my fingertips. I crossed my legs, picked up the ax, and laid it across my knees. Dropping my head in my hands, I let go, crying so hard the sides of my stomach burned.

I didn't notice the neighbor's patio lights click on as two hands slid under my armpits, lifting me from the cold, wet earth. I was cradled against a thick chest that smelled like clean soap.

Surrendering, I pulled in my legs, curling into the fetal position in his arms, and rested my cheek against the warmth of his chest.

I focused on his heartbeat.

The steady, repetitive thumps, the predictability. The calm.

*Easton.*

# Chapter Thirty-Four

## Mia

The rain suddenly stopped beating my face, my body. The comforting scent of the vanilla candle I'd burned while chugging a bottle of wine pulled me back to reality as Easton carried me into the house.

I didn't open my eyes. I couldn't. For many reasons.

Not only because of the *epic* embarrassment of knowing that Easton had seen my stupid breakdown but because I didn't want to face it, go back to reality, to my life, which suddenly seemed an insurmountable burden.

I was at my end. A woman on the edge. And if I'm being totally honest, I was done. In that moment, I wanted to shrivel up and die. That's the truth.

Little did I know it wouldn't be the only time I would feel that way in the coming days.

Easton carried me through the house, pausing briefly in the laundry room. The smell of dryer sheets transported me back to my childhood home, to my mother, to that day.

But this day, I wasn't alone.

I lifted my head from Easton's chest. "Why are you here?"

"I was driving by."

"At midnight?"

He didn't respond, just carried me out of the laundry room and into the living room.

"Easton . . ."

"I was checking on you."

I was lowered onto the couch, secured in place so that I wouldn't fall. A towel draped over my shoulders, over my lap.

"Sit back. Please, lean back."

I did as I was told and closed my eyes.

Easton knelt in front of me and gently ran the soft cotton over my cheeks, my forehead, wiping the hair, dirt, and bark from my face. He didn't speak, didn't ask questions.

I focused on the smell of him, the feel of his touch. I was attuned to it, little beads of goose bumps slowly spreading over my skin.

Once clean, I released my weight against the couch and listened to his hurried footsteps as he walked from one room to the next, gathering a new set of clothes for me, filling the teakettle, setting it on the stove. Pulling the first aid kit from underneath the sink.

Easton returned to the couch, lowered onto his knees again at my feet, and gently took my hand. My eyes flew open as I winced at the pain, registering for the first time that I was injured. My hands were throbbing, a hot, searing pain of splinters and blisters.

And the worst part? *I* was responsible for it. *I* was the cause.

God, I was *done*.

I didn't care anymore. How could I, a pathetic mess, in front of a man who had now seen me at my absolute worst?

As Easton examined my palms, I didn't say anything. What could I say? He gently plucked the splinters, cleaned the blisters, and bandaged each hand.

I focused on the pain, centered myself on it. It was a weird moment. With each sensation, my body told me, *These are your hands; this is your pain; this is what is happening. You're here; you're grounded. You have help.*

Easton remained silent as he tended to my wounds. The birds had even settled, sensing the calmness, the trust between us.

Until the sound of tires against gravel stopped everything.

My heart started to pound.

Easton quickly covered me with a blanket and strode to the window. His shoulders tightened as he peered into the headlights cutting through the rain.

"Who is it?" I whispered.

"The cops."

I shot up from the couch, sending the blanket and towels tumbling to the hardwood floor. The room spun, a light-headedness squeezing my head from the sudden exertion. Yes, I was still very, very drunk.

The birds stirred, angry flaps of wings and sharp chirps, reflecting their mistress's immediate change in mood.

The engine cut off. Boots crunched on the gravel outside.

Easton opened the door as a man stepped onto the porch, the large outline against the blanket of rain igniting a tingle of fear somewhere deep inside me.

Deputy Mason.

The light from inside washed over a hard face and beady, dark eyes that were alert, narrowed, and laced with contempt.

"Mason." Easton acknowledged him with a warning in the tone, as if Mason were on *his* property. As if I were *his*.

Easton squared his shoulders, blocking Mason's entry into the house and his view of me, but it was too late. Mason caught a glimpse of the train wreck that I was.

I stood frozen, next to the couch, in nothing but my muddied nightshirt and bandaged hands. My hair was still wet, hanging in dirty strings around my face, leaving no doubt of my questionable mental state.

I looked like an escapee from the mental ward. The perfect picture of what the town was labeling me behind closed doors.

"We received a call requesting a wellness check at this address," Mason said.

Old Lady Lou had apparently been awoken by the commotion outside—her neighbor hacking at a beautiful tree in the middle of the night, in the middle of a thunderstorm.

My stomach dropped. More humiliation.

"All is well here," Easton said coolly.

"I need to speak with Dr. Frost, Mr. Crew. If you can excuse me."

Easton didn't move.

I grabbed a towel from the floor and wrapped it around my waist to hide the fact that I was wearing nothing but a T-shirt, and also in some ridiculous attempt to make him think that maybe I'd just gotten out of the shower. I wasn't thinking straight. For many reasons.

A bit unsteady on my feet, I walked to the door and grabbed the back of Easton's T-shirt to steady myself, not realizing the intimate touch would do nothing but add to the rumors already flying about me.

"It's okay, Easton," I whispered at his back.

Easton took his time to consider, the tension mounting with each passing second. Finally, he stepped back, allowing Mason to speak to me.

I forced myself to stand strong, to hold my shoulders back and keep my chin up, despite my horrific appearance.

The deputy studied my bandaged hands. "Dr. Frost . . . are you okay?"

"Yes."

"Is everything okay here?" He studied Easton, looming behind me.

The question was loaded. Mason was gauging if I was in some sort of danger from the man in my house.

"Yes. Everything's fine," I said quickly. "I'm sorry I woke Lou."

I needed this man off my doorstep. Needed this night to end.

Silence joined the tension in the room. Me looking at Mason, Mason at Easton, Easton back at him.

Mason scanned the room behind me as he spoke. "We received a call that suggested you were in great distress outside. And that you had an ax. What have you been doing tonight?"

I thought of my current situation. Days earlier, Cullen Nichols had accused me of attacking him, suggesting I was the Black Cat Stalker. And tonight, there I was, drunk and bloodied, after someone had called the cops on me for suspicious behavior with a dangerous weapon.

Holy *shit.*

Things were not looking good for me.

When I didn't respond right away, Mason pressed. "What were you doing outside at this time of night?"

"I thought I heard something outside," I lied.

"And so you went outside with an ax?"

"Yes."

"And what were you doing before that?"

The kettle whistled from the stove.

Easton stepped forward, placing his hand on the door. "As you can see, Dr. Frost is fine. If there's nothing else we can help you with this evening—"

He slammed the door in the deputy's face. We watched from the window as Mason stalked to his car and finally disappeared down the driveway.

I spun around. "Oh my God, Easton, do you realize how bad this looks—"

The words were left hanging as Easton disappeared into the kitchen. Panicked, I stormed after him. "Easton, this is bad." I grabbed my spinning head to steady the thoughts.

Easton calmly poured the boiling water whistling from the kettle into a cup with a tea bag. Without a word, he waited a few moments while it steeped, then removed the bag. Added a dash of milk. A teaspoon of honey. Stirred. Finally, he turned.

"You're shivering." He took my hand, guided me to the couch, and wrapped a blanket around my shoulders. Setting the tea next to me, he said, "Drink this. I'll be right back. Just a second."

Easton disappeared into my bedroom. I wrapped the blanket tighter around my shoulders and picked up the tea. I was trembling. Cold, too, for that matter.

A few minutes later, Easton returned, bringing with him the soft scent of jasmine. "Come on."

I slipped my hand into his as he picked up the tea with his other. Easton led me into the bathroom, where the tub was filling with warm water, big purple bubbles forming below the spout. The lights were off, candles lit. Steam fogged the edges of the mirror. The smell was heavenly.

"I'm going to start a fire. Drink the tea; it will help warm and relax you."

As he trailed a finger down my cheek, my chin, I was speechless for a moment.

"Thank you, Easton."

"Rest."

Leaving the door ajar, I slipped off my nightshirt and stepped into the bath. The moment I sank below the bubbles, tears filled my eyes, and I began to cry.

I'm not sure how long had passed until I felt someone in the room.

Easton hovered in the doorway, his long dark silhouette stretching across the tile floor.

I wiped my eyes. "You can come in."

Keeping his gaze on the floor, Easton lowered onto the tile and leaned his back against the tub, to allow the privacy I needed. He rested his elbows on his knees.

We sat in total silence for a few minutes. Finally, he spoke.

"It's time to talk, Mia . . . it's time."

I closed my eyes and inhaled.

It was time. The walls were crumbling around me.

After all, how much worse could it get?

# Chapter Thirty-Five

## Easton

"I was sixteen," Mia said, her voice small and weak. Although I was sitting with my back to her, leaning against the tub, her pain was evident. I wanted so badly to turn and comfort her but resisted the urge. These were uncharted waters for me—and her, I imagined.

"It was a rainy day just like this one," she continued. "Although it was springtime."

To anchor myself, I focused on the reflection of a candle dancing against the wall.

"I remember the dogwoods being in full bloom, like pink and white clouds floating through the woods. The rain had finally stopped around dusk, and I decided to go for a run. I was working on my time; there was a big marathon coming up. I wanted to win." She snorted out a humorless laugh. "I went to the same jogging trail I'd been to a million times."

"Where was this?"

"Dallas. My hometown."

"What trail?"

"The Sugar Ridge Trail. It's funny you ask that. I kept forgetting the name of the trail after it happened. How weird is that? I couldn't remember it . . . along with a lot of other things."

*It.*

There was a long pause, and my gut clenched. I thought back to Cullen's accusations, my internal questions about if she was capable of attacking someone and not remembering.

"You've had dissociative amnesia, haven't you, Mia?" I asked.

"Yes," she whispered, her embarrassment evident. "That's when the panic attacks started. I'm assuming it was all related to knowing that I couldn't remember such a huge event in my life. Most of the memories slowly filtered back over the years, but ever since the Black Cat Stalker came to town, it feels like I'm reliving it, emotionally, all over again."

The candle popped and hissed, sending a spark bouncing over the tile.

"I was the only one at the trail that day," she said. "Because of the rain, I guess. After getting out of my car, I remember that I felt . . . weird. Weirdly anxious. Looking back, I wonder if that was my instinct telling me something bad was about to happen. But I was young and naive, so I ignored it and took off down the trail."

She paused to take a breath.

"I wasn't very far in, only about a mile or so, when I passed a man. I immediately felt startled—scared, kind of—not just because I was surprised to see anyone on the trail but also because the man wasn't jogging. He was just walking. It felt *off*. He had a black baseball cap on, aviator sunglasses, and a black sweatshirt. I remember thinking that it was too hot for the sweatshirt and too cloudy for the sunglasses. He had long dark hair, tied back in a ponytail. Anyway, I maneuvered to the edge of the trail to put space between us and picked up my pace."

The water splashed as she shifted in the bath.

"He watched me as I passed him. Creepily. I couldn't see his eyes through the sunglasses, but I could just tell he was staring at me. I could *feel* it. Anyway, after I passed him, I was relieved, felt safe again, and just tried to push him out of my mind and focus on my time. I did what's called the Dogwood Loop, a three-mile loop, and had forgotten about the guy until I came back around to the same spot where I'd passed him earlier. I remember again my body telling me something was wrong. My stomach tickled with nerves."

Mia paused a moment.

"*Shit*, Easton," she whispered. "It's been so long since I've talked about this."

I had to refrain from turning around and pulling her into my arms. "It's okay, Mia. I'm right here, but if you can't—"

"Then out of nowhere, something jumped out of the woods beside me. A body barreled into me. I was knocked breathless, off my feet, into the air. We tumbled off the trail, into the woods. My head slammed against the trunk of a tree."

I watched her shadow move along the wall as she reached up, touching the side of her head. "I can still feel the scar," she whispered.

My hands curled into fists.

*Calm down*, I mentally commanded myself. *Calm down.*

"I'll never forget that tree. A bright-pink dogwood *exactly* like the one in my backyard. It was winter when Jo and I moved here to Skull Hollow and I bought this house. The tree was bare then. I had no clue it was a dogwood. If I had, I would have never bought the house. I *hate* that tree."

I now understood the reason for the violence against the tree in her backyard. It reminded her of the past, one that seemed to be slowly coming back to life.

"When I came to, blood was everywhere, and my head hurt so bad—that was my first thought. It wasn't about the man ripping my shorts off; it was that I'd seriously hurt my head. I was dizzy. Nauseous. It felt like a dream. I remember my mind telling me, *You're in trouble,*

*Mia, you need to move, you need to do something,* but my body couldn't move. I was so out of it, I . . ."

Her breath hitched.

I turned, restraint no longer something I was capable of. "Mia . . ."

I lifted to a squatting position, face to face with her tear-stricken eyes. I reached for her hand. Water splashed over the tub as she gripped it desperately, like a child needing to escape.

My heart began to pound. The feeling I had for this woman in this moment was so intense that I knew I would die for her.

"I'm right here," I said, not recognizing my cracking voice. "I'm right here. You're safe."

Mia peered at me with the most electrifying pain and sadness I'd ever seen in another human being. Her beautiful lip quivered, her cheeks pink with emotion. A tear ran down her cheek.

"I just let him do it," she whispered, her voice barely audible. "I just *lay* there, Easton. I didn't fight him. I just let him do it. Even when he pushed back my knees and used the stick, I just cried and lay there."

She collapsed into sobs, then frantically started to stand, bubbles running down her naked body as she desperately reached for me.

"I'm too hot. I want out of here. I'm hot. I need . . . air . . . out . . ."

I surged to my feet, grabbed a towel from the rack, and pulled her out of the bath and into my arms.

Wrapped in a towel, Mia sobbed as I quickly carried her to the bed. I sat and pulled her on top of me, cradling her body as I leaned back against the pillows. She cried into my chest, shuddering with sobs and gasps. It was as if her armor was slowly disintegrating to dust and drifting to the floor beneath us.

"They never found him, Easton," she choked out on a sob. "He's still out there. They never found him. He's back. He's here. It's the Black Cat; I can feel it in my bones. It's him—and he's back."

Rage sliced through me, a sudden and feral impulse to find this man and take his life.

Mia had been brutally sexually assaulted with a stick, while in the woods, out on a jog. Just like Courtney Hayes.

Mia was right—all paths led to the Black Cat Stalker. The similarities were too big to ignore.

I suddenly envisioned the Black Cat's silhouette, a faceless man in front of me, and I was pulled back to my time in the military, to the first time I'd killed a man. That same rush of adrenaline, an uncontrollable, almost delirious fury, ignited like acid through my veins. I literally began to tremble.

I knew, at that moment, that I would kill for Mia. I knew then she was mine.

To protect.

To keep.

To worship.

# Chapter Thirty-Six

## Easton

Once Mia fell asleep, I slipped out from under her and checked the time—2:37 a.m.

After blowing out the candles and taking the empty teacup to the kitchen, I quietly stepped outside and checked the perimeter of the house. Once I was certain no one was lurking in the shadows, I checked the windows, the doors, then filled a glass with water and took it to Mia's nightstand. I replaced the bulb in a night-light I'd noticed in the corner and turned it on. I wasn't sure if Mia used it, but I figured that night she would want the light.

She was going to wake up exhausted. Not only from crying but also from the physical act of chopping down a tree. I'd chopped down my fair share of trees, and never once had I woken up the next day and not been sore. I couldn't imagine what she was going to feel like. The blisters on her palms would be almost unbearable.

I sat on the edge of the bed, my hand drifting to the top of her head, her silky hair threading through my fingers as I lightly stroked.

A few minutes passed before her eyes fluttered open and locked on mine. My heart skittered.

She licked her lips. "Why aren't you asking questions?" she whispered, and I wondered if she'd actually slept at all.

Stroking her head for a moment, I finally said, "I figure if you wanted to tell me more, you will." Truth was, I wanted nothing more than to understand every detail, every feeling, every emotion she'd gone through. But I didn't want to press.

"I've never told anyone. I didn't even tell my mom until hours after I got back."

"What about your dad?"

"Gone. Left us when I was a little girl. Never came back."

"I'm sorry."

"It's okay. I don't know him, and no love lost, I can promise that."

The many layers of Mia Frost continued to peel back.

"What happened after the attack? How did you get home?"

She shook her head, hatred darkening her face. The tears were gone, allowing anger to seep in. "He left me there, Easton. Left me to die. I know the gash on my head wound looked worse than it was. Coupling that with the fact that I just lay there while he raped me, he probably thought I was close to death. He *left* me. Bloodied and broken. The motherfucker raped me and left me to die."

I could practically feel the vile hatred coming off her in waves. "How did you get home?"

"The rain started again, so of course, no one was on the trail to help me. I just lay there in the rain . . . feeling so sick. Finally, after a few hours, I stumbled my way back to the car. Vomited twice along the way."

"Christ, Mia. Did your mom report it?"

"Eventually, yes."

*Eventually.*

"I begged her not to," Mia said. "Oh my God, I didn't want anyone to know. I was *humiliated*. I'd been raped, which is embarrassing enough, but not just that, I'd been raped in the *ass* with a *stick*. A dirty, nasty, degrading stick . . . I was a virgin, Easton. He took the most sacred thing a woman can offer a man, with a stick on the cold, dirty forest floor."

My teeth ground as I tried, again, to rein in my temper.

The pain and torment Mia had gone through at sixteen, such a pivotal age in womanhood, was almost unimaginable. What had it done to her psyche? Her social and emotional development? This single trauma had shaped the woman Mia had become, no question about it.

"Mom cleaned up my head, applied butterfly stitches. We argued about reporting it. Eventually, she took me to the police station the next afternoon. I was interviewed and then taken to the hospital for an examination. The doctor poked and prodded everywhere. *Everywhere.* It was a male doctor too. Can you believe that? I cried the entire time."

I scrubbed my hand over my mouth, unable to sit still and having to physically restrain myself from voicing the vile, violent thoughts racing through my head.

"The cops took my statement, but I couldn't remember much, just like Cullen. I know now it was dissociative amnesia. Anyway, they searched the trail, but nothing turned up. My cell phone had dropped out of my pocket sometime during the attack. It was gone—I'm sure he saw it and took it. The cops were so frustrated I couldn't give them more details. I was so embarrassed that I couldn't. I remember thinking something was wrong with my brain. That the man had messed it up. That he'd made me mentally challenged, which is so stupid, but that's where my thoughts went. I was so, so embarrassed, in so many different ways. Which is fucked up, isn't it?"

"No, Mia, it's not fucked up. How they treated you is. The fact that your mother—your *mother*—didn't make the right decision the second you came home. *You* aren't fucked up, Mia; what happened to you is."

She took a long, deep breath.

"What about DNA?" I asked, my thoughts spinning. "Did they find anything during your physical examination?"

"No, nothing. Not only had it been over twenty-four hours, but I'd showered, and Mom had washed the clothes I'd been wearing. Any of my attacker's DNA that might have been left behind was washed away. There was nothing anyone could do."

"So that was it?"

"Yeah. That was it. You have to realize I wasn't pressing the cops to find him. I just wanted it to go away. Thankfully, I was a juvenile, so my case was kept under lock and key. No one, aside from a few cops, the doctor, and my mother, knew about it. But even though I was promised that it wouldn't get out, I still lived in fear every day that my school friends would find out. Isn't that funny? That's what I cared most about. Not that they found the guy but what everyone else would think of me. That they would think I was gross. That no boys would ever want to date me. That I wouldn't be asked to prom. Isn't it crazy that was my biggest concern?"

I shook my head. "Not for a sixteen-year-old girl."

A minute passed.

"I got really depressed after. Started reading self-help books—which is where my interest in psychology came from. Lost my friends, became the weird girl. Got bullied a bit. Eventually, we moved to Austin, just to get away from town. This is where I graduated from—the new girl, with zero friends. Mom thought leaving town would help, but it actually made things harder. The shame didn't go away. I hated my body, my face, my vagina, my—sorry."

"No. Don't be."

"I hate everything about me, Easton."

*Hate*—not *hated*.

"I started researching and reading stories of rape victims. I learned it's common to feel embarrassed and unfortunately even more common that the victim never tells anyone. Because of the shame. I still regret that I didn't do more. I have a lot of regrets."

Mia blinked at me, then sat up in bed, gripping the towel around her chest, keeping it in place.

"I want to show you something."

"I'll get it."

"No, please. I want to."

I took her hand, helping her adjust the towel so that it wrapped around her naked body, then helped her stand. I watched her pad to the dresser and pick up a small wooden box with a blue bird painted on the side. She pulled out a small red velvet bag. I recognized it as the bag she took outside with her every evening, while I watched from beyond the pines.

Mia crawled back onto the bed, tucking her legs underneath her. I sat down as she opened the velvet bag and carefully spilled out the contents.

Six stones, two twigs, and one bird feather tumbled onto the white comforter. The exact same items I'd watched her meticulously position on the ground before curling into a ball under the tree and crying herself to sleep. The first time I'd seen her.

"These are from the scene, from the trail back in Dallas. I went back a few days later to look for my cell phone. Stupid, I know, but again, I worried someone would find it and start asking questions . . . anyway, I keep these with me. Everywhere I go. To serve as a reminder to never be weak again. To never be a victim again. To remind me to listen to that instinct inside my body. To never make a bad decision again. To remind myself to be strong."

My heart broke for her.

"It's not your fault, Mia."

"I know that. Hell, I'm a psychologist. I've said those exact words to dozens of my clients who have had very similar situations. My rational side knows that it isn't my fault. But I just can't seem to chase it away." Her jaw clenched, her eyes glinting with anger. "I get so mad, Easton. So *mad*. All the time."

"Because to you, that's strength. You regret that you didn't fight back, so you've subconsciously overcompensated, making yourself short tempered. You see getting angry as a good thing. It's solving a problem."

Processing my words, she blinked, considering this for the first time.

"Have you told Deputy Mason any of this?" I asked.

"No," she snapped. "*No*. But to be honest, I'm shocked it hasn't come to light yet. Surely there's a search capability to link other cases where a stick was used in a sexual assault. I'm sure Mason has done that, right? My name will pop up, no doubt, especially being in the same state."

"Has he said anything to you? Implying that he knows?"

"No. And don't even suggest it. I'm not offering up the information, Easton. I can't . . . my business, Jo, my friends. I just can't."

"Okay . . . okay."

She looked out the window.

"Do you think it's a coincidence?" I asked.

"Do I think that it's a coincidence that Courtney Hayes, a young woman who happens to resemble me physically, was sexually assaulted with a stick on a hiking trail in the exact manner I was two decades ago? No, I don't think it's a coincidence."

"I don't either, Mia."

"He's back, Easton. And I don't know why. I don't get it. Did he attack Cullen solely because Cullen is one of my clients? And in regards to Courtney—why such a long time between attacks? And what the hell does he want from me now?"

"I don't know, but I'll find out. I promise you, Mia, I'll find out. I won't let anything happen to you."

She nodded, her fingertip tracing the tip of the feather.

"Now . . . it's your turn, Easton."

"My turn?"

"It's your turn to tell me your story."

I stilled, instantly uncomfortable with this pivot. "How do you know there is one?"

"I can see it in your eyes."

I turned away.

Her hand drifted over mine. "Tell me. Please, tell me."

# Chapter Thirty-Seven

## Mia

I waited through the silence as Easton battled the demons in his head. I knew the hesitation he was feeling, the dread of revealing your deepest, darkest secrets, and mostly, the fear that once the darkness comes to light, you will no longer be accepted. That there is no turning back. I knew these feelings, because I had just crossed that line with him.

Easton knew me now. Not the facade I put on every day, the *real* me.

It was surprisingly liberating, and I wanted him to feel the same release. I wanted us to do this together.

I wanted him to begin to heal from whatever had happened to him.

"Please," I begged. "Tell me what happened to make you give up on life."

"I was engaged. A year ago . . ."

*His fiancée. The accident . . .*

"On the evening of October seventh of last year, two weeks after we'd gotten engaged, I got a call from Sheriff McNamara. She—Rebecca—had been in a car accident. It was a rainy night like this one. She was driving too fast, skidded on a curve, and went into the woods." Easton cleared his throat, controlling the emotion. "I sped to the scene, but I was too late."

*Too late.*

"She died seconds before I arrived."

"I'm sorry, Easton." I squeezed his hand, but a chilly sharpness in his eyes suggested pain wasn't the emotion this story evoked.

"She was driving fast because she was late to meet me. She was late because she was fucking another man."

I blinked, my eyes widening in shock. "Who?"

"Deputy Mason."

# Chapter Thirty-Eight

## Mia

My mind raced to process this new information, replaying every moment I'd seen the two men together, when I'd witnessed the hatred practically oozing from their pores.

Easton's fiancée had been having an affair with Deputy Mason.

"When did you—how did you find out?"

"I didn't know, Mia. I was the *last* to know." He shook his head. "About five minutes after I arrived at the scene, a truck flew up, skidding to a stop inches from the ambulance. Chaos suddenly broke out. I didn't know what was happening then. I didn't care. I was kneeling at Rebecca's body—her *dead* body. Then I heard a scream, like a wounded animal. Someone ran over to me. I still didn't know what the hell was going on. This person—I don't remember who it was—began pulling me away as Mason sprinted toward us, screaming. They told me, right then and there. Literally as I was standing over my fiancée's dead body. The person said that Rebecca and Mason had been having an affair . . . everyone knew, Mia. Literally, the entire sheriff's department, half the town. It took four officers to hold me back. I watched him fall to his knees and cry like a baby over her body, while I tried to get to him so I could kill him."

"I'm so sorry," I whispered.

"The thing is," Easton said, his eyes unfocused, lost in the window, "Mason deserved her."

"What do you mean?"

"He loved her. God, he loved her. I could see it. He was madly in love with her."

"And you weren't?"

"No. I didn't care, Mia."

I frowned, confused but at the same time intrigued. My psycho-analytical instincts were piqued, knowing that this was likely a root to his tree of problems.

"What do you mean, you didn't care?" I pressed.

"I didn't love her. Never had." Easton's body stiffened. "I never cried. Not like he did. I didn't cry once."

"I don't believe that."

"It's the truth. I cared that her life ended, I cared for her family and her friends, but I didn't care that our relationship ended."

He expected me to scoff, to spit on him, but his shield was slowly beginning to lower.

I forced myself to remain silent and let him speak.

"Rebecca and I had a volatile relationship. We'd only dated a few months before getting engaged. I proposed because she gave me an ultimatum. I was forty years old, had never been married, no kids, and I knew I wanted a family. I'd never been in a serious relationship before her . . . never loved someone. I was gone a lot with the Marines, so my relationships were fleeting at best. I wanted more. A partner. And there she was. So what the hell was I doing?"

"So you asked."

"Yes. Because it felt like the normal thing to do. Little did I know at the time, what she saw in me was money, and what she saw in Mason was sex. They'd been in a relationship the entire time. That's what I cared about. It was more about the betrayal of it, not the loss of her. Isn't that fucked up?"

"You shouldn't feel guilty that you don't feel sad about losing someone you never loved."

He looked down.

"Is that why you wear her ring around your pinkie finger?"

Frowning, he blinked at me. "Why do you think it's her ring?"

"Well . . . I—I just figured, I guess."

"No, it's not hers. It's my mom's."

"Your mom's?"

He nodded, his eyes clouding with pain—real pain. "She died. In a car accident. When I was in college. She was on her way to see me."

And it was then that I realized why Easton Crew had given up on life. It wasn't just from his fiancée stepping out on him or from the guilt that he didn't care. It was from the guilt he was carrying from losing two women, both having monumental places in his life, to car accidents as they were on their way to him.

His stare was wide and a bit wild, like that of a scared child finding himself in a situation that he didn't quite know how to navigate.

"I'm not good at this stuff, Mia. With women, relationships, love," he whispered. "I'm fucked up."

"I know the feeling, Easton," I whispered as tears gathered.

I leaned forward and kissed him.

# Chapter Thirty-Nine

## Mia

This kiss was different from the one we'd shared in the woods.

Our first had been an explosion, a release of sexual tension, a surrendering to the lust. He'd devoured me like a man on death row, unable to control himself. It had been hot. Ravenous. The kiss had curled my toes, made me forget my own name. A kind of dizzying rush that, after you experienced your first taste, was all you ever wanted. Like a drug.

This kiss, though . . . this kiss was different. Softer, gentler, his fingertips slowly running down the side of my face as if he wanted to memorize every line of me.

Fingers ran over my scalp, through my hair, sending tingles racing over my skin. I felt a rush of heat below, an unfamiliar throbbing between my legs that ignited every sexual sensor in my body.

The room was dark, scarcely illuminated by the night-light, stealing my vision and increasing the sensitivity of his touch.

When I wrapped my arms around his neck, tugging him on top of me, he stopped. Pulled back.

"Mia . . ."

"No." I shook my head, desperation welling in my chest. "Don't. Please."

His brows creased with conflict. "But Mia, I—"

"No. I'm *not* broken, Easton. Don't treat me like I'm broken. Don't treat me like I'm dirty." I ripped the towel off my naked body. "I'm not dirty. See?" Tears rolled down my cheeks. I was shaking, trembling with emotion. "I'm *not* dirty."

"Oh, baby." Tears came as he leaned in, kissed my lips, my cheeks. "Don't ever say that again."

"Then don't ever treat me like that again. If I were a normal woman, you would take me right now. Take me, Easton," I begged shamelessly. "Take it away, please. Please. Erase it; replace it . . . with you."

He blinked, a tear escaping.

And then, like two magnets, we collided, rolling onto the center of the bed. I remember the heat of him, the smell—God, that smell that was Easton Crew.

As I stripped off his clothes, he took the towel dangling from my hands, the sweep of the soft fibers sending a wave of tickles across my legs. I couldn't get close enough to him. I wanted to crawl inside him. He was everywhere and, at the same time, not nearly close enough.

His tip found my opening, and my breath caught. I braced as he slowly slid into me, two lost souls becoming one. Two imperfect disasters that somehow, when united, found absolute peace.

*"Easton . . ."* My body tightened around him, as if he'd always belonged there.

Our eyes locked as he took his time settling into me, savoring every second of the moment.

I'll never forget how he cradled me in his arms as we moved together, as one, or the tear that dripped down his cheek as we climaxed together. The way he looked at me after, the way he stroked my forehead, gently kissed my face.

There were no butterflies, no fireworks . . . just absolute peace. For a single moment, everything was calm. Everything was right in the world.

"I'm afraid I'm going to fall in love with you, Mia Frost."

"I'm already there."

# Chapter Forty

DOCTOR: Let's talk about intimacy. Have you ever been in love?

PATIENT: No.

DOCTOR: That was an immediate response. Not even for a short time, perhaps?

PATIENT: No.

DOCTOR: This surprises me. Most people your age have experienced love at least once in their lifetime. But you haven't. Why do you think that is?

PATIENT: I'm not that lucky, I guess.

DOCTOR: So only the lucky experience love?

PATIENT: I'd say that's an accurate statement.

DOCTOR: Interesting.

PATIENT: Have you ever been in love?

DOCTOR: This isn't about me. How many relationships have you had?

PATIENT: A few.

DOCTOR: Tell me about them.

PATIENT: Not much to tell.

DOCTOR: Long term or short term?

PATIENT: Short.

DOCTOR: Why?

PATIENT: I . . . just didn't feel the way I was supposed to, I guess.

DOCTOR: So you ended these relationships?

PATIENT: Yes.

DOCTOR: Why do you think you didn't feel the way you were supposed to?

PATIENT: [No response.]

DOCTOR: It would really help me to help you if you allowed yourself to open up to me. Fully. We've been seeing each other for months now, and you have yet to speak openly about why you're here. I can't help but wonder why you keep coming back.

PATIENT: [No response.]

DOCTOR: I remember a few sessions ago when you spoke about the camping trip with your mother and father. You mentioned that when your father built the fire with you, you felt happy and worthy. I was wondering . . . do you still feel unworthy sometimes?

PATIENT: [No response.]

DOCTOR: Perhaps this feeling of being unworthy is tied to your lack of intimacy? Perhaps you don't feel worthy enough of love? After all, you said it yourself: only the lucky get to experience love.

PATIENT: [No response.]

DOCTOR: Okay, let's try something else. Complete this sentence—love makes me feel . . . what?

PATIENT: Indifferent.

DOCTOR: Intimacy makes me feel . . . what?

PATIENT: Uncomfortable.

DOCTOR: Sex makes me feel . . . what?

PATIENT: Angry.

DOCTOR: Why angry?

PATIENT: [*No response.*]

DOCTOR: I can see that you're angry now. Talk to me. Does sex make you angry because sex has been unpleasant for you?

PATIENT: You could say that.

DOCTOR: Because it's uncomfortable?

PATIENT: [*No response.*]

DOCTOR: Painful?

PATIENT: [*No response.*]

DOCTOR: Have you ever been intimate when you didn't want to be?

PATIENT: [*No response.*]

DOCTOR: Have you ever been forced to be intimate?

PATIENT: [*No response.*]

DOCTOR: Or intimate when you perhaps couldn't defend yourself, whether because of drugs, alcohol, size, or age?

PATIENT: [*No response.*]

DOCTOR: I'm sorry.

PATIENT: [*No response.*]

DOCTOR: Let's focus on the anger. How often do you feel this anger?

PATIENT: Every day.

DOCTOR: What does it feel like?

PATIENT: Suffocation.

DOCTOR: That sounds horrible. What is your reaction to this feeling?

PATIENT: [*No response.*]

DOCTOR: Do you cry?

PATIENT: No.

DOCTOR: Do you crawl into your bed and hide under the covers?

PATIENT: No.

DOCTOR: Do you lash out?

PATIENT: [*No response.*]

DOCTOR: Does the anger release in an explosion of emotions? Maybe at the most unexpected times?

PATIENT: [*No response.*]

DOCTOR: Is this anger directed at yourself?

PATIENT: [*No response.*]

DOCTOR: At others?

PATIENT: [*Silence.*]

DOCTOR: Okay . . . then, it's imperative now that this becomes our new focus, do you understand?

PATIENT: [*No response.*]

DOCTOR: Chronic anger, or spurts of uncontrollable anger, is common in people with PTSD. Our bodies' natural response to extreme threat is anger. It's our natural survival instinct to protect life. To fight. You seem to be stuck here, and it needs to be resolved before you get hurt or, worse, someone else gets hurt. How long have you been stuck?

PATIENT: A long time.

DOCTOR: In this "long time," how many things have you done that you regret?

PATIENT: There is no regret.

DOCTOR: None?

PATIENT: No.

DOCTOR: Why?

PATIENT: Because I'm not one of the lucky ones.

# Chapter Forty-One

## Mia

I awoke to the scent of fresh coffee mingling with crisp autumn air from an open window somewhere in my bedroom. I inhaled deeply, noting hints of bacon and toast mixed in there too. My stomach growled.

Then the pain registered.

I winced at the sensations running through my body, my shoulders, my elbows, my back, my head. My palms—bandaged like a boxer's hands—felt like they were on fire. All this from chopping at a tree?

Slowly, the memories of the day before began to trickle back. My mental breakdown. The ax. Deputy Mason showing up at my doorstep. The questioning.

The confession—*my* confession of my past.

The kiss, the *sex.*

*Easton.*

A different soreness registered then. One that sent a rush of heat between my legs and goose bumps over my skin.

I trailed my fingertips over my lips, where Easton's had been only hours earlier. My pulse picked up slightly. Butterflies fluttered in my stomach with an imbalance of feelings and emotions. A swinging pendulum of disappointment in myself for allowing my mental breakdown and pure bliss from making love to the man I was sure I was falling in love with. The only man who had ever made me feel safe, the only man I'd ever allowed myself to trust.

I sat up, pulling the covers tightly around my waist.

He'd kissed me, made love to me—despite my psychotic break-down, despite my confession of being raped in the most grotesque way. Not only that, but the sex had been incredible. I fell asleep within minutes after we'd climaxed together.

My stomach sank.

Had he stayed awake, riddled with regret? Had he showered right after, washing away the dirtiness that was me?

My mind began racing.

Had it been pity sex? Or had it been real?

What did I really know about real?

What was real? What was fake?

A silhouette appeared in the doorway, and our eyes met. Those butterflies exploded into a flurry.

Easton was wearing the same T-shirt and jeans that I'd stripped off him the night before. His hair was mussed. He hadn't showered.

"How are you feeling?"

Just the sound of his voice, so deep and smooth, sent tingles up my thighs. God, I was a mess.

I didn't respond. I didn't need to.

Easton parted the curtains and opened another window. The cool, fresh air rushed in. Sunlight glistened through the trees, sparkling like droplets of gold through the bright autumn colors.

It was a beautiful morning.

My robe was lying at the foot of the mattress. He picked it up, rounded the bed, and lowered next to me, the mattress sinking under his weight, pulling me to him like a magnet.

Our eyes met, two people assessing each other after a night that had changed everything. There was no going back.

When he tucked a strand of hair behind my ear, I melted into his touch.

"You okay?" he asked.

"Are you okay?" I said, cringing at the insecurity in my voice.

"Yes," he said simply. Confidently.

I smiled.

He opened his palm. "Let me see."

I pulled out my hands from under the comforter, and he examined the bandages.

"We'll leave them bandaged today, then clean them up and let them breathe tonight."

"Okay."

Easton stood, the robe in his hand, and helped me out of bed. Warm, soft cotton draped over my shoulders, and then his hand settled on my lower back as he guided me out of the bedroom and onto the back porch, shaded from the rising sun.

The patio chairs had been rearranged—better arranged—with one covered in the same flannel blanket he'd warmed me with the night before. He guided me into the chair, covered me with the blanket. A tray on the coffee table held two cups of coffee, scrambled eggs, bacon, and toast. Next to the napkin was a bottle of aspirin.

Easton placed the tray in my lap, took one cup of coffee, and settled in next to me. Without a word, he contemplated the woods and slowly sipped his coffee.

I followed his gaze.

My mouth dropped with a gasp. The dogwood tree, which I'd marred the night before, had been chopped down into nothing but firewood.

I gaped at him. "When did you do this?"

"Last night."

"Last night when?"

"This morning, I guess. After you fell asleep." He sipped again. "And after speaking with your neighbor."

"What?" I sat up, sloshing coffee onto the tray. "You talked to Old Lady Lou?"

"I did. You really should try her pumpkin pie. She said she put one on your doorstep when you moved here, but you never touched it."

"It could have been poisoned for all I knew." I snorted out a shocked laugh. "What the hell? What time did you talk to her?"

"Oh, she was up, trust me. I waved into the binoculars she was pointing out of the window sometime around four this morning. I decided to pay her a visit, and after an unfortunate incident with the business end of a rifle, she apologized—after realizing who I was—and invited me inside. We had a nice chat about privacy."

"Are you saying she's not going to say anything about last night?"

"Yes, I can guarantee that Old Lady Lou isn't going to say anything about what happened last night. But as for Mason . . ." Easton's jaw twitched, and he lifted his shoulder.

"What did you say to her?"

"Nothing about what we spoke about last night. I didn't tell her anything about your past."

"Thank you." I took a deep breath and sipped my coffee, processing. "What does she look like?"

"The rumor of the wart is true."

"No!"

He grinned. "Yep. Right there on the tip of her nose. Hair growing out of it and everything."

"No." I wrinkled my nose, scowling at the food on my lap.

He chuckled. "Nice lady. Her grandson just joined the Army Reserve. I'm going to take him through our course."

"Ah . . . I see. So *that* was the deal. She stays quiet about seeing me freak out last night, and you give her grandson a free ride through one of the most prestigious tracking courses in the country."

Easton winked, then sipped.

I regarded what remained of the tree, the little red house with the big black truck in the distance just past it.

"Do you think Mason will tell anyone?"

"Yes."

"I do too." I groaned, imagining the gossip spreading like butter over flapjacks at the local diner, probably at that very minute.

Scowling, I grabbed a piece of bacon and shoved it into my mouth.

We sat in silence, watching the sun rise and the woods awaken with movement. I nibbled on my food, realizing my blood sugar was completely out of whack from the amount of wine I'd drunk the night before.

I considered the tree that had once symbolized rape but was now chopped into a hundred little pieces by the man sitting next to me. Easton had literally destroyed a source of pain in my life. He'd taken care of it, *for me*.

*I* was being taken care of.

"Thank you again," I said. "Thank you for everything, Easton."

"I want to know what your story last night has to do with Cullen Nichols."

I blinked at the question that had been apparently bursting to come out of him. *The* question. I should have known he would link the two together. He'd been suspicious of Cullen since day one, and also of our relationship.

I sipped my coffee, buying time while I considered how to respond. In the end, I was too tired to hide anymore.

After all, Easton had seen all my sharp edges now.

"I met Cullen a few months after we opened our business here. Like I already told you and McNamara, he came to my clinic, ironically enough, inquiring about hypnotherapy." I snorted at the irony that hypnotherapy had led him to accusing me of being the Black Cat Stalker. "Long story short, we got into a discussion, and it turns out that he and

I share very similar pasts. He'd also lost a parent at a very young age and had been bullied in school."

Taking a deep breath, I began fidgeting with the napkin on the tray.

"I got the impression he'd been raped, too, but likely hadn't told anyone."

Easton was staring into the tree line, his face tight, his brows pulled in concentration.

"Men get raped too," I said. "Did you know that? And statistically, they're even less likely than women to admit it because they're so embarrassed."

"And so, what? He couldn't get over it, so he came to you?" There was a coldness, a lack of empathy, in Easton's voice that I didn't like.

"Yes. He was seeking alternative therapy like CBT and hypnosis. That's why he came to me specifically. He said he'd tried everything. He was desperate."

"And you began treating him."

"Yes. For obvious reasons, I felt a connection to him that I kind of latched onto. I wanted to help him—like I couldn't be helped. I wanted to know there was hope. First, I set him up with Jo, our psychiatrist, who started him on a conservative antidepressant regimen. Then he and I met once a week for a long time. I thought I was making progress, that I was helping him . . ."

I shook my head.

"Which is why I'm so shocked that he accused me of attacking him. I don't understand it." I looked at Easton. "Do you still think I didn't do it?"

He stared at me for a long moment, long enough to make me think he'd considered it. "No, Mia, I don't think you did it. I don't think you're experiencing dissociative amnesia."

"Why?"

"Gut instinct."

I nodded.

Easton plucked a clear plastic bag from the side of the chair. Inside was a single brown feather. He laid it on the tray on my lap.

I recognized it instantly as the feather I'd gathered from the scene of my attack, that I kept secure and secret in the velvet pouch I'd shown him the night before.

"How closely have you looked at this feather?" he asked.

"I know every blade and dip in it," I said.

"Then you also know there's a strand of hair wrapped around the middle of it."

"What?"

"Yep. There's a small strand of very dark hair wrapped around the middle of it."

My lips parted as I held the feather to the light, examining it closely.

"On the end." Easton leaned forward. "Look closely. There's one, maybe two strands of almost black hair tangled around the middle."

"Oh my God, you're right." My heart was kick-started in my chest. "I've never looked at it that closely. Is it human hair?"

"I don't know."

"It's probably mine," I said, my mind racing. "From when I hit my head on the tree."

"You don't have black hair. You have light-brown hair."

"You're right. It is someone else's—and if it is the Black Cat, this is the first piece of real evidence to link him to my attack."

Easton took the bag from my fingertips, studying the feather that he'd apparently examined last night while I'd been sleeping. "That's exactly what we need to confirm. With your permission, I'd like to have it tested for DNA."

"What if it's an animal's hair?"

"It's not an animal's hair, Mia. It's not coarse like an animal's."

"What would you do? Call Sheriff McNamara?"

"No."

"Why?"

"It would take weeks for him to go through the red tape, and that's assuming he would even do it. Even though there are similarities between what happened to you twenty years ago and what happened to Courtney Hayes last week, you can't deny the huge gap in time between attacks. And not only that, your case isn't his case; it's not his jurisdiction. I spoke with the Dallas PD this morning. The officers that assisted in your case are no longer there."

"But my file is. They have to consider it at least, don't they? I mean, it's evidence, right?"

Easton shook his head as if I wasn't understanding. "Okay. Would you like to drive this feather up to Dallas today and convince them to spend money they don't have, time they don't have, and manpower they don't have, to test for DNA on what may be animal hair—from a twenty-year-old cold case?"

"No, I don't. Hell no, I don't."

"Also, Mia, I don't trust Mason. I don't trust him with this information."

I nodded. I couldn't blame him. "Neither Mason nor McNamara have reached out again about Cullen accusing me of beating him."

"Because they have nothing on you, Mia. He said it under hypnosis after getting his head beaten in. There's no way in hell that any sane person would consider that alone enough to arrest you. They'd need to have something else. Something that proved you were with him, or something like that. Anyway, I'm hoping we won't even have to worry about it much longer if we can get a name from this feather."

I closed my eyes, inhaling what felt like hope. "So what are you going to do?"

"Alek Romanov is a former Fed. I'm going to use one of his resources at the FBI. Have the feather overnighted this morning to Virginia and have them scan it immediately—with your approval."

"But what about the chain of evidence? If they do uncover my attacker's DNA, it won't hold up in court because you went around traditional protocol."

"You know a lot about the system."

"Yeah, unfortunately. I wish I didn't, trust me."

"Well, you're right. This evidence wouldn't hold up in court, but for more reasons than just that. Yes, I would technically be breaking protocol by going around the red tape to get it tested, but *you* broke protocol twenty years ago by removing it from the scene. Who's to say you didn't plant the hair yourself? Or that the hair wasn't intertwined in the feather long before your attack?"

I blinked, processing.

Easton was right.

He continued, "What I want to do with this piece of evidence won't be on the books, Mia. It's the only—and fastest—way I think we can get it done right now. If the DNA is in the system, I get a name; that's the bottom line. I find the bastard. If your attacker also happens to be the Black Cat Stalker, then I'll find something to provide to the police for them to link him, and bada bing, done. This particular piece of evidence will be irrelevant to the case at that point. We'll know it's him and then will put all our resources to finding something else to connect him. Kind of like Al Capone. The police could never link him to murders, even though they knew he was responsible, so they eventually got him on tax evasion."

"And what if my attacker *isn't* the Black Cat? What if it's just some random guy?"

His look sent chills up my arms. "Then I know some people. Off the books."

Meaning what Easton would do when he found the guy also wouldn't be on the record.

Nerves tickled my stomach.

Chewing my bottom lip, I squinted at the withered leaves from the dogwood tree. The chunks of chopped wood scattered along the tree line. A piece of my past obliterated.

I wanted to obliterate it all. Finally face it and finally forget it. And dammit, I was ready to fight.

"You have my permission. Let's get this son of a bitch."

# Chapter Forty-Two

## Easton

I sped up the driveway to our headquarters, the little brown feather burning a hole in my pocket. Beckett and Alek were at the bottom of the hill with a group of trainees.

Heads turned as my truck skidded to a stop next to the front door. Beckett and Alek began jogging up the hill, yelling orders to the trainees to stay put.

I stepped into my office, the men following a minute later. Everyone's focus dropped to the plastic bag containing the feather I'd placed in the center of my desk.

I booted up the computer. "Alek, I need you to reach out to your contact at the FBI. There are a few strands of hair intertwined in this feather that might possibly be linked to the Black Cat Stalker. I need a name."

"You mean you want it tested for DNA?"

"Yes. And I need it now."

"Does this have anything to do with the chewing tobacco you had me send in?"

Beckett and Alek glanced at each other.

"Possibly," I said, choosing to ignore the loaded scrutiny in front of me. "But this hair just became priority number one. Can one of your connections help?"

Alek picked up the bag and examined the feather. "For something like this . . . I'd call a former operative for the German government named Diesel Beck."

"German? What does he do for the United States FBI?"

"Espionage."

"He's a secret agent?"

Ignoring the question, Alek tilted his head, studying the bag. "When do you need it by?"

"Now. Immediately. As soon as possible."

Beckett folded his arms over his chest. "This has to do with Dr. Frost, doesn't it?"

"No root," Alek said, interrupting.

I looked up from the computer. "No what?"

"No root. There's no root attached to the ends of these strands."

"So?"

"So you need a root to get DNA."

"I don't care. Find a way."

Alek sniffed, considering. "There's a new—*very* new—method of extracting DNA from rootless strands of hair."

"Great. Do it."

"It's not that easy, Chief, and also highly fallible. It's cutting-edge technology. They haven't worked out the kinks yet."

"Tell them to work it out on this."

"It's extremely expensive."

"I'll pay."

"Wait just a fucking second." Beckett stepped forward. "What am I missing here?"

All eyes narrowed on me.

"Why are *we* doing this? How are *you* directly involved in the Black Cat Stalker case?" Beckett asked.

I hesitated—something I never did with my team.

What was this woman doing to me?

Beckett's brow cocked. "Or maybe my question should be: How involved are you with Mia Frost?"

"That's none of your goddamn business."

"It is," Beckett said, "if you're about to spend a hundred thousand bucks on some bullshit experimental test, on the off chance you might get a hit from an old strand of hair that somehow involves a woman you just met."

"Without even talking to us first," Alek added. "Do I need to remind you that I am the CFO of this company?"

My spine stiffened as three disapproving faces glared at me.

"The next person to question my instincts will be fired immediately. Is that understood?"

A moment of tense silence filled the room.

Alek spoke first. "Fine—I'll make a call. I'll update you within the hour." He turned and strode into the hall.

Beckett closed the door behind him and turned back to me, scowling. "Listen, man. I don't know what the fuck is going on with you, but you need to look at the facts here. Courtney Hayes made an appointment with Dr. Frost days before she was attacked. Seems like an interesting coincidence, considering that just a few days ago, Mia Frost brutally attacked another one of her clients, the accusation coming straight from his lips—"

"Allegedly," I snapped, noting that the coincidences actually went far beyond those.

Beckett didn't know that years earlier, Mia had also been raped with a stick in the woods, just like Courtney Hayes. He also didn't know that she'd recently gone HAM on a tree outside her backyard, in what appeared to have been a violent mental break.

"Whatever," he said. "Point is, seems to me that this is a very complicated woman, and getting mixed up with complicated and notorious women isn't good for business, Chief."

I opened my mouth to defend Mia, but I couldn't. Considering how it looked through Beckett's eyes, I couldn't ignore that a part of me—the unemotional me—did wonder if she'd attacked Cullen Nichols and Courtney Hayes. If she was the Black Cat Stalker.

Was Mia subconsciously acting out what had happened to her in some sort of fucked-up revenge release? The woman had been through an inexplicable horror at a very young age. The kind of evil that festers and changes someone to the very core.

The memory of her with the ax filled my thoughts. The sheer rage in her. The pain.

*Fuck.*

"I don't want to do this with you right now, Beck."

"I know you don't, but someone has to slap some sense into you. Just answer me this: Are you sure this chick is worth it?"

I looked away. A moment stretched between us.

"We'll see." Closing down that conversation, I refocused on the computer. "Did you talk to Henrick?"

"Yes, as you demanded, I called him this morning. He's back in Louisiana, spoke to the guy myself. Made up some bullshit that I was calling to check on him after you so brutally failed him from your course and derailed his military career. It was awkward as fuck—thanks for that."

"When did he leave Skull Hollow?"

"With the team, two days ago."

"You verify that?"

"Yep. With him and the airline."

That left Mason—and Mason only.

"Where the hell is Loren?" I asked.

"Haven't seen her today. Listen," Beckett said as he took a step back. "I've got to get going."

"Where?"

"Town."

"For what?"

"Errands. Want me to check on your girl?"

*My girl.*

I realized I didn't like him talking about her. I didn't like *anyone* talking about her. The tension was thicker than when the room had been filled.

"That'll be all, Beckett."

My business partner nodded, turned, and opened the door, just as Loren's silhouette disappeared down the hall.

# Chapter Forty-Three

## Mia

Gossip had spread like wildfire. The town was in an uproar with one general consensus: Mia Frost was a sick psychopath.

Innocent until proven guilty? Not in Skull Hollow.

The clinic had been egged, and our mailbox had been beaten to nothing more than a twisted pile of metal.

According to my lawyer, the police had visited Cullen Nichols several times since he'd accused me of being the Black Cat Stalker. Refusing to come to them, he'd remained hidden within the four walls of his home.

But Easton was right. Apparently, the cops had nothing on me, even though they seemed to be searching desperately for anything to incriminate me.

Also, going against my lawyer's advice, I left the sanctuary of my home, pulling myself together the best I could for an emergency team meeting at the office to discuss how to combat the bad press.

Jo, Luna, and Stella showed their true colors that day. A loyalty to both me and the clinic, and a steadfast resolve to do whatever was necessary to maintain business as usual.

I decided to keep to myself the news of my tree-chopping mental breakdown and the fact that Easton Crew had stayed the night with me. I wanted to ride out the short time of anonymity until Mason allowed that news to slip into the public. I had no doubt it would be revealed soon enough—along with the headline of my past, which also hadn't yet been discovered.

More secrets, more hiding. More struggling to keep up the ridiculous charade of my life.

Controlling my anxiety was becoming an hourly struggle. Every decision I made, big or small, was questioned, analyzed, dissected.

Doubted.

I was losing my footing, with myself, with reality, and with the world around me. I'd slipped into a constant state of paranoia, waiting for the past to be unearthed. For everyone to discover that I was nothing but a fraud, a deeply damaged woman who had no right being entrusted with other people's confessions.

Filled with dread, I waited for the memory to return. To confirm that I had, in fact, attacked my patient Cullen Nichols and had simply experienced another bout of dissociative amnesia like I had decades earlier. Perhaps interviewing Courtney Hayes had ignited the pain from my past in ways that I didn't realize, and Cullen had served as the trigger that had made me snap. He and I shared such very similar pasts, after all.

I was also waiting for Easton to push me away, to tell me he didn't think of me that way and wasn't interested in any kind of relationship. The old "it's not you, it's me" speech.

The man was making me absolutely crazy. If anything, I was more confused now than when we'd first met.

Easton spent the evenings at my house, "swinging by" after work, citing some bullshit reason, although we both knew he was there to check on me. He'd stay for hours, though he never stayed the night.

We had sex every night, sometimes the moment he walked through the door. Unable to resist the intense, visceral attraction between us, we surrendered to each other—no words, no drama, no awkwardness, no complications. Just mind-blowing sex that somehow got better every time.

Afterward, we fell into routine, easily. Organically. Comfortably.

Sometimes we would talk about random things, and sometimes we wouldn't talk at all. Sometimes we weren't even in the same room. He'd rake and burn leaves outside, while I remained inside, sipping wine while secretly watching him from the window.

The first night, he finished chopping up the dogwood tree and assembled a tidy pile of firewood for the coming winter. I believe this night he was avoiding my pet birds, who had yet to warm up to having a visitor in the house.

The second night, Easton walked in like a man on a mission, ready to face—*attempt* to accept—the aviary that was my home. He cooked for me that night. Chicken-fried steak, mashed potatoes, gravy, and steamed snap peas. A manly dinner just like him, and dammit, the man could cook.

Goldie had taken an unusual interest in Easton, slowly circling his feet as he moved about the house, the yard, while he hilariously stifled his annoyance and ignored her. A theme, I was realizing.

And yet, despite this, I was in love with him.

And it scared the ever-loving shit out of me.

Deciding I couldn't go on like this, I made the decision to tell him about my feelings.

And then the world turned upside down on me.

It was just after six, and I was on my way home from the office. It had started raining, dark, ominous clouds rolling into town like a black tidal wave, stealing the sunlight and the warmth with it. Temperatures were expected to fall near freezing that night.

I noticed the light as I drove deeper into the thicket, an eerie gray swaying around the pines.

The rain turned into a deluge, heavy drops exploding against my windshield. My wipers struggled to keep up.

I was tired. My head hurt, my body, my hands. The simple knee-length white sheath dress I'd worn to work that day suddenly felt restricting against my chest, the navy jacket over it feeling more like a straitjacket.

When I clicked on the high beams, two headlights suddenly appeared behind me in my rearview mirror. I took a corner, and the car disappeared from sight, then reappeared even closer.

Nerves tickled my stomach.

I shifted in my seat, sliding my hands to the correct ten- and two-o'clock positions on the wheel, keeping one eye on the rearview mirror. I braked around another corner, the vehicle again out of sight, then hit the gas as I came out of the corner. The vehicle emerged from the corner behind me at a speed far too fast for conditions.

It was a truck, not a car, I realized then. A big black truck.

Frantic, I scanned the sides of the road for a place to pull over and let the asshole pass. But there was nothing but long lines of pines and steep drop-offs.

My heart pounded. That tingle of fear, that instinct that I'd ignored so long ago, was screaming at me.

*You're in danger. Don't ignore it.*

I slowly pressed the gas, my sole focus now to get away from whoever the hell was behind me. My knuckles turned white against the steering wheel as panic began to take hold.

My phone was buried at the bottom of my purse. How could I reach it to call for help?

In the rearview mirror, the truck was no more than a few inches from my bumper. Fear zipped through me.

A sharp curve caught me by surprise. I hit the brakes, my tires slipping on the wet pavement.

The steering wheel jerked out of my hand. Overcompensating, I yanked the wheel in the opposite direction, attempting to regain control. The Jeep jolted and then careened into the ditch, clipping a tree. I jerked the wheel again, sending my vehicle shooting across the road.

The last thing I remember was my windshield exploding as my Jeep tumbled over the edge into a ravine.

# Chapter Forty-Four

## Easton

My phone rang from the console of my truck.

"Hello, is this Mr. Crew?"

I recognized the voice instantly. "Ms. Lou, is everything okay?"

"Well, dear, that's why I'm calling. You asked me to call if anything seemed suspicious regarding Dr. Frost . . . you told me I could call anytime."

I straightened in my seat and turned down the radio. "That's right. What's going on?"

"Well, I was just on my way home. You know that really sharp corner right before the turnoff to her house? The one with the steep wooded drop-off?"

"Yes—what's going on?"

"Well, I don't know . . . I could be seeing things, but it seems there are red lights glowing from down in the ravine."

I hit the brakes.

Lou said, "I could be seeing things; you know my cataracts are acting up. And with all this rain and stuff, this weather is just terrible, you know. The roads are slick—"

"Are you saying taillights? When you say red lights, do you mean you think you saw taillights in the ravine?"

"Yes, yes, that's what I'm saying. And I'm not sure, but it looks like a gray car, kind of reminded me of the color of Dr. Frost's Jeep."

As Lou continued, I did a U-turn in the middle of the road, my pulse skyrocketing.

"So I drove to her house instead of mine, and sure enough, her Jeep isn't there. I thought about calling the cops but remembered that you sure didn't appreciate when I called them last time on her, so I thought I'd give you a ring first."

"You did the right thing, Ms. Littles." My tires spun around a corner. "Are you home now?"

"Yes."

"Good. Stay there and lock the doors. I'll be by to check on you in a bit. Don't unlock the door for anyone, do you understand? Not the cops—no one."

"Wait . . . should I be concerned here?"

"No, ma'am. Better safe than sorry."

"All right, dear, you—"

I ended the call and dialed the office. "Beckett, I need you and the boys to meet me on County Road 2883, at the sharp curve about two miles in. Bring the truck, medic bag, everything for emergency rescue."

"Mia?"

"Yes. Now. Come now, Beckett."

I hung up and tried Mia's cell phone. No answer. Again, and again, and again.

My heart pounded against my rib cage as I barreled down the narrow two-lane road, fighting flashbacks of a very similar call only a year earlier. Flashbacks of my fiancée's bloody body facedown on the asphalt, her car a crushed pile of metal in the trees. Memories of my father calling me to tell me that my mother had died on her way to see me.

Panic seized me, and I pressed the gas pedal harder. I had to get to Mia. I couldn't be too late.

*Not this time.*

The rain blew sideways that night, my windshield wipers unable to keep up with the blasts of water pummeling my truck. Lightning pierced the night, a bright violent slash against the pitch-black sky, its jagged tip disappearing into the tops of trees in the distance. A bolt of thunder rattled the truck.

Deciding to take a shortcut, I braked at a stop sign, sending papers flying around the cab. I yanked the wheel and hit the gas, screeching onto a narrow paved road that only hunters used. My back tires spun out before the truck jolted forward. A gust of wind shook the truck, a swirl of leaves obstructing my view as if someone had thrown a bucket of them from overhead.

I was driving blind that night, flying fifty miles an hour over a dangerous country road with nothing but the blurred spotlight of my headlights illuminating the path ahead.

The woods closed in around me, thick gnarled bushes dragging down the sides of my truck like loud squeals of a pig moments before slaughter.

I emerged from the woods and onto the two-lane as a family of deer burst from the tree line, tails up, their white flags flashing in the headlights. I didn't brake, steeling myself for the impact a split second before the last deer leaped into the trees, missing the hood of my truck by an inch.

Below, two red dots glowed through the darkness. I hit the brakes and slid into the ditch.

My heart hammered as I threw myself out of the truck and took off at a sprint down the cracked pavement. Cold rain battered my face like needles as I ran blind, focused on nothing but the two red lights barely visible through the darkness.

It reminded me of that night, so long ago, when I'd lost my fiancée. The pounding buzz of rain against the thick canopy of trees above, the deafening white noise against a chorus of katydids screaming into the night.

My boot heel came down hard in a deep rut, splashing water into the air. I stumbled as I hit another, noting the fresh skid marks on the pavement.

"Mia!"

Flattened weeds and bushes and broken tree limbs led the way to the silver Jeep, hood down, deep in a thicket of trees, its body suspended in the branches of a massive oak spearing up from the bottom of the ravine. The Jeep was covered in leaves and debris from the woods it had plowed through.

The grade was steep, about 20 percent, I estimated, based on the angle at which the car was wedged. Its nose was down, the headlights illuminating the massive trunk just beyond the smashed hood. Wet leaves and raindrops sparkled eerily in the headlights. The smell of fresh sap was ripe in the air.

A large branch lay across the windshield. The *ding-ding-ding* of the open-door alert carried on the wind like a haunting song.

My view of inside the Jeep was obstructed, but I could tell that there was no movement—or sound, for that matter—coming from the cab.

"Mia!" I shouted again, my panic all-consuming.

I crouched and threw myself over the edge of the ravine, securing my footing on a ledge. Brushes grew from the rock's crevices, scraping my arms and neck and face as I climbed down, the wind and rain threatening my balance.

I kept screaming her name, over and over and over again.

I climbed as close to the Jeep as I could, but it was just out of reach.

"*Fuck!* . . . Mia! Answer me!"

Frantic, I looked around, searching for any kind of connection to the tree that the Jeep was suspended in. There was nothing within reach, so I'd have to jump, catch myself on a limb, and pray to God that the Jeep didn't dislodge and fall to the rocky bottom of the ravine.

Holding on to nothing but a few brittle branches for support, I took aim, leaped off the ledge, and caught myself on a branch. Leaves rained around me. The Jeep jostled at the addition of my weight on the tree, the groan of metal against metal sending my heart through my throat before it finally resettled again. I released an exhale. Slowly, I began edging my way to the car, holding on to the branch. I was coming up on the passenger side.

"Mia!" I yelled again. "Mia, are you okay?"

And then I heard it. The sweetest sound, my name from the sweetest lips.

"Mia!" My hands trembled as I slowly edged down the branch, raindrops running down my face. "Are you okay?"

"Yes," she whisper-hissed. Her fear was palpable.

"You're okay. I'm right here. I'm going to get you out. You're okay, Mia. I'm here."

I still couldn't see her. Intensely focused on her, I didn't hear the shouts coming from the road above.

I continued to cross the branch, and to this day, I don't know how it held my weight. Divine intervention is the only explanation.

Finally, I made it to the passenger-side window, one foot on the trunk of the tree and another on a branch. I angled myself so that I could see in the window.

I didn't dare touch the car.

Mia was hunched down in the driver's seat, bent at an awkward angle, having narrowly escaped the branch that had pierced her windshield. The branch was inches from impaling her. She was still strapped into her seat belt, very likely the thing that had saved her life. Her eyes were wild and red rimmed, her skin pale, raw fear etched in her face.

But she was alive.

"You're okay, Mia. Help is on the way. You're okay. You're okay." I scanned every inch of what I could see of her body. No blood or cuts, nothing that appeared life threatening.

She was wearing white, a white dress like an angel's.

A rush of relief washed over me.

*She's okay. Mia is okay.*

With this reassurance, I snapped into rescue mode. "I'm going to make my way around to your side of the car. I don't want you to move—not a muscle, okay?"

She nodded.

"Hang tight," I said, then winked.

The laugh that came out of her sounded like a choking bullfrog.

Carefully, I made my way around the tree, testing my weight on each branch, while also careful not to jostle the one that was holding the Jeep in place. The moment I reached the other side of the Jeep, something dropped onto the roof of the car. I looked at the rope, then up at the three large silhouettes looming over the ledge, backlit by headlights.

Beckett, Alek, and Dane.

Right on time.

I grabbed the rope and yanked a few times, not that I needed to. There was no need to test my team's capabilities.

We were losing light, and the winds were picking up. This needed to happen soon.

I made my way to the driver's side window, and Mia exhaled the moment our eyes met, hers filled with tears.

"Not now," I said, fighting my own emotions. "We need to focus now. Here's what's going to happen. First, I want you to release your seat belt. Then I want you to gently loop this rope around your wrist like this." I demonstrated on myself. "Then grab it with your other hand."

Mia nodded.

I threaded the rope through the open window and watched her grab it like a life preserver.

"I'm going to see if I can open the door enough that you can get out that way. I don't want to pull you through the window because the sudden shift in weight distribution could dislodge it."

She nodded.

A blast of wind shook the tree. I saw the panic in her, so desperate I could feel it between us.

As the open-door alert continued to ding, I slowly opened the door wider, breaking away the thin branches and twigs from its path. Although it was probably only a few seconds, the time this took felt agonizingly long as we both held our breaths.

The door caught on a branch, stuck. I shifted my weight, maneuvering onto another branch, and slowly leaned over, reaching through the gap in the door. Our hands clasped.

We exhaled in unison.

"Good. Good job. Okay. Next, as smoothly as you can, I want you to slide out of the seat, out of the car. I'm going to be holding on to you the whole time. If the car shifts, let go of me and hold on to that rope around your wrist. Got it?"

Another nod.

"On three. One, two, three."

The world seemed to stop as Mia slowly, smoothly shifted from the seat, pulling her legs up and eventually crawling out.

She fell into my arms and heaved out a relieved sob.

Smiling, I gave her frantic, panicked kisses of relief.

"Oh my God," she choked out, her voice shaking.

Hell, I was shaking too.

"I know. Good job, but we're not there yet." I grabbed the harnesses that the team had tossed down while I was opening the door. "I'm going to slip this on you first, then me. I'll hold on to the rope and onto you with my other hand, then swing us out of the tree and onto the ledge. Then it's smooth sailing."

"Swing us?"

"Yes. Just about two feet. It's going to be okay. We're almost there."

Her eyes shot up to the road, a new fear widening them. "Up there—he could still be there. S-someone did this, Easton," she stuttered. "Someone ran me off the road."

"Someone ran you off the road?" Heat shot up the back of my neck, that primal instinct to protect what was mine beginning to rage.

"Yes. A big black truck. Came out of nowhere. Rode my bumper until I drove too fast. I was scared. He tapped my bumper, and I fishtailed around a corner, hit a tree, and lost control. Did you see him?"

"Are you sure it was a man?"

"Yes. I mean, no, I guess not. Did you see him? P-pass him? A b-black truck?" She maniacally stuttered out the half sentences, and I could tell she was spiraling out of control. "A black truck. Did you pass one? Is it there?"

"No." I frowned, her mental well-being suddenly becoming my main worry. "No one was here when I got here. And I didn't pass a car on the way."

She squinted up at the road. "He's gone then. We have to find him." She gripped my sleeve, panic contorting her face. "We have to find him. The Black Cat Stalker, it's him. I know it's him. He ran me off the road and left me to die in the woods, just like he did back then. It's him. I know it. He's here. He's come back for me. We have to find—"

"Mia, stop. Take a breath."

Glancing up, I noticed a crowd had gathered up at the road; then I refocused on Mia. Her face was distorted in the darkness, pale, still etched with panic.

I pictured the road that I'd jogged across moments earlier. There was only one set of skid marks.

*One . . . only one.*

And for the first time, I wondered if the gossips were right.

Had the town psychologist finally lost it?

# Chapter Forty-Five

## Mia

The next few hours were a blur. The rain was abating, the thicket so dark you couldn't see a foot in front of your face. Flashlights had been positioned throughout the scene. Klieg lights were on their way.

Deputy Mason was among the first to arrive at the scene, followed shortly after by the Skull Hollow Fire Department.

In a train wreck of sobs and spasms, I told the deputy everything, including the fact that I believed the man who'd run me off the road was the Black Cat Stalker, and that I believed it was the same man who had raped me in Dallas at age sixteen, blurting out the confession like a prisoner being dragged to the electric chair.

This news hit with the subtlety of a nuclear bomb, stunning the man speechless. I could practically see his wheels begin to turn with all the coincidences:

*The woman who was accused of brutally beating a man happens to be a victim of assault herself.*

*She knows or is linked to both Courtney Hayes and Cullen Nichols, both victims of the Black Cat.*

*Mia Frost is the thread that connects it all.*

Soon, one thing became painfully obvious—Mason, and everyone else, didn't believe me. They didn't believe someone had run me off the road. They questioned my story about being raped years earlier.

They believed I was a dangerous woman who'd lost all sense of reality.

Mason suggested I'd been driving too fast. Distracted, perhaps. Only one set of skid marks indicated this, he explained, as well as the fact that the only damage to my car was from the tree I'd slammed into. There was nothing, not even a scratch on my bumper, to indicate someone had tapped me, thereby spinning me out of control.

Easton remained quiet during the interviews, a looming hostile presence like a bomb about to explode. While he never left my side, he didn't defend me, either, and I couldn't help but wonder if he doubted my story too. Or if he was embarrassed by me.

I hated the stares I was getting.

*No one* believed me.

Despite this, a fucked-up part of me was relieved by the confession of my past. I'd expected it to come to light at some point, and honestly, now that the truth was out, it felt like a weight off my shoulders.

I'd been living a fraudulent life since the day my virginity had been so brutally taken from me, one filled with hypocrisy and secrets, with shame and guilt. I hated myself. I'd built an entire life around helping victims accept and overcome their struggles, while I allowed my own to infect every thought and decision I made on a daily basis. I was a fake, someone pretending to be who they weren't. A mask of perfection hiding an imposter inside.

The Bible says all secrets come to light, one way or another. It is the law of hypocrisy, the final judgment. According to the Bible, the question we should ask ourselves is not how to keep these secrets secure but rather how to prepare for when they come to light.

Luke 12:2–3 says that there is nothing covered that shall not be revealed, and what is spoken in darkness shall soon be heard in the light.

And then there's Ecclesiastes 12:14. "He will bring every act to judgment, everything which is hidden, whether it is good or evil."

The deputy's phone rang.

He glanced at me, and I knew my time for judgment had begun.

# Chapter Forty-Six

## Mia

"Dr. Mia Frost, you are under arrest for assault and battery of Cullen Nichols." Deputy Mason nodded to a nearby officer as he slid his phone back into his pocket.

The baby-faced twentysomething grabbed my elbow. "Arms behind your back, ma'am."

Panic jolted like lightning through my body. "What the hell are you talking about?"

I searched the crowd for Easton but couldn't find him.

"You're under arrest for the assault and battery of Cullen Nichols."

I jerked away my arm, frantically scanning the crowd. *Where is he?*

Deputy Mason glared coldly at me. "I strongly suggest that you cooperate right now."

I focused on the flashlight beams bouncing off the bottom of the ravine.

"Dr. Frost—"

"Get your fucking hands off me."

Why wasn't Easton by my side now? Why wasn't he protecting me as he'd done since the moment we'd met?

A crowd began to gather.

My world spun as my hands were cuffed and my Miranda rights were read. As I continued to search for Easton, my chest felt like it was closing in, and I pulled back.

"*No!*" I barked, struggling again against the cuffs, claustrophobia taking hold. "No!"

"Dr. Frost." Mason gripped my other arm. "We have enough evidence to arrest you for the assault on your client Cullen Nichols. You need to—"

"Because he said it was me? Under hypnosis? That's enough to arrest me?"

"That, and because we now have proof that you were in the woods, in the same area where Nichols was attacked, on the exact day he was attacked."

My breath caught. "No, you don't understand. I . . . I was in the woods that day because I was retracing Courtney's steps to build your profile of the Black Cat." My head began to spin. "I must have wandered . . ."

Where the *hell* was Easton?

My breathing shallowed as I went from alarmed to trying to manage the panic attack creeping up. "Y-you think I'm the Black Cat Stalker? No . . . no, I don't understand," I said breathlessly. "I need to understand. How do you know this, that I was in the woods?"

"I just received a call from Sheriff McNamara. We have video proof of your presence in the woods where Cullen was attacked. According to the video, you seemed extremely upset. Expressing odd, emotionally distraught behavior."

"You're *lying*."

The deputy's hand tightened around my elbow.

"No, ma'am. The LYNX Group voluntarily supplied the video from cameras they have set up in the area to observe their tracking groups."

My heart dropped, shattering to a million pieces at my feet.

"Recorded you clear as day," he said, "visibly upset, crying, running erratically through the woods."

The man guided me to his truck. I stumbled, dropping my body weight, but Mason jerked me upright.

"Dr. Frost, I *strongly* suggest that you remain calm and cooperative for questioning. I have no doubt that your friends at the Dragonfly Clinic will post bail. But if you resist any longer, it's at your own peril. We have the victim saying it was you and now video proof of you in the woods. I need you to cooperate right now."

I felt the blood drain from my face.

Easton had supplied video proof of me? Easton had *betrayed* me?

"Lawyer," I choked out. "I need to call—"

Mason dipped his chin. "That can be arranged."

On the way to the sheriff's department, I didn't speak. Not a single word other than confirming my name, birthday, and address as I was booked into the Skull County Jail.

# Chapter Forty-Seven

## Easton

"Where the fuck is she? Where's Mia—where's Mason? Where the fuck is *Mason?*"

"Chief. Easton. *Stop.*" Beckett grabbed my arm as I frantically scanned the road. We'd been down in the ravine, searching for more clues or evidence. I left Mia alone for ten minutes—ten *fucking* minutes.

"Stop, Easton. Fucking *stop.*"

I jerked out of his hold and spun around to face him. "Why? Why was she taken in for more questioning?"

There was a pause, looks flickering between Beckett, Alek, and Dane.

"Somebody better start talking before I absolutely lose my shit. Beckett, what the fuck is—"

"Our cameras caught Mia in the woods the day her client Cullen Nichols was attacked. Apparently, she was stumbling around, crying, hysterical . . ."

I stilled, my stomach dropping. *Shit.*

"And," Beckett said, "Loren supplied the footage to the sheriff a few hours ago."

*"What?"* Rage flew through me. "Who approved this? What the f—did you know she was doing this?"

Beckett glanced at Alek, then at Dane. They shook their heads in unison.

"No. None of us knew," Beckett said. "Loren said she was heading home for the afternoon. I didn't think anything of it, but apparently she was actually headed to the station."

*"Why?"*

Alek stepped forward. "I think she was worried about you, man. Sticking your neck out for a woman you just met. You know Loren's always had a thing for you."

I blinked, trying to process this insane turn of events.

"She's been acting weird ever since you brought Mia over to the office and started missing work, meetings . . ."

"Yeah, dude." Beckett nodded. "She's been obsessed with you since day one. Didn't you know that? We all figured . . ."

I wasn't stupid. I'd assumed Loren had more than normal feelings for me as a coworker, but I'd never imagined—

"So what's happening now? Where is Mia right now?" I asked, trying to formulate a plan, at the same time trying to understand what was happening.

"Mason just took her in."

*"Fuck."* I slammed my fist into a tree. Of all fucking people, Mason had her. Mason, the man who'd ruined my life, had *my* woman. Trying to control myself, I paced back and forth like a caged animal. "They arrested her?"

"Yes." Alek grabbed my elbow. "Stop, Chief. Pull it together. Fucking *stop*, Easton. *Think*."

"Get your fucking hands off me."

Beckett, apparently done with my dramatics, lunged forward and jabbed his finger in my face. "Listen. Yes, Mia has been arrested and taken in for questioning. It's unavoidable, Easton. She wasn't only directly blamed for the attack by the victim but was now caught on camera on the day of the attack—"

"No." I shook my head. "This isn't what we need to be focusing on right now. Someone is after her, Beckett. She said someone ran her off the road. If so, then that means someone tried to kill—"

"*Exactly.*" He blew out a breath, raking his fingers through his hair. "Shit, man, *listen* to me. Yes, the cops have her, but she's safe right now. That's the point. There's literally no safer place that Mia could be right now. Don't even think about bailing her out, not until we figure this shit out."

I stilled, slowly understanding the point he was making. Mia was currently sitting in a jail cell, with armed guards and under lock and key. Whoever had tried to kill her couldn't get to her in there.

This would give me time to find the motherfucker.

As much as I hated to admit it, Beckett was right.

As I viewed my team—Beckett, Alek, and Dane—an ice-cold resolve settled in my veins. The kind that reminded me of the moment before an enemy breach in a black ops mission. The moment before I was about to kill someone.

I turned, adrenaline racing through my body as I stalked across the pavement, barreling through the crowd that had gathered. I addressed Alek over my shoulder.

"Get me your FBI contact on the phone right now. I need to know about that goddamn hair. If Mia is right, that hair belongs to the Black Cat Stalker."

# Chapter Forty-Eight

## Mia

I watched the deputy close me behind steel bars, the click of the lock echoing off the brick walls of the cold jail cell.

My body trembled. Not with fear or panic but raw, fervent anger.

I pictured Easton's face, the man I'd kissed, made love to, trusted. The man who had supplied the evidence to get me locked up.

My hands curled into fists.

The other shoe had finally dropped—and Easton Crew would regret the day he'd decided to play Mia Frost.

# Chapter Forty-Nine

DOCTOR: You missed our last appointment. Why?

PATIENT: I was busy.

DOCTOR: Too busy to call to let me know you couldn't make it in?

PATIENT: [*No response.*]

DOCTOR: Well, I appreciate you showing up today. How are you?

PATIENT: [*No response.*]

DOCTOR: You seem different.

PATIENT: How so?

DOCTOR: For one, you've never come to your appointment with refreshments before. Is that coffee?

PATIENT: Yes. Does it bother you?

DOCTOR: No. Did you have a long night?

PATIENT: [*No response.*]

DOCTOR: Perhaps that's the reason for your jitters? The coffee.

PATIENT: [*Slides hand to knee of tapping foot.*]

DOCTOR: What's wrong?

PATIENT: Nothing.

DOCTOR: Have you had a panic attack this week?

PATIENT: [*No response.*]

DOCTOR: Are you high?

PATIENT: On what?

DOCTOR: Drugs?

PATIENT: No.

DOCTOR: Sex?

PATIENT: [*No response.*]

DOCTOR: Tell me about the cuts on your arms. The scratches.

PATIENT: I don't know . . . don't remember.

DOCTOR: You don't remember where you got that nasty scrape on your forearm?

PATIENT: [*No response.*]

DOCTOR: You don't want to tell me?

PATIENT: [*No response.*]

DOCTOR: Or you truly don't remember?

PATIENT: [*No response.*]

DOCTOR: What did you have for breakfast this morning?

PATIENT: Why?

DOCTOR: Just curious.

PATIENT: I don't think we need to see each other much longer.

DOCTOR: Why is that?

PATIENT: I think this relationship has gone as far as it can go.

DOCTOR: I disagree. I think there's much room for growth left. I want to help you. If you'd just please—

PATIENT: I need to go.

DOCTOR: Wait . . . just wait a second . . .

PATIENT: Please cancel my next appointment.

DOCTOR: *Wait.* I don't understand. Why?

PATIENT: Because I don't think I'm going to be here much longer.

# Chapter Fifty

## Easton

The road had been blocked off while a crane lifted the Jeep from the debris. The vehicle would be a total loss, but that was the least of my worries.

Beckett, Alek, Dane, and I searched the scene long after everyone else had left, then hoofed it to the junkyard where the Jeep had been towed. After paying the owner two hundred bucks, we were given access to the property and then searched every inch of the vehicle inside and out, hoping to find something that would lead us to the Black Cat Stalker.

It was eleven at night by the time we got back to the office. The rain had stopped, leaving a cold, soggy night in its wake.

Loren was nowhere in sight and also not answering her phone. It appeared that the woman had disappeared after taking it upon herself to report the footage of Mia in the woods to the police. Seven messages I'd left for her, demanding to understand why she'd done what she'd done and why *the fuck* she was avoiding providing me with information on Mason's whereabouts.

She wasn't going to get away with meddling in someone else's life like that, regardless of whether she had my best interests at heart or was romantically obsessed with me or whatever the guys had called it. More than all that, though, I wouldn't tolerate such a brazen decision without going through me first.

Seven unreturned messages.

We settled in the war room, a padded, soundproof room with indestructible doors and a hidden trapdoor in the corner that led to a secret underground bunker. Everything in the room was connected to satellite, so if the electricity was cut, we could still get messages out. We used the room mainly when organizing and planning secret tracking ops for the government. Or, in rare cases, when one of us was involved in an emergency that needed absolute focus.

Dane started a pot of coffee at the small bar in the corner; Alek and Beckett settled around the phone. I couldn't sit. Instead, I paced back and forth, a jittery adrenaline junkie, which derailed any chance to take a load off.

Alek connected his cell to the speaker and dialed his contact at the FBI. No answer.

"Try again," I said.

Again, no answer.

"It's midnight on the East Coast, Chief."

"Try again."

Alek's jaw twitched with disapproval. He dialed a third time, and I turned my back as it rang.

Finally, the call connected, a few bangs and shuffles before a gritty voice sounded through the speaker. "Someone better be dead."

"Diesel, this is Alek Romanov."

"Romanov, it's one o'clock in the fucking morning."

"Midnight, actually. Only eleven here. We've got a situation."

A faint groan followed more shuffling, presumably as Diesel got out of bed. "Talk."

"The feather I sent you—with the strand of hair. I need to know where you're at with the DNA scan."

"No," I said to correct him, jumping in. "We don't need to know where you're at. We need the information *now*."

Dane slipped a cup of coffee into my hand as he passed by, flashing me a look intended to tell me to calm down. It only agitated me more.

I set down the coffee.

"Who the hell is that asshole?" Diesel barked through the speaker.

"My boss. He's good, don't worry. Anyway—"

"Okay . . . the hair . . . yeah." The Fed's voice became stronger as the haze of sleep lifted.

"Any results yet?"

"Christ. Give me a second to pull on my goddamn boxers, brother. Hold the fuck on. And you owe me for this, dude."

"I'll pay my debt. Always do."

We waited silently as Diesel covered himself and booted up the laptop on his nightstand. Because men in his position never slept without their laptop, phone, and pistol in reach.

"The report isn't final yet, but my man is working on it."

After a glare from me, Alek pressed. "Do you have anything you can share?"

"N—wait. That nasty-ass wad of chewing tobacco you sent over, got a partial profile back on that one."

"You get a name?"

"No. But I can tell you that the redneck dipping in the middle of the woods is an aging male, likely in his seventies, and of German descent."

Definitely not Henrick Taylor, at least judging by the age, and also not likely the Black Cat Stalker.

"Give me what you got on the hair," I snapped.

"I just said, the report isn't final yet."

"We need what you've got, even if it's just preliminary," Alek said.

"Off the books," I added, because I needed something—*anything*.

"Listen, *boss*," Diesel said, awake enough now to mock me. "I'm not sure how much information Alek gave you, but this method of DNA extraction is in its infancy. There's still a hell of a lot of testing to do before the process becomes mainstream. If a root was attached to the hair, we wouldn't have a problem, but there was no root. But with that said . . . I can confirm that, of the four strands of hair, three belonged to the same person, and one did not."

"You got two different profiles?"

"Yes—kinda."

"Walk us through the process," Beckett said, always needing to know the whys and hows.

"God, I hate you guys." Diesel took a deep breath, then began. "You see, we can easily extract mitochondrial DNA from rootless hair, which can tell us a few things, like if one strand is different from another, but you need nuclear DNA to get an identity. This is where it gets tricky when you don't have a root. My contact is part of a team that worked alongside a third-party researcher that developed a tool—a kit, if you will—that can recover small degraded fragments of DNA from challenging sources like rootless hair. From there, the DNA is taken through a PCR—polymerase chain reaction—to amplify the DNA, and then it's sent through sequencing to obtain a human profile. There are, like, a million checkpoints along the way to determine if the results are accurate or exactly how accurate they are. They're at about checkpoint ten, with yours."

Alek pressed again. "We just need an idea of who we're looking for—anything you've got. Sex, age, race . . ."

"Well, I can give you more than that."

I looked at Alek, my heart skipping a beat.

"My source was able to extract a small fragment of nuclear DNA from one strand, and he got a hit in CODIS. However, there's still—"

"You got a name?"

"A name and the entire goddamn family tree. We'll start with the brown hair first. The profile wasn't in the system, but I can determine that it belonged to a female, Caucasian, estimated age range in her teens at the time this hair was shed."

*Mia.*

"The second belonged to a male, middle aged, of Caucasian and American Indian descent. Estimated age range between fifty and sixty years old, so thirty to forty at the time the hair was shed. This DNA was in the system, although my contact needs to check a few more things before—"

"Give us the name, D."

"Listen—I don't want to be connected to this shit if it goes sideways, you got me?"

"Got it."

"Okay." He took a deep breath. "The profile of the second set of hair belongs to a man named Mark Swine."

We silently checked with each other. The name was unfamiliar to us all.

"What can you tell us about him?" I asked.

"Mark Swine, age fifty-four years, was born and raised in California. Two Peeping Tom charges, an indecent exposure, and one sexual assault arrest, but he was never convicted. Not enough evidence. Moved to Texas after his last arrest."

"Where in Texas?"

"Dallas."

My stomach dropped. "Do you have his picture?"

The sound of rapid typing on a keyboard clicked through the phone. "Just emailed Alek his mug shot from twenty years ago, his last known picture I could dig up."

Alek clicked a few keys on his laptop and turned it around.

The image was of a man, overweight by a good fifty pounds, his skin blotchy and veiny with a sickly yellow tone that suggested an unhealthy life filled with Doritos and heavy drinking. Long, stringy black hair, tied back in a ponytail. Cracked, thin lips. A long, narrow nose. A mad, evil glint that resonated with me deeply, on some visceral level that I couldn't quite put my finger on.

"You guys don't recognize him?"

"No," Alek said.

Beckett and Dane shook their heads.

"All right, listen," Diesel said impatiently. "I'll send you the final report when it's done in the *morning*."

"Thanks, D. I owe you."

"Yep." The phone clicked.

The room burst with sudden movement, the rush of adrenaline from obtaining our first viable lead.

"Dane, I need you to get me absolutely everything you can on Mark Swine. I need to know where he lives now, where he lived in the past. I want to know what car he drives, if he's married, kids, records. I want to know how he takes his coffee and if the motherfucker uses one or two ply—everything."

"You got it, Chief."

I grabbed my jacket.

"Where are you going?" Beckett asked.

"Back to the LKP—the last known location of the son of a bitch. The scene of Mia's car crash. It was him tailing her—I know it."

I strode out the door.

My guess was that Mason would hold Mia until morning, when she would be bailed out by her Dragonfly comrades. That meant I had exactly six hours to find the man they called Mark Swine.

# Chapter Fifty-One

## Mia

I was granted bail at six o'clock in the morning.

By that time, I was quite literally out of my fucking mind. I hadn't slept, eaten, drunk, or even used the uncleaned silver toilet in the corner of the jail cell.

I was allowed to change back into the white dress I'd been wearing when booked in, an outfit chosen for what I'd assumed was a regular day at the office, so long ago. Now the dress was covered in mud and grime from the accident and still damp from the rain. It had a sickly, musty scent from being stuffed in a plastic bag all night.

I didn't bother with the heels. Figured, what was another germ or two on the bottoms of my feet? After all, the kind of people who spent their nights in jail didn't care about unimportant details like that, right?

Luna was waiting for me in the lobby of the sheriff's department, bundled in a massive red puffer jacket that hung to her knees. The moment I was escorted through the steel door, she rushed to me, mumbling incoherently, crippling concern on her face.

This probably sounds rather ungrateful, selfish, or even bitchy of me, but her pity was the absolute last thing I needed at that moment.

There's something about spending the night in a jail cell that hardens a small piece of you forever. It stirs up a mixture of emotions, really. And if you're not careful, it cracks open the door for an identity shift, breeding an unconscious connection to the devil on your shoulder. Awakening him, perhaps. He becomes a little voice in your head, a whispering coercion to step into this new part of your life. After all, you've survived a night in jail once; why can't you do it again?

*Let's have fun,* the voice whispers. *You're an entirely new person now. Strong, invincible. You don't have to fight it anymore. Release it. Release it. Release it.*

Luna halted in midstride when our eyes met, as if she didn't recognize me.

Not a single word was muttered as we stepped into the cold autumn morning, still dark with night. The scent of rain was heavy on the air. More rain coming.

No Easton in sight. A good thing, considering I didn't know what the hell I would've done if I'd seen him at that moment. All my anger and blame had been funneled to him, and to me, for that matter, for falling for the bastard.

Had Easton ever trusted me? Believed me? Or was it all a game to him? Was I nothing more than a plaything used for his entertainment?

Jo pushed off her truck parked under the streetlight, her dark, menacing demeanor mirroring my own.

I wasn't the only one who had spent time behind bars.

Jo crossed the parking lot, her demeanor hostile, focusing not on me but on the warden watching from the window.

Stella rushed out of the driver's side door, carrying a paper sack in one hand and a drink in the other. A green juice, if I had to guess.

My girls were here for me. They had come, united like always, to help whoever among us was in need. Except I didn't feel like I was in need. I felt like burning down the entire fucking town.

"What the hell is going on?" Jo asked, bypassing pleasantries.

Luna held up her hand. "Take a breath, Jo. She just got out."

"I brought you food." Stella rushed up, still wearing the pajama pants from the evening before.

Jo, on the other hand, was fully dressed, the sleeves pushed up on her black leather jacket. "Let her eat first. She had a hell of a night; give her a minute."

The girls began talking at once, over each other, hurling questions, arguing.

I blew past them, tunnel visioned on Jo's truck parked next to Stella's car. "Keys," I yelled over my shoulder.

A herd of footsteps charged behind me.

"Mia," Luna said in a mothering voice intended to calm a toddler in the middle of a tantrum. "I don't think you should drive right now. We've got a loaner car for you at the office. I've already called several auto shops in town to see if we can get your Jeep fixed. I know how much you love that thing—"

"But if you don't want to drive at all," Stella said, interrupting, "I can take you wherever you want to go."

"She's not disabled," Jo snapped.

I spun around and grabbed the plastic bag that contained my things from Luna's hands. "Keys," I demanded again.

Jo's eyes narrowed, assessing me. "Where are you going?"

"I've got someone I need to talk to."

Thunder rumbled in the distance.

"Jo. Give me your fucking keys."

"Be careful." She tossed them to me. "I'm up. Call if you need anything."

Luna stepped forward. "No way. She isn't driving—"

"Stop. I'm okay. I'm fine. Listen, we'll talk soon."

Jo nodded. "We'd better, because we've got a lot of questions."

I unlocked Jo's truck and slipped behind the wheel. On autopilot, I clicked on the headlights. My hands trembled as I fired up the engine and slipped the truck into reverse.

Tires spun against wet pavement as I peeled out of the parking lot, three worried women in my rearview mirror.

Instantly, I rolled down the window, inhaling the freedom.

I noticed the headache then. Despite the adrenaline, the fatigue from going more than twenty-four hours with no sleep, very little food, and immense stress was wreaking havoc on my body, my brain.

I fumbled through my plastic bag of things, finding my cell phone. When I clicked it on, the screen lit with endless missed calls and text messages.

One caught my attention immediately. I pressed the brakes, slowing to a crawl on the highway.

Frowning, I stared down at the number, my attention flickering between the phone and the dark, lonely road ahead.

I clicked into my voice mails, then pulled onto the shoulder and pressed play. My heart pounded as I waited for the message to download before it finally played.

"Mia . . . this is Cullen. I—I know . . . I think I'm not supposed to be calling you."

Every instinct in my body roared to life at the sound of his rushed, confused babble.

"But I heard what happened—that you got in an accident. Listen. I think . . . I think we need to talk. I know it wasn't you—I'm sorry. I know it wasn't, and . . . I don't think they're done with me."

My pulse thrummed in my ears. The fear in his voice was palpable, like a thick wave coming through the phone.

I got the sense that maybe Cullen wasn't alone, and this instantly worried me.

"I can't," he said, then paused, and after a distant shuffle, his voice hushed to a whisper. "I can't talk right now—I don't think we should

talk over the phone. I need you—come to my house as soon as you can."
He rattled off the address. "I'm so sorry—"

The call cut off.

I looked at the time stamp on the call—12:14 a.m. Six hours earlier.

I dialed the number. No answer.

Tried again. No answer.

I left a voice mail, then replayed his. Again and again.

Called again. No answer.

I plugged the address into the GPS on my phone, then shoved the truck into drive and made a U-turn.

My mind raced as I sped down the dark road ahead, my pulse roaring in my ears.

My innocence was on the line, but what to do? Who to call now?

I didn't trust anyone anymore.

The man I'd thought I could trust had played me like the idiot I was. The entire town thought I was a homicidal psychopath. And I wasn't dragging Jo, Luna, and Stella into this any more than I already had. My name was tarnished, my company now shaded in a questionable light. I had to right the wrong.

My foot slammed the gas.

Cullen would be my—*our*—salvation.

# Chapter Fifty-Two

## Mia

It started to sprinkle as I pulled onto the quiet residential street that led to Cullen's house. It was the type of cookie-cutter neighborhood where each house was exactly the same, on the same one-acre lot, divided by a fence. The only difference between each house was the color of paint. The type of street where neighbors watched through their windows and gathered on the sidewalks during the holidays. The type of neighborhood that made me itch.

Dawn began to penetrate through the blanket of storm clouds, a dim, dreary light replacing the blackness.

The drizzle turned into a steady downfall as I checked my GPS, braking at a freshly painted mailbox on a thick wooden base at the end of the cul-de-sac.

I'd always wondered what Cullen's house looked like, and oddly enough, it was exactly what I'd imagined. Plain, simple, boring. A mid-size two-story monochrome modern home with a peaked roof. The yard was landscaped to perfection, bushes and trees trimmed, decorative rocks and lawn decor meticulously placed. The front porch light illuminated a wicker patio set with brightly colored pillows, and a large flowering plant was centered on the table.

The garage was closed.

As I pulled into the paved driveway, I thought of his story, and I thought of mine. Two seemingly normal people broken by an eerily similar past that neither had expected to survive.

My heart suddenly broke for him, and I felt an intense wave of sympathy for the man who'd accused me of assaulting him. I got it; I understood it. On some fucked-up level, I understood that kind of trauma-induced insanity. Temporary or not.

I shoved Jo's truck into park and, by force of habit, flipped down the visor, and I was momentarily stunned by my appearance in the vanity mirror. The mascara I'd applied more than twenty-four hours earlier had run, giving me a goth, deathly-sick-raccoon look. Circles almost as dark as the makeup shadowed the puffy red rims. My hair was a tangled mess and my dress disgusting. I looked more like the Bride of Chucky than a renowned psychologist.

After pulling the keys from the ignition, I pushed out of the truck and jogged across the small yard, my pulse rate increasing with each step.

A streak of lightning pierced the sky as I stepped onto the porch. The front door was unlatched, darkness beyond the crack.

My internal warning system went off. Something was wrong.

"Cullen?" I called out, lightly pressing the door with my index finger to avoid the knob. "Cullen?"

A sudden bang broke the silence, followed by the clatter of something falling to the floor.

"Cullen!" I charged into the house, following the thuds that led me to the kitchen.

A bowl of oatmeal was burning on the stove, next to a full cup of coffee. The room was dark, the only light from a sickly bulb above the sink. I lunged toward the stove, slid the oatmeal to the side, and turned off the range.

I spun around, heart pounding, and scanned the room. No one was seated at the table, dead on the floor, or lurking in the shadows.

My gaze shifted to the windows. A large, rusted metal garage had been erected along the fence line of the backyard. The side door swayed on its hinges, slanted rain spilling inside.

I crossed the kitchen and opened the back door. I squinted against the gust of wind that blew rain into my face.

"Cullen!" I called out, cupping my hands around my mouth.

A sudden, loud bang carried on the wind, followed by a flash of light inside the garage.

*Shit.*

Ducking my head, I jogged across the backyard, mud seeping through my toes and splashing onto the backs of my legs. I slowed as I reached the metal building, attuned to every sound and movement around me. To my left, a large garage door that was closed. In front of me, a metal door, unlatched.

"Cullen!" I called out again, warily tapping open the door with my toe.

It was a small room, separate from the main garage.

A dim, cracked lantern hung from the ceiling in the corner, swaying in the breeze from the open door, scarcely illuminating a workshop of sorts with rolling tool cabinets, buckets, and landscaping equipment. Long dark shadows stretched across a dirty concrete floor. The space smelled old and musty, turning my stomach.

Another bang, pulling my attention to a narrow door that led to the garage, darkened by shadows.

I felt for my phone in my pocket, then remembered I'd left it in the truck in my confused haste.

"Mia!" Cullen yelled from somewhere beyond the door.

I jogged across the stained concrete and pushed open the door. The moment I stepped into the garage, the buzz of the rain was drowned out with a set of recorded voices, barely audible as they carried on the cold, musty air. It was a male and a female, their voices distorted as if poorly recorded, and speaking in a casual tone. The voices, the topic, felt very familiar.

*"Are you high?"*

*"On what?"*

*"Drugs?"*

*"No."*

*"Sex?"*

After a pause, the recording resumed.

*"Tell me about the cuts on your arms. The scratches."*

*"I don't know . . . don't remember."*

*"You don't remember where you got that nasty scrape on your forearm?"*

I searched for a light switch on the wall but couldn't find one. Squinting, I scanned the space, searching for Cullen. Pops of lightning illuminated the space in intermittent flashes of light. The garage was one large room, empty aside from the towers of boxes and plastic containers that littered the dank space. Wooden support beams lined the metal walls, insulation packed behind them, most shredded by mice.

It wasn't so much a garage, I noticed, but an actual room. Used for what?

The recording continued, from speakers that I couldn't see.

*"I need to go."*

*"Wait . . . just wait a second . . ."*

*"Please cancel my next appointment."*

*"Wait. I don't understand. Why?"*

*"Because I don't think I'm going to be here much longer."*

I froze.

It was me. My voice.

The recording was from my office.

I was the doctor and Cullen the patient.

Except these weren't my audio files. These had been recorded secretly from somewhere else in the room, like a cell phone.

Ice-cold fear trickled up my spine.

*Get out.*

I spun on my heel the moment something burst from the shadows. A blast of pain struck the side of my head, in the exact location where my head had hit the tree years earlier, before I'd been raped by a stick.

I opened my mouth to scream just before the world went black.

# Chapter Fifty-Three

## Easton

Old Lady Lou Littles's owlish glasses peeked around her chained front door. "Well, Mr. Crew, I didn't expect to see you again so soon." She slid off the chain with trembling hands. "Please. Come in."

"Call me Easton, and thanks." I stepped inside. "I'm sorry to drop in so early." The house smelled of fresh coffee, sugar cookies, and mothballs.

"It's six o'clock, dear. I've been up since four."

I didn't doubt it, based on the pink sweater and tan slacks she was wearing and the smear of lipstick on her lips—and her teeth.

"But as happy as I am to see you," she said, "you know you can always call anytime, day or night."

"I was in the area."

Lou closed the door behind me. "Were you?" Her bushy brows furrowed. "Is everything okay with Miss Frost? Was that her car in the ravine?"

I ignored the third question and was unsure how to answer the second. "I'm actually hoping you can help me out."

"Come, dear." Lou gestured for me to follow her to the kitchen. She led me down a hallway lined with stained carpet and faded family pictures. "Would you like some coffee?"

"Please."

We stepped into the kitchen, where a travel mug was lying next to a Bible on the table, the pages worn between at least a dozen bookmarks. A floor lamp glowed from the corner.

"Sit," she said. "Creamer, sugar, whiskey, or Baileys?"

"Black."

"Figured." Lou set a cup of coffee in front of me, then topped off hers.

As she returned the carafe to the counter, I squeezed one finger through the tiny handle of the delicate white, pink, and gold cup. China, best I could tell. Lou Littles didn't get much company but had been raised with southern manners regardless.

Lou settled in across from me and closed the Bible, her curiosity fixed on me. The coffee was strong and fresh, a shot of adrenaline to my system.

"Now," she said. "Tell me what's going on with Miss Frost. Is she okay?"

"Right now, yes, but she's in a bit of trouble, and I'm hoping you can help."

"Anything."

"We both know you keep an active watch on Dr. Frost's house." I nodded toward the tripod next to the floor lamp. A pair of binoculars were looped to the top.

She grinned. "Yes, we both do know this."

I nodded. "I'm curious. Have you seen any unusual vehicles driving down your road lately or parked at or around Dr. Frost's house?"

"I have." Her response was instant, almost as if she'd been expecting the question.

I blinked. "You have?"

"Yes."

"Can you describe it to me?"

"Yes. It's a 1994 Ford F-150 four-by-four. Extended cab, black exterior." She motioned to the window. "Much like the one I have outside."

That was a damn detailed description.

"How many times have you seen it?"

"Four, over the last few months. Twice on the road, and twice turning around in Mia's driveway."

"Could you see the driver?"

Lou shook her head. She'd obviously tried. "Just the silhouette."

"Could you tell if the driver was a man or a woman?"

"No."

I scrubbed my hand over my mouth, my mind racing with this new information.

"Would you like to see a picture?"

"Yes, please."

She nodded, then slowly pushed up from the table. When I started to stand, she waved me off. "No. Stay. Sit."

As Lou left the room, I scanned the detached garage outside, its door closed.

She returned, clicking through the images on a long-shot target camera that probably cost more than the china I was sipping out of.

"Here." She handed the camera to me. "This was taken two nights ago."

The night before Mia had been run off the road.

I clicked through the images of a black truck in Mia's driveway, exactly as Lou had described. I didn't recognize it.

"No full shot of the license plate?"

"No." She rested her hands on her curvy hips. "I wasn't thinking Dr. Frost was in danger. Just thought it was a new boyfriend or something."

My brow cocked. "Has she had many?"

Lou snorted. "As many as I have in the last ten years. Zero."

I smiled, noting my own relief. "Do you mind if I take this camera?"

"Yes, I do. But I can print out the images, and you can have those. Give me a few minutes."

As Lou printed the images, I paced the kitchen, moving from window to window, cataloging all the different angles Lou had of Mia's house.

I turned as she returned and handed me a stack of printouts. "Thank you."

Lou dipped her chin, staring at me a minute. A surprisingly awkward moment passed between us before she asked, "Do you have any other questions for me?"

I cocked my head. "Do you have something you're wanting me to ask?"

She surveyed the pictures of the truck in my hand, and it took me a minute.

Finally, I said, "Ah. Ms. Lou, you worked at the DMV for years, didn't you?"

She nodded enthusiastically as if I was onto something.

"Ms. Lou, do you know who drives this truck?"

"No, I don't."

My shoulders dropped as I let out an impatient exhale. I wasn't in the mood for games, and it was obvious Lou Littles knew something that she'd deemed worthy of my discovery.

"Do you have any guesses whose truck this might be?"

A devilish grin flashed across her face. She held up her hand, curling her index finger. "Come here."

I followed Lou down the hall to a small, messy office with stacks of files and papers. I quickly scanned the stacks, cataloging as much as I could. Most seemed to be irrelevant information about various Skull Hollow citizens.

"To answer your question, yes, I worked at the DMV for seventeen years." Lou plucked a folder from the middle of a stack, knowing exactly where she was going. *Organized chaos* was a fitting description of her office. She began thumbing through the folder. "Do you ever read those true-crime books?"

"I have, yes."

"Horrifying, aren't they? I started reading them when I was a teen-ager. Always into that stuff, I was. The mind of the criminal, all that." She snorted. "Perhaps that's why I'm so paranoid and nosy with my neighbors."

I smiled, hiding my growing impatience.

"Anyway, after I started working at the DMV, I realized how much personal information I had at my fingertips, and well, seeing it as my personal duty to protect this fine, small town, I started making note of anything . . . suspicious."

"Suspicious?"

"Yeah, anyone who came in who seemed off." Her milky, wrinkled eyes narrowed with intensity. Her grip tightened on the folder, now creasing in her hand. "You know those people that just give you a bad feeling the moment you see them? Like you're seeing something evil, something bad, right in front of you?"

I thought back to my tours overseas and nodded.

"Over the years, a few people gave me this feeling. The moment they walked into the DMV . . ." She shuddered. "I just got that feeling."

I stepped closer, eyeing the stack of paper in her hands.

"Anyway, this folder contains information on all those people. The ones that gave me the willies."

"What kind of information?"

"Everything the DMV offers. Some of them came in to transfer vehicle titles, some to get new licenses for changing addresses, and one even came in to get new ID after changing his name."

*Name change.* My heart skittered.

"Can I see this folder, Ms. Lou?"

She hesitated, weighing whether to trust me or not.

"I won't tell anyone you took confidential information from the system, cross my heart."

She nodded, this pleasing her, and handed me the papers.

I opened the folder and thumbed through the papers before stopping on an image midstack. My heart slammed against my rib cage.

I pulled out the picture, held it up. "Do you remember this man?"

"Oh yes. He was the one who changed his name. He had all the necessary paperwork completed for it. And he is one who really gave me the willies."

The pieces of the puzzle slowly began to click into place.

As if completing my thoughts, Lou said, "His name was Mark Swine, but he changed it to Cullen Nichols when he moved here."

I blinked, staring down at the printout Lou Littles had made of Mark Swine's old driver's license—and his new one as Cullen Nichols.

Before taking on his new identity of Cullen Nichols, Mark Swine had lost at least fifty pounds, cut his hair, and dyed it from black to auburn. He'd added glasses and shaved off his beard. He looked like a completely different person—which was apparently the point.

I pulled my phone from my pocket.

"Skull County Jail, how may I direct your call?"

"You have an inmate, Mia Frost. Is she still there?"

"Just a minute . . ."

I peered at Lou as I was put on hold. The seconds ticked by like hours.

"Sir?"

"Yes, I'm still here. Mia, is she—"

"No, sir. She posted bail and was released about thirty minutes ago."

The papers slipped out of my hands as I sprinted out the door.

# Chapter Fifty-Four

## Mia

A wave of nausea hit me like a wrecking ball as I opened my eyes to a blurry body looming over me.

Bile rose to my throat, my body spinning as if I were in some sort of suspended reality, drifting in and out of consciousness.

And then he spoke.

The voice.

I blinked madly, my blurry vision raking over the blotchy red face that I knew so well as an innocent, tortured soul.

How wrong I'd been.

Cullen reached forward, one hand fisting my hair, the other grabbing my arm, yanking both my arms painfully over my head. A searing-hot pain shot through my shoulders. This was when I realized my wrists and ankles were bound.

Everything fell into place like a million different pieces coming together.

The weird connection I'd felt with Cullen when he'd first walked into my office—it wasn't because of his story being so similar to mine. Instead, it was my body remembering his on top of me, my body trying to tell me something that my brain had spent years trying to block out.

And as he pulled me across the cold concrete floor, I remembered every second of that day. The way he'd moved, the smell of his skin, the strength of his grasp, the color of his eyes. I remembered the fear, the panic. It all came back to me.

*Cullen Nichols.*

Cullen Nichols was the man who'd ambushed me, sodomized me with a stick, and left me for dead years earlier.

"Cullen." I croaked out his name, fear running like acid through my veins. *"Cullen."*

"There are many types of rapists, Mia." His voice was eerily calm as he dragged me by my bound wrists across the floor, switching into some sort of weird role-play mode. "The retaliatory rapist, the one who lives in a constant state of anger and rapes when he's triggered by something. Do I fit this profile, Dr. Frost?"

I didn't respond. My head, my thoughts, spun wildly.

"Dr. Frost," he said again. My hair snagged on a divot in the concrete, ripping it from my skull. "Do I fit this profile?"

"No," I said, my voice weak, breathless. I frantically scanned the floor for any kind of weapon. There was nothing.

He continued. "The power-seeking rapist is the one who believes he deserves sex, that it's owed to him by the women he dates. Wealthy men and celebrities often receive this label. Do I, Dr. Frost?"

"No."

He jerked my head, sending another wave of nausea through my body. Chills broke out over my heated skin, that sick feeling you get a few seconds before you vomit.

"And then you have the reassurance-seeking rapist, the most common by far. This man rapes to prove his worth. He has deep-seated feelings of inadequacy. Perhaps induced by his mentally ill father, who took him camping one weekend and, after showing him affection and love, raped his mother in front of him, then raped him repeatedly with a stick, over and over until the boy could no longer walk."

There it was. His story—the real story. The one that he'd never offered details of while sitting on the couch in my office, seeking therapy from me. These details were the center of it all—the catalyst for the making of a psychopath. Cullen's father had raped him in the same way Cullen had raped me, then Courtney.

Tears rolled down my cheeks.

"He is shy, a loner, usually lives alone, either by choice or because of divorce. This man rapes for control, to feel the kind of power that the lucky ones get to feel every day."

I examined the metal wall ahead of us, the chains and cuffs affixed with bolts drilled into wooden support beams that lined the wall. Sticks ranging from twigs to small branches as wide as a closed fist were piled next to the chains.

"He stalks his victims," he said, "eventually interjecting himself into their lives, more often than not developing true feelings for the victim . . . and sometimes, is never able to let go."

Bile rose to my throat. Cullen had interjected himself into my life, had never let me go.

"Do I fit this profile, Dr. Frost?"

Tears dripped onto my chest, the tornado of emotions flooding my body too much to control.

"No."

Cullen stilled, his brows arched. "No?"

"No." Fury, accompanied by an intense hatred for the man, boiled up my neck. "You're forgetting the erotic-aggression rapist. The sadistic motherfucker who uses pain to get off, aroused by the victim's torment. This sick son of a bitch uses tools on his victims, a ritual that means something to his fucked-up brain—like a stick."

Rage ignited like a blaze of fire. There it was, standing right in front of me. *Him—he* was the cause of my bursts of rage, my pain, the internal torment that had ravaged my body inside and out for years.

Adrenaline surged through my veins as I stared into the eyes of the devil himself, the man who had taken not only my virginity but my soul along with it.

Except he'd failed to destroy one thing that day. My brain.

I've treated many patients, men mostly, who use manipulation tactics to get what they want. You might say I learned from the best. That day, I didn't use my fists. I knew I needed to use my brain to defeat my opponent.

I bucked and twisted like a fish on the end of a fishing pole. Clumps of hair ripped from my scalp as his grip tightened. He yanked me violently, but not before I dragged my nails down the back of his legs, leaving long, red, angry scratches.

To my shock, he laughed.

The sick son of a bitch actually *laughed*. And somehow this was more terrifying than if he'd fought back. He was laughing at my fear, my pain. I wasn't going anywhere; he had no question about it.

He righted me again.

I dropped my weight and, this time, was dragged across the floor like a dead fish.

"How many women, Cullen?" I asked after he'd dropped me next to piles of chains and ropes.

A small smile curved his lips. "You mean here or in different states?"

"In total."

"More than anyone has any idea of." His grin deepened. He was proud of this. *Sick fuck.*

"And you've never even been questioned? In all that time?"

"No. I'm not stupid, Mia."

"No, quite the contrary, I think."

He nodded, hooking a chain to a wooden beam. "Just like your approach to healing the minds of the broken, everything is calculated, thought out, each angle explored, questioned, and eventually, the path of least resistance is chosen. I do the same. Mine has never failed me, and it's so damn simple." He jerked his chin to the outside. "Mother Nature. She's a devious little magician when she sheds her leaves, covering tracks, bodies, evidence."

*Leaves . . . the season . . .*

"Autumn . . . you went camping with your family during the fall, didn't you? When you were a little boy? The time that you told me about in one of our sessions . . . the time your dad gave you attention? The time that something bad happened to you . . ."

His smile vanished, eyes darkened. "We went camping every year, every fall, to celebrate my mother's birthday . . . she tried to save me that day." His gaze narrowed on me. "You look just like her, do you know that?"

And there it was—Cullen had formed an unusual obsession with me based on my resemblance to his mother. So simple, yet so complex at the same time.

"She was someone who tried to fix things," he continued, "but never quite hit the mark, you could say. She was the only one who tried to save me, aside from you."

I closed my eyes, the full picture finally coming together. Cullen had severe attachment disorder, common in patients who experience traumatic events in their childhood. In Cullen's case, his mother had represented help and comfort, possibly even love—in his mind—by trying to save him from his abusive father. She'd likely been the one to tend to his wounds, coddle and hold him. I not only physically resembled his mother but also had dedicated my life to helping others navigate the effects of traumatic events. Cullen had subconsciously replaced his mother with me, using me to play out the sick need for help and revenge in his life. Help, because despite his mother's comfort, she'd never fully saved him by being strong enough to leave his father and removing him from the situation. And revenge, for that very reason, as well. Cullen both loved and hated his mother, and I was the lucky recipient of these unbridled emotions.

"I did try to save you, yes, you could say that," I said, "but you tricked me, Cullen. During our sessions. You faked your identity, your story."

"It's all a game, Mia." He laughed. "I manipulated you just as you attempted to manipulate me through therapy. Except I'm smarter than that. I had fun with it—running you off the cliff, leaving you to die, just like I did that day in the woods. It really got to you, didn't it? Fucked you up, didn't it?"

*Revenge.*

He pulled my arms over my head, sending searing-hot pain through my shoulders. He hooked my binds to a chain. "It's fun, Mia. Pretending I was someone else, pretending someone else attacked me in the woods, when in reality, I threw myself off that damn cliff. I literally beat myself up in the woods that day to frame you."

*Revenge.*

A maniacal smile crossed his cracked lips. "And I enjoyed every fucking second of it."

"That's why you refused to go to the hospital after we found you in the woods, isn't it? You were afraid someone would put the clues together."

He nodded, picked up a stick, tested the grip. "And I've never been one to care about scars, anyway."

A chill tickled up my spine. The man was completely out-of-his-mind mad—and who knew how many women had paid the price.

He stepped closer to me, eyes wild, stick in his hand.

I closed my eyes, the same verses running through my head as when I'd been accused of being the Black Cat. Except now, they held a very different meaning . . .

*There is nothing covered that shall not be revealed, and what is spoken in darkness shall soon be heard in the light.*

*He will bring every act to judgment, everything which is hidden, whether it is good or evil.*

I curled my hands into fists above my head, running my thumb along the tips of my fingers. Along the nails that contained specks of Cullen Nichols's skin and leg hair, his DNA.

One day they would find my body.

And that day would be the day of Cullen's judgment.

# Chapter Fifty-Five

## Easton

My truck fishtailed around a corner. I tapped the brakes, corrected, then hit the gas again. I'd called Mia seven more times after leaving Lou's house. I checked her house, then her office, both vacant. When she didn't answer my eighth call, there was no question that something was wrong. I knew he had her—my instincts were screaming at me.

Memories flooded my head. Racing down the road in the rain, discovering my dead fiancée's body. Now, a year later, I was speeding through the rain again.

I couldn't be too late.

I would *not* be too late.

*I* would die first.

I watched the line of trucks behind me, headlights cutting through the curtain of rain. Beckett and Dane in one truck, Alek in the other. Alek always drove alone.

As planned when I'd called them, we passed the quiet residential road that led to Cullen Nichols's—a.k.a. Mark Swine's—house and instead pulled into the small gravel lot next to the neighborhood playground.

The trucks roared to a stop, and the doors flung open.

"You go around back," I said to Beckett.

When he took off, I addressed the others while sliding my SIG into my belt.

"Alek, you take the east side of the house. Dane, you take the west. If the son of a bitch flees, you catch him—do *not* shoot. I'm going in the front. My lead."

They nodded, and we split off, disappearing into the fog of rain like the phantoms we were.

Head up, gun low, I slipped through the shadows, careful to avoid paths that allowed for a clear view by Cullen's neighbors.

A red truck was parked outside his house, crooked in the driveway as if the driver had been in a hurry.

Quietly, I stepped onto the porch. The front door was ajar.

I slowly pushed open the door with the toe of my boot. The house was dark, silent, the charred scent of burnt food pungent in the air.

She was here. I could feel it.

Double fisting my gun, I crept down the hallway, sweeping each room I passed until I reached the kitchen, the source of the rancid scent. Burnt oatmeal and old coffee.

The back door was unlatched, tapping against the frame. My gaze shifted to the metal garage in the distance and a small light on inside, glowing through the rain.

*Mia.*

I slipped into the shadows and silently jogged through the rain. The side door of the garage was open, but the room was vacant.

Gun up, I swept the space as I crossed.

My heart roared as I neared a small, narrow door that led to the main garage.

Centering my sights, I stepped inside.

Mia was naked, her knees up, legs open. Her arms hung limply above her head, her wrists bound together with zip ties and tied to a chain that came down from the ceiling.

A mixture of blood and tears ran down the side of her head, and blood splattered her cheeks as if she'd been slapped around. Her skin was pale and sallow, marked with scratches and welts from where he'd been whipping her with, I assumed, one of the many gnarled tree branches that encircled her.

Cullen crouched between her legs, a stick in one hand, his other sliding up and down his erect penis.

I saw red.

I lunged forward and heaved Cullen into the air, throwing him face-first into the wall. A stack of boxes fell, tools, glass jars shattering on the dirty floor. I threw myself over Mia's body to protect her from the falling debris. A large plastic container filled with pictures of women, news articles, and pieces of clothing fell on top of us, knocking the gun from my hands.

Cullen stumbled backward, slamming into a wooden support beam.

"Cullen!" Mia screamed. "Don't let him get away, East—"

I turned and leaped over the fallen boxes. Grabbing a fistful of his hair, I yanked back and slammed his forehead into the wooden post. Over and over, *thud, thud,* the blood spraying against the stairs.

The next thing I remember is falling onto my knees next to Mia, quickly covering her with her white dress as I frantically looked her over.

Our eyes met, hers wide and wild. She shook her head.

He hadn't raped her.

"Oh God, Mia," I whispered on a shaky exhale of relief.

One minute later, and I would have been too late.

But I hadn't been too late. Not this time.

My focus began to center, shifting to the nasty gash on the side of her head.

"You're going to be okay, baby. Everything is okay. We'll get you to a doctor."

I pulled the pocketknife from my belt and cut her bindings. I noticed my hand was shaking, my entire body was trembling, the emotions uncontrollable.

"I'm so sorry, Mia," I blurted. "I'm so sorry I wasn't there. I tried to call." The words tumbled out of me. "I went to your house the second I found out you'd been released. I went to the office. I called over and over." I cupped her hands in mine, desperately gripping onto them, onto her. "I didn't give the cops the video of you in the woods, Mia. I didn't even know about it until Beckett told me."

Her eyes rounded, filling with tears. "I thought you betrayed me."

My heart shattered. "No, Mia, no, never. Please don't cry, baby, please . . . I'll fix everything . . . I'm so sorry."

"Easton." She shook her head, wiping her eyes. "Stop, please. There is nothing to forgive. You were the only one who believed me. Who stood by me. You saved my life—you saved *me*, Easton." She released her weight and crumbled into my lap, weeping in relief.

I folded over her, squeezing her so tight, and allowed the tears to fall down my cheeks.

"I love you, Mia," I whispered. "I love you—God, I *love* you."

"I love you," she said breathlessly as my focus snapped to the faint sound of movement behind us.

Cullen had awoken and dragged himself across the floor to where he'd picked up my gun. His face was a bloody mess, a steady stream of thick, clotted red strings running from his nose and mouth. Hands trembling, he lifted the gun, a wicked smile revealing his bloodstained teeth.

I shifted, blocking Mia with my body, preparing for the punch of a bullet just as Beckett leaped through the door.

Cullen swung around at the burst of noise. Mia screamed.

"Beckett!" I yelled as Cullen squeezed the trigger, narrowing his sights on the body flying through the air.

The shot went off just as Beckett tackled him, their bodies slamming together with the power of a head-on collision. The bullet ricocheted off the ceiling. The gun flew from Cullen's hands.

The moment they hit the floor, the sound of sirens rang through the air.

# Chapter Fifty-Six

## Mia

*Three weeks later*

I awoke the same way as I had every morning over the last twenty-two days, wrapped warmly and tightly in Easton's arms. He hadn't left my side once, not during the two days I'd spent in the hospital or after I'd been discharged.

The man had practically moved into my house, bringing with him more security than the Pentagon.

Many new locks had been installed on the doors and windows, and cameras positioned at every corner of the house, inside and out. He'd even installed invisible trip-wire alerts that reminded me of an old heist movie, where the spandex-clad heroine deftly maneuvered through the beams before stealing the loot worth millions. If the invisible beams were crossed, the alarms would be activated.

No one could get into my house, to me, without Easton or me knowing about it.

Learning the system had been as grueling as trying to pass advanced calculus in college. But I wasn't the only one being challenged.

Over the three weeks, Easton and my family of birds went through many phases.

The first: complete hatred and utter disdain for one another.

The second: a wary acceptance once both parties realized neither was going anywhere.

The third: curiosity at what one might be able to provide for the other.

For the birds, it was when they realized Easton was the reason for their sudden change in bird food. A welcome change from the discount brand to the premium that included a smorgasbord of seeds for their dining pleasure.

For Easton, it was when Goldie crossed the couch, snatched a Dorito from between his fingertips, and proceeded to eat the chip while perched on his thigh. It was the loudest I'd ever heard the man laugh, much to Goldie's delight.

Easton's Dorito had been devoured and Goldie's heart stolen forever.

Within days after, she'd learned to say his name, calling out for him every hour—on the hour—demanding his attention as most women in new relationships tend to do. Eventually, he started just leaving her cage unlocked, allowing her to perch on his shoulder, her new favorite place.

Most days, I think he forgot she was even there.

In the evenings, while Easton watched the news and drank a beer, Goldie would sit on his lap like a dog or a cat, cooing in his presence. One time, I awoke from an afternoon nap to find Easton sitting on the front porch, Goldie in his lap. He'd been gently stroking her head while staring off into the sunset.

It was the first time I'd seen Easton truly relaxed and perhaps the first time he'd appreciated the therapy that birds can provide. Goldie had him wrapped around her claw, though he'd never admit it.

Easton was adjusting nicely to my crazy household, the evidence of his excitement pressing into my hip every morning.

He nibbled my ear, something else I'd gotten very used to. "Good morning."

I rolled over, squinting into a crooked smile. God, I loved that smile first thing in the morning.

I brought my hand up to my face, cupping my mouth. "What time is it?" I mumbled through closed lips.

He did the same, mocking me, although I knew he didn't care about morning breath. "Seven fifteen."

"It's Saturday. Let me sleep."

"I thought we could do something today."

"Define *something*."

"A hike."

My brows slowly lifted. I—*we*—had avoided the woods since everything that had happened. Too many memories.

Easton tucked a strand of hair behind my ear, sending goose bumps prickling over my skin. "The leaves are just past their peak. Going to start dropping soon. Last chance to see them in all their glory."

"Goldie's going to be mad at you."

"I've promised to have breakfast with her out on the patio."

"Ah. I see. Then you'd better get going."

His hand swept over the lines of my hip, sending a trail blazing over my skin.

He grinned, and I knew that look.

"Make it quick. Those leaves might fall."

"What leaves?" He grinned back, rolling me onto my back.

Forty-seven minutes and two orgasms later, I staggered into the bathroom, unsure of where I was or of my own name. Easton slapped my ass and disappeared to meet his mistress and start the coffee.

I clicked on the radio and slipped into the shower, inhaling the steam and allowing the scorching water to turn me officially into Gumby.

The radio switched from a jazzy new pop song to the local news.

My hand froze on the shampoo bottle as his name came over the speaker.

". . . Mark Swine's trial is scheduled to begin next week."

Trying to force myself not to listen, I squirted out the shampoo and began vigorously rubbing my head.

No matter how hard Easton and I had tried to avoid it, we couldn't avoid the story that had plagued the small town of Skull Hollow—and the nation—for weeks.

Mark Swine had been arrested and taken into custody immediately. A warrant was issued to search his home, revealing a very disturbed man who would later be diagnosed with antisocial personality disorder.

Cullen Nichols, a.k.a. Mark Swine, was the Black Cat Stalker.

The garage proved to be a treasure trove of evidence that included not only the aviator sunglasses he'd been wearing when he'd attacked Courtney Hayes—now cracked—but the bandanna he'd worn in each of his attacks, as well as a plastic container full of sticks that he'd used on his previous victims. My old cell phone, the one I'd lost during the attack when I was sixteen, was hidden in the bottom of the trunk.

I was his first victim, the one who looked like his mom, the one who had stayed with him, the one whom he'd become fixated on. This was confirmed by a shrine of me in his bedroom, along with pictures of all his victims. They all looked the same. Like me, like his mother.

Triggered by what would have been his mother's seventieth birth-day, Cullen had "celebrated" the milestone by executing his final revenge on me—his sacrificial lamb.

Since the news had broken, six other women had bravely come forward with their stories after hearing the brutal, sadistic manner of the rapes. They'd been too embarrassed to admit they'd been sodomized with a stick.

Courtney Hayes and her mother were all over the news, their story making national headlines. Shortly after Cullen's arrest, I'd arranged to meet Courtney for a cup of coffee. This had turned into a twice-weekly date and a friendship that I hoped would help both of us heal.

Courtney had many issues to work through, but she was making the first step toward healing, and that was what was most important.

As was I.

Courtney was only one of a long line of new clients admitted to our clinic after the news of my "assistance" in bringing down the notorious Black Cat Stalker had hit national headlines. The clinic was thriving, but still nothing compared to Easton's business.

A girl had to have goals, after all.

The LYNX Group had hired another office manager after Loren had admitted to her own infatuation with Easton. She'd dropped by my house in the throes of a sobbing breakdown and apologized not only for delivering the videos to the cops but also for her displaced neurosis when she'd realized he had feelings for me.

Good old-fashioned jealousy.

All the pieces of the puzzle had finally come together. Mark Swine would spend the rest of his life in prison and would likely never see the light of day again.

A light that I was just beginning to see, for the first time perhaps.

Easton and I spent the Saturday hiking on a popular ten-mile loop through the wetlands, eating a picnic lunch on one of the small air-boats that he used for tracking training. Snacking on meats and cheeses and sipping Bloody Marys, we meandered through the swamps, slowly, peacefully. We finished lunch under the Spanish moss . . . romantic, to say the least.

It was a beautiful fall afternoon with a sapphire-blue sky, not a cloud in sight. I'd brought my camera and took hundreds of pictures of birds, the wildlife, the glorious nature around us.

The waterway became narrower, the colorful trees closing in around us. Easton guided us into a shallow marsh with blades of green grass poking up through the water.

"Where are we going?"

"You'll see."

Easton pulled up to a small dilapidated dock, barely visible beyond the grass.

"Whose is this?"

"Mine."

"Yours?"

"Yes—barely. My land ends just past that tree line. We use this marsh for training."

"Hard to track someone in here, I'd imagine."

"Not if you know what you're looking for."

Once he'd cut the engine and secured the boat, he slung on his backpack and helped me onto the deck. I slipped my hand into his.

"Ready?" he asked.

For some reason, butterflies tickled my stomach, and I wasn't so sure of the answer to that question.

Hand in hand, Easton led me through the woods, my camera hanging around my neck. My nerves grew with each minute that passed. I could *feel* the energy rolling off him . . . I just wasn't sure why or what it meant.

His grip tightened around mine as we veered off a footpath, pushing through thick underbrush.

"Easton, where the heck are we going—"

I froze at the edge of a clearing, staring at a blazing-pink dogwood with a split down the middle.

"Come on."

I blinked.

He smiled, then winked at me. "Come on."

It was no other reason than me trusting him that I took a step forward, then another, and another.

Easton pulled a small blanket from his pack and laid it on the ground in front of the tree, similar to where I'd lain and cried under the one he'd chopped down in my backyard.

He pulled a drink from his bag and handed it to me, then pulled out one for himself.

"Bifurcation." He nodded to the split in the middle of the dogwood tree. "That's what that is called. It begins with a single weak spot, a barely visible crack or split in an otherwise strong, impenetrable tree. Many things can cause this split, like subzero temperatures, disease, or lightning damage. Most trees don't survive this kind of external assault. Some do, despite the weak spot disrupting the natural course of its life, thereby permanently altering its DNA—though not killing it."

*A victim of trauma finding a way to survive.*

A knot formed in my throat.

"You've been watching too much of the Nature Channel," I said, deflecting.

"It's Goldie's favorite channel." He winked. "I've also been studying about PTSD."

My jaw dropped, and I choked out a gargled laugh. "You have?"

"Yep, Goldie and I have spent many evenings on your deck, reading the night away."

"Should I be getting jealous of this relationship?"

"Shouldn't you know by now that I know when you're trying to deflect?"

I smiled.

Easton took my hands in his. "I've learned that one of the best ways to get over PTSD is to *accept* what happened, accept that it isn't something that you can go back and change, and therefore, you do your best to move on from it."

He reached into his bag and pulled out the small velvet pouch that I kept hidden in my pantie drawer. I watched each item gently tumble onto the blanket.

Six stones and two twigs. The feather, with the hair, was currently in the custody of the FBI.

Next, he pulled off the gold ring he wore on his pinkie finger and set it on top of the pile.

His mother's ring.

"I was thinking . . . there's never going to be a good time to let go." He took my hands in his, his voice cracking. "So . . . let's do it together."

Tears filled my eyes.

He pulled a small trowel from his pack. "Want to bury the past with me?"

A tear ran down my cheek. "But your mother's ring . . ."

He smiled, a sad smile. "Dogwoods were actually her favorite kind of tree. It's time."

I nodded. It was time. For both of us.

He smiled as he wiped the tear away. I grabbed his hand, kissed his knuckles.

We dug the hole together in silence, and together we placed the items into the hole, between the roots of the tree, the ring on top. And we buried them.

I flung my arms around his neck, and we embraced for I don't know how long. No words were spoken; none needed to be. Eventually, I pulled away, inhaling deeply as I wiped my tears away.

"So . . . something else I learned," he said, and I laughed at the sudden chipper change in his tone to lighten the moment, "is about withdrawal after you let something go. The need to fill a hole with something else. This hole needs to be filled with something positive."

"Yes, I'm familiar with this therapeutic approach." I smirked.

Easton pulled a small yellow jewelry box from the front pocket of his pack. My heart tripped in my chest.

He handed it to me, a boyish smile crossing his face. "Just open it."

A surge of adrenaline heated my skin as I opened the box. I gasped. "Oh my . . ."

Inside lay a bright-blue feather next to a gold necklace, the pendant hanging from the chain an exact replica of the feather.

"It's the feather," I whispered breathlessly. "That I found . . ."

"Walking through the woods, the moment before we first kissed."

"You kept it?"

He nodded, then took the necklace from my hands. I turned as he draped it around my neck. Enthralled, I clasped the chain.

He whispered in my ear, "Now you have a new feather to cling to. One that symbolizes hope and happiness."

I turned my face, inches from his lips. "One that symbolizes you."

"I love you, Mia. Have since the moment I saw you."

"I love you, Easton. Have since the moment you correctly cited the definition of maieutics."

Laughing, he took me into his arms and spun me around. A handful of luminescent pink leaves drifted down from the tree and onto the yellow box.

I looked up at the tree, sparkling against the beams of sunlight.

It was a beautiful tree.

# ABOUT THE AUTHOR

Amanda McKinney is the author of more than twenty romantic-suspense, mystery, and action-and-adventure novels. Her books have received over fifteen literary awards and nominations. She lives in Arkansas with her handsome husband, two beautiful boys, and three obnoxious dogs and enjoys hiking, daydreaming, and very dirty martinis (on occasion, all three at the same time).